FIC T584 v.3 1995
Timmerman, John H.
Out of these ashes
Columbia Bible College
34444001017144

P9-EJI-889

Therefore go and make disciples of all nations,
baptizing them in the name
of the Father and of the Son and of the Holy Spirit,
and teaching them to obey everything I have commanded you.
And surely I am with you always, to the very end of the age.

Matthew 28:19-20

THE JERUSALEM JOURNEYS

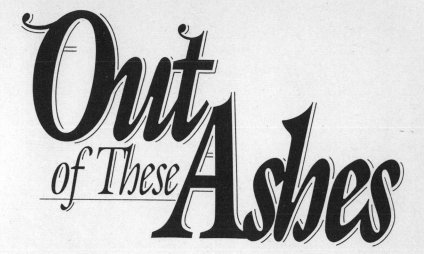

Out of These Ashes

John H. Timmerman

INTERVARSITY PRESS
DOWNERS GROVE, ILLINOIS 60515

© 1995 by John H. Timmerman

All rights reserved. No part of this book may be reproduced in any form without written permission from InterVarsity Press, P.O. Box 1400, Downers Grove, Illinois 60515.

InterVarsity Press® is the book-publishing division of InterVarsity Christian Fellowship®, a student movement active on campus at hundreds of universities, colleges and schools of nursing in the United States of America, and a member movement of the International Fellowship of Evangelical Students. For information about local and regional activities, write Public Relations Dept., InterVarsity Christian Fellowship, 6400 Schroeder Rd., P.O. Box 7895, Madison, WI 53707-7895.

Cover illustration and maps: John Walker

ISBN 0-8308-1678-X

Printed in the United States of America ∞

Library of Congress Cataloging-in-Publication Data

Timmerman, John H.
   Out of these ashes/John H. Timmerman.
     p.   cm.—(The Jerusalem journeys)
   ISBN 0-8308-1678-X
   I. Title. II. Series: Timmerman, John H. Jerusalem journeys.
  PS3570.I46O98 1995
  813'.54—dc20   95-31541
                                    CIP

17	16	15	14	13	12	11	10	9	8	7	6	5	4	3	2	1
09	08	07	06	05	04	03	02	01	00	99	98	97	96	95		

Acknowledgments

A single dedication is far too narrow for this concluding volume of The Jerusalem Journeys series. Thanks are due to many people, but to these especially. First of all, to John and Kathy Van Til, who provided a hideaway for me in their summer home at Northport, Michigan, a land of unparalleled beauty and quiet. There many of the ideas and pages of this book began. Once again, I express my appreciation to Calvin College for its unfailingly generous sabbatical support. I thank the fine editorial staff at InterVarsity, and especially Cynthia Bunch-Hotaling, for both their enthusiasm and their encouragement. I want to thank my daughter Tamara, who not only did peerless computer work on the manuscript but also remains by best critic and literary adviser. Special thanks, as always, go to my men's support group, who once again prayed this work through to the finish. But above all to Patricia, for her unfailing support, and for whom my thanks will never be sufficient.

PROLOGUE

The fields were stubbled by brown husks and windblown clumps of weeds. Stunted bushes dangled bright orange berries that swayed like little lanterns in the mist.

Fog crept everywhere, tumbling in low fields like gray blankets over a restless body. Here and there a weak wind poked holes in it, and then the orange berries shone bravely, the only color in the dreary landscape. Around rocks that lay in piles about the cleared fields, the fog twisted and eddied like a floating stream.

It lay thickest on the lake. Ten feet ahead it was impossible to tell where fog and water separated. The travelers in the boat hugged the shore, alert for fallen trees and underwater snags. The lantern in the prow cast a little orb of yellow light. The creak and rattle of oars in the wooden locks, the smack and heave through the water, echoed against the banks of fog.

They rowed into mist that turned to gray drizzle, then back to a wet, cold fleece. They wore their hoods pulled far forward over their eyes, drops of water screening their vision. The thick woolen cloaks shed the rain, but the fog seeped through, pinching coldly.

To the right, over the brown stubble of field, a hunting bird hurtled through the air. They heard the frantic scurry of feet, the rustle of underbrush, a sudden broken cry, then the wings of the bird beating heavily skyward. They heard it all, sounds amplified by the wet air. But they saw nothing.

Curving around a bend of the narrow lake, the four passengers felt a sluggish breeze move across the water. It momentarily pushed aside the fog. On the shore ahead a small boy, probably no more than four or five, sat on a rock among the weeds. He held a long piece of rope that stretched tautly into the water as if it held some large weight at the end. It lay directly in their path.

Andrew barked an order over his shoulder to Emeth, who was rowing behind him, but he had already seen it and was heaving on the oar to turn the boat out into the river's current.

The boy began hauling in the line, standing with bare feet on the moss-slimed rock. The weight at the end of the line moved ponderously as it broke the surface. It was draped in weeds that hung in black whorls. Andrew and Emeth dug hard with the oars to avoid it.

They saw the man at the same moment, standing back in the mists like some rocky pillar. His shoulders were huge and bent forward, his body wrapped in loose rags. His hair was wet, hanging down before small, receding eyes. He rocked slightly on his heels, his eyes following the boat.

The boy called something over his shoulder. The broad-shouldered man's lips twisted into a grin. He plunged forward on thick, bent legs, splashing directly into the current. The shoreline weeds rose quickly to his chest.

Andrew's eyes darted past the man, and he saw her in the field. A hawk circled lightly about her, then floated to her wrapped wrist, carrying some small animal in its beak. Her eyes were piercing under a tangled mop of dark, wet hair. Carefully she removed the prey from the hawk, then lowered the bird to the ground. She was reaching over her shoulder as the huge man waded toward them.

This close, Andrew could see the broken stumps of the man's yellowed teeth, like kernels of grain stuck in his wide mouth. He splashed through the current as if unmindful of its existence, grabbing the rope from the boy. Effortlessly, hand over hand, he lugged the weight out of their way and lifted it clear of the water.

They stopped rowing, drifting with the current back toward the shore.

The rope was attached to a water-bloated object draped with weeds. The man lifted it proudly for them to see, holding it aloft so that the weeds draped down over his huge shoulders. The boy shouted at him, and he laid the object back on the rock at the boy's feet.

But when he had lifted it, Andrew could for the first time see it clearly. He shivered involuntarily. The rope was tied through the jaw of a severed cow's head. And what he had thought were clumps of seaweed were actually long, thick bodies of eels twined together, attached to the decayed meat.

His stomach twisted, ready to rebel. He raised his head, gulping for air.

She still stood where she had been in the field. The hawk floated now in lazy circles above her head. A bank of fog was rolling back toward her. She had an arrow fitted to a bow, drawn back its full length and pointed directly at Andrew. Her eyes met his. He saw them glittering fiercely as she looked down the length of the arrow, and he knew, as certainly as the strangled beating of his heart, who it was. She had every reason to loose the arrow.

The fog rolled in like a blanket. At the last second she shifted slightly and loosed the arrow. The air whistled, and the lantern in the prow of the boat exploded. When Andrew looked again he could not see any of them in the gathered fog, only the empty rock rising from the river just before the boat drifted on. And then the rock too disappeared in the gloom.

PART ONE
FONTINI VILLA

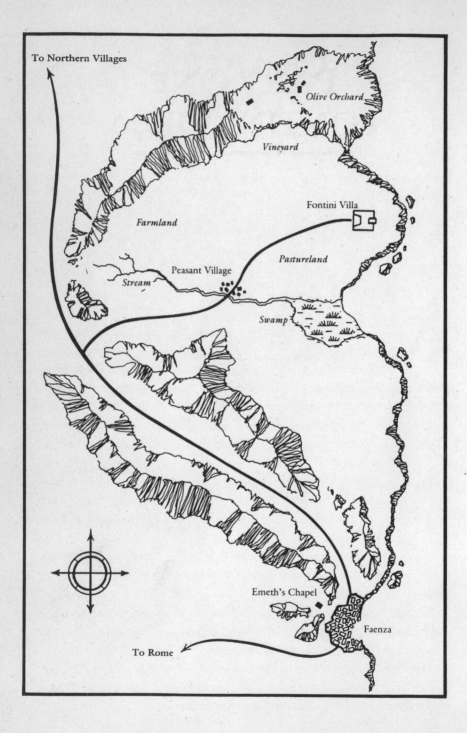

To Northern Villages

Olive Orchard

Vineyard

Fontini Villa

Farmland

Pastureland

Peasant Village

Stream

Swamp

Emeth's Chapel

Faenza

To Rome

CHAPTER ONE

Alone in his bed, the boy convinced himself he had to have one more look.

He did not want to get up in the dark. The wind moaned at the shutters of his window. Every night it came out of the ocean, sighing gently at first. Then as the darkness deepened it began to push harder, its voice angry and powerful against the tower walls. When the wind carried a storm on its dark back, pounding against the house with bolts of lightning and the quakes of thunder, it slipped cold fingers through the shutters right into the room, and the boy was certain the wind would find him and carry him, in one awful peal of thunder, right out into the sea's black heart. Then he huddled under the bed coverings and pretended he wasn't there, squeezing his eyes very tight.

The wind moaned gently at the shutters tonight. It was the regular sea-sounding wind, full of the tangy scent of salt and birds and fish. It would be safe.

The boy knew he would have to do this even if the night storm attacked and he had to fight through shadows and lightning all the way.

He had to see his father one more time.

He pulled back the blankets. Cool air touched his skin, and he shivered. Instead of dressing, he wrapped a woolen blanket about him, trailing it on the floor as he stepped carefully to the doorway.

The other thing he didn't like at night was the stairwell. A torch used to burn there at night, about halfway down where the stone steps circled through the stone walls. He could fall asleep watching its pale glow reach into the upper stonework, leaking into his room. But then he had grown too old for such lights. His mother had asked him, and he agreed. He was eight when they took away the light. Even now, two years later, he still missed the warm glow, especially this night. The stone steps were painfully cold under his bare feet. They always seemed damp.

He walked down the stairwell slowly, dragging the edge of the blanket behind him. He was careful to keep to the center of the steps. Cobwebs seemed to grow overnight in the musty corners. Sometimes when he awakened, especially if it was a gray, rainy day, he was certain the cobwebs would have grown over the entire stairwell, a gray net spun to trap him.

He would take one more look—maybe his last—and then sneak back to bed. But he wanted that look. He wasn't sure he could remember the details of his father's face. It seemed to blur before him now, and he wanted to have it fixed in his mind. He couldn't fall asleep until he was certain it was there in his memory for all time.

*   *   *

The tower rose from the seaward wall of the villa. If one looked at it from the bottom of the hill, near where the peasants who worked in the vineyards lived, the walls seemed to rise out of the hill itself. A curved, gray-stone swelling of the earth and rock, it swept upward toward the point of the tower and beyond to the sea.

He could remember his father and Lycurgus building it. When they had come here, long before he could remember, there had been only the ruined rooms of the villa, with the roof caved in, the walls broken and gaping. There had been a forecourt with a tiled pool, but filled with debris and muck that pigs rolled in.

They had torn everything down and started over. It seemed to the boy that there was always noise as he was growing up, the rasp of saws, the clanging of hammers and tools, the splitting of stone. His growing up was a rampage of play on piles of rock and the warning shouts of his mother pursuing him.

Then, about when his memory started clearly, the twin wings of the villa formed about the courtyard. He remembered his father, clad in an odd sort of cloak utterly unlike anything he himself wore, bathed in sweat, working with the laborers to build walls and rooms. The twin wings of the building swept around the courtyard, meeting in a large room where all of them—his mother and father, and Doval and Lycurgus—would come for their meals.

Each night a fire blazed in the hearth. The cook, Griselde, brought her steaming dishes to the large table. Almost always there were guests. The boy could not remember them all. Sometimes they were joking and loud and the room rang with laughter. Then there were the others, their faces drawn and fearful, and they would rest a night or two in one of the spare rooms and then, by morning light, they were gone.

Mostly he remembered the laughter.

It was a happy house. When the pool was at last cleaned, its blue tiles all shining in the sun and delicate water plants floating on the surface, his father had taken him aside. He led him to an unused pile of rock and stood beside it. Slowly he turned the boy around, facing first the north, where the vineyards sloped along the hillside, winding toward the west in curving green lines.

To the west, at the bottom of the hill, lay a cluster of houses used by the field hands and laborers. Behind the houses stretched pens for the animals that before had roamed freely and small fields for the workers' vegetables and grain. His father and Lycurgus had kept the most trustworthy laborers, helped them build their houses by the stream in the valley and provided them steady work. As he looked, the lad could make out the house of his friend Dominic. To the south lay a rolling plain of rugged ground. From it the building stone had been quarried and hewn. Heaps of slag lay in small mounds as far as the eye could see. Sheep cropped the coarse grass there to the very earth. And to the east, although he could not see it because of the rise of the bluff, lay the ocean.

"I think, Andrew," his father had said to him, "that you need a special place. One where you can see all this daily. See how it all works together when the people are given direction and help and hope. See how the land works."

He had not understood. He was perfectly happy in his old room. Nor did it bother him that he did not understand his father's words. His father frequently said things that were a mystery to him, and sometimes he would not talk at all.

Once when Andrew was quite small, he had wandered across the promontory leading to the sea. The sun shone brightly. Flowers dotted the rocky land—yellow blossoms like splotches of sunlight and fragile little cups of sky blue. The boy felt entranced. And he loved the smell of the sea. He walked until he heard the surf pounding in the distance, a constant booming sound.

Then he heard his father calling. And he started to run away, toward the sea. He remembered the running, a wild summer game. His father's voice chased him, pleading, calling. But he laughed and ran harder, little legs flashing among the flowers, dark hair bobbing. He laughed at the wonderful game. He ran harder, toward the sound of the sea. His father's breath was heaving when he caught up; great gasping breaths shook him. As he doubled over, holding his son in his arms, tears streaked his face.

"Never, Andrew," he gasped, "never, ever go alone."

"But I want to see," the boy had said.

"Very well. Then let me show you." When his breathing evened, he scooped the boy up in powerful arms and carried him to a high bluff where the earth fell away. Below the great cliff, birds swooped and dove. They landed as lightly as air on the rocks far below. They darted up when a great wave crashed over the rocks, sending a plume of spray soaring like a fountain.

The boy trembled and held tightly to his father's neck.

"See. There is great danger here. You must not go alone." He pointed out toward the rocks and the waves. As he did so, his cloak fell back along his arm and exposed a long pink ridge of scar tissue, twisted and grotesque, tracking like a writhing serpent from elbow to wrist. It was the first time the boy had ever noticed it. He shivered and turned his head.

"I don't want to see that."

"I don't want you to fall over," his father said.

"I don't mean the waves. I'm not going to fall." With his head averted, he pointed at his father's arm. "That," he said.

His father fell very still. Carefully he set the boy down. He took his hand and began walking back.

The boy snuck a glance to make sure the arm was covered. He looked up at his father's face. He looked either very sad or very angry. The boy couldn't decide.

"How did you get that?" he asked.

His father shook his head. "Sometime perhaps I'll tell you. Now is not a good time."

"Did it hurt?"

"Very much."

"I don't want you to be hurt."

"I understand, Andrew. I don't hurt anymore. Not at all."

Then, when they were nearly home, his father said, "Andrew, don't ever be afraid of things that are different. Or ugly."

"I'm sorry, Father."

"I know. Sometimes the noblest things bear wounds. And not all ugliness is visible. You will learn to tell the difference."

That was the sort of thing the boy did not understand. It seemed so often that his father found it difficult to talk with him at all. Then, when he did try, like the time about names, what he said was even harder to understand than his silence.

* * *

The conversation about names came several years later, after the tower had been built.

When they had started building the tower, the boy had scurried down the hill to be with his friend Dominic. There was something comforting about Dominic's tiny house in the village. The one room was divided by hanging draperies into living, eating and sleeping quarters. For days the boy left at first light, roaming the fields with Dominic, climbing trees in the valley, building dams in the stream to snare fish that delighted Dominic's mother. When the boy climbed the hill toward home in the evening, the tower looked a bit higher, and his heart sank.

When the day came that it was completed, his father and Lycurgus led him in. They climbed the carefully mortared stairwell proudly. They ran their fingers over the tightly fitted window, pushed the shutters in and out, and studied the stonework lovingly. Lycurgus sat on the bed and watched sunlight flood the room. They talked about its construction, their hours of labor on the scaffolds, the mistakes they had made. They laughed out loud.

Andrew hated it. He was resolute. He refused to sleep there unless Dominic could join him. So for three nights his friend slept with him. Then he was by himself.

17

He felt terribly alone in the tower and longed for morning when he could see his friend again. He was almost used to it when things began to change.

His father fell ill during the winter months, at the very time when the guests arrived. The boy knew these visitors were special. The whole household seemed to hold its breath in anticipation. But his father was sick. That was all the boy cared about.

There were two guests. One was a smallish man with a beard as black as night. His eyes—they reminded the boy of an eagle. Fierce and predatory. The other one was tall and thin. He had long, white hands, the boy remembered. And he remembered the way his mother and his aunt Doval hugged him.

The tall man noticed him first. He stood before the boy then, gazing fondly at him. "So, this would be young Balthazzar," he murmured.

His mother smiled apologetically. "We call him Andrew. It's easier."

The man chuckled. "To be sure! And it is a name from the homeland, of course. A name to be proud of."

Then they had gone in to see his father, and they stayed with him a long time. They left the next morning.

Despite the length and severity of his father's illness, he recovered. But the illness left lingering weakness. When his father climbed the steps of the tower the morning that he talked about the names, he arrived trembling and sweating. He shook his son awake, and Andrew started at the gaunt apparition before him. Then he apologized.

"No matter," Elhrain said. "I'd like to talk with you."

As he spoke in his halting and thick-tongued way, Elhrain's gaunt shoulders seemed to cave inward. His cheekbones flared, the skin so tight and shiny he still seemed to be fighting a fever. But the names he mentioned, the events he described, were like one of the stories of the old Roman gods that his tutor told him. His father spoke of how four kings traveled a long way through the desert to find the True King . . .

"But what is a desert, Father?" Andrew interrupted.

"What is a . . . yes, that's right." Elhrain tried to describe it—"The wind there blows sand until the skin is raw . . . the sun like a white blister scorches the sky . . . the animals there prey on the wanderer without mercy . . ." Then he shook his head and sighed.

"The important thing," he said, "is that they found the True King."

"Mother told me about him," Andrew replied quickly.

"Yes. Yes, I'm sure she has."

"Where is he?"

"Well, that's hard to explain. What I want to say is . . . is this. He has a task for you, son."

"What is it?"

Elhrain paused a long time. The boy grew restless. Light crept into the eastern window. "Well?" he said.

"I don't know," Elhrain said. Suddenly he began coughing violently. He doubled over in a spasm of pain. When he straightened there were flecks of blood on his lips. He tried to wipe them quickly, before the boy could see.

"Are you all right, Father?"

"Yes. I'm all right. I want you to listen." He paused, groping for words, fumbling with ideas. "Listen for the Messiah's voice, Andrew. He will tell you what you must do. You must not refuse."

"How will I know?" The boy looked frightened. "I don't want any . . ."

"No, no," Elhrain said quickly. "It will be nothing to be afraid of. You will hear it inside you, son. In your heart. Listen with your feelings. You will know."

"Why don't *you* tell me?"

Elhrain stared at the light flooding the open window. When the light fell like this, full from the east, it bathed the inside of the tower with a warm golden color. Elhrain had believed it was the right thing to build it. He had wanted his son to learn the ways of the wind. Of the sun, earth and sea. So delicate was the harmony among them, so fragile the balance.

Elhrain winced. "I can't. I wish I could. And now I'm . . . I'm getting older, Balthazzar. Your mother and I both are. Doval and Lycurgus, if they're able—they will help you. I wish I knew what lay ahead."

"Father. You called me Balthazzar."

"Yes. That is one name given to you. After your grandfather. He was one of the kings who sought the True King. The ones I told you about." Elhrain shook his head. So much to tell. He knew he was doing it badly. The words, and the time for words, escaped him. "But for now you are also Andrew. That is your name as well."

"That man, the one who came here when you were sick. He called me Balthazzar too."

"Yes. He is a good man. He has helped many people. In many lands."

"How?"

Elhrain smiled. "Why, to know the Messiah. That is the great task, Andrew."

The lad nodded as if unconcerned. Then, with a glance at the sunlight, he asked, "May I go and play with Dominic now?"

"Yes, my son. Now you may play." Elhrain's voice was utterly weary. Andrew stood up and crossed the room. Standing by the doorway, he turned. "Father, were you one of the kings too?"

"One of . . ."

"With grandfather. Who found the True King?"

"Yes. Yes, my son. We found him."

The boy's steps rang down the stairwell. He did not see his father groan, clutch his abdomen and fall to the bed.

* * *

Dominic was two years older than Andrew, the only son of a tenant farmer who worked in the vineyards and a wife who smiled perpetually, displaying her only two remaining teeth. Although a few inches shorter than Andrew, Dominic was a thick-chested boy, with long, strong arms.

The boys competed in nearly everything, inventing their elaborate games from wrestling to race courses that wound everywhere through the great valley.

There were other children in the village, and sometimes they joined Dominic and Andrew in their games by the stream. But by and by their parents would call them to chores—carefully so when Andrew was there, as if they were asking his permission. Only Dominic seemed to have the complete freedom to come and go as he pleased, to have a special place in Andrew's life.

That place grew deeper by the day, for those at the villa were too old to be interested in boyhood games. His parents kept busy with their pursuits and seldom imposed on the boy, beyond his required school lessons with Desidero.

Desidero and his wife, Griselde, had been a part of the villa for as long as Andrew could remember; it was almost as if they had come with it. Together they ran the day-to-day affairs of the villa with regimented efficiency and graceful good humor. Desidero, who tried to carry his bulky, overweight body with a military bearing as he busied himself with cleaning chores, was mercilessly henpecked by Griselde. After berating Desidero with her sharp tongue, Griselde would turn and beam a huge smile on anyone nearby, as if to say, Isn't he the greatest husband in the world? Where Desidero ruled, however, was in tutoring Andrew and Dominic. Each morning he had the boys for the allotted hours of study. He drilled learning into their heads with enthusiasm, except when he lost the thread of his lessons in some complicated story he was using to illustrate the lesson.

Then, of course, there was Gregor. But no one really knew Gregor. He was a wild thing. Seldom, and then only on the coldest nights, did he actually stay in the villa. Then he would wrap himself in some blankets in the hallway, completely covered from head to toe as if hiding. Early in the morning, even on the coldest days, he would be gone. Mostly, Gregor slept in the hills. Some said he stayed in one of the caves along the ocean shore. Others said that by moonlight his twisted and deformed limbs took on animal form. A few said that they had seen Gregor howling under the full moon by the seashore. Andrew did not believe this.

Sometimes he saw Gregor at a distance when he walked alone in the hills. Gregor would pop up in a thicket or from behind boulders and crouch there watching Andrew.

His hair fell in tangles over his large, misshapen head. His powerful shoulders hunched like some animal. His short, bent legs made him look like he was always crouching. But he could move quickly, soundlessly, on those twisted stumps. And he would pull faces. His lips curled over crooked teeth, and his narrow eyes, which often stared rigidly like pale stones, squeezed nearly shut. Finally Andrew began to understand that Gregor was trying to smile at him, and he grinned back.

At first Andrew was afraid of Gregor. Then he thought little about either Gregor's presence or his appearance. Often he had the feeling of Gregor's eyes following him, but by then he was just one more person in the busy daily life of Fontini Villa.

*　*　*

The day he talked with his father, Andrew told Dominic about the names. He could tell Dominic anything.

The boys had found some scrap lumber left over from building the village houses. Most of the scrap had gone to build pens for the animals kept by villagers. The pens stretched alongside the vegetable fields behind the village.

"Do you think we should take it?" Andrew had asked when they found the lumber.

"Who's going to know?" asked Dominic. He pulled out several long poles and began dragging them to the grove of trees by the stream. "Come on. Grab a couple. We'll build our own place in the trees. Then we'll have a hideout."

"Hide from what?" Andrew grabbed a long pole and dragged it over his shoulder toward the trees. "Besides, they might belong to somebody."

"Finders keepers. They're ours now." Dominic looked back at Andrew. "What's the matter? Scared?"

Pole after pole they lugged. They found the right tree easily, its crotch spreading in a wide arc about ten feet up. By late afternoon the boys had a platform rigged, fully hidden by the tree's branches. They sat there, swinging their legs over the edge.

"This is better than the tower," Andrew said.

"The tower?" Dominic snorted. "Better than what I have, anyway. And it's all ours. Nobody else knows. That's the best part."

"My father talked to me this morning," Andrew said.

"About sex?"

"Sex?"

"Yeah. How babies are made, dummy," Dominic said. His voice was a sneer. "My father didn't talk to me. He woke me up one morning and took me out to the field. An old bull was doing it. You should have seen him, Andrew."

"I've seen the bull. That's not how—"

"How dumb can you be? Course that's how it's done."

"But those are animals."

"So?"

"I'm not."

"It's all the same."

Andrew felt a burning shame. No. It couldn't be. "Anyway," he said, "that isn't what he talked about."

"What then?" Dominic stood up on the platform. He started bouncing lightly. The poles were springy, swaying under Dominic's weight.

Andrew tried to ignore it, but he held on to the tree branch for support. "He talked about my name. He said the Messiah has a special task for me."

"Big deal. Who's this Messiah, anyway?"

" 'The True King,' he said."

Dominic was bouncing harder. " 'True King.' So now I suppose you're going to grow up to be a king."

"I don't know. I didn't understand it. Stop bouncing, Dominic."

"What's the matter, king? Think you're going to fall off?" He jumped harder now, the poles bouncing wildly under his weight.

"Don't!"

"Scaredy . . ." Dominic leaped up. When he landed his foot slipped on the rounded pole. He twisted, grabbing for a branch, and he stumbled. His hand caught Andrew's arm. The poles rolled and clattered. For one moment Andrew thought he could hold Dominic, clutching fast to his arm. But the weight was too much. Dominic tumbled off. Still clutching desperately, Andrew fell with him.

They hit the wet ground by the stream with a thud, and Dominic screamed. He pulled at his wrist, buried in the muck under Andrew's body, and held it in one hand. The hand flopped at the end of his arm, just below the point where the wrist bone poked like a red-and-white stick through the skin. Blood squirted down the boy's fingers.

"You dummy," Dominic hissed, his eyes burning. "Why didn't you let me go?" He bit at his lip.

"I tried to save you. I'm sorry."

"Save me! Save yourself, if you can. It's your fault."

Holding his broken wrist in his other hand, Dominic began walking back to the village.

Andrew ran to his side. Tears were rolling down Dominic's face, but he made no sound. He ignored Andrew.

Several days passed before Andrew saw his friend again. They were supposed to meet each morning in the great room of the villa for tutoring. Dominic's father had resisted the arrangement, but then suddenly agreed after Lycurgus had gone to talk with him. Andrew had wanted him there.

When Dominic appeared for the lessons again three days following, his arm was tightly wrapped between wooden splints. His hand was swollen, the fingers purplish.

"Does it hurt?" Andrew whispered.

Dominic shook his head. "Lucky it was my right hand," he said, "I use my left for throwing."

It was the last they spoke of it. When, after several weeks, the splint and bandages were taken off, Andrew snuck a glance at the wrist. It was still swollen and discolored. Andrew could see the angry red marks where the skin had been stitched together over the swelling. The fingers were still purple and swollen, and the tips twitched when Dominic tried to move the fingers. He did everything with his other hand.

*   *   *

These were the thoughts that crept through the boy's mind as he shuffled carefully down the stairwell. He had wanted to find happy thoughts in his mind, so he tried to think of Dominic. At times Dominic scared him, but he was his closest friend. He wanted to find memories of his father in his mind, so he tried hard to picture him there. His father also scared him sometimes. Not by anything he said or did, but by who he was. Quiet and often solemn, his father often seemed to him to be . . . dangerous. He never seemed to talk about himself, about his past. When he did, it was in cryptic ways. Like the business of names. His father often brooded alone, just out of the boy's reach.

His mother told stories, always about the Messiah and about the teachings of her people. The boy knew he was different. His skin, although not as ebony-hued as his father's, was darker than Dominic's. But that wasn't it. The difference lay in those teachings of his mother—the "law of life" she recited almost daily, the story of the True King and how people still sought him. The True King wasn't even alive anymore. Yet pilgrims came to the villa, and they talked in excited voices. Sometimes they wept, their voices loud with anguish in the night hours. Sometimes they planned eagerly. *Why?* Andrew wondered. When the king was dead. Dominic had told him that much.

His father had been ill for so long now that it had surprised everyone, especially Andrew, when his mother died—just two months ago. Once again his father had climbed to his bedroom, this time with tears running down his cheeks. His voice was hoarse. "It is time to say goodby to your mother, my son."

He waited until the boy got up.

"Is Mother going away?"

"Mother is dying, son. She is going to live with her Lord."

By some strength of will she held death back so she could see Andrew. When he stood before her, she raised her weak arms and enfolded him. Her body felt cold to Andrew. Her breathing was ragged. While she held him, Andrew could feel the arms suddenly go limp about him, and his mother stopped breathing. It was as simple as that. She went to bed in the evening as always, and she died by first morning light.

They buried her in the old way of her people. In the hillside east of the villa, toward the sea, a tomb had already been hollowed out of the rock. She was placed inside and the entrance sealed.

For days Andrew avoided the spot, refusing even to look at it.

Then he began walking out there first thing in the morning. He would sit a few minutes in the growing sunlight, among the yellow and sky-blue flowers, and think of his mother and the things she had told him. Sometimes he found himself talking with her, making promises.

* * *

Doval had come to get him from his play the afternoon before. She looked so much like his mother that Andrew thought for a moment it was she walking down the hillside toward the stream. He had straightened when he saw her and said softly, "Mother?"

"It's your aunt, stupid," Dominic muttered.

Andrew had gotten up and run to her. She did look like his mother. Her hair was graying, but her smile and soft eyes seemed still young, even to him.

As they turned back toward the villa, holding hands, Doval murmured, "Your father has been sick for a long time, Andrew."

"Is it time to say goodby to him too?" he asked.

Doval squeezed his hand. "It is, Andrew."

* * *

From opposite ends of the great room, the twin wings of the villa curved off into two corridors. The north end led to Doval and Lycurgus's rooms, and then to the rooms for Griselde the cook and her husband, Desidero. The south end led to Elhrain's room and, further down, the room Andrew had kept before moving into the tower. The old room was vacant now.

Doval led him into his father's room. Evening sunlight flooded it, touching the wall tapestries with glowing colors. Elhrain lay on a raised bed in the center of the room. He seemed shrunken with age, the blanket trembling over his once massive chest as he struggled to breathe. His arms lay at his sides. Fearfully, Andrew approached the bed. He looked at the ridge of scar tissue twisting from his father's elbow to wrist. It no longer frightened him. Lycurgus stood in the corner, leaning on a long wooden staff that he used increasingly these days. He nodded at Andrew but did not step forward.

Andrew knelt by the bedside and reached out a hand hesitantly, touching his father's arm. He slipped his hand down and found his father's fingers. Gently they squeezed back. Elhrain's eyelids flickered briefly, but they did not open.

Doval knelt beside him, covering their two hands with her own.

"He never told me how he got that," Andrew whispered. His voice was choked. He nodded toward the scar. It did not seem at all fearful now. It was just . . . a part of his father.

"When I was a little girl," Doval murmured, "your father was like a father to me."

Andrew glanced at her in surprise. Her eyes were brimming with tears. When she met Andrew's eyes, her lips tried to smile. The smile broke apart in trembling.

"Some very bad men tried to hurt me. Your father fought them for me."

"I thought it wasn't good to fight. That's what Mother told me."

Doval made a sound like a laugh. Then she said, "Your mother was right, Andrew. But sometimes . . . sometimes it seems the only way."

"How will I know?"

She shook her head. "I can't tell you that. Your father hated fighting. Oh, he hated it. He would rather die than hurt someone."

"But he helped you?"

"Because some bad men wanted to hurt me."

Andrew nodded. But he didn't understand.

They stayed there a long time. His father's condition did not change. When the moon arose they heard the clatter of a horse's hooves outside. A man entered. Andrew recognized him as the doctor from Faenza, a town down the coast. He had come before when his father was ill. Now he bent and peered, then shook his head. "I'll wait a while," he said.

Andrew fell asleep in the room. When he awakened during that deep night, he found that someone had carried him to his room in the tower. But he couldn't stay there. He had to know. Had to know now if his father was dying. He wanted to be there.

How could I fall asleep? he wondered as he creaked open the door at the bottom of the stairs.

The great room was dark and deserted. Embers glowed in the hearth across the room like winking red eyes.

He slipped through the room, sensing more than seeing where the chairs and the large table stood. He found the door to the southern corridor and gently pushed it open. A dim orange glow flickered into the hallway. It seemed to be coming from his father's room.

Andrew tiptoed into the corridor. He touched the wall and his fingers felt sweaty. His heart was hammering. The door was ajar. Orange light leaked through it. He saw a shadow move across the light. Maybe his father was up. Maybe his father could tell him once more . . . about names. He would listen now. He would understand. Or about fighting. When does one have to. . . . Maybe it was not his father there at all. His father was dying.

He wanted to see once more. To know. He needed to see his face clearly. To imprint it on his mind so he would never, ever forget him.

The boy crouched to his knees. He left the blanket lying in a heap. He crawled to the door of his father's room.

But he didn't dare look. The shadow kept crossing the orange light. Andrew heard the sound of something clanking in a bowl. He heard footsteps, someone muttering. His father—he was still alive. One more look.

On his hands and knees Andrew carefully peeked around the corner of the door frame. He saw the oil lamp guttering on the table, casting its dull glow across the room. On the table was a bowl. Some instruments lay in it. The man turned and took something out of the bowl. A knife, its sharp blade glittering in the light. He was the doctor.

Holding the knife delicately in one hand the doctor moved back to the bed. He lifted Elhrain's arm, the one with the scarred ridge, studied it momentarily, then set it down and raised the other one. Then, in one deft movement, he laid the knife against the inside of the upper arm and made a quick, hard cut.

It seemed to Andrew that he could hear the flesh ripping. Then he was screaming over and over, "No, no!" at the top of his lungs. The startled doctor dropped the knife. Andrew rushed into the room, pounding at the doctor with his small fists, and he heard footsteps running in the corridor as he kept screaming and felt hands pulling at his shoulders and Doval's voice calling him. But he felt so very far away then, as if she could never call him back, and then someone's arms were cradling him just before the room started spinning and the light was leaving and everything turned dark.

CHAPTER TWO

The horses' hooves splashed muck from the road, flinging wet clots up onto their clothing, draping the horses themselves in a coat of reddish brown from midwithers down. The rain had stopped, but the air was so humid that the three riders were soaked with sweat. The horses blew long flecks of foam that twisted across their muddy chests like lacework.

When they came to a small river, Lycurgus turned off from the road, dismounted with a loud sigh and led his horse into the water to drink. Andrew and Dominic followed. The cool water felt good against their ankles, and the two boys quickly waded in above their knees.

"Not too far," Lycurgus muttered. "Sinkholes."

Dominic playfully splashed water at Andrew. In seconds the river was white with their kicking and splashing. The horses reared. Lycurgus grabbed their reins and shouted at them.

Andrew turned quickly to help. Dominic wasn't ready to stop. He flung a few more handfuls at his friend's back.

"Stop it," Andrew barked as he took the reins.

Dominic glowered at him. He was no longer willing to wrestle with Andrew. Too often he had been toppled by that lean, rangy body. And it puzzled Dominic. Surely he was the stronger. His arms were thick, his chest like a small barrel. Yet each time he wound up in the mud or dust.

* * *

For the last year a second tutor had been coming to the villa. Desidero doggedly continued his lessons during the early hours of the morning—reading and writing, Roman law, mathematics. They suffered through the lessons, willing them to end soon. Correct answers ensured that. If a point was missed, Desidero insisted on going over it again until the answers were perfect. Often Andrew would sit in a captive rage while Dominic struggled with some point. Dominic was not slow. He simply didn't know how to concentrate during the lesson. In many ways—the way he could manipulate others or talk someone into agreement, for example—Dominic far surpassed Andrew.

Not until the lesson was mastered, however, were the boys free from Desidero's authority and turned over to their new tutor—the *ludus*. Technically he was teacher of games, but his instruction went far beyond that. The *ludus*, a man named Catillo, had served under Lycurgus, that one-time Roman general, for many years. He was no longer young, but nonetheless powerfully skilled in the craft he taught.

Early in their lessons, after several weeks of studying horsemanship and just as they were beginning on the martial arts, Dominic had asked Catillo if he had ever been bested. He had replied, "There was only ever one man who could beat me, and he was one I would throw down my life for. So I never really found out."

"Who was it?" Dominic asked.

"My leader. My captain." Catillo nodded. "He's standing behind you."

Both boys had turned. With a slight smile on his face, Lycurgus stood at the edge of the yard, watching the lesson.

"He's an old man," Dominic said.

"Oh?" Catillo's brows lifted. "What does age have to do with it? If so, then I am old to you. Right? So, why don't you beat me?"

"I bet I could," Dominic answered. He was angry, unaccustomed to being pushed the way he pushed others. At fifteen he was a muscular boy, and few people pushed him at all. "You're not much bigger than I am."

"Would you like odds?" Catillo asked. "Shall I place one hand behind my back?" He did so. "Shall I turn my back, giving you the advantage of surprise?"

He had hardly done so when Dominic leaped out at him, arms spread, legs surging forward in a charge. In one deft movement, so quick Andrew could scarcely follow it, Catillo flicked a hand to Dominic's wrist, bent his shoulder and sent the boy flying into the dust.

Andrew hooted with laughter.

Dominic's face was red with fury. He leaped up and ran at Andrew. Instinctively, imitating Catillo's movement as best he could, Andrew grabbed Dominic's wrist and twisted him over his shoulder. It was clumsy and inexpert. But Dominic landed in the dust once more.

Quickly Catillo stepped between them.

"You've been cheating," Dominic growled. "Where did you learn to do that?"

"I watched Catillo. Just now," Andrew answered.

"Cheater," Dominic muttered. "Besides that, it was my bad wrist. The one you broke."

As time passed, Andrew could tell that Catillo was intensifying the speed and power of his blows. Yet Andrew parried them easily. Andrew was certain that at any moment Catillo could surprise him and overpower him. Catillo himself grew less certain of it by the day.

There were still often guests for dinner in those days. Sometimes they would stay for several days, sleeping in the rooms formerly kept by Elhrain and Taletha. Often they would talk in the strange native language of Doval, a painstakingly complex language that Andrew was just beginning to learn. But when the stories would start, he would sit enthralled. Doval told the old stories of their people, how their Lord would help them in times of trouble, how the people fell into trouble when they had forsaken their Lord. Glorious battles. Angels routing the enemy. Prophets wandering the desert.

"Was my father a prophet?" Andrew once asked.

"No," Doval answered, smiling. "I wouldn't call him that at all. Why do you ask?"

"He spoke about the desert. He lived there."

"True. He did. So did your mother. But not all desert wanderers are prophets. Nor are all prophets wanderers of the desert. Nonetheless, the desert was always close to our people."

"I'm glad it's not here," said Andrew.

"Yes," said Doval. "Yes." But she looked troubled when she said it. And then she closed as always by talking about the One prophesied.

Andrew wondered then, if she had really known this True King, why was she just—Doval? His aunt. Surely a powerful king would make more of his followers.

That was one of the last times Dominic had attended the evening sessions. Andrew walked him partway down the hill to the valley. The moon had risen full, a huge orange globe poking above the summit of the bluff. Like a bowl, the valley filled with its strange light. Trees wore orange flowers for leaves; the stream flowed like a ripple of fruit juice under its light.

Dominic turned back and looked at the moon. "You don't really believe all that, do you?"

Andrew didn't know what to say. He felt embarrassed, like the time Dominic told him people made babies the same way animals in the field do. "Believe what?" he asked.

"That stuff about the True King." Dominic's voice was harshly derisive. "About gods and masters. They're just stories for old women."

"Why shouldn't I believe them? Doval was there. She knows."

"She's crazy, Andrew. So are you if you believe that." Dominic turned and walked down the hill, leaving Andrew standing alone, watching the moon purify to silver as it rose above the broad dark land.

* * *

After cleaning the worst of the muck from the horses' bellies and withers and letting them crop some grass, the three horsemen set out to get mud-splattered on the road all over again.

Andrew only vaguely sensed that, somehow, this was an important trip for him, some change in the course of his life. It had to be, for Lycurgus to undertake it and to take them along. Lycurgus seldom left the grounds of the villa anymore, trusting the buying and selling to envoys who came to him instead. Carried in weatherproof pouches behind the saddles, carefully wrapped, were articles of clothing that also signified the importance of the trip. They were to meet at the port city of Faenza with the important buyers, those who traded wine and produce from the Fontini Villa—as it was known throughout the region—and who in turn invested the proceeds or traded back. It was a passing of authority, an introduction to the heir of Fontini Villa—Andrew. As such, Andrew had insisted that Dominic have a place in it.

But that was only part of the business. The second meeting, also an introduction, was kept secret by Lycurgus. It would be no less important to the affairs of Fontini Villa and the future of Andrew and Dominic. Andrew had also always sensed that Fontini Villa played some larger role that he never fully understood. The night visitors who stayed briefly, then left fully provisioned for other areas were one thing. They seemed to Andrew to be desperate people when they arrived, but people who at least had a sense of hope when they left.

He thought too of the young couple, Samuel and Naomi, who had been given the special task of starting an olive grove on the far side of the northern hill, well past the vineyards. It had been a long time since he had seen them. He almost asked Lycurgus about them as they rode along, but when he glanced at Lycurgus the man seemed wrapped in reflection, and Andrew distracted himself instead by studying the gray, wet countryside they now passed through. Naomi and Samuel had stayed; all the other visitors had eventually left. Andrew wondered now why he had never quizzed his father more closely about it; he had merely accepted it as the pattern of the villa.

But why, he also wondered, *had I never asked?* Somehow he also understood that his father had wanted him to claim some task as his own, rather than having it handed to him. *Hadn't he hinted at that?* Andrew wondered. *Yes, but what exactly?* For the first time Andrew felt himself closer to answers for questions that he couldn't even fully voice.

Andrew's excitement grew as they crested the hill above the port city late in the afternoon and wound down the narrow, paved road lined with small houses leaning at impossible angles. The harbor held several ships, and the docks were a mad scramble of bodies loading and off-loading merchandise. The docks swirled in the mist and heat, in profanity and noise.

They paused on the road above the wharves, pulling their nervous horses to one side as wagons lumbered past. Lycurgus pointed at the ships one by one, identifying them by pennants dangling limply in the wet air from their mastheads. That African vessel bore spices, perhaps ivory and precious metals. That one was from the distant kingdom of Gaul and bore salt or linens. And that one—he straightened in the saddle as he pointed with excitement—that one was from Andrew's homeland. From the east.

What was in it?

Oh, olive oil, no doubt. And perhaps some travelers whom they might meet.

When?

Later. Be patient.

The road skirted the docks, side alleys spindling off between rickety warehouses to the wooden wharves. At one point Dominic hauled back on the reins.

"Did you see that?" he shouted.

Andrew and Lycurgus, riding ahead, turned toward him.

"What?"

"There. By that warehouse. Look. There's a bunch of them."

They looked into the shadows. Suddenly there was a sharp squealing sound. Small brown bodies tumbled and fought.

"Rats," muttered Lycurgus.

"Man, are they vicious," Dominic whispered.

"Fighting for food," Lycurgus said. "There's more of them every time I come here."

While they were watching the melee, the rats suddenly scurried for cover. A shouting voice echoed around the backside of the warehouse. A line of laborers, guided by a huge, bare-chested foreman, walked unsteadily along the planking to the warehouse door. Each was bent over, carrying a large vat across his bent shoulders. Each . . . was a boy.

Andrew sucked in his breath.

Last in line was a boy younger than he. He bent like a crooked letter in this line of sweating bodies, struggling under the load on his shoulders.

Lycurgus had turned to go, Andrew and Dominic following silently, when they heard the crash. The boy had tripped. The barrel spun from his shoulders, rolling with a crash into the warehouse wall. In an instant the foreman was on him, yanking him upright by a handful of hair. In one jerk he flung the boy aside, pointing him toward the fallen vat.

As the horses moved on, Andrew saw the lad struggling to lift the fallen barrel, clawing at its edges, and he felt his own heart hammering.

* * *

They were freshly bathed and dressed in their finest linens. Out of his pouch Lycurgus had produced small golden necklaces that he draped around their necks.

Andrew protested.

"It's part of the custom," Lycurgus said. "Live with it for one night. Tomorrow night we will donate them to a better cause. You'll see."

But tonight at the opulent villa where they met with the traders they wore them, and however out of place in all this shining finery Andrew felt, he noticed that everyone there wore the same apparel.

He couldn't stop thinking of the boy by the docks, his thin body scrabbling for the barrel, while he himself sat amid such luxury. *Why?* he wondered.

There seemed to be a servant for every guest present, young girls in silken garments bustling to and fro. One held a plate of large olives, from which the guests ate freely, grabbing a handful at a time. Another servant carried a silver pitcher, replenishing the wine at every turn. Others prepared the table.

Suddenly all the guests paused. Andrew heard his name called. He was stunned by all the activity, turning slowly to the others. They had raised their goblets toward him, saluting him. He stood gawking.

Dominic was at his side. "Bow, stupid," he hissed.

Andrew did so. The guests cheered.

"What was that for?" Andrew asked quietly.

Dominic smirked. "The new master of Fontini Villa."

The host led the way to the couches alongside the table, placing Lycurgus on his right hand, then Andrew and Dominic next to him as honored guests. Carefully they sat on the cushions. Across from him, a fat, bald-headed man studied Andrew.

"We look forward to continue serving you," he said with a greasy smile.

Andrew nodded.

"And we look forward to your service," Dominic said without hesitation. Andrew flushed. *How can Dominic do this so easily? So naturally!*

The serving girls trooped in a silken rustle, each bearing enormous platters. Some of the items Andrew recognized—sliced eggs, snails, oysters. As the platters emptied, they were whisked way. New ones appeared, bearing roast pheasant, a small roast lamb, slices of large fish, a platter of shrimp surrounded by asparagus. And as those platters emptied, accompanied by loud groans of pleasure and burps by the guests, small baskets of apples appeared.

Andrew felt slightly sickened by it all. It was too much. He noticed how Lycurgus carefully selected minute portions from each dish, eating slowly and methodically. He tried to follow suit. Next to him Dominic gorged himself.

Then the table was cleared, fresh wine appeared, and the discussion, as if on cue, took a serious turn. The room grew warm. Andrew felt sleepy, unable to keep his head erect while the men droned on with details about tariffs and taxes and destinations that made no sense to him. He felt disappointed, both in the proceedings and in his own thorough lack of interest. Lycurgus nudged him several times as if to say, Stay awake—this is important.

When Andrew slumped against Lycurgus's shoulder at one point, Lycurgus squeezed his arm. "You may leave now, if you wish," he whispered. "I will be several hours yet. Go back to the inn and sleep. It has been a long day. But be careful. Go straight to the inn."

Andrew nodded and turned to Dominic. Dominic's head was bent forward, shoulders slumped. He snored so loudly the speaker paused.

Andrew jabbed him in the ribs, startling Dominic awake. His unfocused eyes whirled. "Huh?" he said loudly.

"Come on. We're going back."

"All right." Dominic staggered upright, tripping over the cushion. Andrew caught him and steered him toward the door.

The cool night air jarred them both awake. They began walking downhill toward the inn. Somewhere in the night music played. It grew louder as they walked on.

Two men staggered down an alley. The music, louder now, seemed to come from that direction. They heard voices and rude boisterous laughter.

Dominic pulled at Andrew's sleeve. "Come on. Down here." He turned into the alley.

"No. Lycurgus said to go straight to the inn."

"Who cares what the old man says."

"I do. Come on. It's late."

"I'm just going to look. You coming? Or are you scared?"

Andrew paused. He thought about letting Dominic go alone. But it was their first time in the city. There was so much new to see, so much to learn. "All right. Just a look. Then we're going."

Dominic quickly walked down the alley and was lost in the shadows. Andrew hurried to catch up. Ahead they heard the two men laughing.

The alley opened into a small square. Before them stretched the wharves, the dark ships bobbing restlessly in their moorings, the waves slapping steadily against wooden pilings. In the shadows Andrew saw the shapes of the two men. One stood spraddle-legged. He heard the sound of splashing and the two laughed loudly, then walked into the deeper shadows. Andrew and Dominic stepped into the square. The two men weren't in sight.

The music came from a low wooden building along the wharf. The plank door stood ajar. Torches lit the interior and the air was smoky. Bodies moved like shadows through the smoke. Noise spilled out into the street.

Dominic crept along the walls of the warehouses making his way to the tavern. Andrew plucked at his sleeve. "We saw it," he muttered. "Time to go."

"What are you scared of?" hissed Dominic. "Let's get closer and take a look."

They stepped through a mud puddle, nearly stumbling, then regained the wooden planking. A small window was open-shuttered in the tavern. Dominic crept below it. He lifted his head, peered inside and sucked in his breath. "Come on. Look at this," he hissed to Andrew.

Andrew crept up beside him. At first he saw only careening bodies in the glare. Bodies moving together. Women and men. Directly on the other side of the window, a woman suddenly stood up. A man clawed at her shoulders. She erupted in drunken laughter as the man pulled her back down.

Andrew felt his stomach churning. The noise and the hot, sweaty stink of the place were overpowering.

He pulled at Dominic's shoulder. "Time to go. Now!" he said.

"Are you kidding?" Dominic said. "Look at this. Look at what they're doing! Right out in front of everybody."

Andrew heard a hissing sound, the scurry of claws across the wooden wharf. He whirled as a rat darted into the shadows under the planking. And he looked up into the faces of the two men they had followed.

One was grinning broadly, his large teeth glowing luridly in the light through the window. The other stood behind him, shoulders bent, arms flexed.

"Look what wandered into our hands," said the grinning man. "Two little rich boys."

Dominic turned slowly at the sound of the voice. "Oh, no," he moaned.

"Oh, yes," chortled the man. "My, my. What fine clothes. And what's that around your necks? Would it be . . . could it be . . . gold?"

He lurched forward to grab at Andrew's necklace. Andrew batted his hand away, and the man's grin disappeared.

"Okay, rich boy," he muttered. "I'll feed you to the rats."

Dominic broke, trying to run. The second man grabbed him and flung him heavily to the planking. The first man reached out again for Andrew's necklace.

Later Andrew could not say how it happened. All the lessons meshed without thinking. He instinctively grabbed the outstretched hand, twisting it violently and pulling the weight forward. The heavyset man careened past him, smashing headlong into the building. The wooden planks of the wall shuddered and someone inside yelled. As the man got to his knees, curses foaming at his lips, Andrew lashed out with a round kick. He pirouetted on the ball of his foot, bringing the full weight and force of his body behind the kick. It connected high, but it staggered the drunken man, toppling him over.

The second one released Dominic and leaped on Andrew's back. His weight brought Andrew to his knees. An elbow thrust, driven solidly back into the man's sternum, rocked him backward. Fingers clawed at Andrew's throat, squeezed down on his windpipe.

Then suddenly the hands went limp. Andrew heard a sickening thud. A body slumped to the ground. He knelt, gasping for breath. A hand reached under his shoulder helping him stand. He fought against it at first.

"Shh," came the voice. "Easy, Andrew. You did well."

Andrew turned. He looked into the grim face of Catillo.

"You did well. But it was unnecessary. You failed to obey. That was the first step. You chose to disobey and this is the consequence." He nodded at the two prone bodies. "Always, there is a consequence for your choices. For good or evil."

Andrew nodded. "But—"

"No. Please, no buts." For the first time Andrew noticed a man standing some distance behind Catillo. He wore a brown cloak that blended into the night. Regardless of the darkness, Andrew could feel the man's eyes probing him.

Catillo turned to Dominic standing in the shadows. "Was it worth it, Dominic?"

Dominic shook his head angrily. "I didn't do a thing," he muttered with shame and anger. "I just stood there . . ."

"Yes. And now it is time to leave."

Catillo turned. The boys followed him, but Dominic walked several paces behind, his footsteps ringing angrily against the wharf. The man in the brown robe seemed to float eerily in the fringe of darkness.

Andrew wanted to say something to Dominic. To tell him not to worry about it. But his neck hurt where the man had grabbed him, and he followed Catillo silently back to the inn.

CHAPTER THREE

The next morning Andrew, Dominic and Lycurgus rode far into the hills above Faenza on a roundabout course, traveling leisurely across hillsides and meadows. Catillo was nowhere to be seen. Yet Andrew was certain Catillo knew precisely where they were. All that time he had never been far away.

Dominic rode head down, refusing to speak. When Andrew said something to him, Dominic glared angrily.

Lycurgus, if he knew about the events of the night before, said nothing. Catillo had escorted them back to the inn. "I trust you'll stay here now," he had said at the door. Andrew nodded for both of them. Catillo disappeared into the darkness.

By midmorning the sun burned away the wet mists. The landscape was green velvet. The horses' hooves made damp sounds against the sod. They were frisky this morning, occasionally breaking into a quick trot. They kept wanting to edge off the trail and sneak a mouthful of the lush grass. One of them would let its head droop low, then lower, with exaggerated weariness. Then, as the scent of clover grew overpowering, suddenly its nose would be buried in the grass as it tried to walk and crop at the same time. It became a kind of game, letting the reins relax until the temptation grew too great, then goading them back onto the trail.

Lycurgus seemed in no hurry today, content to watch the rolling landscape and to enjoy the warmth of the sun. For a long time they could watch the sea recede behind them as they climbed into the hills. Then there was only the quiet whisper of the wind among trees, the call of signaling birds and the dulled clop of hooves. When they stopped high in the hills for lunch, Lycurgus let the animals crop freely. He ate, then leaned back on the turf. In moments his chest rose and fell as he slept.

Andrew studied his uncle then, and thought to himself, *He is getting old. Very old.* The powerful chest rose and fell. The sun flickered through the shading leaves of the overhead trees. It lit Lycurgus's face in a myriad of wrinkles. His mouth dropped open and his breathing deepened. He snored and Andrew chuckled.

Dominic sat a slight way off, pulling blades of grass. He twisted them through his fingers over and over, knotting them into tight green balls that he tossed down the hillside.

After a while Dominic got up. He stood looking at Lycurgus. "Did you ever think," he said slowly, "about just taking that?" He stuck out his leg, pointing with his sandal to the small leather pouch tied to Lycurgus's belt. That morning Lycurgus had collected the three golden necklaces again and jammed them thoughtlessly into the pouch.

"No," Andrew replied. "Why should I?"

Dominic's eyes were filled with something that chilled Andrew. "That's right," he said. "It's yours anyway."

"No, it's not," Andrew protested, but Dominic had gone to retrieve the horses.

* * *

They arrived at the stone building at evening, after circling down through the hills into a green valley. The building itself was clearly the remains of some old fortress, long since abandoned to the ravages of time and scavengers. It overlooked the valley through small windows above a ruined wall that lay in collapsed heaps of stone. The walls once curved into the rock of the hill, enclosing a small, quiet space. A stream issued through a gap in the wall, wound down the hillside, disappeared into a thicket and emerged in a small lake that nestled in the valley like a blue jewel. It winked as clouds danced across the sun.

Following Lycurgus, they dismounted inside the gate. To one side was a stone building, once the main assembly of the fortress. To the other was a row of wooden stables, some caved in and lying in ruins. They stabled the horses in the tightest structures. Between the stable and the main building little stone paths ran among gardens where a profusion of flowers ran riot in color. Behind them, in the face of the hillside, was the dark mouth of a cave. A stone wall had been built partway up and across its entrance. The place of last resistance, no doubt, in time of attack. Andrew wondered if blood had been shed here, if battles from some long ago past carried the noise of swords and armor and arrows cascading up the hillside. Now there was only the sighing of the evening breeze that brushed thickets and flowers. Andrew noted where the stream issued from the cave, darting in a silvery thread under the rocky wall.

An old man stood upright among the flowers. He held a small shovel in his hand. He grinned broadly at them, showing a mouthful of gums. He waved his shovel.

Lycurgus waved back to him and finished unsaddling the horses with the two boys. They found brushes and began currying the animals. The old gardener entered the stable, went to a side room and began forking out hay that the horses fell to eagerly.

"We're a long way from Faenza," Andrew observed. He rubbed his sore backside and grinned.

"Actually," Lycurgus said, "Faenza lies just over the backside of this hill."

"What! We've been riding all day," Dominic said in disbelief.

"Yes. We have been. But we've been riding in a circle, through the hills."

"Why?"

"Because," Lycurgus said evenly, "I want you to know these hills. And I wanted to give you time to think. You both had things to think about, didn't you?"

"Catillo told," Dominic muttered.

"That's not the point," said Lycurgus. "The point is, What do you think of what you did?"

"It was my fault," Dominic said. Andrew was surprised how easily and readily he said it.

"Really?" Lycurgus's eyes seem to pierce Andrew, rooting through his soul.

"I'm sorry, Lycurgus," Andrew said. "Are we really that close to Faenza?"

"There is proof," Lycurgus said. He pointed toward the cave. A large brown rat was wriggling under the gap the stream had made, into the cave. "But now," he said, "to the real purpose of our coming all this way." He pointed to the stone building. "This was once a Roman fortress. During the Etruscan Wars. Now we call it a chapel." With that he strode across the garden path toward the stone building.

The chapel door seemed not so much an entrance into a room as a separation of worlds. The verdant beauty of the hills soared outward, rising from valleys up along hillsides to the blue vault of the skies. But when one passed through the chapel door, one seemed bathed in an inward quiet, as if removed from the earth for a time. It was a haven, a safe place for going inward and for circling the hills and valleys of one's own life.

Andrew paused by the doorway, letting his eyes adjust to the muted light. The construction was simple in design, and the place was not large. Plain wooden benches were placed here and there, several of them pushed back against the walls. The floor was leveled rock of the hillside, swept clean and polished by years of boots and sandals across its surface. Narrow window slits stood high in the walls. Andrew thought back to its original design as a fortress. It was nearly impossible to imagine now, but surely the window slits were built high so that men could stand on benches or catwalks inside and rain arrows down on some foe. In the evening sunlight that filtered through the slits, Andrew imagined ghostlike warriors, sweating at their tasks, the twang of bows, the clash of armor echoing from outside.

Not now. Bird calls fluted in from the garden like an evening hymn.

At the north end, several low steps led to a raised dais. Of course, in times long past that would be where the captain of the men sat at his table. Now a low wooden kneeling bench rested on the stone.

In the center of the chapel, tables and benches had been arranged for the evening meal. Already Lycurgus mingled with a small group of men and women. A priest of some sort, wearing a loose brown robe and sandals, greeted Lycurgus with a hug. Their embrace seemed slightly embarrassing to Andrew. Deftly, almost casually, Lycurgus unfastened the pouch at his waist and handed it to the man. *Lycurgus is the one embarrassed,* Andrew thought with a start.

The brown-robed man turned momentarily in Andrew's direction.

Those eyes! They were like hawks diving inward, irresistible. *The same man from the wharf?* It couldn't be.

Then, one by one as he was introduced by the brown-robed priest, Lycurgus turned and embraced the others assembled. They seemed nervous and tentative. Some clung to Lycurgus like hope itself.

A girl walked through a small door on the other side of the chapel, holding the hands of two young children. Three other children followed them. The children skipped and danced. They were dirty from play. They were happy and tousled.

Not the girl. She looked a mere wisp in her brown cloak. She released the children's hands, and they went bounding to their parents. The girl herself walked alone to a bench at the table and sat, her legs tucked under her, hands folded in her lap. Her head was bent down, the hood of her brown cloak pulled forward. Her dark hair curled out from the hood, hiding her cheeks. She lifted her eyes, wide and brown and glistening wetly, and Andrew could not take his own eyes off her. She seemed to feel him watching her. She lifted her gaze once more, met his and gave a nervous smile. Then her lips trembled and she bent her head again.

He was halfway across the room when Lycurgus called to him and Dominic. Andrew stopped and blinked. He glanced again at the girl and then at Dominic, who was leaning against the wall inside the doorway, surveying the room casually with his dark probing eyes. Then Lycurgus was introducing them to the people. Soon everyone began sitting at the tables, the young children scurrying and jostling each other for chosen spaces, and several of the women carried in food from the door the girl had come through.

Andrew wasn't hungry. The bread was warm and fresh, the cheese tangy, the lamb stew as sweet as honey. But his eyes kept straying down the length of the table. She kept her head down, methodically and slowly eating her portion as if without enjoyment, without thinking. Just once, when a neighbor asked her to pass the cheese, she looked up. Again her eyes lighted on his. This time she held his gaze for a moment before turning away. Andrew remembered thinking, *They are the saddest eyes I've ever seen. And the most beautiful.* It was a moment before he remembered the bread in his hand, held halfway to his open mouth.

When the meal ended, and the empty plates removed, and when the people fell to talking softly, Andrew could not take his eyes off her. He only half heard the words.

"Safe places will be found," the priest was saying. "Some of you will go further north. There are settlements. Joseph," he said, addressing a young man across the table, "I understand it is your desire to bring the way of the Lord to the northern people. Perhaps Catillo can direct you. I don't know the way. There is an old man named Rafeo—he has been with us from the start . . ."

"Must be a very old man by now," someone said.

The priest smiled. "Yes, indeed. Like some others I know of?" His comment was a question, and he smiled at Lycurgus when he said it. "Lycurgus too has been here since the start. Someday perhaps you will hear his story.

"But this Rafeo is hard to find. Something of a hermit, really."

"What good are hermits?" someone asked. "At a time like this."

"Each has a calling. Rafeo knows the northern mountains. And the language of the people. That is his calling. Perhaps he will find *you*, Joseph."

The young man nodded.

"It doesn't sound safe," one woman said.

The priest raised his eyebrows. "No. It isn't," he confessed.

"What do you hear from Rome?"

"As you know," the priest said, "when they seized the Apostle, I left. He . . . he was an orator. He wanted to have his voice heard as a Roman citizen, even at the cost of his life. His words have been recorded. A copy of one of his letters circulates even among us here. It encourages many. It is not my calling, however, to be a defender of the Way in such a manner. It was the Apostle himself who insisted I leave."

"I heard he was crucified," someone said. "Head down. He thought himself unworthy to die in the same way as the Messiah. He was crucified that way by his own choice."

The priest lowered his eyes. "It is not my place to speak of these things."

Lycurgus's deep rumbling voice broke in. "Yet you deserve to know the truth. You have had to flee the homeland for different reasons. Except for Joseph and our brother Gaius there," he nodded toward the end of the table, "who are from the church in Rome, each has left under a threat, each has lived for the cause of the master, each is seeking a new life of service.

"Perhaps it was the Apostle's most important teaching not to forsake the affairs and needs of this world while awaiting Christ's return. No. There are no hermits among *us*."

"Only martyrs," the man named Gaius murmured. Andrew saw Dominic look up then, nodding approval as he caught Gaius' eye. No one else seemed to notice.

"The church in Rome is under siege, much like the church in the homeland," Lycurgus said quietly. "Each with its own dangers. In the homeland the persecution is often subtle—multiplying the taxes, taking someone's land." A husband and wife, who sat with two of their sleepy children, nodded vigorously.

"In Rome, it is often more barbaric. During the last years some of our brothers and sisters have been torn by beasts in the amphitheater. As sport. Or burned alive. As entertainment.

"So," Lycurgus said, "we don't minimize the risks. It is costly to walk in the Master's way."

"How much has it cost you?" Gaius interrupted. The table fell silent. The words were out. Gaius hesitated. "I mean . . ." he faltered.

The priest stood up. Anger flashed in his eyes.

Lycurgus held out a hand, motioning him down. "I am not here to tell my story," he said gently. "Only to help you tell yours."

From where he sat Andrew studied Lycurgus in a new way. Yes, he had heard stories. Overheard them. He could not help it in the old days when his father and mother were alive and would sit with Doval and Lycurgus by the tiled pool, and they would wonder aloud and reflect and remember. His mother had told him stories of the homeland. But he had been young then, and only half-listening, anxious instead to run off and do something with Dominic. For the first time there arose within him a burning curiosity about his homeland.

While the others continued talking he mused to himself on the stories his mother had told him. He found himself wishing that he had listened closer. He had missed so much. And now she, they, were no longer there to tell him. For the first time in a long time he felt the old overwhelming sadness rise in him, and he nearly felt tears in his eyes.

He blinked rapidly, lifted his head and saw the girl watching him. She did smile then.

They were breaking up from the table. They would sleep here tonight, unrolling pallets and blankets on the floor, and leave for their new homes, their new destinations, tomorrow.

Andrew and Dominic were sleepy after the long day of riding. They followed Lycurgus and the priest through the back door. On the other side of the chapel, by the ruined wall, was a squat little house, probably the priest's quarters. Apparently they would sleep there.

Lycurgus walked beside Andrew. The boy paused suddenly and spoke. "You gave him the necklaces."

Lycurgus chuckled. "Yes. That's how it works."

"How what works?"

"That's our contribution now. It was your mother's idea. To make the villa a working farm, not an old people's home to hide away in. Last night you met the people we trade with. Tonight you met the reason we trade with them."

"I see," Andrew said. "The gold? It helps these people find new homes?"

"New homes. New communities. To further the Cause. Unfortunately," he murmured, "one of them died on the way over. A woman named Rachel. Her husband had been seized, and he died in prison." Lycurgus paused as if remembering. "The daughter has no place to go," he said, "no one to go with. So she will be going with us."

"What is her name?" Andrew asked.

Lycurgus eyed him keenly. "Hadesseh," he said. "She will join us in the morning when we leave."

Suddenly the priest stood before them, melting out of the darkness.

"This is also one other you should know," Lycurgus said. "His name is Emeth."

Andrew looked up into the hawklike features of the man, seemingly carved out of silver in the moonlight. He nodded slightly.

"There will come a time . . ." Lycurgus began. Then he stopped. "Enough for now. It is time to sleep. I have a few things to discuss yet with Emeth."

CHAPTER FOUR

C ome on, come on." Andrew whirled and parried a leg blow.
"You're getting old, Catillo. Old and slow," he taunted.

Both men were bathed in sweat, but their breathing was even, carefully controlled. The hot summer sun beat upon their naked shoulders. When one twisted and feinted, flecks of sweat spun off like light rain.

"I bet you're just getting tired now. Need to rest, Catillo? Just tell me and I'll pop you in the ocean. You can float all day. Like an old man in his bed."

Catillo spun. He feinted a side kick, his body as limber as a dancer's, then flicked a chopping blow at Andrew.

Andrew was caught. He went with the blow instead of resisting it, diving into a side flip that would bring his legs around, the right leg coiled to strike out. Even as he spun he imprinted in his mind the spot on Catillo's leg where he would land the blow.

Catillo was a brown blur against the ocean waves. Sunlight flashed like tongues of flame over their long white crests.

Grinning with expectation, Andrew drove his hand down into the beach sand to execute his flip. Then, below the surface of sand, his hand struck a sharp rock. His wrist twisted at the sudden impact, the kick was off target, his body tumbled awkwardly.

With one lightning kick, Catillo caught Andrew's upside-down body right in the buttocks. Andrew spun head over heels, tumbling down the beach. He lay spread-eagled, face to the sun, laughing. A wave crashed up the shore and foamed over his body.

"Oh, you were lucky that time," Andrew said, wringing his wrist.

"Lucky?" Catillo asked in amazement. "Always expect the unexpected, Andrew. Know how to use it to your advantage." He reached out a hand to help him up.

Andrew was tempted to twist it and flip his tutor into the waves. He grinned broadly. Catillo probably expected that. Instead, he clenched Catillo's hand and bounced upright. Then he turned, ran into the waves, dove in and swam back.

Catillo was sitting on a rock, watching.

"Come here," he said.

Andrew walked to him.

"Lift your arm to strike. No! Not like that. Like you mean it! Strike me!"

In a blur Catillo's fingers jabbed the striking arm. It was like a serpent, so swiftly did the hand strike. The fingers caught Andrew's arm precisely inside the forearm and squeezed down on a nerve. His entire arm felt paralyzed. He gritted his teeth at the numbing pain.

"You know the blows, as well as I. Better. You would have beaten me— again," Catillo added with a smile. "But now you must learn how to do it *without* blows. Like this." He squeezed suddenly on the nerve. Andrew felt as if the bone itself would rupture, but he struggled not to move, not to cry out. "Very good, Andrew," Catillo breathed as he released the hold. "Very good."

"Yes, well," Andrew muttered, "it's all a game anyway."

"Oh?" Catillo lifted his eyebrows.

"When will I ever need it, running this?" He flung his hand upward.

They were at the base of the promontory. Above them, unseen from the shore, lay the vast lands of the Fontini villa.

"I don't know," Catillo admitted. "It was Lycurgus's wish. I don't know why."

Both fell silent, thinking of the hillside sepulchre now holding three bodies. There was only one empty shelf within it.

They climbed over the rocks that littered the shore toward the path they had cleared up the face of the bluff. Andrew wore a pair of brown peasant trousers, loose and baggy, held at the waist by a dark sash of cloth for a belt. He tugged the baggy shirt over his shoulders. "This . . . this is just . . . exercise," he muttered. He looked out over the shore as if to signify everything that had occurred there that morning.

Catillo shook his head. "No. More than that. You have a gift for it, Andrew. The quickness, to be sure. The strength, yes. But also the instinct."

"Bah! What good is it?" He began climbing the narrow path among the rocks.

Once again the dark memory of the Faenza docks slipped into his mind. He fought against it. He *had* been tested that night, and he knew he could have taken the two thugs, even without Catillo's help. It seemed a long time ago. In terms of his skill, he was just an infant then. Now he found himself thinking, with increased frequency, what he would have done with the skills he *now* possessed. Would he be able to control it? Temptation. *But you can prove yourself*, another part of his mind insisted. The living test!

"Lycurgus thought it had a purpose," Catillo said, as if to say, That's reason enough.

"Playing. That's what it is. While I have this place to run. Maybe I should just let Dominic run it all. He has the head for it."

Catillo climbed behind him. "Some would say he runs it too much already," he said softly.

"What's that supposed to mean?" Andrew looked down at Catillo. They were high above the shore now, clinging effortlessly to the steep windings of the trail.

Andrew leaned back against the rock, his long muscular body relaxing easily at the precarious height. He never tired of watching the ocean. Its infinite restlessness. Its deep power.

A gull swooped suddenly from a small ledge above him. It was the ugly bird with the mottled pink flesh above its beak. Andrew could tell by the way it flung itself into flight, dropping like a stone until it caught the wind in its wings. Sometimes it seemed to plummet nearly to the rocks before it miraculously caught an air current.

Andrew glanced along the rocky bluff. Perched on an outcropping from the face of the bluff, under a slight overhang that could be a cave hollowed by the sea winds, squatted Gregor. His long, powerful arms were splayed across his knees, and he watched the bird soar gracefully now. It almost seemed Gregor himself was going to spring out, take flight. Then the misshapen head turned toward Andrew, fixing on him that peculiar look—half-scowl, half-smile. Andrew waved and Gregor turned away, shifting his thick haunches like a resting animal.

"I'm not sure I meant anything. Next week," Catillo said as he paused and looked out over the ocean. This high up the wind whipped his hair and had already dried the sweat on his body. "Next week you go to meet the traders. You'll see Emeth."

"Of course."

"Why don't you ask him about these things? I am not a wise man. Never pretended to be. But if Lycurgus believed in it, then it has a purpose, Andrew. Trust him."

Andrew climbed over the top of the bluff. He stood there, scanning the vast sweep of the hillside and valley before him. Suddenly his eyes lightened. He saw Hadesseh moving around a thicket on her hands and knees. *Probably looking for her precious herbs*, he thought. He grinned.

Ignoring Catillo, who began walking to the villa, Andrew set out toward the girl. Her back was to him. On her hands and knees she suddenly began digging with the small pointed shovel. Andrew decided to make a game of it. He darted to a pile of rocks left from the quarrying. He could hear her humming softly. Her voice was like a bird singing—so light, so gay.

At that moment a bird called out from deep in the thicket. A perfect imitation followed. Hadessch. Andrew crawled through the knee-deep grass toward her. The calls echoed back and forth. He heard her giggling.

How she had changed during the two years she had been here. The sadness wore away like hours, and a cheerful, childlike gaiety emerged. And she was quick. Within months under Doval's teaching Hadesseh had learned the language of the land. Still, she and Doval would often sit by the tiled pool speaking in their native tongue. Andrew had tried but never had mastered their language. Compared to Latin and Greek, it seemed a maze of incoherence.

Andrew lifted his head. He could see her clearly, sitting cross-legged by the thicket, arranging some plants in her basket. Here was another thing she had learned from Doval: this pharmacopeia of plants and herbs. They all looked alike to Andrew, but to Hadesseh and Doval they were remedies for illnesses and pains beyond counting. Her perfectly oval face was bent forward, studying the plants. Framed by the sun and lifted by the sea wind, her dark brown hair blew out with tousled reddish highlights. She straightened, stretching with her arms uplifted as if to loosen a kink in her back. Andrew sucked in a breath as the sun defined her figure. *She's not a little girl anymore*, he thought with sudden embarrassment. He felt a pang of guilt for watching.

Andrew lowered himself, slithering quietly through the grass toward her. He lifted his head, searching over a small boulder. *She must be close now*, he thought.

He looked around, raising his head higher. She was gone. How did . . .

He felt something sting his leg. Another. A pebble struck him on the ankle.

Where did that . . . He stood up. "All right," he shouted. "Where did you go?"

Hadesseh darted out from behind a nearby rock. "A fat old bear was sliding through the grass." She laughed. "So clumsy and slow. I had to wake him up." She hurled a small stone at him.

Andrew caught it easily and flipped it aside. He began to chase her through the grass, dodging, darting. At last he caught her. They fell to the grass tumbling and laughing. Hadesseh was giggling and wriggling like a slippery fish. Andrew caught her knees, began to tickle her as he had when she was younger. Hadesseh squirmed with laughter.

He stopped suddenly. He lay back, his heart pounding. "So, I'm old and slow, huh?"

"Maybe just clumsy," she said laughing. "And besides, you don't know how to listen."

"Listen?"

"To the wind. To the land, silly."

"So the wind speaks? What does it say?"

She smiled at him, as if to say, If you don't know, how can I tell you? But then she answered, "I hear it. It talks to the trees. It makes grass sounds. It brings stories from the sea. It tells me when a clumsy man tries to sneak through the grass."

Andrew stood and reached out a hand to help her, but she bounded up like a skittish lamb. She fetched her basket, and they began walking back to the villa.

"You know," Andrew observed, "you're growing up."

"I am."

"I probably shouldn't chase you anymore. Tickle you. It's not for grown-up girls."

A shadow crossed her face. "I'm not so very old, brother," she said.

Andrew chuckled.

Suddenly she held up an arm, stopping him. "Shh," she whispered. "Don't move."

Andrew was going to ask why, but suddenly she drifted off in a circle, moving so silently and smoothly through the grass, around the rocks, that Andrew marveled at it. She moved out, then began angling softly back to a large outcropping of rock only a few feet ahead. And Andrew saw what she was moving toward.

The snake lay in a light tan coil against the rock. It had sensed their footsteps and had raised its head, forked tongue slithering in and out, tasting the air. Hadesseh crept behind it, and Andrew noticed now that her shadow fell behind her, away from the snake.

He was going to shout, "Don't!" when suddenly she bent and flicked out her hand, snaring the snake directly behind its blunt, triangular head. She lifted the snake delightedly, its body coiling about her arm. She held it out. Andrew stood rigidly.

"You're afraid," she said in surprise.

"No. Put it down."

"Yes, you are. Admit it."

"Just don't touch me."

"It's harmless. And even if it weren't, it could do no harm. See." Hadesseh jabbed the head toward Andrew, its jaws agape but futilely immobilized under her fingers. Andrew jumped backward.

"Don't," he repeated.

"Very well." With a shake she dropped the creature into the brush where it slithered away. "They all look dangerous," she said. "The trick is knowing which ones really are."

As they approached the villa, Andrew saw Dominic standing down the road, talking to a strange horseman. Andrew couldn't make out the man's features at this distance. Yet he felt it was someone he had seen before, someone he had met. The horseman looked up at him, wheeled his horse and galloped down the road.

Dominic turned and walked to meet them.

"Who was that?" Andrew asked.

"No one. Just a traveler asking directions." Dominic averted his eyes and walked ahead of them toward the villa.

He had moved into a room there during this past year, down the northern corridor from Doval. They had rooms to spare, Hadesseh having moved into Andrew's old room, next to the empty room of Elhrain and Taletha. It was easier for Dominic to live there in many ways. It freed up space for his own parents in their tiny house. And from the villa Dominic could better oversee the tasks of the laborers. When Lycurgus died, Dominic had easily stepped to the task. He had nearly complete charge of running the daily affairs of the villa now, gradually displacing Desidero and Griselde from that role also.

As Dominic walked toward the gate, he turned suddenly and called, "You're still going to Faenza?"

"Yes, surely," Andrew said.

"I have to talk with you before you leave."

"Yes. Tonight, then. At dinner."

Dominic nodded and walked inside.

*   *   *

Hadesseh ran on ahead of Andrew. He slowed, watching her. "Brother," she had said. Truly, Lycurgus and Doval, who married too late in life to have children of their own, had found in her the adopted daughter they had always longed for. And now that Lycurgus had died, Hadesseh was Doval's closest companion, like mother and daughter. *Cousin, then*, thought Andrew, *but in ways so much more than brother.* He found himself at once comforted and unsettled by the deep place she had taken in his thoughts and heart.

Inside the gate, Hadesseh knelt in front of Doval's chair. Even in the warm sunlight, Doval had a blanket wrapped about her thin shoulders. Her skin was like worn parchment, so thin it looked. Yet her eyes glittered when she saw Andrew approaching, and she lifted one hand weakly to wave.

She sat, as she so often did these days, in the chair by the pool. For hours she watched the light ripple on its surface. The large white and pink flowers of the water plants floated as if on sunlight. Occasionally one of the fish nosed the surface, begging a scrap of food, and the water parted in neat concentric ripples. Each morning Hadesseh helped her out to the chair, and they would sit for hours, sometimes talking in soft murmuring tones, sometimes just sitting in absolute quiet. *Listening to the wind?* Andrew wondered. And what stories did she see there as she gazed at the water's mirrored surface? Did it reflect only sunlight and warmth, or were there darker passages in the watery depths of memory? Sometimes Andrew sat with her, asking questions, begging stories. Her answers were always cryptic, confusing more than clarifying.

One thing emerged clearly. At the center—the very heart—of all their days and ways was the strange, mystical figure of the Messiah. Mystical to Andrew. To Doval, as to his parents and to Lycurgus, he had been a physical reality. Andrew wondered over this. Kings lived and died. They ruled and were replaced. This, they said, was the one eternal King.

Increasingly, as age rendered Doval less able to tell him, Andrew desired to know more and more. Knowledge was a raw hunger in him. His mind searched for answers. Doval's eyes would brighten at first under his questions, then she would tire even as she began talking. She would shake her head, lapsing into her native tongue before she dozed off under the blessing of the warm sun. Her gray head would lean forward, and Andrew wanted to will her awake, to will her into providing answers for him.

So often then, as he sat by her side by the pool, the image of his father and his mother would float into his mind. It was nearly impossible to think of them as young . . . as two people who fell in love, and loved. And the other stories—of their wanderings in the desert, their flight from the homeland. When he had probed Doval for answers, pleading with her, she would smile at him and say something like—"Your father wanted you to live your own story." Or something that made no sense at all—"The Messiah has his own story to tell through you."

Was this it? This villa? Was this to be his story? Oh, the work seemed important enough and only since Lycurgus's death had Andrew realized the full complexity of it. The villa had been Lycurgus's inheritance, and for this final chapter in their lives it had become a means of helping others in flight as they themselves had once had to flee.

Quite some time after his father died, Andrew had wandered into his parents' room early one morning. When he opened the window shutters dust motes spiraled through the sunbeam. The polished tiles of the floor held a light layer of dust. Andrew simply stood there a moment, studying the spare furnishings of the room. The stone walls were covered by hanging tapestries as in the other bedrooms. He studied their strange patterns, the intricacy of the designs. It felt to him like he was invading someone's privacy, or that he might at any moment see his mother enter with a smile on her face, or his father sitting quietly on the bench, face turned toward the sun, watching. He felt . . . like he did when he had first entered the chapel at Faenza—as if he were in a holy place where something more than merely human life lived. Then he remembered his father's body on the bed, the dark physician preparing the body for burial, and he shivered.

Silently he walked to the curtained alcove and drew the hanging aside. The drapery opened on a small bench, worked into the stone of the wall. The bench itself was a wooden covering, tightly fitted to the stonework. Andrew had wondered about the alcove. He could not remember his father ever sitting there. The curtain was always drawn. Carefully, as if disturbing something fragile, Andrew sat down on the bench. The wood shifted, ever so slightly. He stood up.

He had always assumed the wood had rested directly upon stone. He studied it, tapped the thick wood in several places. *What if it covered something?* His fingers explored the edges; tightly fitted, inset to the stonework, no gap appeared. His exploring fingers found a knothole in the upper corner. He was surprised that one finger could slip into it rather easily. Excited now, he tugged, and the wooden covering slid out.

He lifted away the covering to find three small chests within. One by one, he drew them out and opened them, hesitant at first, then as if by some compulsion. The first held clothing, carefully folded and layered. So few. And, to his surprise, he found his childhood blanket folded among the clothes. As he fingered it, his throat constricted suddenly. So long ago it seemed now. Carefully he refolded and replaced it.

The second chest held odds and ends from their daily life at the villa—records and notations. He found a long list of family names and destinations—some places familiar to him, others not, and tidy notes indicating some payments. He didn't think they were in his father's handwriting. Although he couldn't be certain. The third box was smaller. He didn't expect it to hold anything of importance. On top lay a ribboned tube of several pieces of parchment. When he opened it, a stoppered bottle of ink and several quills slipped out. Andrew caught them in his lap. He was kneeling now. The parchments were all blank. He laid them aside.

Under them was an odd piece of cloth. Andrew lifted it, shook it out.

It was an old cloak, sun-scorched to a pale color, its hem ragged and torn, its fabric worn so thin at spots he could see through it. He wondered at the garment, why it should be kept there, so old and worn and worthless it was. He set it aside.

Under it lay an equally worn leather pouch. It was heavy. He opened it, the leather strips stiff and unyielding in his fingers. Five gold coins. He held one to the light. It was embossed with the figures of two intertwined serpents. They seemed warm and alive in his hand. Nervously Andrew slipped them back into the bag and cinched the drawstring.

He lifted the last object. Even before he unwrapped the carefully folded cloth, he could tell by the feel of it what lay inside. It was a knife, its blade a dark shining color, its handle worn as smooth as polished stone. He held it and studied it a long time before he rewrapped it.

Andrew sat there a moment wondering. So this was it? This was all of it. Mementos of a past. There was nothing to guide him. Empty parchments. A few coins he had no need of. A knife and a worn rag of a garment. He replaced the objects one by one. The parchments, quills and ink he held back. He thought he would use them himself, but when they had lain for several weeks in his room in the tower, he tied them all together and presented them to Hadesseh for her amusement. It was not unusual in the weeks following to find her sketching one of the plants she had found, rendering it in such vivid detail it looked a perfect copy. Often she used some materials she had found—earth, stones, plants—to make dyes to color in the parts of the drawing.

* * *

Andrew saw her now sitting beside Doval, laughing with her, and he smiled to himself. *Probably she was telling Doval how she had frightened him with the snake,* he thought.

He stood before his aunt and took her hand. It was like holding a bunch of tiny twigs, so fragile and thin were her fingers. Doval smiled at him. *Why,* Andrew wondered, *does she always seem able to read my mind?*

"Tomorrow you go to Faenza?" Doval's voice was thin and reedy, yet she smiled as she spoke.

"Yes."

"Sit by me a moment, Andrew. Hadesseh, perhaps you could get me something to drink."

Hadesseh bounded off.

"So much happiness she gives me." Doval sighed. "As do you, Andrew." She looked at him. Her lips were stretched thinly in her smile. "As do you. You are precious to me."

"You are to me, Doval. I sometimes wish . . ."

"What? What do you wish, Andrew? That you knew more?"

He nodded. He looked aside, seeing the villa past the courtyard as Doval could see it. The muscular green shoulders of the hills rose toward the blue sky. Vineyards laced them in dark green rows.

"I'm sorry," she said. "Your parents have told you what they were able, or what they wanted. What they served, what they believed—those are the important things." She was silent a moment. Andrew followed her gaze to the shimmering pool. It seemed bottomless, like the past.

"They told you all you need to know, Andrew. Anything else is your own story." She smiled weakly, but her brown eyes glittered with a fierce light. For the first time, it seemed, Andrew clearly noted the flecks of gold coloring in her irises. *It must be the light,* he thought.

"Only this," she added. "This is what I wanted to say. Hadesseh . . ."

"Yes?"

"Protect her. She had been sent to you as a sign."

"I don't understand." He paused, "*We* took her in."

Doval shook her head. Her face was angry. "No. She was sent. Whatever the circumstances. Look to her to guide you. Always."

Just then Hadesseh came out of the villa. She carried a goblet filled to the rim with spring water. She wiped the dripping edge and handed it to Doval. Before drinking, Doval's eyes met Andrew's.

There is a fire there, Andrew thought. He turned away. *But for how much longer?*

* * *

Two things happened at dinner that put such thoughts out of his mind. They were served in the great room as always, but their numbers were much diminished now and there were no guests. As they finished eating and Griselde cleared away the dishes, Hadesseh stood and helped Doval to her room. The older woman seemed to lean on her, and Andrew's eyes followed them out of the room.

When they had left, Dominic passed a small tally sheet and a leather pouch toward him. He sat watching Andrew, his face a stony mask. Andrew scanned the sheet quickly. He frowned. He opened the leather pouch, his fingers nimbly counting off the thin pieces of pressed gold that made up its weight. He looked up in surprise. "That's all?" he asked.

Dominic nodded. "You'll see when you get to Faenza. Times have changed. Besides, we lost that one shipment to thieves. Remember? I'm sure I told you about it."

"But . . . this isn't half of what we usually give."

Dominic waved a hand. "It's plenty. We also had to put more money into the villa. I had to hire more laborers to work in the village after the storm. And guards. Did I mention that? We hired two guards."

"Guards? What on earth for? We've never needed guards before."

"Think about it, Andrew. I don't want to bother you with these things. But the peasants in the countryside are getting restless indeed. There is a sickness starting."

"Sickness?"

"In Faenza. Some other port cities. It isn't anywhere here in the country yet. It happens from time to time. No one knows why. The rats, some people say. But when that happens the peasants get rebellious. I'm convinced that some people among our own engineered the theft of that shipment."

"Oh, come on. They are all—"

Hadesseh entered. She offered them more wine from a flagon. Andrew thoughtlessly waved her aside. She went to some pillows near the hearth and sat quietly, watching, listening.

"We don't know, Andrew." Dominic sighed. "This is the best we can do. This time. I don't know if it will get better or worse. See what you can work out with the merchants."

Andrew leaned forward. "We should do much better," he said in a low voice. "It's why we're here, Dominic. The grapevines are better than ever. The sheep . . . how many do we have? A hundred? Two hundred?"

Dominic merely nodded.

"And grain?" Andrew added. "We seem to increase, yet we come up with less."

Dominic banged his goblet down and stood. "You run it then! If you don't trust me." His eyes burned like coals. His thick shoulders bunched dangerously.

59

Andrew sighed. "Of course I trust you, Dominic. It's just . . . well . . ."

"Well, do the best you can, Andrew." He turned toward the door. "If you want, I can send one of the guards with you."

"No need. I want to go alone. And I'll be leaving early."

"It's not safe."

Andrew merely looked at him. Dominic turned and strode out of the room.

"Brother?" Hadesseh's voice was a whisper.

Andrew looked at her, startled to see her still in the room.

"Yes, Hadesseh?"

"May I come along?" Her voice was tentative.

He chuckled. "Come along? I'm afraid not. Why on earth would you . . ."

"I'm scared. Alone. With him," she whispered. Her eyes turned to the empty doorway.

Andrew frowned. "Don't worry. Besides, Doval needs you. You'll be perfectly all right."

He kept watching her. After a moment, Hadesseh nodded and stood to leave.

"Good night," she whispered.

CHAPTER FIVE

———————————

A long the docks of Faenza crept scores of the small brown-gray bodies. Stiff hair bristled as their black whiskers swept the air for signs of danger. Their claws were sharp, honed by scrabbling along the uneven planking of the wharf, digging into stony ground, tearing at wooden and canvas coverings over the precious grain they sought. Sometimes they milled together—a swift and silent blanket of twisting brown bodies.

When one of them scented a spill of grain, they descended like a brown avenging cloud. They were one body then, of many independent parts moving ferociously to feed. Sharp yellow teeth ground like gears, jaws snapped and hissed, lean pointed snouts dug like hard shovels.

In the darkness of the docks the clicking of their sharp claws across wood and stone rose and receded in waves. Occasionally a sudden hiss, a squeal of terror, the harsh noise of a fight. Then the brown blanket moved on, relentless, primeval, a new one following on its wake like the endless flow of the sea.

Knots of sailors and dock-laborers moved to and from the taverns and the cheap hovels that lodged them for the night. When they passed, noisy and drunken, the rats scurried to dark corners. A few of the bolder ones, reluctant to part with a spill of grain, held their ground and hissed.

None of the sailors saw another figure, dressed in the loose brown trousers and shirt of a peasant laborer, creeping through the shadows. He moved quietly, his sandaled feet silent on the wharf, gliding among the shadows like a bit of night wind.

Only hours before, Andrew had been attired in splendid garments, adorned with a glittering necklace, as he met with the traders. He had questioned them sharply about the tally sheets, about the stolen shipments.

"True. There has been some theft," old Luchesi was saying. "Gangs of outlaws roam the hills now. But they have stolen nothing of Fontini, I dare say. Only, your shipments have been down. Far down. Why is that? Is there trouble?"

No, no trouble, Andrew assured. *Someone is lying,* he thought. He could trust no one.

"Perhaps," someone opined, "the Fontinis are finding it more profitable to trade with another market. The north, perhaps? Venice?"

No, Andrew insisted. But he detested the threat in the comment. These arrangements were not easily broken. And he sensed a change in attitude among these merchants. They did not fully trust him—this young, rich upstart. It had been different before. He remembered the abject deference paid to Lycurgus. It was absent here—had been eroding throughout his last several trips. He only saw it now.

He tried to keep his voice even and conciliatory, although anger began to saw at his nerves.

By the time he left the ornate villa on the hillside where he had met with the merchants, and walked back to the inn, his outrage had left him drained. He tried to sleep, lying on the cot while a hot sea wind pummeled the room. Flies had gotten in around the cloth over the windows and buzzed in his ears. He wished he had taken Catillo along—someone to talk to! But Andrew had insisted on going alone, and had insisted that Catillo not try to follow.

"I'll know," he had warned. "I'll know the moment you climb your horse, the moment you set foot on the road."

"But it is not safe," Catillo protested.

Andrew hushed him angrily. "Then you have taught me nothing all these years."

As he lay sleepless on the cot, his sweat dampening the cheap blanket, Andrew's thoughts turned over and over to the brown peasant garb in his bag. *Why did I even take it along?* he wondered. *Because you expected to use it!* his mind answered. *No! There is no need.*

Yes, to prove yourself.

He had slipped soundlessly from bed, changing in the darkness, even as his mind shouted, *This is not the way. Never as the aggressor.*

That can be managed. He smiled grimly. *I need to test myself. Let others come, then.*

Silently he peeled back the cloth covering over the window and slipped through it. The darkness swallowed him instantly.

* * *

He was not nervous now. He breathed easily in the shadows. He watched the rats swarm like surges of waves over the wharves. He watched the crowds of drunken men as they drifted back and forth and began to thin. A sliver of moonlight suddenly filtered through the clouds, trapping the docks in a preternatural bluish light. It disappeared quickly as the clouds heaved their shoulders over the sky.

Even in that moment of illumination, however, Andrew failed to see the figure in the shadows opposite. He stood as silent as a wooden plank, raptorlike eyes peering out from under a brown hood.

After several minutes, Andrew spotted the ones he had waited for. There were three of them, clad in ragged clothes, tough and watchful. They were the predators, waiting for a lone sailor to wander across the dock. They would beat him without mercy and strip him. If the sailor was particularly unfortunate, they would roll the unconscious body into the waves. Predators. Andrew smiled. They were his prey tonight.

He staggered loosely from the shadows as if hauling himself erect from a drunken stupor. His legs trembled. He hunched over. He muttered a few incoherent bars of some song he had heard issuing from the tavern.

Yes. They were turning toward him.

Andrew staggered toward the back reaches of the docks, to the land of shadows and filth. A rat squealed suddenly, nearly underfoot. Andrew thrust his head back and laughed uproariously.

He heard heavy footsteps behind him. The steps were angling apart. So they would come from different directions, distrustful even of the drunken sailor he pretended to be. He stood, spraddle-legged like a blown horse, then staggered on. He jingled a few coins in a leather purse at his waist. Enticing. Entrapping.

The first leapt in from the right, aiming a rude, roundhouse blow at

63

Andrew's head. In a flash of motion Andrew seized the wrist, spinning the man over his hip. The body slammed into the dock with an explosion of breath. But Andrew was whirling, his body a blur. His foot, rigid as stone, caught the second man just below the rib cage. He doubled over with a groan. Blow followed blow. The man's head rocked back, his knees buckled, he collapsed.

The third man stood a couple of feet away, stopped in his rush as if he hit a wall. He stood there, arms raised as if frozen, his jaw gaping.

Andrew took one step forward, smiled. "Well?"

The man barely shook his head, then, without a glance for his mates, he wheeled and fled across the dock. The sound of a crash echoed as he tripped on a barrel in the darkness, then hauled himself up and ran on.

Andrew shrugged, loosening the tension. He felt vital, charged with energy. It was intoxicating. He felt giddy, free, wanting more. He looked down at the two unconscious forms and toed the closest one. Too bad the other one got away. He wished there were more. Next time—

"Well, Fontini."

Andrew whirled. The man stood, covered head to sandaled feet in a brown cloak, the hood pulled far forward, features lost in darkness.

"Are you satisfied?"

Andrew recognized the voice. "What are you doing here?"

"I could ask the same," the hooded figure said. The voice was atonal, a lifeless chill of dispassion. He stepped closer to Andrew. His dark eyes pierced the shadows of the hood, holding Andrew transfixed. "I come to seek the lost," he murmured. "These are my people."

"You can have them," Andrew said. But his voice was shaky, covering uncertainty with anger. This was to be a triumph, his own personal testament to skill and power. Instead he felt sordid. "Take them—filth and vermin. Like . . . like your rats. Take them all." He turned on his heel.

"Andrew," the voice called. It was not raised, yet it impaled him like a blade. "They are not the only ones lost. Some know it and seek my help. You too must look to the ones that can help you."

Andrew glanced back. A cold shiver slashed through him. In the brief glare of moonlight, he saw a rat nose the unconscious man. It tiptoed to the man's face, brushing broom whiskers against him. The pointed snout lifted to the man's ear. In an explosion of movement, Andrew leapt forward, kicking out as he landed on one foot. He put all his force behind the blow, the foot rigid at the end of the lean muscled leg. He felt the furry ball wrap around his foot, bones breaking. It was not a wounding kick, not a parrying kick. It was a blow to kill. The foot followed through, carrying the limp, shapeless mass high in the air, rising across the face of the silvered moon. It landed with a dull thud at the end of the dock. A small splash followed as the lifeless body of the rat rolled into the water.

Sharp claws skittered everywhere across the wharf.

A voice boomed out. It was the tavern-keeper, stepping outside for air. He was a huge man, tested in more than one brawl. He reached back in the tavern, plucking a torch off the wall, then he walked toward the hooded figure. "Oh, it's you," he said to Emeth.

"Yes." He turned about. Andrew was gone. Emeth bent to the prostrate form. "Help me with these two, will you, Julius? If we leave them the rats will claim them."

Together, the brawny tavern-keeper and the brown religious man bent and carried the two bodies up the wharf to the side street. They were awakening then and struggled fearfully for a moment. Then quieted as the religious man tended to them.

* * *

Andrew rode up the hillside path warily.

He did not want to do this. He did not want to face the brown-cloaked figure again.

At one moment he told himself angrily, stormily—*I am the master of Fontini Villa. I don't need these people. They need me! It is my gold I hand over. They should be on their knees. Grateful for what I have done. That* priest! *That know-it-all Emeth, wandering around the docks. Looking for the lost! If they're lost, let them go. He especially should be grateful. Instead . . .*

At the next moment he thought about turning around, riding back and forgetting the whole thing. He had been found out. He fought it terribly, but a sense of shame twisted in the pit of his stomach like a bad meal. *Just turn around and ride away.*

And what of the necklace? This means for conveying—secretly—the Fontini support for the work of . . . of what exactly? Refugees from the homeland, he knew. And what was this homeland? And what were they fleeing from, or running toward? What did he owe them—after all these years? They were nothing . . . Hadesseh. In his mind's eye he saw her, on the day she had ridden back to the villa with them.

Was it only four years ago?

She seemed to have been a part of his life forever, so much a part of his life had she become.

He chuckled a moment, forgetting his errand, remembering something from a few days prior.

Hadesseh was always roaming the hills, studying, collecting her plants. Discussing them with Doval. Some of them she brought to the peasant village, he knew. Just why, he wasn't certain. Medicines, he thought, although he had never needed any. And he had found her once in the great room, a flowering plant set before her, roots tied in a wet strip of cloth to keep it vital. And on a piece of parchment, given from Elhrain's supply, she was drawing the plant. It was immaculate in detail—the plant on parchment an exact duplicate of that in nature. With her ingenious dyes she had shaded leaves and stem, colored the sky-blue petals, the tiny orange pistils.

Andrew had pulled an oil lamp over to the table to study it more clearly.

"Careful," she whispered suddenly.

"Why?"

"It will . . . go boom."

He laughed.

She glared at him angrily. With the edge of a knife she scraped some glittering powder—which he now saw she had been using to color the roots of the plant—onto a tiny scrap of parchment. She moved to the hearth, poking among the dead coals until she found the piece she wanted, then ground it up with the powder, sprinkled in some reddish powder from a small vial and mixed it together. She wrapped the parchment tightly into a small tube and carried it outside.

Hadesseh told Andrew to stand back, which he did with a bemused smile. She placed the tube among some rocks, struck at it several times with a flint, then raced back toward him. She was still running when the mixture exploded with a harsh crack and a puff of gray smoke. Little pebbles bounced in the air.

Where had she learned these things? Did she just *know*?

Suddenly from behind the boulders poor, deformed Gregor had sprung up, howling. His twisted limbs seemed to sway. He leaped, arms shaking, hands upraised, mouth open in a sustained howl, and started running up the promontory toward the sea.

In a flash, Hadesseh ran after him. Gregor's bent limbs were no match. In seconds she caught him, folding her small arms around his huge, hairy shoulders. She hugged his deformed head to her breast the way one would a frightened child.

"It's all right," she crooned. "Don't worry, Gregor. Hadesseh won't do it again."

Gregor shot a pained look back at the rocks.

Hadesseh laughed. "No. The ground didn't do that, silly. It was just Hadesseh." She stroked his huge head soothingly. "Hadesseh was naughty." Gregor shot a scowl back at Andrew. "It's all right now."

Slowly Gregor relaxed. He held one of Hadesseh's hands in his hairy fist and limped back to the villa, his eyes glancing nervously at the rocks where he had been hiding.

The remarkable thing, Andrew remembered thinking, *is that he understands her. Or, that she understands him.*

So thinking, Andrew crested the hill above Faenza, in the open ground now. The scattered shops and houses that held to the lower reaches of the hillside looked from here like little dark rocks surrounding the wharves in a graceless arc. He could pick out the wealthier villas of the traders and merchants, their polished tiles and pristine pools winking in the sun. Far out to sea a small ship hove toward the port. Its sails were faint tan smudges in the distance. Continuing on the path down over the hill, he saw the chapel, and old Petra the gardener looked up and waved, and there was no longer any turning back.

* * *

Andrew stabled the horse where it could feed, but he did not unsaddle it. He did not expect to stay long. He drove the fork into the hay mound. Three brown rats, their bodies thick and wriggling, scurried out from behind the pile and darted for the safety of the back wall. Two ducked through a hole gnawed in the wood. The third stopped, stared boldly at him with black glittering eyes as if taunting him. Andrew heaved the fork at it like a javelin. The rat bared its fangs, then slipped through the hole as the fork clattered harmlessly off the wood.

He walked slowly through the garden, pausing to enjoy the flowers. Or to delay the meeting with Emeth. Coral flowers trembled in the sunlight, shifting under a vague breeze that danced up the hillside. In a bricked circle, a volley of lilies held their white trumpets gaudily toward the sky. Small yellow buds of some creeping plant rampaged around their feet.

It was quiet in the garden. Andrew heard the trickle of the stream over rock. The dirt around the flowers still sparkled wetly, like pale blue diamonds strewn against a black cloth.

He heard a shovel ring against stone. Then an enormous grunt. He turned behind the chapel. A small grassy plot spread from the back of the chapel toward the hillside. There old Petra was bent double, working a large rock out of freshly dug ground. Andrew stepped over to him, bent and helped him pry the rock loose. He lifted it, carried it over to the ruined wall and set it down in a empty space. The rock left red marks on his forearm. He brushed away the dirt. Petra threw up a huge shovelful of dirt over his shoulder. His face and arms were dripping with sweat.

"Digging up more gardens?" Andrew asked. He didn't know if the old man understood him.

Then Petra grunted. "Graves," he said.

Graves?

Andrew went to the chapel. The room inside was quiet and darkened. Andrew paused, letting his eyes adjust to the subdued light. Gauzy curtains had been hung over the high window slits, casting the whole chapel into a warm, gray darkness. He made out Emeth, clad as always in his brown cloak, kneeling beside a bench across the room. His hood was pushed back, cowled thickly about his neck.

Andrew noticed with surprise that the man's hair was thin, a bald spot shining damply at the back of his scalp. He seemed to be peering intently at something before him. A body. Lying on the hard bench. Emeth's hand dipped. He was washing—no, dripping water over the form. Andrew stepped softly forward.

"You may come ahead, Andrew." Emeth's soft voice seemed to float in the empty room. He did not turn around.

Andrew approached and looked over the priest's shoulder. It was a man, his face twisted in agony. Gently Emeth laved the swollen features. For a moment Andrew thought it was one of the men whom he had attacked the night before. He was nearly turning to leave. He didn't want to see him—this effect of his violence!

Emeth tugged the man's shirt open. Purple swellings rose under his armpits, spreading across the chest.

Andrew nearly gagged. Emeth glanced up at him briefly. Above that long beak of his nose, his eyes flashed angrily.

"What is it?" Andrew whispered.

"No need to whisper. He can't hear you." Emeth straightened wearily and stood. He flung the rag into the bowl of water.

Andrew looked at the man on the bench. His open eyes had gone rigid. His cracked lips hung open as if screaming silently.

"He just died."

"Petra . . ."

"Yes. Digging his grave. This is the third one now. I don't know—plague? Like the others, he is a dockworker. I think he was bitten. By the rats."

"One of the lost ones," Andrew murmured, remembering.

"Lost? Yes, well, one could say that. But that isn't what I meant." Again Emeth held Andrew with those fierce eyes, like hawks diving into Andrew's very soul. He sighed wearily. "I haven't eaten yet today. Will you join me?"

He wiped his hands carefully on a towel, then turned to a doorway at the back of the chapel. Andrew followed quietly, casting one glance back at the stiff form on the bench, the terrible pain impressed on the man's features.

* * *

Emeth's private room was small and virtually empty. A pallet lay rolled in the corner. Andrew couldn't help thinking, *He sleeps on that?* Emeth did, winter and summer, abetted only by some blankets. It was his preference. As was the spareness of the room itself. A slit window emitted a thin band of light that fell across the stone cell. A small desk with an oil lamp on it stood in one corner. There was a fireplace built into the west wall. That was it. It was not a room for receiving visitors; it was a retreat. And at the moment, a retreat from the death in the outer room.

From a small arrangement of goods on a wall shelf, Emeth took a wineskin—unusual in these parts, Andrew noted, where ornate pottery was the rule—and in a quick, practiced motion filled two small cups. One he handed to Andrew.

Andrew waited for words. For accusations. Something he could fight against. Or use to defend himself. Emeth said nothing. He spoke only with those piercing eyes.

As Andrew took the cup, he lifted the golden necklace and handed it toward Emeth. He held it there, arm outstretched. Emeth did not move.

"Don't you want it?"

"Of course. And our work *does* appreciate the work of Fontini. Put it on the desk, please."

Andrew did so. He felt provoked. Insulted. The necklace felt warm and heavy in his hand as he dropped it noisily on the desk.

"Did you wish to keep it, Fontini?"

Andrew shrugged. "It's the way my father taught me to do. The way it has always been done. I'm just not sure *why* it is done."

Emeth nodded and finally looked away. "Your father told you, surely?"

"The resettlement of pilgrims. Those fleeing persecution. From the homeland. From the church in Rome."

"Yes. Over the years many new lives have been started. The gospel has been spread. Your father—no, all of them: Elhrain, Taletha, Lycurgus, Doval—they knew want. They knew persecution. Out of their pain grew compassion. They knew how to give to help others. Not from their excess, but from their calling. It was the end of their life's work, and it started new lives for many. Without them . . ." He lifted one hand and shook his head.

"Why do you tell me this?" Andrew asked. "I brought the necklace."

"Yes. You did. Dutifully, Fontini—"

"Call me Andrew. Why do you keep calling me 'Fontini'?"

For the first time, Emeth smiled slightly. "Because you are the keeper of the trust now. The Fontini Villa, as it has been known for years. It is yours. I know that. Andrew? Him I am not certain I know."

Andrew stirred angrily. "What is it you want from me, religious man? There." He pointed to the desk, the glittering necklace. "I gave it to you. Help whomever you want with it. I don't care."

Like living coals Emeth's eyes burned through him. His words also burned, although they were given in the softest of whispers, in that slightly husky, quiet voice, as if Emeth were unused to talking at length.

"What do I want? Do you dare hear it, Fontini? What it is that I want?" He stared relentlessly.

Andrew stood rigidly. He refused to avert his own eyes.

"I'll tell you what I want, then. I want your rich clothing, every stitch of it. I can cut it up and use it to warm pilgrims who have had to flee to the northern hills and mountains. The snow falls there like the very clouds have descended to earth and opened their ripe bellies. The cold . . . the cold air drives inward upon them, sapping every ounce of warmth. Oh, it is a dangerous thing to ask what someone wants, Fontini. For I am not done yet.

"I want your money, Fontini. Every cent of it, because the people who find their way here, fleeing by night with only the clothes on their backs, those people have lost everything. They have no hopes or expectations anymore and sometimes a few coins, as we convert this," he waved at the necklace, "can start them once again on a path toward hope. Toward wholeness. I want . . . I want—I could go on and on, Fontini.

"From you I want not less than everything, until you are reduced to a condition of complete simplicity and then—only then—can you ask the question properly. *And I can't give you the answer!* Only you can."

Emeth's voice had raised. He stood thoughtfully a moment. "Now ask me an easy question. Ask me what the Lord wants of you. Ask me. Go ahead. I can tell you easily.

"No? You hesitate? Very well, I'll tell you anyway.

"He wants nothing of what you have, Fontini. He wants not a thing less than everything you *are*.

"Wait, Fontini! Don't be quick to respond now. Listen to me. Count the cost, my young friend. Count the cost, for this too will cost you not less than everything. There is no room for bargains in the matter. These golden baubles are here today. They will be gone . . . within a month. This will cost your heart and soul and mind and strength, and it will last not a moment less than forever.

"No. Don't protest yet, Fontini. For I know what you are thinking. So, good. I ask you to think, not to talk. For I am almost done talking, and *you* asked the question, after all."

Here Emeth did in fact smile. And Andrew was held by those eyes, and he found himself strangely without anger. He listened as if studying the man the way one studies a problem—abstractedly, coolly, politely.

Emeth seemed to sense it. Yet he continued.

"What does God want of you? I'll tell you, Andrew—allegiance. That one thing." His voice softened. The iron glare died in his eyes. He shook his head slowly, the slightest perceptible movement.

"Andrew," his voice was hoarse, nearly a whisper. "Money will come and go. The proceeds of Fontini Villa, its generous gifts, have been valuable beyond counting. They have fed the hungry, clothed the naked, comforted the sorrowing. But if there were no Fontini Villa—if no Lycurgus and Elhrain, those old warriors, and if no Taletha and Doval, if no Andrew—we would get by. Others would help. Maybe not in this place but in some place. It is never, *never* the offering that matters—only the heart of the one who offers.

"Allegiance, Andrew. The heart can be as slippery as starlight upon a desert wasteland, or as true as the star that gives the light. That's what your parents learned. What they offered to you. What the Lord requires. Allegiance will be written as the first fruits in the Lamb's Book of Life." Emeth shook his head. For the first time ever that Andrew knew, he actually chuckled. "Sorry," he said. "Perhaps you don't know those terms. But now you know the cost. I gave answer to your question."

Andrew had started for the door.

"Fontini."

He turned. "Yes?"

"The girl. Hadesseh. How is she?"

"She's well, priest."

Emeth's eyes lowered. To Andrew's surprise, he detected some slipping in the chiseled features, some . . . weakness. "Please," Emeth said. "No defenses. She is gifted, Andrew. Beyond one's wildest dreams. Once in a . . . lifetime? No, rarer than that, such a one comes along. Trust her, Fontini. She will chart a course for you."

"Maybe," Andrew spat back, "she just wants to be . . . who she is! Not called. Not gifted. Not chosen. Oh, yes. I have heard those words. Just once my mother spoke them. She was wise enough, priest—wiser than any of us—to leave it there. But the words are still stones in my path."

"But you cannot ignore the stones, can you, Fontini? They show you the path itself."

"Leave Hadesseh alone, priest. Let her be."

Emeth nodded. The slightest smile crept across his features. As Andrew left he said softly, "And farewell to you too, Andrew."

Andrew paused in midstep, then hurried on.

CHAPTER
SIX

F *or the horse's sake,* Andrew was thinking, *I should have waited until morning.*

The moon had long since faded as he entered the lower end of the valley. As he rode through the forested stretches, the night had been so black that he wasn't certain where he was or where he was going. The horse somehow kept to the narrow road, guided by the familiarity of scents along the way. It had moved wearily, shaking its head from time to time in sheer protest while its legs slowly, mechanically moved up and down hill. Andrew sat slumped in the saddle.

When the hooves clopped over the wooden bridge below the peasants' houses, the change of sound jarred Andrew awake.

I should have waited until morning.

He had left Emeth's presence confused and angry. There was good reason to leave. The chapel reeked of illness, that peculiar sickly odor of suffering and bodily wastes and impending death. Impending! He had seen the man die, his body swollen, discolored, suffering.

And there were no pilgrims that night. They were frightened now. The persecution was everywhere. Fewer made their way to Rome, settling instead in safer cities along the coast of the Great Sea. Only the most desperate now straggled north. *Where did they go from here?* Andrew wondered. They had nothing. Few knew the language. To the north lay wild, hostile lands. Vicious, marauding tribes, he had heard, roamed the wooded and mountainous wastelands of the north, held in check only by the power of the Roman Legions. Even these seemed in decline. The age was a wasteland. The madmen in Rome were killing for sport. How could life in the hinterlands hold any value?

How had Catillo endured it? Andrew wondered. Not until shortly before his death had Lycurgus told Andrew of Catillo's past—how after military service he had been trained for the gladiators' games in the great Roman circus. Smaller of stature than many of the other gladiators, Catillo had studied the art of warfare, of life and death, with intelligence rather than strength. He had perfected his unorthodox patterns of blows and parries—a dance of devastation—so successfully that he had been a hero of the games.

But the awful results—the inevitable bloodshed and the grotesque cheers of the crowd! These had driven Catillo from the games even as his fame grew. He escaped. Quite literally, for when he failed to show one day for a long-expected bout at which the Emperor himself was scheduled to appear, there was a price on his head. Somehow, through that secret network of men who had served with or had known about Lycurgus— one-time heroic general in the Roman army, illegitimate son of an emper- or and reclusive owner of an inherited estate—Catillo had escaped to the relative safety of these northern hills.

Such thoughts wandered aimlessly through Andrew's mind as he rode through the darkness. Wanderings of the mind. Accident or design? he wondered. What brought them—him!—to this place? *Calling! Chosen!* What did the words mean?

Fragments of an uncertain mind—that's what they meant, Andrew thought.

The small peasant houses lay silently in the darkness. A dog barked noisily as he passed. There was Dominic's house. Where was he? No longer the peasant boy, to be sure. His friend. Boyhood companion. Chosen? For what?

I wish, Andrew thought, *I could find answers.* By going back? He had heard all the stories of the homeland. Suppose he went there? Talked to the people in the stories. Were any still living? He had asked Doval about it. She had shaken her head. "I don't think that is your story," she had said. What did she mean? Was it possible to go back? To find answers from any fragments of the past that still lived on there?

Unlikely, if not impossible. It could have been . . . nearly twenty years ago, Andrew thought. *Still . . .*

The barking of the dog receded. The small gathering of dwelling places, scattered aimlessly alongside the stream, slept on. The muffled sounds of the horse's hooves on the dirt path disturbed no one.

The grove of trees rose ghostly and still. Andrew felt them more than saw them. In their midst stood the triumphant old oak he and Dominic spent so many carefree hours in. Andrew wondered if the rude boards they had eventually tied and hammered into the crotch still remained. Did other boys come there to play now? Had they all been torn down, or blown apart?

As his memory worked backward, almost in conjunction with the trail to the villa now winding uphill, past events slid through his mind. He remembered his father sitting with him high on the hillside when he was very young. So young he couldn't remember his age. It was before awareness of time started.

His little world was all low and green then. Windswept grass and flowers on the hillside. They had been near the grapevines. No sea sounds reached there, only the soft sound of the wind making its grass noises and leaf sounds.

His father lay back in the grass. A tiny bug crawled up his neck and Andrew tried to pick it off. His chubby little fingers poked and probed, and his father started laughing and pulled Andrew down for a hug. Then he cradled him in one arm.

Remembering, Andrew seemed to be reliving. The night wind now became that summer wind.

He had lain flat on his back, head on his father's shoulder, following the pointing of his father's finger stretched high into the sky, almost touching the bottom side of clouds. Andrew held his breath, waiting for the rain to come.

The sun kept shining, and the fleecy boats kept drifting across the blue sky, their great white sails billowing.

"That's a horse running," his father said. His finger traced the outlines. It seemed to Andrew that he *made* the horse, his hands caressing it into shape out of its blue bowl. "It took us to the coast of our homeland," his father said.

"There were other men chasing us. See? There they are. See those little horses way in the distance?"

Andrew watched the sky-horses give chase. Oh, they were drawing closer.

"Now," his father said, "There comes the boat. Right there. Yes. Mother and you go on ahead. Oops! Look what happened to all the men chasing us."

The wind had scrambled the little figures.

"So for many days you and your mother sailed. Lycurgus and Doval were with you. Then for many days I sailed. Oh, I was trying to hurry. I wanted to see you."

And then he squeezed the boy cradled in his arms, and the boy laughed.

"Why are the bad men chasing you, Father?" Andrew remembered asking. The answers were vague.

Now, as he rode in the darkness, Andrew couldn't remember ever having gotten one clear answer. Just bits and pieces, most of it overheard from the elders as they talked in the great room at night.

He gave a sudden start. The horse was standing still, lifting its large head and blowing. They stood before the villa gate. Andrew shook himself.

He climbed down, led the horse to the stable and quickly, as if in a dream, unsaddled it. He was tempted to let the grooming go, or to awaken someone to do it for him. But there was something cleansing about caring for the animal. He forked it some hay and grain, then barred the stable door and walked across the courtyard. A frog grumped noisily by the pool then quieted. Half asleep, Andrew moved by darkness through the familiar corridors, through the great room, toward the tower doorway.

He nearly tripped over the girl in his path.

* * *

Hadesseh huddled on the steps inside the doorway. When Andrew pushed the door open, she at first cringed away fearfully, as if startled from sleep. Then she clung to him.

"Shh," Andrew whispered, although she was not crying. She held on to him, trembling. "Shh. What is it?"

For a long moment she said nothing. Then she spoke. "I'm scared. I want to sleep with you."

"Scared? What of? Shh, quiet now." He led Hadesseh by the hand to the table in the great room. Andrew poked through the coals in the hearth, found some live embers, took one out with tongs and from it lit a wall torch. It spumed smokily into the large room. In its light Andrew studied Hadesseh. Her eyes were wide and fearful; they clung to him. He sighed with relief when he found no marks or bruises on her. For a moment he had thought . . . *No, just a young girl's nightmare,* he thought.

Andrew reached across the table and held her hand. "What happened?" Hadesseh's fingers trembled and her lips quivered. He thought she would start weeping, but with an effort of will she fought it back. In that moment Andrew felt his heart breaking for the girl. He realized suddenly that she had no one else to turn to.

"There was someone watching me. Last night. Through my bedroom window."

"Someone watching you? Who?"

She shook her head.

"Did you see him? How do you know?"

"I heard him. And I smelled him. He wanted to hurt me, Andrew." Her eyes were pleading. She turned them away.

"I believe you," he said quickly. "It might have been anyone. Someone walking by." *Who?* he thought. "Maybe Desidero," he said.

She shook her head. "I know it wasn't Desidero. It was someone under the window. He looked through the shutter. He was watching me."

"It was dark."

"I *know.* He wanted to . . . to do things to me. I lay still. I was afraid. Then I said, 'Go away! I can see you!' It was very quiet for a while. Then I heard him moving away."

Andrew said nothing. *Someone hurt Hadesseh? How could they?*

"I looked out the window then, and . . . I saw Gregor. Standing by the rocks. On the hillside."

"You don't think . . ."

Hadesseh shook her head. "No. Not like that. Gregor was watching *over* me. Protecting me. But something . . ."

"What?"

"When I asked him the next morning he wouldn't talk to me."

"Gregor! He doesn't talk anyway."

"Yes. To me he does. In his own way. When you learn to listen."

Andrew nodded. "Why didn't Gregor do something then?" Andrew thought of those powerful arms on the misshapen body. He had seen Gregor lift a rock in the old quarry once, lift it and toss it playfully. Gregor hadn't known Andrew was watching. Later Andrew tried to lift the rock. He could scarcely budge it. "If he was protecting you, why didn't he do something?"

Hadesseh shook her head. "I don't know. Maybe . . ."

Andrew finished her thought. *Maybe it was someone Gregor knew.*

"Tonight I heard him again. So I hid on your stairs. I was going to sleep in your bed, where it's high up and no one can look in and no one can hurt me." Her words came in a rush. She bent her head fearfully.

"Shh," Andrew whispered again. The small hand in his was trembling. "Shh. It's all right now. No one will hurt you."

"I want to sleep with you tonight."

"You're a big girl, Hadesseh. You can't sleep with me. It wouldn't . . . be right."

"By your bed, then. On the floor."

"You have a bed. I can't have you sleeping at the foot of mine like a dog."

Her lip trembled now.

Andrew squeezed her hand. "Yes, then. Listen, tonight you sleep in my bed. Just for tonight. It's very late. I'm not tired though. I'll sit here and make sure everything is all right."

"Will you look first?"

"In my room?"

Hadesseh nodded.

"Sure." He took the torch, leading the way up the stairs. He remembered how they had frightened him when he was little. Now . . . they were just stairs. He opened the bed and tucked her in quietly. He leaned forward to give her a hug. She wrapped her arms around him and held on tightly. He found it hard to let go.

* * *

The morning light surprised him. Andrew did not remember dozing off. He had bent his head forward on his folded arms on the table, and his neck felt stiff and sore.

Dominic was there, dressed and ready to get going. He stepped to the cold hearth and kicked angrily at the dead coals.

"Good morning," Andrew said.

Dominic wheeled, startled. "What are you doing here?"

"I live here."

"I mean . . . I didn't expect you back this soon."

"Got home late last night." Andrew studied the thick muscular body of his friend. He wore a tunic of rich linen. Andrew couldn't remember seeing it before.

"Old Desidero," Dominic muttered. "I ought to fire him. Can't keep the fire going. And where's breakfast?"

"It's early yet."

"Yes, well, I have things to do."

"What things, Dominic?" Andrew stood up. His body felt sore its entire length.

"Lots. Get the peasants working. Too much to be done."

"And yet our produce falls off." He paused. "The merchants were surprised. Two shipments never appeared as scheduled."

"I told you about that," Dominic retorted. "Robbers. Thieves. Outlaws. They're all over. What with the sickness. They're all over the countryside now. I'm doubling the guard on the shipments."

"You told me one was lost."

"Two. There were two lost. I'm sure I told you. The shipment of wool and . . ."

"And?" said Andrew. "And . . . there were two shipments of wool lost, Dominic. I saw the trader's records."

"Maybe they're lying." His eyes shifted. He bent to the coals, raking the embers, and threw on some wood.

"Maybe. Tell me this, Dominic. Who could have frightened Hadesseh?"

"Hadesseh? Who knows? What, frightened? She's just a girl, Andrew. They're scared of everything."

"No. She was scared of *someone*. And she is not a girl. She is a young woman."

"You know how the girl is."

"Why don't you tell me 'how the girl is.' "

"A dreamer. A foreigner. Like all these foreigners. They're worthless."

"I too, Dominic, am a foreigner."

"Bah. There was no one there."

"Where, Dominic?"

"At her . . ." He stopped, catching himself. "I have a lot to do," he muttered. "Have Griselde send me something to eat in the fields."

Dominic paused by the door. "Surely you don't mistrust me, Andrew. Just give the word, and the complete handling of the Fontini Villa is yours. And I will go back where I started from." He shook his head. "Andrew, Andrew. If you can't trust me, who can you trust?" He walked through the door shaking his head.

Andrew got up from the table. He stepped outside into the early sunlight. Already he could see the peasants walking up the hillside to the grapevines. They seemed, from this distance, bent and weary shapes. Suddenly Dominic wheeled on horseback from the stable door. He galloped off toward the distant vineyards, his horse heaving clots of turf as it thundered up the hillside.

Andrew walked outside the wall of the villa. He bent under the slitted window of Hadesseh's room. Imprinted in the damp earth was a series of footprints, the ball of the foot impacted deeply, as if someone had knelt there a long time, listening, waiting.

CHAPTER
SEVEN

F or a long time that morning Andrew brooded silently. Things were
going wrong, getting confused. Just what and how it was so, he
wasn't certain. Some vague portent—the feeling one has when midnight
approaches or a storm hovers in the green underbelly of clouds on the
horizon—seemed to be creeping silently about the villa grounds. Something out of place.

At midmorning he saw Hadesseh help Doval out to her chair by the
pool. Griselde brought them something cool to drink.

Andrew heard the sound of a broom sweeping and a ragged, off-key
humming that occasionally broke into words. A door popped open and
Desidero backed out, his ample hindquarters bobbing with the motion of
the sweeping. His head was down and swirls of dust rose about his ankles.

He paused and tried his voice loudly on some chorus. It cracked, struck
a half-dozen wrong notes in a row, then Desidero stood laughing and
shaking his head. From inside Griselde shouted something about not
butchering squawking chickens in the courtyard. Hadesseh giggled.
Desidero looked around, suddenly embarrassed, and fell to his sweeping
with renewed vigor, if not dignity.

Andrew smiled as he watched Doval and Hadesseh talking. No. It was Hadesseh talking. Doval merely smiled and nodded. When Hadesseh pointed
at something, Doval squinted her eyes, but appeared to see nothing.

Well, Andrew thought, *there's work to be done. I'll get Catillo and . . .* Catillo. Abruptly, Andrew scanned the grounds.

No matter how late he had come in last night, Catillo would have heard him. And would have risen to greet him. The man could drop into or out of sleep in a second.

Maybe he went . . . no. He had not gone to Faenza. Andrew insisted on going alone because . . . because he wanted to try his experiment, test his skills. A hot shame crept over him as he stood remembering.

Andrew walked over to Desidero. The portly man bowed ponderously, despite the fact that Andrew had told him a hundred times not to bother. Once, long ago, Doval had whispered to him, "He really wants to, Andrew," whereupon Andrew shrugged his shoulders and gave up. Now this morning he enacted the practice he had adopted instead—he bowed back, deeply, humbly. As always, Desidero's face went flame red, then he stood there laughing genially.

"Yes, master," said Desidero. That too Andrew had forbidden, also to no effect. It had started the very day, several years ago, that his lessons had ended.

"Desidero, have you seen Catillo?"

Desidero stood as if searching his mind for recollection. "No," he said. "That's funny. I haven't."

"Do you know when you last saw him?"

"Indeed, master. The morning you left."

"That would be . . . four days ago, then?"

"Yes. He followed you down the path. A long ways. That was it. The last time I saw him."

"No, it was not," Griselde's harsh, crackly voice broke in. She stood in the doorway where she had been listening, a wet rag dripping in her hands. "Think sometimes, dear. I saw him come back."

"Ah, but did I, my sweet?" Desidero puffed out his chest. "Did I? No. Desidero saw no such thing."

Griselde ignored him. "Yes," she said to Andrew, "he came back up the path, on foot mind you, later that morning." She tossed the wet rag toward Desidero. He missed it as he juggled the broom in his hands and the rag wrapped around his thick neck. Griselde continued as if nothing was amiss. "He came back, and sat in the great room a great long time too, he did. Just sitting. Then he walked back out."

She stood there a moment. Desidero had unwrapped the wet rag. He knelt by the pool, carefully polishing the outer tiles. He kept edging further away from his wife. Andrew knew the routine, knew Desidero's constant evasion techniques.

"And that," Griselde declared, "was the last I, or anyone else, has seen of him."

"He didn't come back?"

"I would have known if he would, wouldn't I, master?"

"Yes, Griselde. I'm sure you would." Andrew was wondering if Catillo had followed him into town after all. And what had happened to him. But nothing *could* happen. No one could harm Catillo. Yet, Andrew remembered Catillo's own lessons—advantage lay in surprise. Anyone could defeat another by surprise or by deceit.

*   *   *

By midafternoon Andrew's concern deepened to worry. Surely Catillo had no requirement to be here or to remain on the villa. His loyalty had been to Lycurgus. Yet he had willingly remained, and Andrew had been glad to have him. In a hundred different ways Catillo had proved useful, but mainly his presence—his steady, powerful presence which seemed inherited from Lycurgus himself—was valuable. He was important because he was there, always dependable.

Andrew saddled his horse and rode out under a fall sun. The hillside swarmed with insect sounds and the lazy drone of bees. The land was moving toward ripeness. Soon it would be time to harvest the grapes. Then for weeks, every waking hour, the entire villa would be absorbed in the huge task of harvesting, pressing, curing and bottling. Thinking of that, Andrew rode first to the peasant village where much of the actual labor would occur.

He had not been here often since his days of childhood play. It was Dominic's domain now. As he approached, Andrew acknowledged the value of Dominic on the villa. These were his people. He knew them, understood them, in ways that Andrew never did nor could. They were fiercely loyal to him.

As he rode through the dirt path dividing the small dwellings, some of the women nodded politely to him. A gang of young children frolicked by the stream, and Andrew felt a sudden pang, remembering the hours he had spent there with Dominic. He wondered now at the cross words spoken that morning. It would pass, soon be forgotten. Dominic was working hard and was entitled to his moods. Indeed, he had much to do. Andrew was more than willing to accept the blame for pushing his friend too hard.

With surprise Andrew noted several new huts on the edge of the village. In fact, two men were working on new ones. They had built the walls of baked brick and clay mortar and were presently cutting log poles for the thatch roof. They merely glanced at Andrew as he paused to watch. Andrew didn't recognize them. There was no reason why he should. Yet, they troubled him vaguely. They didn't look like Fontini people. They looked like . . . dockworkers.

He heeled his horse closer. One of the men glanced at him, then ignored him. They were thick-shouldered men, sweating under the afternoon sun.

"How are you doing?" Andrew asked pleasantly.

The one who had looked at him muttered, "Working. What does it look like?"

Andrew stiffened in surprise. *Don't you know who I am?* he wanted to ask. There was no need. They did not know. And didn't care.

In the grove by the stream, where the pressing vats stood under the cool shade of some trees, Andrew saw a new vat, unfinished. Its wooden staves were loose, several lying on the ground.

The vats were large, able to hold two pressers at a time. It was essential that they be built tight, to hold both the weight of the grapes and the motion of the pressers. Each season they were cleaned carefully, and if any signs of weakness appeared they were dismantled and rebuilt.

"Are you going to work on the presses?" Andrew asked.

The one man heaved a long pole up to the roof. The other began binding it down. The man on the ground turned to look at Andrew squarely. "When we get to it," he growled. "A man has to have a place to live before he can work." He turned his back as if to say, That's enough for you.

He didn't think it would be worth asking, but he did anyway. "Have either of you seen Catillo?"

"Who?"

"Catillo. The . . ." Andrew paused. What was Catillo's place on the villa? Tutor? Protector? Guide? Andrew just described his features.

84

The man shook his head without turning around. "Never heard of him," he muttered. "Never seen him either."

"Do you know who you work for?" Andrew asked abruptly.

The man looked at him angrily. "Of course. For myself and . . ." Slowly some recognition dawned in his eyes. He turned his head and bent back to his work.

Andrew sat a moment and rode on slowly. To his surprise, two of the houses—there were about a dozen in all—looked vacant. He dismounted by one and walked to the door. The room was cleared out, but a small mound of rubble lay in the center of the living space. *Well*, Andrew thought, *it is several weeks yet until harvest.*

Past the animal pens, holding a few pigs, a few young cows, some birds in coops, lay a few vegetable and herb plants. Some peasants had started their own small grapevines. Andrew nodded approvingly. He knew that that was Elhrain and Lycurgus's plan from the start—that the peasants worked their own land, calling this place their home, as much as working the villa.

He turned the horse uphill. It moved slowly, still weary from the long travel of the night before.

Andrew was thinking then of riding past the grapevines to the backside of the hill, the windward side facing the ocean. It had been one of his parents' last experiments. Andrew remembered Elhrain and Taletha walking out there with him one morning when he was still young. They had climbed the long gentle sweep of the hillside past the trellised grapevines, pausing often to hold a handful of young fruit from the vine, studying it, commenting. It was a happy day, the sun bright, the breeze as subtle as a breath. The long rows of vines stood like sentries rising on crooked brown legs. An old dog was sleeping in the sun and ambled over to them when he heard their voices. He let Andrew scratch his ears, then suddenly ran off yelping as he scented some small animal invading his vineyard.

Then they had crested the hill. The sea breeze gusted over them, its scent tangy with salt and shoreline odors. The backside of the hill, hidden from the villa itself, fell away in a long gentle swoop, ending in the shaggy brow of the cliffs along the sea.

Elhrain and Taletha walked slowly. They bent often, fingering a handful of the soil lifted from the base of the long grass. Their voices were excited. They talked about vines and trees and which would be better. They pointed and gestured at the land, then joined hands and simply stood looking while Andrew ran among clumps of wildflowers. Unlike the promontory above the villa which was riddled with rock outcroppings, or the wild land of the quarries to the south where the sheep grazed, the hillside here had few stones underfoot.

When they returned that night they were still talking excitedly.

It was several months before the wagon appeared, full of little seedling olive trees from the homeland. The seedlings were grafts onto wild stock, and each one was carefully wrapped in damp fiber. For several days laborers hoed and planted. Elhrain and Taletha were among them, returning at evening weary and caked with dirt and sweat. Andrew remembered those as some of the happiest days he had ever spent at the villa.

And then, when the planting was done, a crew of several men began building a small home on the hillside. It was unlike those in the peasant village, larger and roomier, and Andrew wondered who would live in this special place.

When they came he was disappointed. It was a young couple, Samuel and Naomi, from the homeland, and they had no children. They too were fleeing the persecution. Andrew remembered their voices in the great room late into the night. He remembered it because it was the one occasion when Emeth had come to the villa. There were two or three others whom Andrew did not know. He heard later that they were from Rome, that great and distant city. Much of the day was spent in anxious preparation. Griselde's kettles were steaming all day. Desidero swept as if a dust storm had struck.

Griselde and Desidero served the guests in the great room like a couple of clucking hens tending their brood. Occasionally Griselde prodded Desidero into some pose of formality that she thought the guests merited.

"Desidero," she hissed, loud enough for everyone in the room to stop eating and take notice. Desidero was the only one not to take notice. He had been dipping his fingers into a stew, taking out a choice piece of meat that he savored with pure enjoyment. Griselde sidled her bulky body over to him and drove an elbow into his ribs. Desidero bent over, face aflame, gasping at the food stuck in his throat. Griselde hammered him once on the back in a way that would stun a mule. He straightened up, beaming. "Thanks, my love," he said loudly. "Nearly had me there!"

Then she gestured at the meat juices on his chin, making furious wiping motions. Desidero stared at her blankly.

"Your chin," she hissed and thrust a cloth napkin at him.

Whereupon Desidero nødded, smiling broadly, and swiped away at his chin as if polishing it.

Worst of it was when Griselde tried to make her polite inquiries regarding the well-being of her guests. Desidero often thought about making the inquiries about half a step after she did. As Griselde would politely ask, "Can I get you anything more, perhaps a bit more of . . ." Desidero would boom out, "What! Not done already? Here, let me get . . ." And Griselde would deliver another of her expert blows to her husband's rib cage, smiling benignly at the guests all the while.

There was always more than enough to eat at Griselde's table. The guests left well-fed, happy. And entertained.

The next day Elhrain and Taletha walked the young couple the long way over to the new house. They wept when they saw it.

It would be years before the olive trees began producing, but always it was a special place. Andrew could remember his father wondering aloud about it. Taletha often cautioned, "Wait, Elhrain. They know what they're doing. Now let them do it. Leave them alone."

The wait was long. Year by year the trees grew. In the springtime their branches were full of white blossoms. The young couple pruned and cultivated. They grafted new seedlings, letting the orchard sprawl over half the hillside in time. But they grew no children, and in time Andrew lost interest. They were just the people from the backside. Andrew did know that often pilgrims from Emeth's chapel would stay there a few weeks, even a few months, before being located elsewhere.

Thinking of it now, Andrew regretted that his parents had never gotten to taste the fruit of those trees. It had been over a decade now since they were started. Perhaps there would be some this year. But then, Andrew reflected, it was not, perhaps, the fruit itself that they so relished as the expectation. The sign of a promise. A hope.

The horse's hooves clicked against a stony path. Rocks that had been dug up in the vineyard had been used as dividing walls among the trellised rows and had been laid out in narrow paths. Down a row Andrew saw workers tying up the heavy fruit with cloth strips. Some fruits already held a faint purple glow of near ripeness.

Andrew's glance moved upward along the path. At its head, astride his horse, sat Dominic, one fist cocked at his waist, watching the workers. The hard sun chiseled his features like the dark-hewn rock. His eyes passed over Andrew dispassionately. Andrew kneed his mount up alongside him and halted there, the wind drying the sweat on his body. The horse leaned forward and cropped.

"Nearly ripe," Andrew observed.

Dominic merely nodded.

"Listen," said Andrew. "About this morning. I'm sorry."

A slight smile parted Dominic's lips. For a moment that old affection surged up in Andrew. "I was tired," he said. "Not thinking clearly."

"Forget it, Andrew. We all get busy."

"Yes."

They sat silently for a few minutes. Down an unseen row some worker called out. Another answered, laughing.

"Where are you headed, Andrew? It's unusual to see you out here."

"I was going further. To the olive groves. See how they're doing."

"Don't bother. Nothing will ever come of it."

"Well . . ."

"Ten years of work. And nothing to show for it? Besides, it's getting late. Stay here for a while. It's good for the workers to see you take an interest."

There was a note of accusation in his voice that bothered Andrew.

"I rode through the village. I noticed some new workers."

Dominic lifted an eyebrow, as if to say, So? Instead he said, "The harvest is almost upon us. We need more help. Besides, I had to let a few people go."

"Go? Without telling me?"

"They were getting old, Andrew. Old and worthless. They did virtually no work at all. They should earn their keep."

"But . . ."

Dominic seared him with a glance. "But what? Don't you trust me, Andrew? Then who can you trust? We grew up together, Andrew. We're like . . . brothers." Dominic smiled warmly. "Trust me to do my job. In all things, Andrew."

Andrew nodded. But there was protest on his lips. Something rattled inside him. But he dropped the subject. "Actually, I was looking for Catillo. Have you seen him?"

Dominic appeared to be reflecting. After a moment he averted his eyes and said, "Yes. I didn't know if I should tell you, Andrew." He sat silently, frowning as if struggling with something.

"What?"

"No. I should not bother a friend with this."

"Go ahead."

Dominic sighed. "This would have been yesterday. Two days ago—the day after you left. I lose track, I get so busy. We had been working late. There were many details to take care of. I ate with the workers in the village."

Andrew knew this was not unusual. Dominic's parents, after all, still lived there.

Dominic sighed. "It was well after bedtime when I came back to the villa. Everyone was sleeping. I could not sleep. Too much to think about."

Again he sat a moment, tossing the reins from hand to hand. The old dog bounded past, then circled and settled in a patch of shade. He laid his large head on his paws in the dirt and looked up at them as if begging a compliment.

"I stabled my horse," continued Dominic, "and I sat for a while on the terrace. It grew very late. I began to doze. Then I heard something . . . there in the darkness. I listened, I followed. Then—I don't know if I should say this."

Andrew's heart was pounding.

"I walked along the outer wall, past the sleeping quarters. As I passed Hadesseh's window I saw someone crouch down. I crept up on him."

"Catillo?"

"Catillo. I was so angry I was about . . . never mind. I told him to leave, then and there. I followed him inside, watched him pack his things."

"I can't believe—"

"I followed him to the crossing at the stream. Yes, believe it, Andrew. I caught him with my own eyes. My own hands."

"Then Hadesseh was telling . . ."

Dominic looked at him sharply. "It is better she doesn't know. I didn't want *you* to know. But I see it's a matter of trust, Andrew."

"Still—"

"Or a matter of blood. Of tradition. We have to protect that. We've been here a long time, Andrew. We can't take risks. Think back now.

Who had opportunity to move freely around the villa?"

Catillo, Andrew thought.

"And who knew the traders beside you and me? Only Catillo. And who do we know least on the whole villa?"

Again he paused, letting it settle in.

"Oh," said Dominic, "I had begun to suspect him for some time. It was too convenient. Several shipments had been lost. Thieves? To be sure. But how did they *know*? We keep our shipping plans and our routes secret."

"I didn't know that."

"There's no need for you to know. A simple precaution. But Catillo knew. I'm certain." Dominic sighed. "Well, he's gone now. Maybe I should have waited. I hadn't put it all together when I sent him on his way. There's an appropriate justice for traitors, Andrew." Dominic turned toward Andrew and smiled broadly. All the old warmth, the friendship, the love were there. As hard to believe as the things were, Andrew felt an ill wind had blown away and a fresh one sprung up. He nodded.

"We have to stick with pure blood, Andrew. Those we know."

"Pure blood?" said Andrew. For the second time that day he reminded his friend, "Technically I'm a foreigner, not Roman born at all."

"Hah!" Dominic chortled. "You know what I mean. You *are* Fontini Villa, Andrew. And I am your protector. What I have to guard you against is the preying of others. The defilers. We should purge them. Trust me."

Andrew saw Dominic's eyes turn cold, and the coldness touched somewhere deep inside his own being. He shivered.

"Yes," said Dominic. "We should get rid of that half-wit too."

"That what?"

"That creature. That animal that runs around the hills. That thing that Hadesseh hangs around with. Who knows, Andrew, what the creature is trying to do with her." Dominic was trembling in the saddle, his eyes blazing. Suddenly he caught himself. He laughed nervously. "Sorry," he said, "I just want to protect you, Andrew. And I will."

Andrew nodded. He wheeled his horse back down the stony path. He could visit the olive grove another day. He had lost interest today, and felt suddenly very weary.

CHAPTER EIGHT

Nor was Andrew able to visit the cottage in the olive grove for some time. Even his lingering questions about Catillo had to be set aside.

He rode back down to the villa as the evening sun laid its heavy light across the fields. Greens deepened to emerald. Distant grain fields shone with a rich golden hue. In the dusk the walls of the villa itself took on a rich glow of pewter.

A strange thought struck him then. Doval and Taletha had talked often about the Messiah's return. He had ascended, they said, in a cloud of glory. He would return, they said, in the same way—but the heavens would crack open, the clouds roll down, the legions of heaven accompanying him.

What will he see when he returns? Andrew wondered. *The same things I do? The beauty and the tension? The golden bath of light on the verdant hills? The restlessness that grips the villa and its surrounding lands?* For a moment, Andrew pretended he was *him*—the Messiah looking down. *Oh*, he thought, *it must be lonely to look down, always apart.* How little this all looked to him then. The villa sparkling on the hillside below, the peasant village, the harvest. They would all pass away. Who would tell their story, and what would be worth telling about finally? What really endured, so that when—if—this Messiah returned he would find something of worth? Andrew could not shake the feeling of disconsolation. As the horse stepped down the hillside it jarred every bone in his body, but it could not jar loose the sadness that settled on his mind.

I'm just tired, he kept telling himself. *And confused.*

As he neared the villa, his eye picked out the pool in the courtyard. Yes. Two figures sat there. Hadesseh and Doval, aglow in the light. Then the hill dipped, and when he rode out he was beneath the wall line of the villa and saw only its gray stones rising.

Desidero met him at the gate. His face was grave. "I'll take your horse," he offered. He reached for the reins. "They are waiting for you."

Doval looked tiny in the chair, wrapped in a woolen blanket. Her gray head was bent slightly, and she seemed to be wearing a smile, although from the gate Andrew couldn't be sure.

Hadesseh lifted her head when she heard his steps. Her face was tear-streaked. She held Doval's hand, and as Andrew neared she pried her thin fingers loose and laid the hand tenderly on Doval's lap. It lay there open, unmoving. Then Andrew looked, and he knew.

"When?" he whispered.

"A few minutes ago. She saw you coming down the hillside. She asked, 'Is that Andrew?' 'Yes,' I said. 'Then I can go now,' she said."

So quickly, Andrew thought. *Couldn't she have waited until I got here?*

He bent to the chair and lifted her easily, so thin and light Doval had become. Without her spirit, she felt even lighter to him, nothing but a thin shell like the chambered feathers of a seagull. For a moment, as he held her, Andrew imagined her so. Imagined the incredible brightness of her spirit taking wing, gathering new form as it soared heavenward.

Then his vision had not been all wrong, after all. But it was not the Messiah coming down. It was Doval rising that moment when the sun shone its last golden rays of the day. He looked back up the hillside to where Doval must have watched him coming, but tears blurred his eyes and he saw nothing clearly.

As he held Doval, Hadesseh tucked the loose ends of the blanket about her. Andrew carried her into her room so she could be prepared for burial. The shadows inside the villa deepened, as if it too had held its breath—waiting.

* * *

They bore Doval's body to the tomb the following evening, Desidero

92

and Andrew carrying the linen-wrapped corpse upon a litter. Dominic had not come in from the fields on time, and Andrew felt a pang at his absence. And he missed Catillo—he was part of Doval's life. Once. Regardless of what he had done or where he was now. There were only the four of them, the two litter-bearers followed by Hadesseh and Griselde.

As they approached the tomb Andrew couldn't help thinking, *This is the last of them. The last of the four to be laid to rest.* Doval's body would fill the only remaining shelf.

Rest in peace, brave hearts, he thought. All the stories! They rested with them.

They laid the litter on the grass, in the same golden light.

He and Desidero bent to the gravestone in its grooved track. Earlier, Desidero had gone out to clear the track once again, for a final time.

Andrew felt weak and lightheaded as he fingered the huge stone. Desidero bent beside him. "Now?" Desidero asked.

"Now." They heaved together.

The stone would not budge. It had settled with time. And always before there had been several men to help them. Now only two. They heaved again. The great stone rocked slightly but did not move. *Oh no,* he thought. *Do I have to carry her back? Get more men? Try over? Why couldn't Dominic be here now!* He bent wearily, futilely, against the gray rock. The sun flickered over the western hills. It would be dark soon.

Hadesseh and Griselde moved forward to help. As they came, Gregor stumbled out from the thicket behind the tomb. So squat and misshapen, he resembled a piece of earth moving. His thick torso swayed over the stubby bent legs. His long arms came near to the ground.

Gregor made deep grunting sounds in his throat. His hair was all wild and windblown. The horribly disfigured face looked up at them with a primitive longing.

"What?" said Hadesseh gently.

Gregor grunted noises at her. Andrew stood transfixed. *Like a beast,* he thought.

"You want to do it?" Hadesseh asked.

Gregor nodded. He made deep, coughing noises that, even to Andrew, sounded like, "Gregor do it." Again he nodded.

Andrew shifted to make room. Maybe together . . .

"He wants to do it alone," Hadesseh said sharply.

"What?"

"By himself. It's his gift. For Doval."

For some reason he didn't understand, Andrew stepped back. He looked at Desidero. The man's face was flame red from his effort. Sweat stood out like bright shiny pebbles on his broad forehead. He nodded and stepped back also.

Gregor fingered the rock for a moment, as if reaching for its heart. The broad, spatulate fingers, hairy to the tips, caressed the stone. He found points to grasp it. The short legs squatted further, and the huge shoulders bunched under his brown rags.

Gregor's face dipped alongside the rock. The cords of his neck stood out and his color deepened. Then steadily, as if by a machine, the huge rock rumbled and moved in the track. There was no rocking. It rolled smoothly under brute power. Nor did Gregor pause when enough space was cleared to enter. He kept moving until the dark mouth of the grave stood utterly open to the last golden light of the sun.

That light flooded the dusky cavern and made it suddenly seem a palace. As they bore the litter in and laid it tenderly on the last shelf, Andrew was thinking, *They are the last kings and queens. True kings. Loyal queens. The last of their kind.* And then the tears were blurring his eyes, and the chamber seemed bediamonded with light as Hadesseh and Griselde tenderly lay their wreaths of flowers about the linen-wrapped body.

Again, Gregor refused assistance as he rolled the huge stone back in place. Perfectly so. The fit proper and tight. It was his gift, his tribute indeed, to the fallen kings and queens.

Tomorrow Andrew and Desidero would mortar in the permanent seal. Certainly no predators would enter tonight.

Andrew looked around as they began walking down the hill. Gregor had disappeared. Hadesseh slipped her hand in his, and he held on tightly.

* * *

Life affords so little time for mourning.

Andrew wanted to set things in order, to pause and to reflect. He wanted to live for a few days through Doval's eyes, recapturing the things she had said, the things she valued or discounted as of no worth. As he walked the rooms or the courtyard of the villa, however, he felt only fragments that remained at the end of many years. When he looked deep into the past, it was not Doval he saw, nor the others. He saw himself.

Sometimes he wept when he revisited those early memories of a time long past. But they were not tears of anguish. It was a kind of stripping off of necessities that bound him to the present. Increasingly he wondered if he could go further back, perhaps back to the places where it all started.

His father had told him of the farm they had had in the homeland. Of the house where he was born—in the care of friends who loved them. But he had also warned that the land was changing, not the land itself but the rulers of the land. It was a land of conflict. In fact, Elhrain had cautioned him *not* to go back. That very caution created the yearning in Andrew. He had nearly resolved to go. He wondered whether he should take Hadesseh. It was her homeland also.

Then the harvest was upon them. And the mourning and the recollections were pressed underground in his mind for the necessities that never leave one alone.

It was nearly two weeks since Doval's death when the first laborers began carrying the heavy bunches of grapes down the hillside from vineyard to presses. At first, when he stood by the villa gate that morning, Andrew wasn't even certain what was going on. They moved slowly, a few at a time.

He remembered Dominic once saying to Doval that they could save a lot of effort by building the presses up by the vineyard itself rather than in the valley.

She had shaken her head. "No. The sun is too hot there. It would ruin the juice."

"This way is too far," Dominic protested. "A waste of labor."

Doval smiled. "But it is the people's time. The pressing should be a holiday. It always occurs in the village. In a shady place."

And that was the end of it.

So now the people still walked down the hill, bent under huge bunches of grapes. They came slowly at first, all morning, and the excitement seized him. He walked down toward the village. Already the mounds of grapes began to rise beside the presses. Some women and children had begun the hard work of stripping the bunches. Some people, Andrew knew, simply threw in vine ends and all. It was easier, and the woody pieces settled in the mash at the bottom of the press, but Fontini Villa had always insisted on the old way. In some places, Andrew also knew, they were even starting to use the stone wheels used for pressing olives on the grapes.

Every so often one of the children would seize a particularly good bunch and begin stripping the grapes off one by one to make raisins. Andrew smiled. He remembered how his mother loved that special treat.

The mounds grew throughout the day. Once begun, the process took on a life of its own. It would not cease until the last grape was pressed, the last weary legs staggered, the last drop bottled for juice or casked for wine. The carpenters Dominic had hired were busy now with the casking work.

There were several more of them, Andrew noted. In fact, some villagers he had known from the old days were not there. He saw Dominic's aging father, too old for fieldwork, supervising the stripping. He smiled when he saw Andrew approaching.

"It looks like a good harvest," Andrew said as he greeted him.

"Wonderful." The old man beamed. "One of the best I can remember."

"Dominic has done a good job," Andrew said.

"Yes. And thank you."

"For what? He has helped me! He knows the fields and workers better than anyone." He paused. "But some are gone."

A shadow slid over the old man's face.

"The sickness," he whispered. "They fear the sickness."

"What sickness?"

The old man shook his head. "Not here. But we hear stories. About the rats. And the sickness. It is close. Maybe we will escape it."

"I see."

*   *   *

For days the harvest consumed every working hour. When the mounds of grapes grew to a suitable mass, the pressing started—in gaiety at first, then to the plodding rhythm that simply got the work done. When the end was in sight, the momentum would accelerate again. The lines of finished casks and stoppered bottles grew. The first two wagonloads, manned by Dominic's carpenters, left for Faenza.

Andrew himself spent little time in the village. His mother and father had been familiar and welcomed guests there. Lycurgus and Doval had mingled easily with the people. Andrew felt more at home in the fields and vineyards, so the supervision of the village fell entirely to Dominic. Several times Andrew had himself shouldered a load into the village.

Dominic reprimanded him. "You shouldn't do that."

"Why?"

"You are Fontini. Not a peasant."

"I don't care."

"Ah, but the people *do*. Think of them, Andrew. Not of your own wishes."

It puzzled Andrew. Dominic was from them; he should know. "There are so many new workers," Andrew said, surveying the presses. "It seems all changed." There was a note of disapproval in his voice. Many of the laborers looked like the rough, cursing men of the Faenza docks, rather than the men and women formerly of the village.

Dominic shrugged. "We need workers. So many of the old ones have left now. I get who I can." He looked at Andrew through weary eyes. "What? Do you want the fruit to rot on the vine? Or the ground?" He smiled. "It doesn't do anyone any good then."

Andrew walked the long way back up the vineyard path. He had left his horse picketed above the vineyard. Instead of stopping—either to work or supervise, he hadn't decided which—he kept walking, found his horse and mounted. The old dog, excited by the sudden motion, barked at their heels.

He turned the horse northward. It had grown fat and perky these last weeks. Andrew felt the coiled energy in its muscles. The horse shook its head from side to side, ornery and restless. Hitting the uphill meadow, Andrew suddenly heeled the horse hard, gouging the ribs, and it exploded into motion. The wind felt like a warm blanket passing by his side. Andrew let the animal have its head, unleashing it into a long, powerful gallop. The dog's barking faded behind them. The thundering hooves floated over the uneven ground. Like an arrow they drove toward the crest of the hill, hot into the eye of the sun. Foam whitened Andrew's legs, the horse's flanks. Almost to the hilltop, paralleling it, easing upward. Andrew thought of the olive grove on the other side. Why not now? He kneed the animal. In a lunge it crested the hill. Andrew hauled back on the reins in sick surprise.

In the distance sea and sky shimmered together in a white haze. The long sweep of the hill rolled down toward the rocky head of the coast, and at one glance Andrew read the ruin there. Slowly he dismounted, coiling the reins of the snorting horse around a rock. The old dog came panting up to them, and when Andrew knelt, the dog planted a wet, sweating lick of its tongue on his cheek. Andrew reached out and slowly scratched the dog behind its ears.

The taller, older trees were planted near the headland of rock, to serve as protection for the younger trees that stood in decreasing ranks behind them, rising up along the sloping hill. Even from this distance Andrew could tell that the older trees had borne fruit. Their boughs sagged heavily. He wondered for a moment why no one had bothered to check them. He wondered why Dominic had not. He wondered why *he* had not. But they had been forsaken, and the reason seemed plain.

Midway up the hill, in a slight declivity protected by rock, were the remains of the small house. Fire had gutted the roof and the interior. Its collapsed roof poles thrust charred dark ruins toward the sky. The stone walls were blackened where door and window frames were burned out.

When? he wondered. *I would have seen the smoke. Someone would have seen the smoke!*

Unless . . . unless it happened during my last trip to Faenza.

Still, someone would have seen it! And why did no one tell me?

Unless someone didn't want me to know.

Andrew walked heavily down the hill, feet dragging. As he neared the house the dog whined anxiously and held back, its body sidling in nervous circles.

The fire was not old, Andrew noted. Probably no more than a few weeks. On the backside of the hill, would it have blazed unseen from the villa? Impossible! But why had no one told? Had no one seen? And what happened to Naomi and Samuel? Perhaps they had fled in embarrassment at the destruction. Perhaps they thought it was their fault. But the orchard. All the work they had put into it! How could they leave it?

Andrew looked inside the ruined house, and the desecration was thorough. Furniture lay reduced to ash. Scorched blankets piled in the corner rose from the charred ruins of a bed. He remembered now that Lycurgus had had the bed made and sent over so that the couple wouldn't have to lie on pallets on the floor. The entire room still stank of smoke. The only whole pieces remaining were some blackened pieces of cookware by the ruined hearth.

98

Andrew stiffened suddenly. The grayish-brown shape slithered from behind a charred pile by the cookware. It stared at him with beady eyes, then darted past him through the door. Andrew's breath hissed out in a slow stream of tension. Rats. Even here. They were drawn to ruin, to desecration.

The old dog whined, then barked in harsh warning.

Andrew stepped outside. Again the dog barked. It stood near the spring, by a thicket of brush that clumped out of the soft, wet earth there. And Andrew wondered for a moment, *Surely there was enough water here to fight the fire.* Out of curiosity he lifted the lid on the cistern behind the house. It was full. The stream from the spring babbled freely, not more than a dozen feet away.

Again the dog barked, its voice trailing into harsh growls. Andrew saw it pawing at the soft earth past the spring. Its neck fur stood up like a warrior's plume. Its head bent low in a fighting pose as it growled at something on the ground. Andrew walked over to it. The dog backed off, growling nervously.

Something white lay on the ground where the dog was digging, its claw marks stripping it. Andrew bent. A piece of cloth. He pulled. Harder. He pulled against the sudden feeling of weight. The white cloth shifted, breaking the surface of earth where the dog had dug away the dirt. Andrew pulled again, and the cloth broke partially free.

The thing blurred before him. He felt his stomach churning and turned aside, sucking in deep breaths. When he turned back, what he had seen was still there. It hadn't disappeared, like the dream he wished it had been. Protruding from the dirt was a hand, fingers rigid and clawlike, its wrist and forearm pulled loose from the ground as if it were groping at the sky.

Breathing deeply, Andrew rose and walked back to the tool shed behind the ruined house. The door was unlatched and standing ajar. There were few tools, far fewer than those needed to run the orchard. Had someone stolen them? Preyed upon the remains of the dead? Set the fire as a coverup? His mind reeled. He found a shovel with a broken handle.

The late afternoon sun glanced with a wicked heat off his shoulders. Several times Andrew thought about quitting, about riding back to the villa for help. Something drove him on to do this thing, even as the splintered handle of the shovel raised blisters on both hands and his palms turned raw and liquid. He exhumed both bodies. Several times he turned aside to gag into the stream, until finally he only retched dryly. Something compelled him. Something spoke primitively of threat and danger in the back of his brain. He had exhumed both bodies, wondering as he did so why he felt it necessary. *Because they deserve better*, his brain insisted. *Because . . . because.*

And he knew why when he brushed the dirt away from Samuel, using a handful of broken branches from the nearest bush. He found the sunken spot on the back of the skull, matted and filthy. He had been struck, clubbed from behind.

Andrew straightened slowly. The dog, who had been waiting on the other side of the stream, peering steadily over crossed paws he laid his head on, whined at him.

Instinctively Andrew kept digging. Below the spot where Samuel and Naomi had lain.

He knew by the clothing who it was. His digging grew frenzied then, as if hurrying against the dying light of the afternoon. Already shadows crept languidly into the copse of brush. He could not stop. The shovel was slippery in his hands. He uncovered the legs and feet first, as if unwilling to see. But he knew.

Gently he brushed away the dirt from the face and shoulders. He looked into the hollowed eyes, the already decaying flesh, and fell to his knees. He knew. But what drove him to his knees was the length of thin cord still wrapped around Catillo's neck.

Choked, garroted. And buried here. Why?

Andrew stood upright nervously, thinking, *I have to get help.* He looked uphill. The horse had pulled loose from the rock and wandered toward the sweeter grass of the overgrown orchard.

Help? Who? Who had done this? Whom could he trust?

Well, of course, Dominic.

Anyone? Can I trust anyone? Andrew wondered.

The distant crashing of the surf pounded on his hearing. He felt it inside his skull, pounding questions.

Can I trust anyone?

Hadesseh? Her only? But she needed *him.* And what could she do, this—girl, he was about to say. But that was no longer true. She was a young woman now. Beautiful. And he thought again of the watcher she had felt outside her window. Not Catillo, then?

Thinking of Hadesseh, he thought of the death of her mother at sea.
He looked down at the three bodies now.

They deserve better, he thought again. *They should not be buried with their
violence, like . . . rats tossed into the ground. Like garbage. They deserve the
dignity in death that someone denied them in their dying.*

There was no doubt they had been murdered. Brutally. Violently. All
three of them.

But what now? Carry them back to the villa for proper burial? He would
have to get others to help. And if the murderers were on the villa—he
wondered about the new faces in the peasant village, the disappearance
of the old families—why multiply the threat by having them know *he* had
found the bodies? But he couldn't just dump them back in the ground
here, to be torn and ripped by animals in this shallow earth. They had
to have been killed recently, within weeks, else surely the creatures of the
wild would have found them.

He thought again of the story of Hadesseh's mother. It had been fitting,
she had said. Having no land to call their own, no ground to make sacred,
the captain of the ship had wrapped the body of her mother in linen and
committed her to the sea.

In the ruined house Andrew poked among the charred pile of blankets.
Their very density had protected them. He found three serviceable pieces.
With strips torn from the other blankets he bound them around each
body. The limbs were rigid and bloated. He had to turn his head as he
cinched the knots.

He whistled to the horse. It came partway down the hill, shying away
as it caught the scent of the dead.

The sun was lowering now. The hillside lay stitched with shadow. It
took a long time to move the bodies. One at a time Andrew hoisted them
over the horse's back while the animal skittered away, twisting its head
against the reins, white eyes flashing. Then he walked the animal down
the long hill to the headland rocks. The olive trees near the coast were
full to bursting. The overripe fruit nearly broke his heart. It seemed an
odd thing to him then—death through neglect and death through violence. Each violated some fundamental harmony.

He moved Catillo last. He wanted to carry him but did not have the
strength.

He stood then at the headland. The rough gray rock dropped away fifty or more feet to the surf below. The tide was in, the waves washing in huge white and gray swells against the rocks that chained them. Their pounding became a death song in his head. The sun had dipped behind the westward hill, casting that peculiar, lonely light over the empty sky that comes only at evening. The sea looked dark and heartless.

As he lifted each body and dropped it to the cold arms of the sea, Andrew's heart was throbbing with anger.

When at last he mounted, turned his back on the charred ruins and rode toward the villa, he was afraid at the anger and violence breeding within him.

CHAPTER
NINE

W ithout physical proof, Andrew didn't know whom to accuse, whom to trust. Outrage coiled in him like a nest of snakes, waiting, seeking opportunity to strike.

* * *

In the days following his gruesome discovery, Andrew spent time with Hadesseh, trying to distract himself. Several times he walked with her across the grassy plain toward the sea that she loved. He began to understand her attraction: the sea, somewhere, held the body of her mother. Over the sea, the body of her father reposed in her homeland. Andrew did not tell her that the sea now also held Catillo.

Andrew questioned her several times. Did she feel safe? Had anyone bothered her? No, she insisted adamantly, walling in whatever fear she felt. Whether she felt rebuffed by his earlier treatment of her or whether she had simply decided that there was no threat to her Andrew couldn't determine. She still grieved deeply for Doval and talked often of her. And then, without his fully realizing it, she would turn the questions on him. Did he believe as Doval did? As his mother, father and Lycurgus did? And Andrew answered, "Of course," but in his heart found the questions unsettling. Did he? he wondered. Had he ever? Or was it just something he accepted, as casually as the morning sun, the presence of friends and family? Without ever appropriating it as his own. *No,* Andrew thought, *I don't own it. But neither does it own me.*

When he grew tired of her questions and his own musings, he would leave Hadesseh with her plants and parchments, her marvelously detailed drawings, while he went back to the labor of the harvest.

But even there he felt like the outsider, and as he brooded on it he wondered if he was being shut out. Why? he wondered. He did not want control, but he also did not want to feel *without* control. As he brooded over the work, done mostly by strangers now, he thought of a plan. He would work from the inside out to find some answers. Go underground. In the Fontini Villa there was a serpent coiled. To find the serpent, Andrew had to become—the snake. And he *would* strike.

* * *

The wine was fermented in several stages. The early wine for export was ready within several weeks and was shipped to the coast in huge wineskin bladders upon a single cart. Not until the season had slid into the cool days of autumn did they begin to ship the superior wine. The Fontini shipments would be expected eagerly in Faenza.

When the first of it was casked, laborers carefully stacked several of the casks on their sides in the wagon bed of a team of oxen. The very placement of the wine signaled its worth, as did the three additional men who rode guard on the wagon as it made the trip to the city. Shipments would be made at odd times, supposedly on varied routes as the drivers followed country paths to the main road to Faenza.

Andrew forced himself to patience. He studied the pattern of shipments, weighing options. Where was the missing link? Were shipments being taken en route to Faenza, as Dominic claimed? Were the Faenza merchants deliberately falsifying accounts? If so, in cooperation with whom? Or, simplest of all, were shipments being diverted north to Venice?

Think like the serpent, Andrew warned himself.

He waited.

* * *

October winds trailed mists over the wagon and riders. They moved slowly, the creak of the wagon like a wailing in the darkness, the shapes of the horsemen ghostly in the gloom.

In the shadows Andrew moved afoot, well off the road. It would be no particular effort keeping up with the heavy wagon. The path wound along the valley, paralleling the stream. Soon it would intersect the main road, one of the many stoned roads the Romans had built to knit their dominions together in the cloth of commerce. Andrew knew the road; he knew the way. He knew no hurry. He wondered only which direction the wagon would take—south toward Faenza or north toward Venice. Still further on, after one passed through Faenza, the road angled west toward Rome. The crossroad, Andrew decided, would tell the story. If someone was diverting Fontini goods, what more natural step than simply to turn north, instead of south? There other roads led to remote places. Further north into the wild mountainous lands beyond which lay Paris. East to strange barbarian nations.

* * *

Andrew crept down the hill. His worn black trousers were wet with dew to the thighs, the peasant shirt dirty and hanging loosely from his shoulders.

He had waited on the hillside for as long as he dared, wondering whether to come out. The wagon had not yet come by. Below him, where the rural wagon trail intersected the main highway, a small campfire glowed. Three figures huddled around it.

Watching them, Andrew thought about remaining where he was. From here he could tell which way the wagon was headed. Surely that, he thought, would answer his questions, for he had successfully convinced himself now that if shipments were missing, as the traders claimed, someone was diverting them north to Venice. Who? And what was done with the profit? How long had it been going on? Years now? The profits would be considerable indeed. Andrew thought of the warm weight of the golden necklaces. And that had only been the part of the profit turned over to the cause after workers and the villa had been provided for. *The Cause.* It seemed distant to him now.

Andrew crept closer. A spring wound down the hill, its soft gurgle covering any noise he made. He could see the three men plainly now. He had been thinking they were outlaws, but then discarded the thought. The fire was built as protection against outlaws, who had their own camps back in the wild places from which they preyed on travelers. No, these seemed ordinary wayfarers, banded together at evening to summon strength in numbers against the night dangers.

He saw a mule now, staked in a grassy area. And a wagon, its ox also staked out.

Andrew studied the men. The one in peasant clothes—probably a farmer, himself returning from trading in Faenza and too poor to take a room at an inn there. The other, a tall thin man as he stood up to toss more wood on the fire, was dressed in a black cape. A professional. Maybe an itinerant lawyer, perhaps a physician making his way to some northern village. The third was younger, a lad not much older than Andrew himself. Andrew winced inwardly—he felt old here hiding in the hills, his world crumbling around him. He felt like . . . Fontini, not like Andrew. Like the snake going underground.

The lure of the fire drew him out of the damp and darkness. He reasoned that when the Fontini wagon passed no one would recognize him. He didn't even know the men driving and riding. The new men.

He approached the fire carefully, standing a short distance off and clearing his throat in the traditional manner of a guest awaiting welcome. Heads turned. Andrew felt their eyes probing him. He stood silently, undergoing their scrutiny.

Finally the thin man stood. "Well, you might as well come and share our fire, then," he called.

Andrew stepped forward, slowly, letting the men study him, assuring them he bore no threat. He noted that the farmer relaxed his grip on a clublike log by his side.

Andrew joined them, sitting cross-legged by the fire.

The farmer dozed. The physician, for so he introduced himself, stared silently into the flames. It was the boy who talked. Indeed, to Andrew's increasing annoyance, he wouldn't stop talking. His tone was haughty, the voice of one sophisticated in the ways of the world.

"I don't suppose *you* have ever been to Venice," he was saying.

Andrew couldn't remember ever having been interested in going to Venice. Nor could he imagine why he should. "No," he agreed.

The lad shook his head tolerantly, as if dismissing another country bumpkin. "Ah," he sighed. "I can't wait to get there." He looked at Andrew, waiting for Andrew to ask the right question. Finally Andrew gave in.

"Why?"

"I have dreamed of Venice! Because the great Salerno is there." He waited Andrew's response with doglike eagerness. "I have sold most of my books to go study with Salerno."

"Salerno is a teacher, then?"

"Indeed. But not just a *teacher*. I have studied with those in Rome. All it is is oratory. He who talks best wins. But what good is talk unless something is said?"

"And what does Salerno say?" Andrew stiffened slightly, picking up the distant creaking of a wagon in the wet mists.

The student looked at him as if his ignorance were a pitiable thing. "Salerno has used the mathematical derivations of astrological patterns to prove the existence of the Divine."

"He has proven it?"

"What?"

"That this . . . divine . . . exists? And what is that divine? Is it Zeus? The old myths? Is it some other god?"

"What you name it," said the student haughtily, "is completely irrelevant. Even distasteful. We deal with principles. First principles. Of course he has proven the Existence. Mathematics does not lie."

"Oh? Why?"

"Because it is given of the Divine."

"Perhaps the divine lies."

"Impossible."

"Among some it is said that with God all things are possible." Yes, Andrew did hear it now. He kept talking to establish his cover. He wanted to see who was on the wagon. He was hardly mindful of what he was saying.

But the student had grown angry. "Except lying," he was saying. "The Divine cannot lie, for it is truth itself."

"Then he is not all-powerful."

"Of course the Divine is all-powerful. Else it would not be the Divine."

"Then he can lie."

"Able to, perhaps. But it does not."

"Perhaps that is his chief lie."

"How so?"

"To make us believe he does not lie." The wagon rumbled toward the intersection. Andrew prepared himself. If it turned north, toward Venice, he was willing to run all night following it. To find out the deceit. He was sure it would turn . . .

The wagon slowed. The driver cursed at the oxen. The horsemen guards splashed by. Then all of them turned down the road toward Faenza.

Andrew breathed a sigh of disappointment. He wanted to catch . . . someone!

"I will question Salerno about this," the student was saying.

Andrew turned abruptly. He stood to leave. "Listen," he said to the student. There was no longer any need for friendly conversation. "Who can pretend to know the mind of God? You? Your pathetic Salerno? I tell you, if you use mathematical derivations to prove the existence of God— as I call him—then I guarantee you that in a short while someone will use those same derivations to prove there is no God."

The student stared at him, mouth agape.

Andrew couldn't resist. He was angry. He too had been so *sure*. "Listen, boy. It's when you're certain you know something that you should doubt yourself the most. Understand? There's more bravery in doubt than all the Salernos in the world possess."

Andrew disappeared into the darkness. He angrily pummeled his way up the hillside. An inner voice cautioned him that he didn't have to be cruel to the lad.

Well, he responded inwardly, *if truth is cruel, then so be it*.

As his energy waned along the dark footpath in the hills, so did his anger. At least, he thought, the student was reaching—still asking questions.

Andrew found, somewhat to his surprise, that he thought seldom about such matters. He tried to convince himself that he was too busy. For his parents the spiritual life had always come first. And somehow it made their life seem so . . . simple. It was not, he knew, but so it appeared. Orderly and simple. Their God, and his son the Messiah, rested like a massive centering point right at the heart of their lives.

What was it Emeth had said? *Allegiance*. But what does that mean? Andrew wondered. He felt a pang of guilt over his glib talk with the young student.

He felt also the pang of failure. He had been so sure. It would be the easy way—to divert the shipments northward. That would make sense.

Then it would point to someone inside the Fontini Villa. Someone who knew the schedules. Who? Dominic? Surely not. But he did control the process.

But what if that theory was all wrong? Like the student's Salerno, whose warped logic wanted to find God creeping out of some human system. Any human invention could *not* be God, Andrew thought angrily. Any fool knew this.

Wait. The traders at Faenza had told him about the missing shipments. Why worry about Venice? If it were the merchants themselves . . . then they would find it altogether too simple to cover their crimes. Some skillful juggling of accounts and, by magic, there was *no* crime—only profit. Perfect. *Oh, look to the obvious. You have lost yourself in subtleties,* he thought. And, yes, if this were the case—and already he had nearly convinced himself it was—it would clarify all his questions about Dominic. Who else can you trust? Dominic had asked. Who indeed? How he hated it when those doubts wormed through his mind. Circles within circles.

If only Catillo were still here to guide him. Yes, and what of Catillo? *Murdered.* For the first time Andrew let the word slip fully formed through his mind.

Well, someone from the past, then, from Catillo's past. He was, after all, a man with a price on his head for forsaking the Emperor's games, and it was hard to escape the long reach of Rome—even here in these hills. So, someone from Catillo's past had found out, had probably collected a ransom. *Probably!* Andrew wondered how he could know anything with certainty anymore. Everything orderly seemed to be crumbling, and he stood confused in the rubble.

For some reason he thought suddenly of Hadesseh. With Doval's death, her own links to a past seemed irrevocably stripped away. His heart felt her loneliness as he realized that, with everything else that had happened, he had neglected her. He would talk with her. Spend time with her. Tomorrow, he vowed.

Then Andrew was crossing the familiar bridge over the stream by the peasant village. He walked in a dream, weary and distracted. He thought at first the sound was from some animal. Low and guttural, it rose out of the darkness and bubbled up suddenly into a scream of pain. He was running toward the peasant huts when it rose again, breaking apart in a strangled sound. It was followed by a lamenting wail as if from a young child.

It came from one of the new huts, on the edge of the village.

He approached the door. A hog was feeding, untended and unpenned in the front yard. It was huge, and snuffled over into Andrew's path. In the thin, cloud-choked moonlight, it appeared like a squat, ugly growth moving before him. Andrew kicked out savagely, striking the animal behind the ear. It snorted angrily but moved away from the door.

He fumbled inside the doorway for the oil lamp. He heard the child whimpering. The lamps were always inside the door, on the shelf by the flint. It was the custom. But here there was no shelf. Andrew crossed to the little low hearth and blew on the embers. He threw a handful of twigs from the pile on their glowing. Light ate into the darkness.

The child, scarcely more than two years old, sat naked on the dirt floor of the hut, clutching a strip of burlap which she fondled for comfort. Her cheeks were tear-stained and red. She sucked her thumb, holding the grimy burlap up to her nose.

When she saw Andrew, she crawled across the dirt floor to a pallet on which a woman lay. Andrew bent over the woman, feeling the fierce heat of fever rise like an aura in the cold air. The heat seemed to palpitate against his palm held to her forehead.

Andrew stood and looked around the squalid room. He had been in several of the peasant houses when he was a boy. They had been nothing like this. The emptiness and the rude stench of sickness assaulted him.

The little girl clutched his leg, struggling to stand. Andrew picked her up and laid her on a small pallet that was enclosed by woven willow shoots to form a crib. She sucked noisily at her thumb.

Andrew found an oil lamp lying in some rubble by the door. The fluid was nearly gone. Finally he got it started. He placed it by the woman's pallet, studying her in the feeble light. Her blanket, a filthy rag, was sweat-soaked. She trembled violently under it, then would fall into a deathlike stupor before the trembling started again. Andrew thumbed up one eyelid. The pupil stared out glazed and unseeing.

He lifted back the blanket. The swelling started in her lower neck and rose in angry purple lines, like thick worms crawling under her flesh. When she tossed on the pallet the swelling held her neck rigid as if in chains. The ropes of swelling stitched above her breasts to angry purple lumps in her armpits. With growing dread, he pulled the blanket back. Her groin was swollen with buboes, huge lumps arching up from her inner thighs. Plague!

Andrew stood up, aghast. The sickness lived in this room like a fiery presence. It reached out to touch him in the woman's moans and the child's whimpers.

He wanted to get out.

Suddenly her body twisted in a spasm of pain. Her breath heaved, gurgling in her throat. Her eyelids opened. When she fell back, her eyes stared rigidly at the ceiling.

Andrew drew the blanket back over her lifeless form.

Cradling the infant carefully in one arm, Andrew seized a burning stick from the fireplace and he stepped outside. Moving rapidly, he set the roof ablaze at three separate points. The fire rushed greedily at the dry straw, lapping at the support poles. As he walked through the village, holding the little girl carefully, workers came running out of their huts.

Andrew shouted them back. He did not speak the word *plague.*

He started up the hill.

Dominic drew up on horseback. "Where have you been! What's going on?"

Andrew glared at him. "Those peasants you hired. Those thugs. I want them gone. Every one of them."

"The harvest, Andrew. We have to finish shipping."

"Then we'll do it ourselves. I'll talk with you later."

Dominic stared at Andrew's strange clothing, at the infant in his arms, but said nothing.

* * *

Awakening several hours later, Andrew dressed hurriedly and tended first to the little girl.

From the looks of her, Griselde had scrubbed her within an inch of her life. Andrew had not breathed a word of the sickness, but he sensed that somehow Griselde knew. He looked about the spotless kitchen, the shelves and tile floor scrubbed to glowing. Sunlight danced through the large window and sparkled on the culinary tools. Even the mammoth hearth was swept clean. He shivered, thinking of the squalid hut.

In a chair in the corner Hadesseh sat smiling, holding the infant, who sucked greedily at a flask.

"You gave her wine?"

Hadesseh giggled. "Porridge," said Griselde. "It will do." Whatever her place on the villa, the kitchen was her undisputed domain.

"She seems to like it," Andrew observed.

"Porridge with fresh goat's milk. Who wouldn't?" Griselde stood with thick, work-roughened hands propped on her ample hips.

The little girl suddenly slapped the flask away and laughed up at Hadesseh. A wreath of golden curls played about her head, capturing sparks of sunlight. She wiggled off Hadesseh's lap and tottered over to Andrew. She tugged at his trousers.

"She wants to be held," Griselde said.

"Held?"

She nodded. "In your arms."

"Very well." Andrew picked her up, looked into her blue eyes full of laughter. Suddenly he understood everything.

After a moment he placed the girl back amid a clutter of pans, which she banged unmercifully.

"Will you see to her needs, Griselde?"

"Of course, master."

He paused at the door. He motioned for Hadesseh to join him. Clearly she wanted to stay with the little girl.

"Griselde," he said, "from now on you are in charge of the villa. Of everything. You and Desidero."

She nodded, as if to say she had been all along. "But my cooking," she said. "It is all I can do to prepare for the dinner parties . . ." She paused, then added, "When you have them."

"Yes," Andrew said. "It has been a long time, hasn't it? But there will be no more parties."

*   *   *

Andrew spent the entire afternoon with Hadesseh. They wandered along the coastlands, talked in the shade of some headland trees stunted by wind and sun. With backs leaning against smooth stones, they talked.

Anything, Andrew thought, to avoid thinking of the peasant house, the stench of decay and dying, the harsh whorl of flames.

He had seen no one in the fields all day. Well, he told himself, harvest was now nearly done.

But mostly he looked at Hadesseh. She had grown so beautiful. Her face was still deeply tanned by the long summer past, and sprinkled with freckles over the bridge of her nose and the tops of her cheeks. The wind tousled her dark hair. Yet there was a haunted look about her, as if she were forcing something dark to the back of her mind, fighting hard to present a face of joy.

Even as he studied that face, Andrew began to realize how very dependent she was on him. Perhaps that caused the slight uncertainty that slid over her face now and then like a cloud in the pale sky. He was all the more startled when, at precisely such a moment, she turned to him and said, "Well, do you want to tell me about it?"

He did. Beginning with the fire and the woman's death the previous night. As he talked, he realized that he too was dependent on her. He had no one else.

"You did the right thing," she said. "Only fire can cleanse the plague. I saw the fire start."

"You saw it? It was nighttime."

"I don't sleep very much anymore."

"I'm sorry. Has anything—frightened you?"

She shook her head. "Remember when I wanted to sleep with you?"

"It seems like a long time ago."

She smiled with embarrassment. "I was too old. Even then. But so many things frighten me. Catillo . . ."

She sensed Andrew stiffen.

"Tell me, Andrew. I can't help unless I know."

And so he told her. Everything. The bodies in the house in the orchard, the suspected theft of shipments, his fears about Dominic. Finally he even told her about Emeth's chapel now turned into a hospital for victims. While she sat leaning next to him, glancing upward with her wide dark eyes that seemed bottomless, he told her these things. When Andrew was done talking he was surprised to find both his hands entwined in hers.

As they walked back to the villa, he found himself thinking, *I wonder if she knows how much I have come to love her.* He wondered how he could ever tell her. *I could not stand having her say, I love you too, but thinking of me as a brother.*

She seemed to sense his thoughts, as she did so often. She leaned up and kissed him quickly on the cheek, and then darted on ahead through the fields. *I wonder what secrets she keeps,* Andrew thought. *And why haven't I asked her about them?*

He had done too much of the talking; he should have been listening, letting her talk too. *Next time,* he vowed. *Next time, so I can know her heart.*

* * *

Andrew would have liked time to stop right there. Just when awakening from the horror to find the day pleasant after all.

Several events over the next several days were to prove the lie to his hope.

Not until the next day did Andrew talk with Dominic. Andrew wanted all the laborers hired in recent months released. Immediately. He wanted only families working on Fontini Villa, as in the past.

Dominic protested. Families had left. They were afraid of the sickness, of the rumors. They had moved north. The harvest had to be finished. Couldn't Andrew see that! And now there were only two more shipments of wine scheduled. Let them remain for that, then dismiss them for the winter months.

Yes, they live in squalor, these ruffians. Still, the work got done.

And finally Andrew agreed to let them finish with the shipments. He would spend the winter locating new families. Perhaps Emeth could help.

Three days later the drivers and horsemen returned from the latest shipment to Faenza. Dominic had agreed to send to Andrew the man responsible for the care of the dead woman and the little girl immediately upon his return.

When the man knocked clumsily on the villa gate he did so with anticipation—perhaps the master would reward him for his suffering.

And perhaps that deed, customary on the large villas, did pass momentarily through Andrew's mind—until the peasant came in and everything fell in place.

He was hulking and surly when Desidero ushered him into the great room. He stank of alcohol, of sweat and filth. His piggish, red eyes squinted in the dim light of the room, and he had trouble navigating to the table where Andrew sat. Andrew recognized him—one of the workers brought aboard just before the harvest, the same one who insultingly ignored him while he worked on the hut. The same hut where the woman was found.

114

Yes, things fell in place. Andrew felt anger surge through him like liquid flame. When he leaned forward his body was trembling with it. He did not invite the peasant to sit, even though he swayed drunkenly.

"How long have you worked for Fontini Villa?" Andrew rasped.

"Oh, a long time, master." The man fumbled for words. "Months now. Since before harvest."

"Months? Since your daughter was born?"

The man lifted his eyebrows. His eyes went wide, wondering. "Yes, blessed dear," he murmured.

"What is the name of your blessed dear daughter?"

"Master, I . . ." He groped for words as Andrew silently eyed him.

"Don't know? Try this then." Andrew stood. Face to face with the man, his odor was overpowering. "Who hired you to work here?"

"Ah . . . I don't know, master. I was . . . sent."

"*Sent?* From where?"

"Perhaps I should not say. I was told there was a house vacant. It was a lie, of course." He said the last in an aggrieved voice. "I had to build my own." The nugget of his brain was working against the alcohol. How much to tell, how much to hide.

"Do not forget your place," Andrew chided. "I am Fontini."

"Yes, master."

"Tell me, what was your wife doing in Faenza?"

"Faenza, master?"

"She died of plague. Plague, peasant! There have been cases along the docks. None here."

"Ah, she shopped."

"Shopped! No Fontini families need shop in Faenza. Goods are available here. *Everything* is provided for your sustenance."

The pig eyes worked furiously now, blazing with the effort to avoid confusion. "I don't know that she went to the city, master."

"Why? Because you are absent from your duties? Or because you brought her along from Faenza? To continue *her* work here?"

Silence.

"Your daughter, your unnamed blessed dear, is strangely bred, wouldn't you say? Blond hair, fair skin?"

"What of that?"

"Your own hair, peasant, and that of your wife, is black."

The man shifted his bulky body forward, crouching slightly as if to spring. The anger was ready to explode. *Rub this ulcerous sore, then,* thought Andrew.

"She was not your child, peasant."

The sound that came from him was a growl. Lips flared back over yellowed teeth.

"And where would your wife become pregnant with such a child?" Andrew leaned forward over the desk. "A child from a blond-haired, fair-skinned stranger? Why, only at the docks of Faenza."

"Enough!" The man stood quivering with rage.

"Where you took her, peasant. To sell her body along the wharves. Where you took her still after the child's birth. Where she contracted the plague that killed her. Where you killed her, peasant! Was the money worth it, to sell your wife to the northern sailors? Did you watch them while you jingled their coins? Or did you run to the tavern then?"

A strange growl rose in the man's chest. He heaved himself over the table, launched like a battering ram. Andrew struck him behind the ear. The blow was rigid, landing precisely on the knot of muscle where the neck joined the skull—one of the points of vulnerability Catillo had so carefully taught him. The man toppled. He thrashed and gagged on the floor. Spit dribbled from the corners of his mouth like a winded animal.

"Tell me, peasant," Andrew hissed. The man's eyes rolled upward. "Were you at the docks last night?"

He shook his head. "No."

"You were with the wagon. Last night. The night your wife lay dying. Who were you with?" Again the man's eyes flared with fear. "Stealing Fontini goods. For what? For a few coins and a flagon of wine. Get out of here!"

He fell over on his first attempt to rise, staggered, leaned against the wall while his breath flagged noisily. His eyes slid toward Andrew, wide with fear. The look sickened Andrew.

"Go," he hissed. The man slid backward along the wall, reached the doorway and bolted out. Andrew followed him to the gate, watched him stumble down the hillside to the village. The man paused by the ruin of the hut but did not stop. He paused only to talk angrily for a few moments with his other teamsters also just arrived from Faenza. Then he began walking down the road and disappeared into the trees.

When Andrew turned back to the house, he was trembling. Desidero stood by the pool watching. He asked if Andrew needed anything. Andrew shook his head and started to wave Desidero away. Then he stopped. "The little girl," he said. "How is she?"

Desidero grinned broadly. "Fine, master. As full of life as—"

"She doesn't have a name," Andrew interrupted. "Why don't you and Griselde give her one?"

"Master," Desidero flushed and half-bowed. "Griselde calls her by a name."

"Yes?"

"Helena. It is after her own mother. If that's all right . . ."

"Helena. Yes. So it shall be."

* * *

The final event was no less upsetting.

The next evening a lone courier rode up to the villa. His horse was a powerful animal, but it stood winded from hard travel. When Desidero ushered him in, the courier handed Andrew a note sealed and ribboned.

It was from the merchant association that he traded with in Faenza, carefully signed and sealed by the head official. The note inquired politely, in formal terms, why only one shipment had been received, and when, since the end of the shipping season was drawing near, they might expect the others.

Andrew paid the courier who bowed and waited for a written response. Andrew shook his head. The courier turned, immediately mounted his horse, and rode off.

The note was crumpled into small jagged bits in Andrew's hand.

* * *

Late that night, Andrew stepped into the quiet emptiness of his parents' bedroom. The room itself seemed to breathe memories. He stopped for a moment, remembering, seeing them standing there, smiling, talking. He shivered and shook his shoulders as if warding off a chill. He stepped to the small bench behind the tapestry, opening the secret compartment that he had examined so long ago. He dug hurriedly through the objects. He set aside the worn cloak, still puzzled by its mystery. The small leather pouch of gold coins was there, undisturbed. His fingers felt the object he was looking for through its protective wrapping. He unrolled the oiled cloth, letting the knife fall out into his hands. Its blue blade winked dangerously in the moonlight. The bone handle felt cool and smooth to his palm; it felt light in his hand, superbly balanced and crafted. He ran his thumb lightly across the blade, and its sharp edge neatly creased the outer flesh. He tucked the knife into his belt and again lowered his shirt. He would craft a sheath for it in the morning.

CHAPTER
TEN

Late November mist clung to the flanks of hills, muffling all sound. It caressed the wet grass silently; it wound among the leafless branches of the rambling thickets; it snaked about the dark black trunks of dripping trees.

Andrew heard only the rasp of his own breathing, and it seemed to him the loneliest sound in the world.

So utterly alone in darkness and fog. The cold mist caught on his face, barely exposed under the hood of the cloak he had flung on over his peasant clothes. It clung to his skin like tears, dripping crooked trails.

He paused by the trunk of a wind-warped tree and leaned against it, letting his ragged breathing even. He tried to keep his mind on the objective. He had insisted, *demanded*, that the teamsters take all three wagons, heavily laden, and get them to Faenza for marketing and shipping. He remembered the look in Dominic's eyes as he argued with him.

"It is too much risk," Dominic protested. "We should go singly. This way there are too many drivers, not enough guards to keep watch."

"We have lost shipments with guards! You can go with them to guide them."

Dominic shook his head. "We surely cannot risk this."

In the end Andrew had insisted. The son of Fontini had declared it.

And was the quick, harsh light in Dominic's eyes then fear? Or anger? Or greed?

Andrew had wanted to force the truth. Make a prize that couldn't be turned down. Answers! He wanted answers. And he was ready to follow—on foot—all the way to Faenza to know the how, the why of the deceit. And who was deceiving.

Having decided already to take risks, Andrew decided to compound them. Instead of leaving by the safety of daylight, the small caravan would leave at night. Here too Andrew was plotting ahead. An attack by outlaws, usually in the late afternoon or evening hours, could be considered a normal threat. The three wagons would act as an attraction: a rich load to be carried so. It would also act as repulsion: the numbers of men with the wagons. It would, nonetheless, be a tempting target. The numbers, Andrew knew, were more show than substance. Few workers had remained to the hard end of the harvest and processing. Those riding guard would be strung out, the numbers less than they appeared.

But at night, at deep night, if there were an attack on a moving target this large, it would have to be coordinated ahead of time. There would have to be signals sent—from inside Fontini Villa. *Enough proof*, Andrew thought. The risk was worth it.

As he topped a long hill and stood for a moment, ankles wrapped in ground fog, heart beating heavily in his chest, Andrew knew well his anxiety was not only for this mad plan.

* * *

Before leaving he had walked quietly to Hadesseh's bedroom. He didn't know then how long he would be gone or what would happen. He had actually started out, just after the wagons left, when he stopped suddenly and returned to say goodby to her.

He had pushed her door open gently, stepped slowly across the bedroom floor, letting his eyes adjust to the darkness. Only the tiniest flicker of light crept from the great room, down the hallway, into her room.

She looked so peaceful there, curled in the soft blanket, her raven hair spread like wings. He knelt by her bedside, the way one would by a child. He watched her for what seemed a long time. Unconsciously he was fastening her in his memory, and for the first time a trickle of fear slipped through his anger and touched his heart. Fear for Hadesseh. This was her safe place. Nothing could—nothing *should*—threaten it. He reached forth his hand, touching her forearm flung casually across the blanket, letting his fingertips trail with the lightest touch across her skin.

And he felt her whole body stiffen rigidly. It was like a palpable signal, burning through his fingertips. *Dreaming,* he thought, and he laid his hand on her arm to calm her.

Suddenly Hadesseh bolted upright. She flung her arm up before terrified eyes, her face transformed into a mask of stark terror. Her mouth opened, but no sound came. Her eyes shrank from him, her body recoiling rigidly against the wall, where she huddled like a struck puppy. She shook her head wildly.

"Hadesseh, Hadesseh," he whispered.

"No," she groaned. "No."

"Shh. It's only a dream. It's me, Andrew."

"Andrew?" Her voice evened. But her thin body shook and trembled. "What are you doing? Why are you here?" Her voice hissed through tightened lips.

"Shh. It's all right."

"No!"

"Yes, it is. You're only dreaming."

For long moments her breath heaved. Slowly she relaxed. Yet she shrank from him.

Andrew stood up, puzzled. This fear—it was more than a dream. "Are you all right? Do you want me to get Griselde?"

"No!" She was silent for a moment. "Don't get anyone. I thought . . ."

"What did you think? Hadesseh?"

"Never mind. Go away, Andrew."

"I am. I wanted to see that you were all right. I'm sorry."

"It's too late."

The words bewildered him. He turned to go.

"I tried to tell you, you know. Long ago." Her words were like darts. Angry. Accusing.

"I'll be back in a few days."

Hadesseh said nothing. He couldn't see her as he stood in the doorway to go. But he was conscious of her eyes. Out of the darkness they seemed to rake his soul. Too late? Quietly he shut the door and slipped out into the hallway, out of the gate, into the darkness—the cold, the fog, the great open darkness.

* * *

The cold settled on him, eating inward as he knelt among the bushes. He shivered and tried to ignore it.

He recalled the night long ago when Catillo had awakened him from a deep sleep. Suddenly his teacher had been there, shaking him awake. Andrew protested angrily, half-awake. Catillo reached over and flung off the blanket. He put a finger to his lips and motioned Andrew to follow. He refused to let Andrew put on sandals or clothing, pushing him naked save for a loincloth into the hot summer night. Outside, the insects whined and buzzed at his ears. Wordlessly Andrew had followed Catillo out of the gate, down the hill, then south along the stream. Never once did Catillo look back. He expected Andrew to be following. It was as if he held Andrew on the leash of his own will.

They entered the stream, walking along its graveled bottom. The water felt cold on the hot summer night, icy against Andrew's calves as they splashed downstream. His feet numbed. Pebbles spiked against his soles; he barely felt them. Downstream the waters broadened into a thick grove of brush. Andrew felt the sudden shift in temperature as they walked from the water's flow into a low swampy area, his feet sucking at mud now, algae gathering like moss on his thighs. Low hanging branches swatted out of the darkness, pulling his hair, raking across his naked flesh. They slowed as the swampy muck deepened around their ankles, clinging, sucking. Andrew felt something slither across one calf and he shivered. The water here was thick and warm, the air humid and stinking of decay. And then Catillo stopped.

"What do you think . . ."

"Shh," Catillo hissed. "Not a sound." He held up a hand. "Do not move."

Insects whined and stung. Catillo stood rocklike in the darkness.

Andrew slapped at a mosquito. Catillo caught his arm in midblow, pressing against the nerve at Andrew's elbow that paralyzed his arm. "Do *not* move." The words struck him like a forked tongue.

And they stood there. Andrew fought the temptation to move, to run back. Then he remembered the breathing. In through the nose; out, slowly out, through parted lips. As Catillo had taught him. *Control.* There is no victory, Catillo had said, without control. He breathed evenly. His heartbeat steadied. The whine of insects seemed a noise far away. Inward. Go inward. A bug landed on his nose, tracked to the corner of his open eye. Breathe. In and out. In and out.

Andrew had been surprised when the sky reddened finally. He flicked his eyes at Catillo. The man smiled at him and nodded.

When Andrew tried to move his legs they seemed rooted in place. He had sunk into muck nearly to his knees. He felt trapped. He had to fight to move. The muck sucked at him. They moved back to the stream, to the cold water, the good water. It was numbing and clean. He was moving outward. Catillo started running and Andrew kept pace. They ran uphill, algae and muck slimed across their bodies. Sweat cut rivulets through the muck as they ran, past the villa, into the eye of the red rising sun, to the rocky coast. They clambered down the rocks and flung their bodies into the crashing waves, letting the salt water sting and purify as the sun whitened above them and the sky silvered.

When at last they returned to the villa, Andrew felt clean, reborn.

Remembering the experience, he shook his head as he crouched in the bushes while the cold fog pinched his flesh. Catillo! How he missed him.

His legs grew numb. The knife was sheathed at the small of his back, under the loose peasant shirt. The bone handle pressed into his back. When he heard the creaking sounds of wagon wheels and harness, he could not at first sort out what it was. As if wakening from a fuzzy dream, he shook his head. Drops of cold moisture flicked off.

The wagons groaned heavily down the path. Voices cut through the air. Andrew recoiled. A torch had been fastened to the lead wagon, its gaudy yellow flame bobbing through the gloom. The drivers laughed and cursed now. For whatever reason, they knew no fear of outlaws. *Of course not,* Andrew thought. *Not if they themselves were the outlaws.* They reached the fork in the path and ground to a halt. They dismounted wearily, stretching their legs, stepping off to the side of the road. A flagon appeared and made its rounds.

Why are they stopping? Andrew wondered. He shifted uncomfortably in the brush.

Dominic dismounted and walked down the road a few paces, into the darkness that squeezed like a fist. Suddenly Andrew heard the muffled beat of hooves. Three horses stopped in the darkness, milling about Dominic where he stood in near darkness. One rider dismounted. He walked back with Dominic, toward the light. He gestured and pointed. Grinning now. Yes, that smiling face. It took a moment for Andrew to recognize him. Gaius. The man he had met long ago at Emeth's chapel. Was he the Faenza contact, then? There had to be another!

Andrew shifted in the brush. He stumbled over a fallen branch, his feet slipping on the slick sod. The branch caught between his ankles. He flung out his arms to stop himself. The small knapsack he carried over one shoulder caught in the branches. He twisted, falling heavily into the bush.

The men stopped. A shout. The torch moved toward him. Someone drew a bow and arrow. Another waved a sword. They moved toward the underbrush.

Andrew forced himself, with every ounce of his will, to lie still, flat to the ground, his heart hammering against cold, rocky soil. If he were found out now . . . The footsteps neared. Torchlight glittered off the tops of the bushes. He waited, breathing evenly, in through his nose, out through his mouth.

Andrew heard something stir in the brush near him. His own muscles tensed, ready to run blindly into the thicket. He could hear the men breathing now, their gasps short and angry as they worked uphill to where he lay. Nearer.

The deer suddenly knived out of the nearby brush, hooves hammering uphill past Andrew. The arrow zinged through the night, falling harmlessly beyond Andrew where he lay frozen in the bush.

Hoofbeats pattered lightly away. The men swore loudly, laughing at each other, calling each other names. They walked back to the horses and wagons, still laughing. Andrew heard the creak of gear. Then motion. The whole group turned south at the Faenza road, Dominic and Gaius riding in the lead.

Andrew listened closely until the creaking of the wagons disappeared, then slowly pulled himself upright. His clothing was soaked. He wrung water from his shirt front. Then he gave up. It was cold, bitter cold. He shivered. He stepped out of the brush and began running down the road. He eased into a steady pace that he could keep up as long as he had to.

It was a long way to Faenza. But he knew where they were going now and had no intention of stopping until he got there.

* * *

When Andrew arrived in Faenza, a pale November sun had cut through the seaside mists. Gulls careened noisily in the air, the surf sang against rocks and wharves, and for a moment one could have thought everything was at peace with the world. He was tempted to stop at a tavern and eat a long, slow meal.

He had run much of the night to keep up with the wagons. Through the long hours he threaded his way over hills, through brush and forest, always keeping as near the caravan as he could. The cold deepened with the night, sapping his energy. When he arrived at Faenza, slightly ahead of the caravan but certain it was headed toward the docks, his body was numb with weariness. But he could not risk being seen, and he desperately needed rest.

He climbed into the hills above Faenza, huddled in some bushes and opened his knapsack. The bread was damp. Even the cheese seemed soggy. But the raisins were sweet. And it was good to rest. He drained the small flagon of wine and leaned back. The sun struck him, warm against the damp shirt. So warm for a cold November day. In a moment he was asleep.

He wakened to a sound in the grass. He felt something brush against his outstretched arm. His eyes peeled open slowly, fighting against the inner fog of sleep. Shadows were deepening on the slope where he lay. He startled upright. The movement sent several rats who had been foraging greedily in his knapsack scurrying into the underbrush. For good measure, he flung the nearest rock after them.

The knapsack was empty. Andrew flung it angrily into the brush. He stood up. Evening. He was too late. He had slept too long. He plunged downhill toward the wharves and warehouses of Faenza.

Dusk was falling when he spotted the wagons. They were standing empty by a row of warehouses, the horses still harnessed, snuffing restlessly at some piles of hay thrown carelessly before them. Rats crept about the fringes of the hay, dancing away from stamping hooves. Andrew's anger surged higher. The horses were to be stabled, fed grain, rubbed down before the return trip.

But if they weren't intended to be returned?

He crept along the warehouses in the growing dusk. The clouds had thickened, and the wind was rising in the cold air. Little pellets of spray needled his skin.

There was one of them, walking through the shadows toward the end building. One of the Fontini drivers. Wrong! One of Dominic's men. Andrew slipped through the shadows, following as silently as a breath.

The door to the warehouse stood ajar. He peered around the corner, body pressed carefully against the wood. The torchlight inside flickered. Andrew studied the figures, taking count. Dominic, Gaius. Three—no, four—other men. They had been stacking the shipment. They stood now nearly finished; the hired men slouched wearily.

Andrew leaned forward.

The blow to his kidneys sent him reeling through the doorway. He stumbled, tripped and sprawled full length in the dirt at the feet of Dominic.

The guard who entered behind him laughed heartily above his prone form. He shook the club he had used, paused and kissed the tip of its dark wood.

Andrew pulled himself to hands and knees, head down, sucking for air. He felt exhausted, as if he could collapse right there. He stared at the feet encircling him—worn sandals, a pair of boots. One of the boots lifted, the toe catching him under the chin, forcing him to look up. Into the eyes of Dominic.

"Stand up, Andrew," he said.

Andrew pulled himself to his feet. He wiped sweat from his forehead. *Strange*, he thought, *how I can sweat on a cold night*. He looked around the circle. Peasants. From the villa. Some he recognized. Not all. They were grinning, but not from friendliness. Andrew understood that to them he was the enemy. There was a sign of triumph in their eyes—triumph and hatred. Gaius stood to one side, his eyes wandering nervously.

"Strange place to find you, Andrew. Has it been a cold trip?"

Andrew looked into Dominic's eyes for the first time. There was no gloating *there*, no triumph. Nor any affection. They were . . . vacant. Dark, blank orbs.

"You may not believe me," Dominic murmured, "but I am sorry you made it. Now there is only one choice for me. Oh, I will not regret the act, for I have always hated you, you know."

"Hated . . ."

"Of course. You were Fontini!" He spat the word out like a sour taste.

126

"I, your peasant."

"No. No, Dominic. My friend."

"Your friend!" Dominic's voice was a snarl. "How could I be your friend? Everything . . . everything you beat me at!" His face reddened. "And at night I had to slink back to that worthless hovel like some trained dog. Come here, Dominic. Do this Dominic. Nice—"

"No!" Andrew shouted. "I—I loved you."

"And I hated you. But now you see my revenge, Fontini. For years I have plotted this. And you never knew. You with your pathetic *trust*. You were such easy prey, Andrew. And now it's all over."

Andrew stiffened. For the first time he understood his peril. He wouldn't leave this place alive. He whipped a glance around the circle of men. They were no longer smiling. Five of them. And Dominic and Gaius. Seven. Impossible.

"You're not going anywhere," Dominic hissed.

"Except for a swim," one of the men blurted.

"Silence!" Dominic snapped.

"How long?" Andrew asked.

"How long have I hated you? Since I first was sent—*sent*, mind you— to that villa to entertain you. And at night I had to walk back down to that cramped little—"

"No. I mean, how long has this gone on?"

"Oh. You want answers? I no longer care. It no longer matters. Practically since that first night I went to Faenza with you. For years, Fontini—"

"Call me Andrew."

"I'll call you what I want. I saw the way to get back. I took bit by bit at first. It was so easy. A diversion. In time I spoke for Fontini, you understand, so I gave the orders. Then I had to pay off certain parties. To Venice first. Then right through here, little Faenza. It's all gone, Andrew. And it's untraceable. I have my own villa now. After tonight I am leaving for good."

"Where?"

"What does it matter? To the north, where I'm safe—lord of my own land. Gaius here has everything in place."

Gaius nodded soberly.

Andrew reeled. The word *why* careened in his mind. Dominic's anger was feral, dangerous. How had he kept it contained? My betrayer. Andrew's own outrage rocked him. *Revenge!* he thought. His hand began to move toward the knife sheathed at the small of his back.

"Poor little Andrew. Wondering why. Money, Andrew. Wealth! It's all mine now. Mine! And mine alone. For you, it is all finished." His voice lashed. "Take him!"

Dominic took a step backward as the men pressed in. A hand grabbed Andrew's shoulder. He bent, seizing the wrist, then exploded into motion, twisting the heavy body in a blur over his shoulder. The man thudded to the floor with a whoosh of breath, his legs tangled in some lumber.

Move! Andrew darted, feinted, using his surprise. A side kick exploded against a man's sternum. He felt the impact jar along his leg. No time. He whirled, fending off the blows that clubbed his head, his shoulders. He ducked low, somersaulting, and drove upright with fists striking. The weight of his body, his pure outrage drove the blows. He recoiled and parried, dancing the macabre dance Catillo had taught him.

The old lessons came back. He felt as if Catillo himself were standing there, directing. He whirled, bringing his elbow like a sword stroke into an opponent. Darted away. Sweat poured into his eyes. *Too many*, he thought. The club one peasant used swung in from the side. He saw only blows and targets now, not men. He parried it with his forearm, inches from his temple, drove in on the attacker with rigid blows. Someone screamed. There were only shapes now. Blurred, distorted shapes in the darkness. One lurched at him, hesitant, fearfully. Andrew's rigid palm caught him precisely under the jaw, driving the blow upward. The man collapsed at his feet.

Andrew spun in a cold rage, transformed. *Revenge! My friend.* His bitterness exploded in each blow. He wanted nothing now. Only devastation. He heard a screaming sound, rising and ringing with each blow. Then he realized there were no more targets—nothing, and the screaming was his own fury.

He stood limply, shoulders slumped, in the puddle of muddy light. His breath sounded like a pumping bellows. Andrew grabbed the torch from its wall bracket. Bodies lay crumpled in impossible postures about him. But not the one he wanted. Raising the light, he screamed out, "Dominic!" The sound echoed off the walls.

He stepped to the doorway, bearing the torch like some demented wanderer. He saw Gaius huddling behind a barrel.

"Where did he go!" snarled Andrew.

Wordlessly, as if stricken dumb, Gaius pointed out the door.

"Get those men out of here," Andrew snapped. He turned and flung the torch far into the recesses of the warehouse. He bolted through the door. "Dominic!" he screamed. The sound echoed down the length of the dock.

Nothing. Nothing but the scurry of rats' claws in the alleys.

Andrew dashed down the wooden planking toward Faenza. A barrel tipped somewhere ahead. Footsteps pounded. Andrew saw a dark shape scuttle through the shadows. "I have you!" he screamed.

He ran through the mazelike alleys, following sounds more than sight. They were delusive sounds, shredded and carried away into the dark by the noise of wind and waves.

The streets of Faenza were empty now. He was working uphill. Yes. He caught a glimpse. A ragged dark shape far ahead, running.

Past the inns, wind-whipped and shuttered against the cold. Uphill, past the villas of the merchants just outside Faenza. And Andrew knew with a sickening certainty where Dominic was going. The one place he believed himself safe.

His breath rasped. His legs felt rubbery as he ran. The untold number of blows he had taken slowly took individual places on his numbed body. His head throbbed. As he trudged he fingered a swelling at the back of his head. No blood. Good. Then as he looked at the top of the hill, he saw the dark shape he pursued suddenly outlined against the night sky. A darkness swallowed in darkness. Yes, Andrew knew where Dominic was going. He flung himself at the brambles and bushes of the steepening hillside, clawing upward.

CHAPTER
ELEVEN

I
n a moment, crossing over the ridge of the hill, it seemed to Andrew
that he had entered into another world. Behind him an orange
glare rose from the warehouse fire. He could neither see nor hear them,
but he could imagine men running from taverns and inns to battle the
flames. It would not last long; nonetheless, it would consume the last of
the Fontini shipments.

Then as he crossed the lip of the hill, the darkness was profound. The
icy air stung the sweat trickling down his body. He saw nothing; he heard
nothing. Only the moan of the wind in naked trees.

Andrew made his way across the broad slippery slope. He located the
gurgle of the stream and followed the sound upward. He stood finally
beside the ruined wall, silently probing the empty spaces.

A faint light issued from the chapel. Surely Dominic wouldn't dare!
Nonetheless, Andrew crept to the door. He pushed it soundlessly ajar.

The stench hit him first. Like a wall no door could penetrate, it rose
solidly before him—the sick odor of dying flesh, of rot and human decay.
No blow could have repulsed Andrew more effectively.

He stared into the chamber, his eyes adjusting to the light of the oil
lamp. On the stone benches rimming the outer wall, on flat benches
propped here and there, on pallets scattered haphazardly about the floor
lay the bodies of the doomed and dying. Lying in the stench of plague.

One figure moved in the shadows. It was Emeth, rising from prayer before one sufferer. His shoulders slumped wearily.

Gently Andrew closed the door. The oil lamp flickered in the draft and Emeth's head turned. But by then Andrew had stepped back into the darkness.

Where could Dominic have gone? If he had expected sanctuary in the chapel he would have found only death. Yet he had to be here.

Andrew stepped silently toward the garden.

He sensed it in the darkness—the tremor of air parting, the motion out of nowhere. He ducked. The rock careened off the side of his skull, erupting into a violent swirl of colliding lights. He fell gasping to his knees. Footsteps pounded through the garden. Andrew staggered upright, pursuing. Into the darkness.

The cave! Surely not. There was no escape. Andrew heard the sounds in there. He paused. Sounds too loud. Too obvious. Drawing him? Well, then, let them. He stepped over the low wall, splashing in the frigid water on the rocky floor, eyes piercing the gloom. There was an odd phosphorescence from within, the decay of algae and stagnant water, that cast an opaque green glow inside the cave. Andrew stood panting, his own breathing clearly audible, the only sound beside the solemn drip drop of water and the occasional whine of wind as it keened against chinks in the stone wall. When he stepped forward, it was like walking into a greenish pall.

Somewhere in the darkness he heard the breathing of another. Yes, there it was. Andrew fought to control his own breath. He took a careful step forward, expecting a blow or flight out of darkness.

"Andrew." The voice was empty. "Andrew."

"I hear you, my enemy. And I will repay you."

"Can we talk? I can make life good for you."

"I hear the noise of rats' feet, traitor. Soon they'll feed on your bones." Andrew stepped forward. His body trembled. His fists clenched. He traced the sound of Dominic's voice. He thought he could see him now— a dark shape in the odd green light. He stood on a raised ridge of stone at the back of the cave.

"I see you see me, Andrew. There's no hiding, is there?"

Another step.

"You are a dangerous man, Andrew. Think about it. You don't have to do this. What would your parents have said? Could you live with my blood on your hands?"

"My parents are dead, Dominic. As is Catillo."

"No, no. I didn't do that. It was Gaius. He insisted. When Catillo followed . . ."

"It doesn't matter."

"What do you want?" His voice rose, cracking. "What do you want? Tell me! Anything."

Andrew tried to focus on the voice, the shape. Want? He had lost everything. It wasn't . . . fair. "What I want, only you can give me, Dominic."

"Tell me! Anything, it's yours."

"Your life."

"No. Wait. I'll tell you where it all is. I'll draw a map. You'll never find it without me. It's all far away, Andrew." Dominic's voice rose hysterically. He shouted at Andrew. Treasures, he said. There were treasures hidden. In his place. *His* villa.

Andrew closed in. His legs seemed to drag. The figure before him, *above* him, gestured wildly. Dominic's voice howled. "I'm taking *her*, Andrew. Do you want her? Your little girl, Hadesseh. I tell you, I take her as my whore! You should know—"

Andrew's scream echoed off the walls of the cave. He lunged forward. Up the rise of rock, the surface slippery with moss and water, flinging himself at the green-hued demon, and he tripped, on the rotted wood covering the old cistern. The old wooden lid split beneath his feet like rotten twigs. He tried to lunge sideways but there was no support.

He plunged into blackness.

The hole sucked him down like a throat. He pitched down, banging against rock, smashing into the bottom. He lay there a moment, stunned. Slick walls, dripping slime rose around him. The bottom muck oozed over his body. The shaft of the knife at his waist jabbed angrily into a kidney.

When at first he looked upward, tracing the dark walls of the cistern toward the opaque green light—like swimming under filthy water and peering toward the begrimed surface—he saw nothing. Then the head and shoulders of Dominic leaned into view. He laughed harshly. "Yes," he whispered. "My enemy." Casually Dominic flipped a small rock into the cistern. Andrew twisted to avoid it, his limbs moving like dead weights in the slime. He struggled to his knees.

"Shall I torment you?" Dominic called. He rolled a heavier stone over the edge. It careened against the wall, bouncing off Andrew's hunched back. Andrew bolted upward, tearing at the slimed walls, scrabbling for hand or footholds. His breath stormed. He fell back exhausted, huddling hopelessly in the slime. Small stones bounced off his body. He wrapped his arms over his head and bent against the wall.

There was silence then. Andrew peered up cautiously. He heard the scratch-scratch of flint. A dim light wavered. Dominic reappeared, holding a tiny torch. "How convenient," he giggled. "Someone left me a torch to work by. Enjoy it, Andrew. While you can." He positioned the light nearby. Andrew's eyes clung greedily to the thin rays. Then the first piece of wood was slammed over the cistern opening. A second. The rays diminished. Dominic worked quickly then, and wordlessly. He repositioned the boards of the rotted covering, one by one shutting out the light. Andrew heard him placing stones upon the boards to weigh them down. Then his steps retreated, and there was only the desolation, and Andrew cringed at the bottom of the pit.

* * *

The lid was hardly necessary. Escape was impossible. Andrew clawed at the slimed walls until his arms and legs trembled. Impossible. Years of seepage and neglect had scaled the stone. The calcined surface was draped by sheets of moss.

Andrew wondered why the cistern no longer held water, and for the first time the thought slipped through his mind, *It would be a blessing to drown myself.* Years of seepage had opened minuscule cracks in the rocky bottom, other needle openings for the relentless press of the water toward the sea. What was left was the slime of decay, the clotted muck rinsed from the cave.

* * *

A strange scraping sound, like knives being sharpened on a whetstone, awakened him. Andrew knelt cradled in a ball, his body wet and stiff. He awoke to a wave of pain. The swelling from the blow to his head was crusted in blood. He peeled the dried edges from his hair. His shoulders and back ached at a dozen points from the rocks Dominic had flung down. It reminded him—he could not stop the picture—of years ago when he had seen the young boy beaten on the dock of Faenza.

Sensation slowly spread to other areas of his body as he tried to stand, a wave of pain twisting against a blessed numbness. His feet were numb with damp. They sank into the mucky debris of the bottom of the cistern. His skin seemed withered to his touch. He stamped his feet to restore circulation, but the movement splattered cold muck up his calves. Stones shredded the puckered skin of his feet.

He heard it again: the knives scraping.

He looked upward, eyes reaching for the trickle of daylight worming into the cave, outlining the patchwork of slats above him. Andrew recoiled in cold terror. They were all around. He heard their claws scraping on the stone now. The faint light outlined the slats and gave definition. Andrew could pick out the dark shadows of the rocks Dominic had piled on. *Like gravestones,* he thought. Impossible to move. Like climbing out of the grave.

"I will try," he muttered. "As long as I have breath in my body, I will try."

He could see their gray-brown bodies scamper over the gaps in the lid and between rocks, drawn by their frenzy for food, uncertain how to get to it. *I,* he realized, *am their prey.*

One of them stuck its quivering snout through a gap. Andrew picked a small stone out of the muck and hurled it upward. The rat recoiled, hissing with anger. The brown wave of bodies retreated. The hard claws scuttled nervously on the rock.

Another gray snout poked through. It was light enough now to see the quivering whiskers, the black bead of an eye fixed downward. Again Andrew heaved a stone. Missed. The gray body, driven by greed, suddenly wormed through. Into the cistern. It thrashed in the slime. Andrew kicked at it, beat at it with his numbed feet. His hand reached for the knife at his back. It sprang easily into his hand, as if made for this. He waited, plunged, felt the blade sink into the writhing flesh. Felt it fall still. Still he twisted, then hurled the body loose. Before it was free another slithered through, splashing into the muck.

Plague! The bite of rats. Furiously he struck with the knife. Not enough light. Andrew twisted and kicked. His hand closed on the writhing, snapping body. He drove the knife in like a madman. Felt it enter. Waited for another.

No more.

What did they sense? Had primitive fear overcome hunger? Were these the leaders; the followers now fallen back? Perhaps the scent of kindred blood drove the others back. How long? How long until the scent of the blood itself drove them wild with hunger? No good. Andrew knew he could not battle them if they came two, three at a time. He had to get out!

* * *

Slowly now, he groped for the gaps that had to lie in the stone, digging at the moss, probing for weaknesses. He used the knife to scrape away slime and calcification. He worked by touch. There was barely enough light to see if progress was made. Small crevices appeared. The wooden lid seemed impossibly distant. Andrew gained a toehold, leaned against the opposite wall for leverage, hands twisting and sliding on the black slime. But he was moving. Upward!

There they were again, gray snouts attracted by the motion and quivering through the gaps. Andrew screamed aloud. "No!" One rat slipped, claws scrabbling to remain upright on the rotted wood, then it dropped soddenly into the muck where it scurried wildly in the scum and the bodies of its two fellows. The creature hissed in rage, its claws raking madly and futilely at the slick stone.

Andrew ignored it below him, continuing his slow climb. Minutes passed dully as he dug out clumps of slime to gain another few inches. Stone tore at his fingernails: he could feel the skin abrading and turned his will against it. Claw to the very bones if it meant life. Another few inches, balanced treacherously over the pit of slime. The hissing of the rat below stilled to a furious gurgle and then silence.

His fingers touched wood. Careful now. With one free hand he tried to tear the rotted wood loose from the gaps and small stones cascaded down. He had no strength left to work the wood loose, no leverage to push upward. He beat weak fists upon it with futility.

He hung there panting, exhausted, wanting to weep from self-pity, every muscle screaming with tension as he hung poised on the slippery stone. *I don't deserve this!* Light was fading fast now, shifting almost tangibly from the reaches of the cave. *Only one chance*, Andrew decided. He would seize the lid itself. Leap and force it. The risk: the tumble of rocks Dominic had piled upon it.

135

Pounding again on the cover to scare away the rats, he carefully tensed the muscles of his legs, poised and ready for the spring. His breathing slowed from heaving gasps to a barely discernible rhythm. In and out. Then, a suck of air deep into the lungs that charged his muscles, and he leaped, fingers reaching for the gap in the wood, clawing, grasping.

With a great scrape, the wood tore loose. The rocks spilled through, flinging him back down. Down to the muck. Down to a burning pain in his ankle as it struck a stone in the muck and twisted crazily. Andrew heard the snap of bone above the tumble of rock as clearly as a thunderbolt just before his body plummeted into unconsciousness.

* * *

Oddly, what awakened him was not the scurry of clawed feet around the lip of the cistern, although it was the first sound that assailed his senses. Nor was it the pain of shattered bone in his ankle. It was the vague, unsettling sensation of itching. Andrew awakened clawing at his legs. They seemed alive with something biting, tormenting worse than the throbbing ankle. There was no relief from the itch. It rode up his body in fiery waves, the skin, as he clawed at it, rising in weals. Recklessly, he tore slime from the rock and plastered it over the already filthy, raw broken flesh. Anything to get relief.

Looking around, Andrew saw that rocks now littered the entire floor of the cistern. The battery had killed the remaining rat. Its body lay against the stone wall.

He looked up and saw the rats, momentarily baffled by the sheer drop into the cistern, ringing the opening. Andrew tried to stand to heave a rock at them when a scream of pain roared from his ankle, collapsing him once again into blackness.

When he awakened, again to find his hands clawing at revolted flesh, it was dark. Night had fallen. It was then that he willed the final act, willed death itself—the sweet, black comfort of oblivion—to consume him. To end the weeping pain of shattered bone. To end the torment of itching flesh. The sound of rats' feet! His jaws yanked open in a scream. He reached for the knife, his body aching at the action. He held the bone handle and it was terribly heavy now. He thrust the point toward the softly beating vessel in his neck and . . . it stopped. It would move no further. Again he pressed the point under his chin—*just so*, he thought.

Now, exhale, and jam it upward. End it! His whole arm trembled with the effort. Then shaking, he dropped the knife and let the spinning blackness carry him away.

*   *   *

The gray light of morning pierced the cave. To see the sun! He had not wanted to awaken. He had willed death, and failed. He felt the knife lying on his stomach and, twisting, slipped it into the sheath at his back. The itching subsided to a fire that raged unabated. So intense it no longer mattered. Pain itself the anodyne to pain. *I had raised the knife to my throat,* he remembered, *felt its tip rest on the great artery. So easy. So easy. What, then, stayed my hand?*

He wanted so badly to die in order to end it.

Andrew watched the light inch, minute by minute, hour by hour, along the stone. How slowly! He had never watched light move before. He picked a point, watched it slowly dissolve in gray light. Picked another. It seemed his mind floated with the light.

Of course, he thought. *You are losing your mind. This is how it is.* Tortured to extremity, the mind frees itself, leaving behind a wracked shell.

Watch the light move. Down. Now up. So it was afternoon. Watch the light. Focus up.

For the first time Andrew began to understand the meaning of the word *prisoner.*

He thought of it as an absence, for every degree of imprisonment is marked by an equivalent degree of privation. Having had everything he wanted, Andrew now knew the complete loss of those things. *As a prisoner,* he decided, *one is, first of all, thrown back on himself. What do I want? Things? No longer. Instead, freedom.* To see the sky, to touch—to touch earth, to touch grass, to touch a baby's face. These are the things of freedom, not understood until they are impossible.

Many long for things. A little more grain. Two candles instead of one. A change of clothing. Not one fish for dinner but two. Not satisfaction of hunger, but fullness. Many are free to long for these things. They are possibilities; and as long as they are possibilities the dreamer is free. Deprivation is theft of possibility. *Was I ever free,* Andrew wondered, *to seize possibility? Was I a prisoner even of Fontini Villa?*

Andrew fell to the muck, his sobs transformed to a harsh guttural laugh. What does it matter anymore? Imprisoned.

Fontini Villa! The words echoed like curses in his mind. He tried to banish them; they brought him again to tears. He saw sun-splashed fields. He saw . . . Hadesseh. A spasm twisted his heart. For an instant he felt the same terrible impulse to claw at the walls for a way out, or to die trying. He laughed feebly. He was dying, he thought. To be imprisoned is to die; it is removal of life.

But Hadesseh! What had Dominic said? And what did he mean? He could not imagine it, even while his mind insisted on it.

A black refrain echoed through Andrew's mind. *I am here! Alone.*

Alone. Die here alone? In this stinking, filthy cavity? The cell is a black mouth.

Suddenly it seemed terribly important to Andrew to know how long he had been here. Desperately he tried to tick off the hours, counting backward. Everything obscured. Two days? Three days in this pit? Alone.

I do not want to die, Andrew insisted. Yes, I had held the knife to my throat. But I drew it back! Something out of the sluggish awareness of his imprisonment screamed out: *I do not want to die!*

It seemed only a very small sound in the black mouth of imprisonment, but it slowed the abandonment to nothingness.

The green rock dripped to the pool of muck. Andrew realized in the silence broken by the trickle of the earth's tears that he had been screaming, screaming at the top of his lungs: *I want to live!* In the eerie stupor of exhaustion. The only sound the mocking echo of his plea careening against the insensate heart of stone.

The only sound . . . the scurry of rats' feet . . .

No. He listened harder. It was there. Hesitant. Footsteps. *The enemy returning to mock me?* Andrew wondered.

The scraping of flint echoed through the vault. Andrew could not bear to look up again—if it was only to see the face of Dominic.

The candent light of a torch flared suddenly. And the voice. "Is someone there?"

A demon then. Mocking him from the pit of hell, a pit seemingly higher than that in which he lay.

Again the voice, "Understand that I will help you." The voice moved into the heart of the vault. "Whatever you have done, whoever you are, I will help you."

Help me! "Father," he screamed. "Help me!"

Footsteps ran to the lip of the cistern, someone thrust the torch over it. All Andrew saw was light, an eruption of light so fierce it pained his eyes. He cowered in the slime under an upraised hand.

"I'm sorry," the voice said. The light drew back. Andrew could see his face now, the hawklike nose thrust forward under the cowled hood. Those eyes that always seemed to pierce to his heart.

"Andrew?" he breathed.

"Help me. Please, please help me."

Carefully Emeth laid the torch aside on the rim of the cistern.

"Don't take the light away," Andrew pleaded.

"My son, I shall leave it here. And return."

He ran off. The minutes ticked by, thudding to the beat of Andrew's heart. The light transfixed him. He held it with his eyes, gathering its rays, drawing them in. Emeth returned with ropes, looking about for a place to secure one end, darted off again. He returned, dangling a heavy rope into the cistern.

"Tie it under your arms. I will raise you."

Andrew fumbled desperately with the rope, swollen fingers tugging ineffectively with the thick coil. "I can't," he whispered. "I haven't the strength."

Again Emeth darted off, returning moments later with a rope tied about his own waist.

Behind him Petra's haggard face appeared. He looked like an old, stone savage in the torch rays. Petra wrapped his muscular hands around the rope and braced his feet against rock.

Then Emeth did this impossible thing. Brown robe swirling about his gaunt body, he lowered himself down into the pit. He stood in the muck beside Andrew. He struggled to tie the other rope about Andrew's torso. With the rope secured, Emeth clambered back out on his own lifeline, clots of muck dripping from his cloak, then with Petra's help steadily, slowly hauled Andrew's limp body up. And Andrew's only thought, as his eyes sucked at the light, was this: *He had to come down for me to rise. He did this. For me, he did this.*

CHAPTER TWELVE

Andrew awakened lying on a thin pallet, swaddled in a woolen blanket. Feeble winter light fell into the sanctuary, touching the wooden benches with its pale glow. He shivered. Through squinted eyes he saw the altar, rude and unornamented, at the head of the benches.

Emeth knelt there, hands clasped in prayer. When he rose he turned to the back of the sanctuary where he made his living quarters. *Good,* Andrew thought. He did not want to talk to him now, knowing that he owed at least an explanation.

It must have been he who carried me here.

How long have I lain here? Andrew thrust back the woolen blankets, damp with his fevered sweat. He was naked. His body, scrubbed clean, was a patchwork of weals. They no longer itched, although the memory of that torment nearly drove his hands clawing to the raw flesh. He tried to move his leg and felt its clumsy weight. The ankle was splinted and bound by strips of rawhide. The skin lay swollen against the strips.

"So at last you're awake."

Emeth stood shrouded in his robe, hands lost somewhere in its folds. Only his hawklike brow and nose, framing those piercing eyes, protruded. Andrew lay on a bench in a stone alcove of the chapel, and Emeth's body seemed to fill the space.

"Thank you," Andrew said.

"You have suffered much, and the only remedy is rest."

"My ankle?"

"I did what I could. But that may not be enough. The bone was shattered. If you will ever walk," he spread his arms, his hands appearing miraculously like white doves from the folds of cloth as he shrugged, "only time will tell."

Andrew was silent. To crawl like a cripple along the docks. Begging.

"More serious," Emeth said, "is your skin. Were you bitten?"

"Bitten?"

"There were rats in the cistern."

"I killed them."

"So easily?"

"They were rats."

"Then perhaps you will escape the plague."

Andrew shuddered. "My clothes?"

"We will find new ones for you. This also is yours." From the folds of his robe, he palmed the sheathed knife and laid it on the pallet. Andrew stared at it as if it were a strange thing.

"The rats did not bite me," Andrew said. "I will leave soon."

"You may leave when you wish, of course. When you are able. You still have fever. I will bring you something to eat, as soon as I feed the others."

"Others?"

Emeth stepped aside. Andrew saw them then. The wonder is that he had not seen, nor heard them before. Slowly the memory of his earlier glance returned. Even now as he looked, he saw a shape twist and moan in an alcove on the opposite side of the chapel. The small sanctuary was ringed by tiny alcoves, seven to a side. Each alcove had a prayer bench. On all of those, shapes lay huddled under blankets.

Andrew recoiled. Emeth held out a hand to calm him. "If you have not been bitten, I don't think you have anything to fear. I saw no bites on your body, but," he waved a hand toward Andrew's flesh, "you bear affliction enough."

"Why do they come here?"

"Where else would they go?"

"How did you find me?"

"The Lord led me; is that what I should say?" He smiled then. His white teeth flashed behind the rusty beard and held a trace of mockery. "I was returning from a trip to Venice," he said. "There I can purchase certain powders for the ill. They don't do much, but they seem to make the pain easier. In fact, I was crossing the courtyard when I heard you cry."

"I cried?"

"You cried out, Andrew. I heard you. It is enough. Rest now."

But he could not rest. It was not just the fever alone, nor the pain of the broken ankle and tormented skin. It was . . . another pain, beyond words. Andrew watched Emeth move from pallet to pallet, a tall, gaunt shape in brown. Through the haze of fever, Andrew could not tell what he was doing. And then he moved again to Andrew, pouring a broth from a large pot into a clean wooden bowl. He ladled a spoonful to Andrew's lips. Andrew sipped weakly, fell back.

"The plague," he asked again. "Will I get it?"

"I don't know. I believe God has a work for you. Even so, I don't know."

"What might this work be?" Andrew was barely conscious of his own words. His breathing was labored, and he felt dizzy from sitting up, propped on one elbow. The words seemed to come from some voice other than his, some dream voice.

"It will be revealed to you," Emeth answered.

"But the plague. It is death."

"Some die of it."

"Have you known any who haven't?"

"No. But you said you weren't bitten."

"True. I killed them."

"You are efficient at killing."

Andrew pictured in his mind the men in the warehouse, the sudden hot flash of flames. Had they escaped? Or burned to death? And did Emeth— this strange man who seemed part apparition—know all about it?

"You disapprove, of course."

"Of course. There are other means to health than killing. But sometimes health can only be attained by dying."

"You riddle me, Father."

"You yourself are the riddle, Andrew. Let me feed you."

Andrew let Emeth prop him upright, accepted the broth spooned through his parched lips.

"There are more rats on earth than are dreamt of in your heavens," Andrew said.

"Put it behind you, Andrew. This is the dying you must do."

"Why do I live, then, Father?"

"You yourself are the answer, Andrew. You are riddle and answer. I can only feed you now." He held out another spoon of broth and Andrew took it, gratefully.

* * *

The slant of sun on this winter afternoon bore the weight of sickness. As if they were dying themselves, the feeble rays crawled across the gray stone of the chapel. They fell momentarily upon the recumbent shapes huddled in alcoves, lit a fragment of glass with candent brilliance, then waned. Each of the alcoves across the chapel held illness. Plague. Encapsulated in human flesh. Having taken over the body like a succubus. The very air breathed the odor of illness, and Andrew could not stand it.

He still felt imprisoned. He wanted answers. What happened to Hadesseh? Why hadn't she come looking for him? Did she think he had abandoned her? *It's too late*, she had said.

He tried to rise, propped on one elbow while the chapel tilted dizzily. He pushed himself upright, the air a cold buffet to his fevered skin. He would have tried to stand, but Emeth was suddenly there to stop him.

"Have you slept well?"

"Have I slept?" His voice was groggy. The room seemed to be spinning crazily.

"A long time. I fed you again while you slept. And now, perhaps, you would like to go for a walk?" Again, that trace of mockery licking the heels of his words.

"Out of here! I want to leave."

"Surely. Any time you wish."

"But I can't, can I?" The words seemed forced out of some hollow place deep within him. He was barely conscious of what he was saying, only of his own weakness.

"I think not. Not unless you can hop on one foot. But you have surprised me often. Perhaps if I fashioned a crutch for you?"

"Anything to get me out . . . of this stinking charnel house." Andrew spat the words.

143

"It is a house of God."

"A decayed house for a dead God."

"Ah, but it does not house God. And, true, those who built the place never sought his presence here. But the place is the same when its purpose is fulfilled."

"Again you speak in riddles. Do you mean to mock me?"

"Not at all. You are the riddle."

"You keep saying that. I am Andrew. Master of Fontini Villa."

Emeth studied him a long time. "But you do not know yourself, Andrew. Here is the riddle each person contains, and is never content until the answer is found."

"I *do* know myself. I am prisoner in this . . . stinking . . . house of God!" He thrust the blankets aside. Andrew would have stood then, tried to walk, or crawl, out of there with its stench of suffering flesh. He tried. He actually poised his legs on the stone floor when a pain, not the sharp fire of broken bone, but a leaden coldness in the blood, stopped him. It pulsed terribly through his legs, knotted at his groin, doubled him over with nausea. Andrew toppled to the floor, vomiting against it uncontrollably.

Emeth lifted him as one would a child, scooping him up and raising him to the pallet. Emeth's face was rigid with concern. He placed a hand on Andrew's forehead and muttered, "Fever. It's worse. You're burning." He turned away then to the others.

But it could not be denied.

In the morning his arms felt stiff. He probed gingerly with nervous fingers, finding the lumps in his armpits. When Andrew sat up to urinate into the chamber pot, the pain in his groin was excruciating. The urine burned. And then he could see them. The raised lumps in the groin, like gray wads of dirty fat under the flesh. He averted his eyes, sickened by his own sickness.

Across the chapel bodies groaned and writhed. Andrew swore he would not let it get that far, to the point where he was the victim of his own body. He reached under the pillow stained heavily with his own sweat and drew out the knife. It was so light, so perfect, its blade a blue jewel. He laid its tip upon the hideous gray bubo at his groin. He squeezed his eyes shut and drew the blade along it. The hard, clean tooth separated the flesh like water. The swelling erupted and flowed down his legs.

He fell back, gagging with revulsion, hearing the knife clatter against the stone floor. He remembered Emeth running, his eyes wide with horror. Even as Andrew gave way to fever, he felt Emeth's strong hands bathing the mess from his legs.

And a crooked hand, affixed strangely at the end of Andrew's own arm, floated from his body, waved feebly, found a cuff of Emeth's cloak. It clutched tight and drew him near.

"If nothing else," Andrew gasped, "find him. Kill him. He must not live!"

Before sinking into the black froth of pain, he saw Emeth's eyes fixed on him—eyes wide, terrified. But also full of anger.

* * *

The days passed, swallowed in a haze of gray fever.

The day after lancing the hideous buboes in his groin, Andrew laid the knife to the swellings under his arms. It seemed a terrible release from nearly unbearable pain. Again Emeth ministered to him, washing his body tenderly, unmindful of his own contamination, silent and anxious.

The pain was unceasing. Streaks of white fire twisted inside his body. There was a flame in his brain that no water could wash out. It worked its way from the base of the skull along the temples and tried to drive out through his eyes—demons of the plague.

Over and over Hadesseh's face flashed through his fevered mind. One moment she was a little girl, laughing. Then the face of terror, turned to him the night he left. How long ago? Then, as if her face danced in flames of fever, it shifted and became the face of Doval, or of his mother, and he twisted helplessly on the pallet as the images burned in his mind.

Through it all, like a brown cloud, Emeth hovered nearby. Not just to Andrew, but also to the others. They came; they suffered; they died. Somehow Emeth found the energy, the strength to minister, to bear off the dead, to bury them in the cold earth outside.

Then one morning, through the delusion of fever, as if through a gray haze, Andrew saw Emeth leaning over him. Emeth's eyes pierced, cutting the way a knife blade severed the bloated sacs of poison. The force of those eyes ransacked Andrew's spirit. He felt impossibly weak. He seemed to hang in midair, looking down on Emeth's bent shape over the lifeless body below. Removed utterly from his own life. What he saw made him weep, although his glazed eyes found no tears.

I am dying.

Andrew felt light. Light in weightlessness, freed from the ill flesh. Light in transparency, freed from the press of darkness. Emeth hovered in a shaft of winter sun that fell feebly into the church. Andrew watched him make the strange signs of the cross over his body. He wanted to laugh. He was weeping instead—tearless, inward weeping like suffocation.

He felt he was not there at all.

Ah, but you are, a voice answered. *You are not ready yet.*

Emeth's words were quick, urgent. The words of the dead: "In the name of the Father, the Son, the Holy Spirit . . ."

Emeth bent his head—in weariness, Andrew thought. People lay scattered on the floor now in this house of the dead. The alcoves were full. They pressed their fevered bodies into the cold stone. Black lines inked their flesh. And on the altar! The hard, blue shine of the knife! Its blade shone cleanly next to a basin of bloody water. Emeth had been lancing the buboes. So much poison!

Emeth's grim feral eyes peered intently into those of Andrew. Andrew stared fearfully back. Emeth was the hawk. The raptor diving! Andrew wanted to scream. *Let me be!* he tried to shout. *Let me be. Can't you see, I have had enough of dying?*

But Andrew saw Emeth's hand reaching toward him—a strong hand, wrapped in a brown robe. His hand stopped on Andrew's forehead, but something reached further, diving through his body. Andrew shuddered and started back. Emeth's palm extended, waiting. Andrew reached forward tentatively.

He looked up, and for one moment another face took shape behind the brown robe. It was a face Andrew never remembered having seen in his lifetime. For an instant it was the face of Emeth. For a moment the face of another. And, then, the eyes! The grief imprinted there. Andrew seized the hand roughly, pulled, screamed.

And found himself looking up into Emeth's hawklike eyes.

Emeth held on to Andrew's hand with both of his. Sweat poured from his face, but he smiled.

"I have come a long way to find you, Andrew," he said.

"Thank you, Father." His parched lips shaped the words although no sounds leaked through.

"My name is Emeth," he said.

"Emeth," Andrew whispered.

"All shall be well. The fever has left you."

* * *

But if all was well, the reversal of dying carried its own weight of pain.

The simple process of eating, for example. After weeks of warm broth, Andrew's body cried out for solid food. That first solid morsel—a piece of goat meat—weighed heavily on the tongue. Tentatively his tongue savored it, brushed it against the palate. Almost reluctantly he swallowed. Each bite exploded against his starved throat.

After three or four such morsels Andrew was exhausted. He lay back on the pallet as if having devoured bowls of food. In such a way—a few slow bites, then rest—it took over an hour to finish the small helping of meat.

One day there was fresh milk. Andrew had heard the cow bawling in the yard, a donation or a readily accepted stray. The first time he held the cup of warm milk in his hand, he nearly trembled; like a starved infant he begged for more.

In such a way a week passed before Andrew could sit on the edge of his pallet, another week before he could stand. Time had lost sequence or meaning.

When he first sat on the edge of his pallet, feeling the warmth of a January sun on his ruined flesh, he looked at his naked torso and felt a surge of nausea. Muscles lay flaccid against bone, thin strips that barely responded to his commands. Even the most feeble commands. Hold a cup and drink. Raise the spoon to your lips.

The flesh lay like a wrinkled landscape of raised, purple weals, sores that still oozed around raw edges, on white valleys of enervated skin. The shattered ankle had knit crookedly, and hurt terribly when he tried to move it.

The halls of the church were littered with victims. Soon Andrew hobbled along behind Emeth as he tended the ill. Gripping a rude crutch, he hopped from form to form like a crippled surgeon. For such he became. The blade was light in his palm, wielded now against the black swellings at groin and armpit.

Most distressing were the children. Andrew could not bear to lay the knife to those tiny shapes, limp with fever, the helpless eyes staring up through a veil of pain. Yet while Emeth whispered the words of the benediction, Andrew made the hard, clean strokes into the writhing body. Perhaps he could forget the stink of that place in time, the overwhelming odor of illness. Perhaps the smell of the sea, the scent of flowers somewhere, would obscure the vile memory. Perhaps he could forget the writhings of pain, or become inured to it. But he knew he could never, never forget the eyes of those children.

As the pilgrims continued to enter the church, the cemetery expanded. Old Petra worked hours each cold winter day just turning earth. They piled the corpses into the holes. Sometimes two or three adults and several children layered into one pit before they shoveled the earth over their bodies. After a time, they didn't even weep as they turned the dirt. It was a work of necessity.

Andrew would not have bothered with the surgery save for two facts. The terrible issue brought almost instant relief from pain. The cut was nothing to the relief it brought. And, second, there had been at least one cure. His own. Then, as that terrible winter waned toward spring, there were several more. The treatment became more of a ritual, less desperate. Those who came early in their sickness were plied with liquids until they were ready to burst. Some women from the hill country left herbs and potions at the door of the church. From the knowledge Andrew had gleaned long ago from Hadesseh, he knew which were efficacious against fever, against vomiting and diarrhea. They mixed these with broths and soups and ladled them out generously. Against the plague itself there was little they could do save for the ministry of the knife and the whispered words of Emeth. Those who came to them late received only the latter before dying. The medicines from Venice had long since disappeared, and there was no time to replenish them.

But in this way of plying potions, liquids, constant scrubbing and mopping, using the knife with care and quickness, a few others survived. If *survived* is the proper word. The relics who emerged were death-haunted skeletons, their flesh pitted with scars. Two women who survived remained with them to do the cooking. A man from the docks, a burly worker named Philip, who seemed nearly to have lost his reason in his grim struggle, toiled endlessly in the cemetery with old Petra. When not excavating graves, he planted and trimmed the grounds. He spoke no words and avoided looking directly at anyone. When Emeth walked past, he would fall to his knees despite Emeth's protest. When the man continued to do so, Emeth blessed him gently and continued on his way.

No child lived. Not one.

Until late April.

Emeth and Andrew had begun, in those warming days, to take an hour to themselves in the garden at sundown. Philip had seen them there one afternoon, in the mangled little space between overgrown hedges, and had immediately begun carving a retreat for them. He trimmed back the hedges, pruned the trees and bushes, and began spading earth for flowers. It became the quiet place during those lengthening spring days that Emeth and Andrew could retreat to. They rested there one evening.

"Not having time for prayers, I've forgotten how," Emeth remarked. His eyes were weary as he lifted them to the encircling hills.

They sat on the greening turf, watching the sun fade across the hills. The sun had grown warm from its ghostlike winter disc and was a pleasure to behold. The spring wind was cold in the evening. Sea birds wheeled above the hills, darting like brown arrows in the sky, cawing and wheeling across the face of the sun.

"Your work is your prayer," Andrew answered.

"And you, Andrew. You are at peace?"

"I have been too busy to wonder. I suppose I am. A large part of me, anyway."

"Perhaps that is the best we can wish for. Any of us."

Andrew, however, had forced peace on himself by a conscious act of the will—and so it was no genuine peace at all, but a kind of resignation. He had simply understood that whatever had happened, he could no longer do anything about it. His emaciated body grew exhausted after an hour's work. Fontini Villa seemed to have receded in distance as it had in time. Now it seemed impossibly distant, beyond hope of recovery.

Nor did Andrew really think he could recover it. That life . . . it was a thing of the past. Something that had in fact died during his ordeal.

Only one thing did not—his inconsolable yearning for Hadesseh. He wanted to know . . . something. And not able to know, his mind filled with the worst fancies. That Dominic had taken her away. That she had contracted plague and suffered a lonely death. That she, in his months-long absence now, had believed herself abandoned and had willingly left. Where though? Or that she just no longer cared.

And, he wondered, who could care for his own ruined flesh, save for those equally ruined? *My kinsmen, fellow sufferers*, he thought.

* * *

The wind stirred in the leaving branches of trees. The sea birds above the hill cawed. Andrew reclined on the damp turf, hands held behind his head. Through the limbs of the gnarled hemlock, he saw the spire of the chapel rise against the sky. It seemed strangely blurred against the purple heavens, a scar of suffering, a sign of hope.

"I hadn't noticed the cross before," he said suddenly. It was a defiant symbol, Andrew knew, and a dangerous one. Why now? he wondered. But he realized it was a sign of hope to the endless stream of suffering pilgrims washed up on its doorstep these winter months.

"Petra repaired it last week." Emeth said. "He is also repairing the mortar between the stones. See the scaffolding there."

"A strange man, Petra."

"No more than any of us," Emeth observed. But then he sat up and stiffened, peering intently at the broad sweep of the hill.

"What? What is it?" Andrew pushed himself wearily upright.

Emeth pointed and Andrew shielded his eyes to peer hard at the distant hill.

A lone mule plodded slowly down its flank. It stumbled slightly, utterly spent. The woman aboard it was hunched over. She seemed to be kept upright only by the presence of a small bundle before her. But it was not a bundle. It was—holding the reins, propping the woman really—a young girl. And in the sunlight her flaxen hair shone. And Andrew and Emeth were up then, stumbling along the hillside, hurrying to meet them.

"Griselde!" Andrew called when he was certain. He saw her head lift, then grimace painfully, and he knew.

They led the mule to the chapel, Andrew propping Griselde on it while Emeth tugged the reins. When Emeth finally stopped before the chapel door, Griselde slumped and fell into their arms. Little Helena climbed down slowly, nearly tumbling off the mule. She followed Petra into the stable as the old man came to gather the reins.

With the macabre whimsicality of the plague, old Griselde survived. While young bodies were eaten into husks by the virulence, Griselde's sinewy strength somehow defeated it. She underwent the torment, and

150

bore the scars. She lost all her teeth, a phenomenon they had not seen in others. The first dropped out when Emeth was ladling broth to her and tapped a tooth with the wooden spoon. It was no more than that, a tap, and the tooth simply fell out. Curious about this, and concerned lest a tooth should choke her, Emeth tested others. Two more dropped out at his touch. Within two days he had removed every tooth in her mouth. They simply fell out to the touch.

Anxiously Andrew hovered around her during her recovery, waiting to ask the questions that burned in him. Each time he stopped. Staring at her pale flesh, her eyes sunken to dark pools, lips pulled tightly over toothless gums, he could not intrude on her suffering.

When it came at last, Griselde initiated it.

"They must have come during the night, master."

"Griselde, please. Call me Andrew."

"Yes, master. During the night."

"Who? Why? How many?" Suddenly the questions burned to his lips, hot and urgent.

Griselde shook her head. "I don't know. I don't—but it had to be during the night, for the next morning Hadesseh was gone. I thought, at first, she had gone off somewhere on her own. I waited, master . . ."

Her words were a rush now. Tears scalded her eyes, and her voice was weakening.

"I waited and waited," she moaned. "Then I began looking. Her room . . . all a mess. Someone took her, master."

"Andrew."

"Yes. Who? Who would do such a thing. She is—was so precious . . . Andrew. So—"

"When, Griselde? When did it happen?"

"Oh, months ago. Shortly after you left. Dominic came back, looking all wild he came. He said you had died—in a warehouse fire, he said. Then he hitched up the oxen to the wagon and took the horses, and he had two others with him and . . ."

"Shh," Andrew said. "Maybe you should rest, Griselde." *No!* he said inwardly. *I have to know.*

She sighed deeply. Suddenly her eyes startled wide open. "He? Would Dominic—" She shook her head. "He left the next morning, the wagon packed with everything he could lay his hands on."

"When, Griselde? Was this the next morning, the morning you discovered Hadesseh missing?"

She moaned again. Suddenly she wept openly. She nodded. "Would he—would he do that?" she groaned.

Andrew hung his head. His breath felt short and ragged. A pain drove up into his chest like a knife wound. *My enemy.* He sat silently.

"They were all gone," Griselde whispered. "All the peasants. Even Gregor. I haven't seen him since . . . that day. Just the three of us, Andrew. And Desidero, poor dear, so old he was. His heart, Andrew. It was . . . like it was broken.

"Then the first of them came. Marauders. Outlaws. They raided the huts first. They took supplies, all the stock from the harvest. What was Desidero to do?"

"Shh, Griselde. It doesn't matter."

"Oh, but it did to Desidero, master . . . Andrew. So when they raided the sheep, he went out to stop them. They beat him then. But he was already sick then. I don't know how. But he never recovered. Then there was no one. And I felt the sickness . . ." Her voice was trailing off. "I had heard about this place, of course. Griselde heard. And I called my little Helena to get the mule . . ."

She was asleep. Andrew tucked the blanket around her. He leaned forward and kissed her worn cheek. *Wherever she has gone—or been taken,* he was thinking, *I'll follow. To the ends of the earth, I'll follow. But where do I start?*

He slumped beside Griselde's pallet, weeping with his own helplessness.

Griselde survived, and joined the two women from the docks who now cooked for them. These three, the toothless crone and the younger women, worked side by side in the kitchen, their tasks spiced by loud talk and laughter, their work faultless and endless.

Day by day they watched Helena for signs of plague. They never came. Whether her northern blood granted her some fierce power of immunity, or whether God had placed a seal upon her, they could not say. But she brought to that cold chapel a light its inmates desperately yearned for. Into the charnel house she skipped gaily, mocking death with naiveté, unmindful of the sorrow, unstinted in her frolic. Her mass of golden curls bounced here and there like a comic sun. No one hindered her. She was light and gaiety and life. When Griselde toiled in the kitchen, little Helena followed Petra with the fidelity of an adoring pet, joining him in planting and laboring, chattering to his furry ears in a ceaseless noise which he responded to with a patient smile. He would have died for her.

There was not one in the chapel who would not.

* * *

As the days passed, the grip of cold now thoroughly loosened under a spring sun, Andrew felt increasingly restless. Yet his energy seemed completely gone. It was as if the illness still lingered, draining energy from him. About the farthest distance he could walk without getting utterly exhausted was down the long slope of the hill to the small pond.

That place, that still point where the hillside rivulets mingled, strangely attracted Andrew. He watched insects flit across its surface among the reeds. He pondered the glide of sun and shadows across it.

As he knelt by the weedy bank one sunny day, a curious slant of light sent his own reflection mirrored back to him.

The face that appeared was scarred and pitted. A shock of hair hung raggedly about his ears. Andrew looked into this face he saw and thought, *how ugly! How thin and pitted these features are. One would not know him. Outcast!*

But the eyes held him. He looked deeply into them, and at that precise moment a small fish arose. Its mouth bubbled up through the reflected eyes.

It seemed to suck him deeper and deeper; the mirrored image overwhelmed him—a spirit so scarred and pitted it was horrifying. Loathsome. No one could love this thing reflected in the water. Andrew reached a hand into the pool to brush it away. With a spasm of its tail the fish dove.

"There is an easier way!" Emeth's laughing voice boomed down the hillside. "Hook and line will work. Fat spring worms for bait." His tall, gaunt body angled down the bank, brown robe flapping in the breeze, the hood thrown back so that the sun raked his hawklike features.

Andrew leaned back and smiled at Emeth. But his hand ran unwillingly along his cheeks, feeling the scars that pitted the flesh.

"May I make a suggestion?" Emeth asked suddenly.

Andrew looked at him a moment, then nodded. The waters of the pond wrinkled under a spring breeze. Lights winked off and on in it as clouds passed overhead.

"You don't know what you're going to do now, right?"

Andrew merely looked at him quizzically. How could he say what was in his heart?

"The plague seems to be passing." Emeth said. "At least for now."

"For now?"

"Until it returns again, Andrew. As it surely will. The prophets spoke of it; we just don't hear them anymore. Our ears have grown deaf to the voice of the Lord."

Andrew leaned on one elbow and studied Emeth. He had grown accustomed to the man's roundabout way of making a point. Emeth spoke rarely—when he did, it was with weight and reason. As he watched him now, Andrew couldn't help perceiving a twinkle of excitement in his eyes. Emeth's rough-hewn face, Andrew thought, was so homely it was handsome. *Distinct.* That's the right word. Like wind-worn granite along the shoreline, like . . . like one of the old prophets themselves.

"Well," Andrew said. "Go ahead. Let me hear it, then."

Emeth chuckled. "You're tired?"

"Not too tired to hear about dreams. I wish *I* could; I might as well hear yours."

"Very well. But it's not a dream really. It's . . . a calling."

"Call away." Andrew lay back on the warm grass. How good it felt after the cold and suffering of the wet winter. Overhead tiny wisps of cloud took on colors of evening.

Emeth waited, cleared his throat, as if wondering how and where to begin. Where he began startled Andrew entirely.

"It was many years ago when the Apostle came here," Emeth said.

"The Apostle! The one my parents spoke of? The one—"

"The same. He was later crucified during the madness in Rome. Oh, he visited with your parents once. You were just a boy. I doubt whether you would remember." He looked at Andrew, who shook his head. "That was when the calling of this chapel began to change, Andrew, for then, as you know, we became a safehouse. For those fleeing the persecution and those locating further north.

"But even before the Apostle stopped here we had a mission. He wasn't the first, you know, to bring the word of the Way to this land. There were others earlier. But he authenticated it, sharpened it, gave direction.

"He traveled here with three others. One of them, a young man named

Joseph, was gifted in languages. A strange man, this Joseph was. Indeed, I had already heard stories about him—he carried a letter to authenticate his message. And he was a brave man, for he carried it to the northern kingdoms, taking the good news of the Way."

"Where the settlers went?" Andrew asked.

"Oh, far beyond. I don't know just how far north our refugees have settled. I doubt whether any went past the huge mountains that rise to the north. Perhaps. But it was Joseph's dream to go far beyond.

"That letter he took with him was a letter from the Apostle, outlining the good news and the life of the Messiah."

Andrew remembered the stories of Taletha and Elhrain, of Doval and Lycurgus. They too had been witnesses. "Go on," he urged.

"It was Joseph's dream to study the languages of the northern tribes. To translate this gospel for them. To go to the uttermost ends of the earth."

"And?"

"And we have no idea what happened. The earliest reports had Joseph making it to the mountain ranges. We rejoiced. That in itself was a feat. But then we lost contact. All these years. We have no idea how his work went, whom he contacted, whether he succeeded at all."

Out of the corner of his eye, Andrew studied Emeth. The man's face was eager, the eyes glistening with excitement. *I wonder*, Andrew thought, *how long he has held this dream in.* "And you want to find out," he guessed.

Emeth turned toward him. His raptor eyes were fierce. "Oh, more than that, Andrew. I want to finish it. I want to carry on."

"To the uttermost ends of the earth?"

"Well, say as far as the Lord grants me."

"Why?" The simplicity of the question was thunderous.

"It's a matter of allegiance. Remember?"

Andrew turned his head. "Yes," he murmured, "I remember."

"It's not whether one succeeds or fails. In earthly terms, in human terms, such are immeasurable. What does it mean to succeed? Does it mean perfection?"

"Heaven help us," Andrew muttered.

"Precisely."

"What is it then?"

"The commitment to at least try. To pursue this no matter what. To know that you have done all you could."

"It's never enough."

"No. It never is. That is where heaven helps us, as you say. It is the mystery of the Lord's will. And power. For us, it's a matter of trying."

"Mysteries. I don't know, Emeth."

"I will go alone if I have to. My work as I have known it is nearly finished here now. It can be given to others. But I would prefer not to go alone."

Those hawklike eyes fixed on Andrew. He stared back a moment, blinked and turned away.

* * *

The following morning Andrew found Emeth on his hands and knees scouring the floor and benches of the chapel. The door was wide open, the window-hangings stripped down, and sunlight flooded the room.

It seems so small now, Andrew thought. *How could it ever contain all the suffering of these past months?* For truly, apart from Emeth the chapel was empty at the moment. No new cases had come for several weeks. It had been a full week since the last burial. When a peasant had appeared at the door a few days ago, it had only been for a toothache. Emeth himself had extracted the man's tooth with a pair of tongs.

Empty. And it seemed so . . . calm in the absence of suffering. Little Helena bounded in the back door and Emeth scolded at the muddy footprints. Helena stopped in her tracks, looked at her feet, whispered, "Oh-oh," and backed out. From outside, Emeth heard Petra laughing. He whistled to the little girl, who met him in the garden.

"I've been thinking about it, Emeth," Andrew said simply.

Emeth rocked back on his haunches, looking up at Andrew with an eager light in his eyes. "I am not a young man, Andrew. I need help."

Andrew nodded. "I will join you. Just one thing."

"Yes?"

"Just this. Do not expect me to go as the humble penitent, groveling on cut knees."

"Of course not. But how shall you go?"

"As I am, for better or worse."

"God made you as you are. I trust him, and you. As, I pray, you will learn to trust yourself."

Trust myself! "Yes, that is the question, isn't it?"

"You too must understand something, Andrew. They are not pleasant words."

"Go ahead."

"You have changed. You have been transformed, but you are still Andrew. Everything you were—Andrew—everything! You still are. And it will be no holiday. We are not ready to leave yet. We have many preparations to make. The land ahead is rough. The people savage and uncivilized."

"So unlike fair Faenza with its civilization?"

He laughed at the sally. "They say every priest has a death wish. To go out with the gospel is to go out greeting death."

"The roaring lion and all that?"

Emeth laughed. Andrew welcomed the sound he had heard from him more frequently during these later days. "You will make of me a philosopher, Andrew. No, I want to go only to satisfy two things: a vision that commands me and a curiosity that consumes me."

* * *

Once having committed themselves, on nothing more than the words passed that morning, they were in no hurry to leave, nor, it seemed, to make any special preparations. They waited, preparing inwardly, recovering strength for the journey.

In Andrew's mind certain words kept echoing—"To the north, where I'm safe . . . lord of my own land . . . I'll draw you a map. You'll never find it . . . I'm taking *her* . . ." But when he remembered Dominic's cold hatred as he spoke those words, Andrew also felt a sickening fear.

Who do you think you are? he asked himself.

I am a twisted thing, scarred, ruined—a desecration.

Yet it would be worth everything to look once more on Hadesseh's face, to let her know I really had tried, if only to have her loathe me.

Strangely, Andrew also heard his father's broken, urgent words, "The Lord has a task . . ."

* * *

When the last, the very last, of the needy came to them, their work was done. This too was not a case of plague at all. The man had a fever—from a cold. They let him sleep for the night, fed him some broth laced with herbs and sent him home.

That morning Andrew took the blued knife, wrapped it in an oiled skin and placed it in a crevice behind the altar where it wouldn't be easily found. Its work too was finished.

It was an undoing, an unmaking of a past that could never be undone.

It was late summer when Emeth and Andrew walked in the cool of the evening toward the rivulet running from the cracked cistern. Andrew stared at the darkness inside the cave, the place where life had ended and started, the still point, the intersection of time and the timeless. He had not dared look at it since the day Emeth lifted him from its maw.

They entered together.

It surprised him now. The cavern was still dank, the shadows moist and heavy on the walls. But it was only a hole in the face of the cliff. Nothing more. Still, he trembled seeing it. They stood there a moment, peering at that round pit, so innocent in its design. Andrew reached out a hand to touch Emeth's cloak. They turned to go.

The rivulet issued in a whisper of water from the arched cave, a quick, silver spasm in the evening light. They walked alongside it, beyond the confines of the chapel. Behind them the building stones shone with a soft pink glow in the evening sun. The summer grass, thick and moist against their sandaled feet, made a soft, swishing sound. Save for the endless cawing of the gulls and the bleat of sheep on a distant hill, that was the only sound in the stillness of evening.

They reached the convergence of streams and heard the light gurgle of water in the stony throat of the main stream. The rivulet widened, cut a white swath through the bank. It ran rapidly downhill, curling, folding, springing sharply. Silver streaks foaming together toward the quiet point of the pool. They walked side by side into its water. For a moment Andrew saw the spasm of a blighted fish, turning its tail toward them. It seemed to swim toward the sea. The water rose to their hips, cool fingers enfolding them.

Emeth placed his hand behind Andrew's neck. Andrew leaned backward, seeing as he did so the glowing spire of the chapel reach its angled peak above the green crest of hill. Then the waters flowed over him, and there was only the light of the evening sun, the deep blue chasm of the sky shot with violet and the softly running words, "I baptize you in the name of the Father, and of the Son, and of the Holy Ghost."

I who have died am alive again this day.

158

PART TWO
TO THE ENDS OF THE EARTH

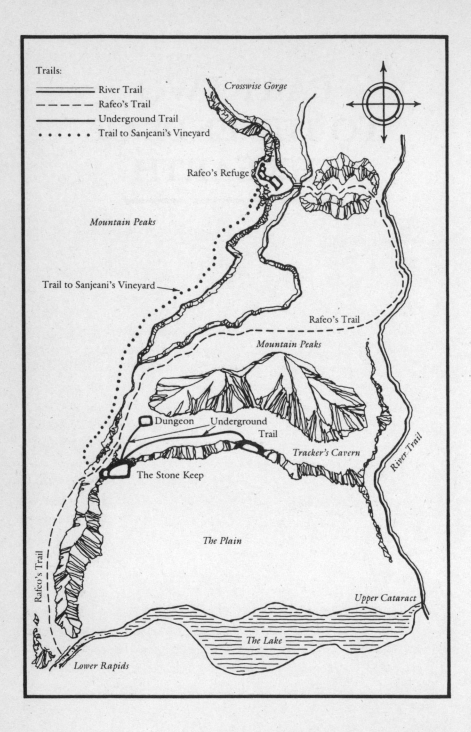

Trails:
─────── River Trail
- - - - - Rafeo's Trail
─────── Underground Trail
· · · · · Trail to Sanjeani's Vineyard

Crosswise Gorge

Rafeo's Refuge

Mountain Peaks

Trail to Sanjeani's Vineyard

Rafeo's Trail

Mountain Peaks

Dungeon   Underground Trail

Tracker's Cavern

River Trail

The Stone Keep

The Plain

Rafeo's Trail

Upper Cataract

The Lake

Lower Rapids

CHAPTER
THIRTEEN

Nearly two more years passed before they left.

Andrew's once supple and athletic body had been wasted by plague to the point of gauntness. For a long time he had barely the energy to do the few chores given him. He helped Petra do some work in the garden, and within an hour his limbs were trembling and cold sweat stood on his forehead. He walked along the hillside, on the way to the stables perhaps, then suddenly had to sit, right where he was. He sat so for hours, letting the sun's warmth rekindle energy in his body.

An overwhelming grayness afflicted him, something that lay deep within him and daily infiltrated every pore. It went beyond bodily weakness. It clung to his mind like a vaporous cloud, clogging thought and memory and will. Thoughts would not connect; they spun helplessly into anxiety. His will, any desire to do or achieve something, stumbled against a black wall of irresolution.

For a long time now they had heard no news of the surrounding countryside, nor of Fontini Villa. It was as if the plague had severed communication, as if even the chapel, which had been so long a refuge, was now itself in quarantine—empty, self-contained, virtually forgotten.

As that second summer gave way to autumn, Andrew could not resist the lure of seeing his land once more. The rhythms of planting and harvest were in his very bones. Even though Griselde had brought report of the despoiling of the villa during those final days of the plague, when bands of dispossessed peasants roamed the countryside looting and pillaging in a mad effort to survive, Andrew wanted, once more, to see for himself.

He went alone, walking. One slow step at a time. He remembered how he had run up and down these hills in his mad pursuit of Dominic. *That was before,* he thought. His desecrated body now felt each labored step. He wore a brown religious cloak, the hood flung forward to hide his ravaged features. His body was a network of scars, his face brutally thin and pitted. He wanted to meet no one, and he succeeded.

The countryside was desolate, as if gone into mourning.

Andrew carried a small knapsack holding only bread, cheese, wine and a blanket. He slept at night on the leaves under the trees, their dry crackle a kind of lullaby. By nightfall he was so exhausted sleep came instantly. With each step also, the trip seemed more like a dream than a reality. The land felt unreal.

After nearly a week of traveling he drew near the footbridge by the stream. He had not yet dared lift his eyes. Now he did. The peasant huts were bare ruins; all burnable materials reduced to ash, the brick walls scarred black. Here and there small, improvised fire pits were littered by the bones of livestock. The marauders had slaughtered and cooked them on the spot. Looking uphill, Andrew saw the vineyards run wild in tangles. *Impossible,* he thought, *that they could run to ruin so quickly.* All the trellises had been broken down; the vines lay in twisted humps. Slowly he walked through the village, along the path to the villa.

Even from the valley the story was clear, but having come this far Andrew wanted to see all of it. The walls were broken and the front gates hung askew. Surprisingly, the tower still stood, although its flanks too were scarred by fire. He stepped through the broken gates into the courtyard. The pool was algae-laden, the blue tiles broken and corrupted by filth.

His home lay in emptiness; it was a desolation. Andrew remembered Doval, the last of them, in her chair by the pool when the sun was warm and the water pure and the tiles sparkling like chips of precious stone and knew those days were gone forever. Perhaps in years hence someone would pass this way, stand here and wonder over the building blocks lying heaped recklessly about. Or perhaps the land would reclaim it by then— the stone worn back to earth, the brush and grass overgrowing everything.

It lived now only in his memory.

Andrew stepped into the corridor leading past the individual rooms to the great room. Miraculously the roof and beams here in the southern wing had escaped the fires, unlike the north wing that housed the kitchen and the rooms of the help. That was all gutted by fire. He peered into Hadesseh's room, pausing before stepping in. He drew a deep breath, but no sign of her presence remained. It was as if she had never been there—the room stripped to bare walls, everything gone.

The room of Elhrain and Taletha was different. Litter was strewn throughout—scraps of broken furniture, shards of pottery, and linens lay ripped and strewn. The tapestry on the east wall was criss-crossed with cuts, as if someone had attacked it with a knife but had been somehow repulsed. There was something about it—something in the design or fabric or symbols that had rebuffed even the most malevolent of the marauders. Through the dust and dirt that now coated it, Andrew could still decipher the ancient design: the centered seven-tiered candelabra in light filigree, the crosses at the four corners, the star in the upper center. All now slashed in long jagged rents.

Andrew drew the tapestry aside. Behind it lay the stone bench. Carefully he fitted his fingers to the recesses in the wooden seat, lifted and heaved a sigh of relief. The chamber was nearly airtight, and the contents undisturbed.

But someone had disturbed them! Andrew sensed it. He picked up the child's blanket, worn smooth by his own hands. He pictured himself as an infant, clinging to its ragged edge, and self-consciously he raised a corner of the blanket to his nose in that old, instinctive gesture. He rubbed the smooth fabric, worn thin by his once-wandering fingers, against his nose, and let memories flood over him.

He was on his knees then, head cradled on the blanket, tears flowing in helpless abandon. How innocent were those days; it hurt to remember.

It was with his forehead against the folded blanket that he first felt that something lay wrapped inside. Something stiff; something that had not been there before. Hastily he unwrapped the blanket—a cloth packet, rolled and tied with a scrap of ribbon.

Andrew undid the ribbon carefully, fingers trembling. The sheets of parchment were still clean and crisp. Andrew moved toward the window, carefully studying the sheets he held. Drawings. Intricate and detailed.

How much time they must have taken! The dyes, extracted from different plants and minerals, were laid on with infinite patience. He nodded, remembering the long hours Hadesseh had labored over these. He had hardly noticed at the time. They had just—kept her busy. And in those final days she had hidden them here once again.

The first drawings were stunningly accurate representations. A series of plants tightly crowded each page—four pages in all—each labeled in a strange, runic language that Andrew recognized as his parents' native tongue. Under the plant, in the Roman language, were applications for the plant: For headache. Mixed with mustard, a poultice. With weak wine, for diarrhea. In paste, a salve for burns. And so on. Four leaves of parchment crammed with these. Many of the plants Andrew recognized from Hadesseh's tutoring.

He had watched her drawing—it almost seemed that he could see her again, head bent over her designs as she worked in the great room. But nothing prepared him for the drawings that followed.

There were six in all. Predominant in each was a tree—in the early drawings a lithe, slender tree, in the later drawings one grown thick and gnarled. The tree was positioned differently in each portrayal, the first centered on the page with the background foliage muted and distant. The tree seemed gay, happy—its lines stroked quickly and carefree, as if the tree were a living thing, dancing. Etched in the corner was a leaf from the tree, and the label: Myrtle—peace.

In the sequence, the position of the tree changed. It drew nearer and nearer the eye of the beholder; about it sprawled a mass profusion of rioting growth. The colors of the dyes rampaged about the tree, which itself grew progressively dark. In each the tree moved closer to the eye; details grew more stark—whorls appearing beneath scarred bark, the bark shaggy and weighty.

And in the sixth, which Andrew looked at with a chill, he realized the intention of the artist. For the tree now covered the page, and only through a knothole did one see the world outside. This was it: the tree was a living thing, the artist—Hadesseh—was inside the tree, no, was the tree itself. But in this final portrait that detailed so intimately grain and bark of the tree, its bark open so that one peered through the knothole, that space opened not on a world of profuse growth but on a night sky, drawn in thickly, in which pinpoints of white space, like random stars, shone in the darkness. And one star was brighter than the rest.

There was a final page, unfinished—one last image impressed hurriedly upon the parchment. No dyes were used. The design was muted by cross-hatchings of light and dark. It was a face—a face only. Andrew looked longingly, for the face appeared at first to be a self-portrait. Then he realized it was only the shadow of Hadesseh, but belonged to another— the way a child mirrors a parent. Yes, that was it. It was the face of a very young boy. An infant's face.

For a long time Andrew studied the figures on the parchments, spreading them out on the floor beneath the window. His eyes roved over them again and again. Was there some secret in the sequence—from knowledge of the plants, to the tree? No—to living inside the tree. Captive? Of what? Of some secret knowledge? And knowledge of what—the boy? Sequence? Or was it all just a random collection? And why had she wrapped them like this, in his old blanket? Had she been trying to tell someone—himself?—something?

Andrew didn't know what to do with the parchments. Were they left for his eyes to see? And how did Hadesseh know about this hiding place? Did she know that it was his old blanket? On impulse Andrew rewrapped the parchments in the blanket and placed them carefully in his knapsack. Perhaps he could find a place for safekeeping in the chapel. Perhaps little Helena would like the old tattered blanket. She had little enough.

Quickly Andrew sorted through the other items. As he did so, he wished he had never taken the knife. Here too there were questions. What was its history? On what long past journey had his father found need for it? And why had he kept it? The knife now seemed to him an emblem of violation, of sickness, of wrongness. At least now it was hidden where it would work no harm.

The old cloak Andrew set aside. His fingers fastened on the small bag holding the golden coins. Intact. His fingers felt them under the cloth. No need to examine them. He didn't want to. But with these the journey northward could be possible. Mules. Supplies. It could work. Quickly he stuffed the bag too in his knapsack.

He turned in the hallway, started toward the great room and on to his old tower room. He stopped. He didn't think he could bear to see it now. Besides, several steps down the hallway he could see the dark charring of fire. What had stopped it here? Rain? A thunderstorm, probably. The great room too would be burned, beyond recognition. Better to preserve it in memory.

He walked back down the hallway, into the courtyard. He ran his eyes once more up the vineyard hill, violet now in the evening light. Perhaps some day someone else would find vines, or those olive trees over the hill. By then, perhaps, it would be too late. They would all be overgrown. It was a savage land in the aftermath of the plague, and it was no longer his land. He had no heart for it; the memories cut too deep.

As he walked down the long hill, through the peasant village, he felt good, for the first time, about the prospect of going north with Emeth.

CHAPTER FOURTEEN

The intense suffering of the plague nurtured curious signs of hope. Truly there were despair and despoliation enough. While some families emerged virtually unscathed, most had undergone the fiery torment of loss. Oddly, when their lives began to be reordered in the months following the plague, they did not forget those who had given succor in the time of need. Strange gifts were left at the chapel door—a few pence wrapped in a piece of cloth, a bundle of candles, odds and ends of clothing found in the home after the death of a family member. There appeared items of food—for those who still suffered or were in need. One day a sheep was found tethered in the stable. On another, a ball of cheese lay inside the chapel door. Then sacks of grain and flour, or a flagon of wine, appeared during the months that followed. Andrew and Emeth distributed the goods to the needy in Faenza. And a community grew out of the ruins of the city.

After a time, the growing community began gathering at the chapel. Out of suffering, hope took root and grew. They ate together, sang songs, talked and prayed.

They also worked. For too long old Petra had labored too hard on the grounds. Philip, the former dockworker who had helped him, had simply left one morning. To look for his own family, Petra thought. Now it was unusual on an evening not to find several people laboring quietly. The stables were rebuilt and replenished. Several people worked to fill the old cistern with rock and to create a new drainage channel toward the stream. They created odd little winding courses to water Petra's gardens.

Even as the little community grew, it at once both held Andrew and Emeth and encouraged them to leave. New ties had sprung up. Among these people Andrew felt accepted; his pocked features startled no one. Here the maimed were the normal: all had suffered and so accepted each other with understanding. No questions were asked; nonetheless, if someone wanted to talk there was always someone to listen. But with the little community, this primitive church, growing week by week they also began to feel free to go. The community could continue without them.

Of particular delight to Andrew was the way old Griselde, with that bouncing bundle of energy that Helena had become never far from her side, assumed a role as unofficial greeter and hostess of the chapel. Griselde truly loved the preparations for communal meals, the relentless bustle and noise. Then her olive cheeks took on a red glow, her back was a bit straighter, her toothless smile broader. Helena danced among the people like a blond-haired whirlwind, skillfully avoiding the relentless hugs pressed on her.

That then became the one obstacle to leaving. For Griselde and Helena insisted on going with them.

Emeth was adamant. "We don't even know where we're going!" he exclaimed.

"Very well, but you're going in a direction," Griselde said. "We can too."

"No. No, you can't."

"Why not? Do you think I'm too old? Helena too young?"

"No. That is not it at all. You have a place here. At the chapel."

"No. Our place is with you. And it's a place you need if you're ever going to get along with others."

"We'll get by," Emeth insisted, shaking his head hopelessly.

"Yes, you'll get by, won't you? Two odder creatures I've never seen than you and Andrew. Why, you'll scare people off! And you think you'll preach the gospel to them. Listen to me. Listen to *old* Griselde. I know the way to people's hearts."

That she did. And where she went, Helena did also.

In the end the four of them prepared for departure.

* * *

If suffering is an inward journey which can nurture outward hope, traveling is an outward journey that finally and always turns the traveler inward.

They prepared carefully. Months passed. Emeth converted the strange gold coins through a contact in Faenza, purchased two mules, packs and ample supplies. Most of the leftover money, apart from what they took for the journey, he put in the care of a young couple who would be taking their place in the chapel.

As another winter waned and the land warmed under a spring sun, they set out, Andrew and Emeth leading the mules on which Helena and Griselde rode, surrounded by supply packs.

The journey began, and so very slowly.

For the first days they were mindful simply of the ground covered. Not even distance—simply terrain. The monotonous placement of one foot before the other, the slow ache that crept along untested muscles—all reminded them of the *act* of the journey. Then muscles tightened, the ache deepened. *How long can I walk before resting?* each wondered. *How long may I rest before walking? How far to that grove of trees by what looks like a stream?*

Then a strange thing happened. Each began to realize that there was no staying because there was no longer any place to stay; nor any place to return to. Expectations arose. What *might* lie in that grove of trees? And what if it is a stream? The journey outward had become the journey inward.

They struck out going inland, wanting to get the sense of the land in their hearts, the feel of the land under their feet. As they turned northward, they walked on clear roads meandering through broad valleys. Other travelers passed them by, caravans of goods from the north toward Rome, a troop of soldiers, individuals on horseback or afoot. Life seemed to be rejuvenating in the plague-stricken region, but everywhere the effects of the desolation were still evident. Small clusters of houses stood empty. A herd of pigs gone wild rooted for food at the forest edge. A solitary cow grazed forlornly in a field.

Gradually even such signs as these disappeared as they headed north. Villages were small and bustling, if much farther apart, and when they turned off from the road to Venice, continuing north rather than east, villages seemed to disappear altogether.

So the days kept turning. But with the slow pace of travel, each felt a vague stirring, a sense of renewal that accompanied the slow, peaceable routine. At night the campfire sputtered; forest leaves hung thick-tongued under a spell of flame. An owl called in the distance. The sky flashed with a spiral of stars. Finding a small village after several days of seeing no one, they replenished their supplies, not knowing when they would have the chance again.

They forgot to measure days; now there was only the journey. When at last they saw the mountain peaks in the distance, it was clear that summer was on the wane. Faint blushes of gold and red touched distant hills. The peaks appeared so distant at first that they thought they saw clouds. They followed the road northward, even as the peaks grew less distant with each day's travel. Only once a merchant caravan passed them. The drivers spoke a foreign tongue, calling to them as they passed.

"How do we know," Andrew asked one night as he made camp with Emeth, "when we've come to the right place?" The question had been gnawing at him for some time now. "I mean, do we just plunk down in some village? 'We're here now. Listen to us'?"

Emeth chuckled. "Probably something like that. I know that we will have to make our way over the mountains."

"Over the . . . mountains?"

"Or around. Or through. There are ways. There are always ways, Andrew."

"And we just wander around until we find the ways? We'll turn old and gray, Emeth. We'll be preaching to rocks."

Again Emeth smiled. It came easier to him these days. "Don't forget snow and ice," he added.

Andrew shook his head, an only half-mocking gesture.

"I heard from Joseph once," Emeth said. "He gave me a rough idea of the way. And it is the way we're following. He had found a sort of shelter in the mountains. He had started work on his translation. I'm not sure how . . . or just whom he met among these people. The final stage is to learn the language, of course."

"Of course. Then we'll have a reception committee, of course. Road signs. All of that."

"Andrew, Andrew. We'll find the way."

Andrew sighed. "I know. Remember my past, Emeth. The villa ran on organization; it lived by schedules. It had to."

"Are you sure? Or did it only seem that way to you?"

Andrew reflected. It was true. His parents, along with Doval and Lycurgus—it was a cause for them, not a schedule. Andrew often wondered what strange peace infiltrated their lives. It seemed somehow to have escaped him. Too often the recklessness of those last years seemed to rise up against his memory—the time when things were careening out of control no matter how hard he tried to impose order. And it had escalated into deceit and violence. Too often yet, even after several years, the violence at the docks, the blows, the fire, the ordeal in the cistern, seemed to rise unwilled and unwanted in his memory. *Who was I?* he wondered. *What had I become?*

Was it possible to put violence behind him forever? He remembered bits and pieces of Elhrain and Taletha's stories—the few they told. There always seemed to be a darker side shadowing their joy. Was it possible to have only the joy? *Am I,* he wondered, *also doomed to violence by a nature bred in me?*

No more! He vowed. It is behind. The offering of the knife hidden behind the altar was the symbol of it.

* * *

Apart from morning and evening prayers, one would be hard pressed to know their mission. Andrew still knew little about Emeth's past, but he sensed this much about his present: spirituality also was the way, not just the journey. He paid little heed to the rituals and trappings of the religious life, beyond his brown cloak which he wore like a symbol of the faith. For him, spirituality, in all its raw, brutal power, was a way of living. The mark of the divine was carved with fingers of fire on his soul. He had swallowed the fiery torch of God and let it burn in his life.

They were camped one night in a valley they had followed for days. The mountain peaks were clear now, stretching away in capricious waves to a distant haze. As the valley narrowed before them toward the shoulders of the mountains, the landscape grew more focused and intense. Where they camped they could clearly see the granite flanks rising beyond the forest.

They sat that night around the campfire, when suddenly Helena's eyes flashed open.

"I'm afraid," she said. She held the old tattered blanket from Andrew's childhood, clutching its blue edge to one cheek.

"It's a dream," Griselde murmured. "Go back to sleep. Here. I'll wrap this blanket around you."

The night air had grown chilly. Wounded fragments of cloud scudded across the stars.

"No. Hold me," said Helena. "There's something out there."

A sudden chill at his back made Andrew speak more harshly than he intended. "Hush, Helena. Go to sleep."

* * *

Andrew no longer had any idea of where they were. For many days they had met no other travelers as their way led deeper into the mountains. An eerie sense of forsakenness hung in the morning fog. The sky drooled thick, gray wisps. Nor did the fog lift as the day wore on. They followed the sound of the river and moved on up the valley.

The thick fog and the cold, damp air signaled the presence of autumn. They had left the chapel in early summer and had been afoot for several months. They had expected to winter near the mountains, but somehow had thought they would have the leisure to select the place. Now the weather sharpened their need. For the first time they found themselves thinking of shelter, longing for an indoor fire, for walls to hold the cold mists back. As they entered the foothills, they carefully packed all the remaining supplies on one mule and bundled as much firewood and kin- dling as possible on the other one. The beast looked like a walking bush, twigs sticking out of the bundle in crazy angles. It meant that Helena and Griselde had to walk now, and their pace slowed still more as they moved up into the hills. Their guide was the river. What path there was seemed to follow its winding course.

The mist hung thickly all the next day. Their steps grew leaden beneath its weight. Toward late afternoon Andrew noticed that Helena had hardly spoken all day. Her incessant chatter had snuffed out like a wick. She marched steadily in place, clinging to Griselde's skirt.

They stopped early that evening in a rocky clearing in the foothills. Hour by hour the land had grown more rugged, strewn with huge boulders. The grass had thinned out altogether. Rocks dripped water about them. All day they had moved through mist. They sensed they were climbing steadily upward, even though the land twisted and turned, rose and fell. They had little sense of a path at all except the few steps before them. The brown cloak of Emeth, cowl up to ward off the weather, bobbed steadily ahead. Often they followed the tapping of his staff rather than the man himself. When they stopped at the clearing, the fire was hard to start, the wood that they had bundled on the mule burned fitfully, casting only a feeble light against the encroaching darkness.

There was no dawning. Dark night drifted to gray and the gray held. Andrew thought they were well among the mountains by now, following the river's course. They knew they were climbing by the steady ache in their legs and by the slow plodding of the mules, punctuated by snorts and pawings. The animals grew more ornery and reluctant with each step. As they moved upward it was always into thickening mists, as if the clouds had dropped wetly about them.

The river was their only guide. At times it was a noisy cataract rolling down a rocky gorge, then at other times a wide, shallow body gurgling over stones. When they camped this night, the gray clouds punished them, squeezing them in a cold wet grip.

Andrew looked across the fire at Helena. It was a mistake to bring her and Griselde, he thought now. They should have foreseen this. Helena huddled close to Griselde. Griselde herself was weary, holding the girl tightly against the night chill. During the night Andrew heard whimpering and could not tell if it was from the girl or the woman.

In the morning, Griselde passed slowly by Emeth and Andrew as they packed. She spoke softly, so Helena could not hear, "Have you heard it?"

"What do you mean?" asked Emeth.

"Something is out there."

"I have heard nothing."

"Listen." There was nothing to hear. Only the dripping of moisture from the rocks.

Still, Emeth peered hard into the gray light, so hard that he trembled.

"I'll take a look," said Andrew. He walked back on the path and was immediately lost in the vapor. It was a strange world of unrelenting mist. Andrew stood as silent as the weeping stones about him, and heard nothing. As he stood he sensed the deeper shadows, felt them like the pressing weight of stone on his nerves. It was the weight of cold darkness—the cistern, the slime and stink of death. The very air breathed warning.

He walked hurriedly back to the camp. "I heard nothing," he said. But his hands sped with the preparations to leave.

Griselde and Helena rode together now on the one old mule, slumped like scarecrows on a balky animal. The other mule bore the packs and remaining firewood. The trail still dipped and rose, often falling off sheer to the right. The river they had followed for days became a rushing torrent here. When it was lost in the fog below they heard the plunge of its rush. The sound grew throughout the morning to a grinding roar as they wound higher through the pass. At one point Emeth stepped aside, let the mules pass and joined Andrew in the rear. He walked silently for a while, tapping his staff against the rock.

"Well, what is it?" Andrew finally asked.

"Winter comes upon us more quickly than I thought." Emeth's face was grim, a drop of moisture beaded on his beaklike nose.

"We could have traveled faster," Andrew said. He was thinking of those slow days in the lower regions—the lush valleys, the sun of daytime, the quiet fires of evening.

"Could have, perhaps. But it was necessary, wasn't it?" His breath heaved in steamy clouds. "We all needed it. *You* needed it."

"I don't regret it, if that's what you mean. Still, we need shelter for Griselde and Helena. If only until the fog lifts."

They came to a small cataract flowing down the side of the mountain, crossing their path. The mule stopped at it, refusing to go on even though the bed was shallow. Griselde and Helena dismounted, led the mule across and proceeded on foot, still leading the stubborn mule. It was only a small stream. The mule should not have balked. Andrew and Emeth stepped across it easily, prodding the pack mule ahead of them.

"Perhaps we should not have brought them," Andrew said when they regained the trail.

"I was wondering the same," Emeth said. He was silent a few minutes. "Who else do they have? If we could find shelter, good shelter, maybe they could stay while we went ahead."

"Do you know of any?"

"I have not been in this country, Andrew. But I know this much. The route I chose was a caravan route."

"We haven't seen a caravan for days! Nothing could pass on this path."

"True. We have been off the trail for days now. We must have taken a wrong turn in the fog."

"This is a wretched place, Emeth. If it is a trail at all, it's been years since anyone has used it. We have no idea where it leads. Shall we turn back?"

"The fog may lift. Everything seems strange in this mist." Emeth's eyes were worried, even as he fought for some fragment of hope. "When it does, we might be able to tell where we are."

"We could turn back, try to pick up the main road."

"Andrew, where would we turn? I don't know where we are. We have passed many turnings in this fog, I would guess. But to where do they go? More twisting little trails? Dead ends? My thought is that we should continue until a sign is given."

"Very well."

Helena and Griselde no longer rode the mule for it balked at uncertain places and stumbled often. This was a creature of the plains and gentle hills of Faenza, not this rocky desolation. They stopped again in the late afternoon, built a small fire and prepared for the night.

"We are almost out of dry wood," Griselde remarked. She couldn't hide the edge of worry in her voice.

"It is still light enough to see," Andrew said. "I'll look for some up the trail."

"Don't go."

"Only for a few moments."

Trees and brush could appear from the heavy flanks of the mountain in random places—bulging from a declivity, tucked in a rock fall or a tiny clearing off the trail. Andrew went slowly, scouring the trailside for such a spot. A *fire*, he thought, *a good, roaring fire would make all the difference. At least for this one night.*

The mists swirled in the uncertain light of late afternoon. Andrew had walked some distance, and thought of returning now before darkness fell, when he came upon an opening in the mountain's face. It would have been a good place to camp, he thought, better than the hard stone ledge under an overhanging rock where they had stopped. There was a line of brush where a stream flickered along the glade.

The wood was wet and hard to break off the brush. Andrew twisted branches back, stripping them of autumn leaves, ripping the branches to tear them loose from the bark. It was green wood and would burn poorly, but it would burn, and night had become an enemy to be beaten back.

He gathered his arms full and turned back down the trail to the campsite. They could dry some wood by the fire for the next night's camp at least. Fire had become something precious.

Andrew walked carefully back down the trail. The world compressed to a gray swirl of mist against the approaching dark. He thought he was nearly there, but it was impossible to be certain. Everything looked the same. A harsh bray of the mule suddenly shattered the air. A scream followed. A human scream. Andrew dropped the wood and ran.

The guttering firelight threw the scene into a swirl of shadows. Griselde huddled against the wall holding Helena in her arms. The mules kicked and brayed. Emeth clumsily struck with his staff at the wolves, trying to beat them back from the mule they had targeted. There were three of them—gray, haggard shapes. Already one had its fangs sunk in the neck of the mule, and while the old beast shook and brayed, the body of the wolf swung to and fro, like a leech locked to its neck. Emeth struck wildly with his staff. Suddenly the other mule bolted free, galloping back down the narrow trail, its hoofbeats soon lost in the darkness.

One of the shaggy mountain wolves leaped upon Emeth from behind, knocking him to his knees. The sharp coughing of growls ripped the air. The wolf coiled to lunge for Emeth's neck.

Andrew was already moving. It seemed a growl rose in his own heart, from old, cold reaches. In a slashing movement he leapt between the wolf and Emeth, kicked out, his foot snapping into the wolf's neck with a force that rocked his leg. Andrew whirled.

The third wolf had also leaped on the mule, sending it skittering across the slippery rock. The mule staggered, the two wolves locked by iron jaws to its body. It went down thrashing with hooves. The beasts rocked and surged. Andrew froze. There was nothing he could do in that furious frenzy. With an agonizing twist the mule rolled, and tumbled over the edge of the cliff.

Even above the roar of the river below, Andrew heard the body hit the rocks. A broken wail rose from one of the wolves and shut off in a choking gurgle. Andrew turned to the body of the wolf by Emeth, its legs still jerking, trying to claw life from the stones. He grabbed it by its wet hide and dragged it over the cliffside. The weight was huge and repulsive to his hands. He shoved it over the edge and stood there panting.

All their supplies. Lost!

Emeth crawled toward him on hands and knees, his cloak torn about his body. Andrew helped him to his feet, steadied him, led him to the fire where Helena and Griselde huddled against the rocks. As Andrew sank to the ground, he heard Helena say, "It's still out there. It didn't go away."

Andrew knew her fear. Suddenly it struck him like a physical blow. Out of nowhere the wolves had come! But they couldn't materialize out of rock.

Andrew shook his head angrily, replaying the scene in his mind—the wolf at Emeth's back, the claws digging . . . He looked across the fire where Griselde tended Emeth's wounds.

"They're gone, Helena," Andrew said. "The wolves are gone."

"Not the wolves," she said. "Something else."

"Andrew," said Griselde softly, masking her own fear, "just before the wolves attacked I heard something."

"What?"

"I don't know. A call. A voice."

"Hush." He said it too sharply. Helena turned into Griselde's arms, burying her face.

Emeth stood up and walked to the cliff, peering downward. Slowly he began unpeeling his torn cloak. With the colder weather he had donned a loose shirt and pants underneath. They were plastered to his gaunt body with sweat. It was the first time Andrew had seen him without his cloak. It seemed slightly obscene. Involuntarily Andrew turned his head.

Emeth handed the garment to Griselde, who took it and began foraging for mending implements in the small supply pack she hand-carried. Emeth moved back to the cliff, studying the precipice in the dim light of the fire. He walked back and forth. In the shadows his shape resembled a gray pillar.

"What are you doing?" Andrew rasped.

Emeth didn't look around. He bent to the edge, testing the rocks. Andrew stood, guessing Emeth's intention.

"I said what are you doing?"

"I have to go down."

"Don't be a fool. You'd never make it."

"There were still supplies on the mule. I was unloading when the wolves attacked."

"And now they're washed away in the river."

177

"No. I don't think so. I heard the body hit the rocks, but no splash. I think I can make it down there. See."

A tumble of rock, broken loose from the cliffside by erosion or lightning, formed a treacherous channel in the face of the cliff.

"You'd never make it. Nothing on the mule is worth it."

"I want to try. It will be dark soon. The body may not be there in the morning. It will wash into the river."

"Then I'll go." Andrew shoved Emeth aside. He pulled off his own cloak and flung it behind him. *It can't be any worse than the ocean cliffs by the villa,* he was thinking.

To reach the rift of fallen rock Andrew had to dangle from the lip of the rock beside the trail and lower himself.

He could gauge nothing with certainty in this light. When he dangled from the cliff, his feet hung in the air. He held there a moment, remembering the sickening thud of the mule on the rocks below. It would have been easy to say, "It's impossible. Let it go. Nothing is worth it."

Leave it, a part of his brain insisted. *This is not the way it's supposed to be. The old life—the worry, the violence—all that was supposed to be done. You're supposed to go out to people who welcome you with open arms. It should all be so easy. Not this—this madness. Go back. Quit! No God could have meant it to be like this! It's too . . . cruel.*

"The rock is just below you," Emeth called. Andrew looked up into his hawklike eyes and let go.

The rock was slippery where he landed. Andrew clawed for balance, falling to all fours like a cat. Momentum carried him down. He slid, pebbles cascading about him, before finding his balance. Then it was a slow descent, boulder by boulder, into the deeper darkness of the gorge. He moved from fingerhold to toehold, the rock wet and cold. His ankle, for the first time on this long journey, began to hurt terribly from the strain. He repeatedly had to place full weight on it at awkward angles. He had to hurry, racing the night shadows, thinking, *I still have to go back up.*

The cliff leveled onto a stony ledge just above the river. The roar of water drowned all other senses. Had the river been higher, fueled by spring rains, it would have washed over the ledge, but now the jagged outcropping shot into the heart of it, the froth of water swirling about the edges and splashing the rock. The body of the mule hung on the very edge of this outcropping. Emeth had been right. By morning the carcass would have washed into the river. Whatever was bundled to it had better be precious.

Andrew stepped carefully out onto the rock, its surface slick under his bare feet.

He could focus now, eyes sucking at the last light in the canyon.

He saw that the wolf still had its jaws clamped in the gray throat. Half its body had landed under the mule, shattered by the weight. Still those terrible jaws held, locked in death by its primitive urge. It was a creature of unbearable ugliness, and yet incredible beauty in its single-minded purpose. Destruction. A pure violence. Andrew shivered and moved around it. He didn't see the other wolf. It must have tumbled into the river.

Andrew dropped to all fours, crawling over the rock toward the mule. He reached across the mule's belly for the bundle of supplies hanging askew on its back.

The sound rose above the noise of the river like some primitive growl, deep, coughing, malevolent. Andrew whipped around as the eyes fixed upon him, twin fountains spewing hate. The second wolf was crippled, terribly so. Yet it dragged its battered body to a leap. Andrew saw the legs gather with forces he could not imagine. The huge head shook, the jaws gaped, the eyes spat fire. With a coughing grunt it launched itself, hurtling through the air.

And Andrew surged to meet it. He turned, leg outthrust to meet the charge, precisely as he had practiced a thousand times with Catillo. Along the rocks of the coast, the waves pounding in the background. Whirl and thrust. The weight hit his foot, claws raking his leg. But his aim was true, even in the mad dance of shadows. He met the force, let it carry over him by momentum, then thrust the creature far into the river. Its splashing was lost immediately.

The force of the blow drove Andrew backward. He slid on the rock, clawing for a hold, and slid into the carcass of the mule. He felt it give way, and as it did so, he turned to rip at the bundles on its back. Two broke loose, just as the mule, the other wolf still locked to its throat, slipped into the rush of river. The carcass revolved, hooves pointing skyward, and dragged under.

Andrew sat panting, every muscle enervated. He could feel the cold trembling throughout his body. And he still had to make it back up. He raised his hand from the rock and felt the sticky wetness of unwashed blood.

Andrew carried the heaviest pack to the cliffside, tying it carefully to the rope Emeth had let down. He jerked on it and Emeth began hauling it up, banging and bouncing against the rock. He returned and picked up the smaller pack. *Time to get out.* It was almost thoroughly dark. He could see the cliff only as a black mass. Quickly he strung the smaller pack over his own shoulders and began climbing.

The pack felt strangely light. Why had this been so important to Emeth that he was willing—no, ready—to go down himself? How could he have survived it? Andrew had no reason to doubt the courage of the gaunt man.

He searched the rock for cracks and seams. Slowly, laboriously, he made the climb, stones shifting underfoot, the roar of the river dissipating below. Below! He dared not think of it. Up, inch by inch. Now he could see the globe of firelight rimming the rock. And the outthrust form of Emeth, peering into the gloom.

Andrew reached the drop-off, stood upright, and found the lip of the rock several feet above him. He could find no holds in the smooth face of the rock. It had broken off as sheer as a knife's blow.

"Wait," cried Emeth.

"I can do nothing else," Andrew muttered.

Emeth returned with the rope. Griselde stood beside him, holding it with him.

"Once again, Emeth?" Andrew asked.

"The last time, I hope." Emeth chuckled. It seemed strangely comforting to Andrew. He wrapped the rope under his shoulders. He felt himself pulled upward, inches at a time. The roar of the river diminished to a muted rumble, that sound they had lived with for days now.

"I heard a sound. A growl," Emeth said. Andrew lay on the flat rock, gasping for air.

"It was the third wolf. He was not dead."

Emeth's eyes bored.

"He is now."

Emeth nodded.

Andrew stood up and shrugged the pack off his back. He handed it to Emeth.

"Thank you, friend. But it is not for me."

"But you were going to go for it."

"Perhaps for us. Open it."

Andrew undid the bundle. Extra cloaks lay on top. Extra pairs of sandals. Then, still wrapped in its oilskin, lay the blue jewel of the knife. It gleamed malevolently in its sheath.

Andrew stared at Emeth, anger scalding him.

He raised the knife to hurl it into the river. Emeth wrapped his arms around Andrew, clenching him tightly. Even then Andrew could have thrown it, but did not. He let Emeth hold him while his breath raged.

"Wait," Emeth said. "If it must be so, then I will do it. But listen. This too is a part of you, Andrew. Given to you."

"No! No longer."

"All right, then. It was for me. I was afraid."

"Afraid! You want me to be *that*," he swept his arms over the cliffside, "the person who does *that* so easily, for your fear? You were *not* afraid. I don't believe it. Next you will say a dream told you to take it."

"Don't mock my dreams, Andrew."

"I am done with it. Do you know how easily it came back? No. I will not use violence. I have enough blood on my hands." But in one quick motion, Andrew tied the sheath securely around his waist. He pulled the cloak over his body, trembling.

He sat apart from the fire, nursing his rage. Even among these he now felt like an outcast. *Because I can destroy things!* he thought. *It is all I am. A destroyer. A monster.*

Even Griselde's soft crooning to the fretful child could not quiet his anger.

CHAPTER FIFTEEN

They slept fitfully that night.

Emeth volunteered to tend the fire, but after several hours of tossing against the wet rock under the outcropping, Andrew got up and sat by him. Weariness had sapped the anger from him. Neither of them said anything more about the knife, as if in unspoken agreement.

After a long time Emeth murmured, "The wolves."

"Yes?" Andrew's voice was languid, his lips chilled by the night air. The fire wisped in the drafts that wound up through the rocky canyon. It glowed brightly one moment, softened to a mere gray heat the next.

"Where did they come from?"

"Probably out of the mountains. Where else?"

Emeth shook his head, although Andrew couldn't see it. "They're predators. They need game, lots of it. It got me thinking. Their prey lies in the valleys," he said. "Down below."

"We're too high up now?" He was trying to follow Emeth's logic.

"I don't think so. I don't think we're that far from the main path. I *know* there's a caravan route through these mountains," Emeth insisted. "Marked out. I think we'll hit a pass, a valley, that will connect us with it. If the wolves are here, then that valley can't be too far away."

"What we need is shelter. What if winter hits? Who knows when it snows up here? Why, right now it's so cold . . ."

Emeth shivered. "Don't remind me." He tossed a few more branches on the fire. "That's near the end of it."

"If the snows hit, *when* they come, Griselde and Helena . . ." Andrew left the thought unfinished.

* * *

They broke camp in weariness, taking stock of their diminished supplies. Andrew and Emeth both fashioned heavy backpacks. Griselde and Helena toted lighter packs, strung together over their shoulders with rope. It was cold enough now that they simply donned the extra cloaks as additional outerwear. They wrapped their feet in strips of woolen cloth and wore the heavier sandals that strapped up the calves, leaving the lighter ones behind where they had made camp.

They moved slowly along the trail. Increasingly Andrew's ankle pained him. Finding some fallen brush and old trees in one of those sudden openings on the trail, he fashioned one of the stouter limbs into a staff. They collected firewood for nightfall and moved on.

They ate tiredly at noon, and Andrew and Emeth in particular fought off the urge to nap. The fog shifted now and then to a cold penetrating rain that turned the rocky trail slick and dangerous. They welcomed the rain because for a few minutes it granted a bit of clearing. At such times they could see the river, sometimes like a twisting snake in the gorge far below, at other times nearly at their own level as the trail dipped and rose.

They were no longer sure it was a trail at all.

It was afternoon; the mists had fallen again. Andrew hadn't noticed Helena beside him, nor how long she had been there, until he felt her small fingers fumbling for his hand. Instinctively, he wanted to shrink away. Then he grasped her small hand. It was warm in his. They walked so until evening. Not one word passed between them for a long time.

When she spoke, the words didn't seem to reach Andrew at first.

"What?"

"We should have turned back there." Helena pointed back over her shoulder with one hand.

"Turned? Why?"

"Back where the stream came out into the river. I saw trees there."

Andrew stopped suddenly. They had crossed a stream, another of those countless mountain cataracts. They had stepped carefully from rock to rock across its bed. To their right it had plunged down the rocky cliff into the river. Just one more mountain cataract, one of dozens they had crossed. And crossing it, Andrew and the others had focused every bit of attention on the crossing itself. One slip, and someone could end up carried by the current over the waterfall. At such points they had developed a routine. Andrew went ahead with one end of the rope, tying it to a rock as a lifeline. Griselde and Helena crossed, then Emeth brought up the end of the rope.

No, Andrew had not noticed any trees. He had been watching every step.

"Trees?"

"I heard you talking," Helena said like an accusation. "You said you wanted to find a valley. You told Emeth that. That was a valley. I saw. Up beyond the rocks."

Andrew squeezed her hand.

Quickly he dropped his pack and darted back down the trail.

It wasn't far. He called to the others as he clambered up the rocks of the stream's throat. For one moment the valley spread before him as rain gusted through the fog. He could not see far. The stream was the overflow of a long, narrow mountain lake, spilling through a narrow tunnel of cliffs. For one moment, Andrew thought he could see a plain on the other side fringed by forest before it met the mountain flanks. He called again, but by the time the others got there the mists had lowered once again over the face of the water.

Just inside the narrow canyon that the stream ran through, the mountain valley opened. They walked through to a small clearing, ringed by mountain pine, right at the lake's edge. In the gathering darkness they made camp under the shelter of the great trees, a fire crackling from wood they had dragged from the underbrush.

In the darkening mists Andrew walked a short distance along the shoreline. The world about was shrouded by eerie patches of fog. Sounds seemed oddly magnified. He heard a fish splash in the lake and a dove cooing mournfully from the pines. They had set up camp on a spit of land protruding into the lake. It held a tumble of rocks, then pebbly bottom, then clumps of weeds and water plants. He heard the smack of another fish on the water. He walked further, certain he could find his way back easily, wondering if they had anything from which to fashion a fishing line and hook.

It was then, when he rounded a rocky point of shoreline, that Andrew found the boat.

*   *   *

The boat looked less promising by morning light than it had in the evening mists. It appeared to have broken loose during a storm and washed up on the spit of land. It lay on its side, the lower edge half-buried in muck and algae. It had been there a long time. As Andrew pressed on the wood, he was surprised to find it still solid. No sign of decay. He and Emeth pulled it upright. The boards were rough-hewn and warped, but with some bailing it would keep water out. The prow curved upward in what had once been a graceful swoop, but it had broken off and now ended in a stub of raw wood. Miraculously, a small oil lamp still hung from the gunwale near the prow. One oar lay in the bottom, caught in a coil of rope and a fishing net. The oar was warped and useless.

They worked throughout the day in a nearly constant drizzle. There was nothing they could do about the leaks in the boat. They tried packing stones, twigs and muck into them, but such packing would last only a few moments. Well, Helena and Griselde would bail then. Furiously, perhaps. But the prospect made them eager. They sensed a way out now. Andrew and Emeth spent the evening by the campfire fashioning oars from fallen hardwood. They tied them in place with rope to the rotted oarlocks.

They set out the next morning in a lowering fog with the first faint hope they had felt in many days. Andrew and Emeth hugged the shoreline in the frail craft, afraid that at any moment they would have to swim for it. They rowed steadily against a light current, fighting against the flow toward the pass they had entered. But soon the currents shifted. They felt, as much as saw, small feeder streams entering the lake. They sometimes fought hard against the currents that grasped the fragile boat. Boulders shot up here and there, sending a whirlpool of froth in their way. They wondered, as the day wore on, if they wouldn't be better off walking. No! The ache in their shoulders wore deep and persistently, but they had all had enough of walking now. The boat was a sign of hope that they clung to. As the fog thickened, they lit the little lantern and pushed the boat steadily forward.

Until that moment when the wind momentarily brushed the fog aside and they saw the boy fishing, the huge, hunched man, and the strangely garbed woman who unleashed an arrow that smashed the lantern.

* * *

The mists closed down; the shoreline disappeared as if it were never there.

"Hadesseh." Andrew breathed the name. His body seemed without will, frozen into immobility. The air seemed sucked of any sounds—only the ragged twist of water pushing and pulling at the wooden boards broke the profound silence. They sat stunned, forgetting for a moment the dangers about them.

"Was it really she?" Griselde asked.

"You saw her too?"

"I no longer trust my eyes, Andrew. But I am certain that was Gregor. There can't be two like him."

"Gregor, Gregor," Helena shouted. "It was him. We're home."

Andrew groaned. Then suddenly he grabbed at the oar. "To shore!" he shouted. "We have to find them."

As he plunged the oar in, he felt the current stiffen. Emeth was already rowing, his body contorting powerfully. "Something's wrong," he hissed.

Water frothed about the boat.

Suddenly Griselde became aware of her forgotten chore. Water swirled around their ankles. The old boat was wallowing dangerously. "Bail!" she shouted to Helena. The two of them bent to the water, splashing handfuls overboard. For a moment they seemed to be making headway. But a slight chop in the lake flung more water into the dangerous boat.

"Row!" Andrew shouted.

"I can't. I can't pull against it. The current . . ."

* * *

The current had changed powerfully, as if redirected now in midcourse. It swirled against the boat, pushing and shoving. They seemed to be moving more rapidly.

When they broke into a patch of clear air, the fog momentarily whipped aside by some freakish wind current, Andrew was amazed to see mountain rock pressing down toward the water. The plain had disappeared. And the rock seemed to be spinning past at an astonishing speed.

In a moment he understood. "Row!" he screamed. "For your very lives, row!"

The others were suddenly frantic. *No good,* Andrew thought. The upper end of the lake was merely a higher spillover. *We're headed toward the lower end, where the lake empties into some other river or some branch.* And moving much more powerfully. They felt caught in a giant's grip.

The boat glanced off an underwater boulder that sent the wood shuddering from bow to stern. Water frothed along the shoreline. There was barely any shoreline left. The deep roar of water echoed off stone cliffs.

As a boulder approached, Andrew raised his oar, praying it would hold. Emeth paddled furiously in the stern. "Get ready!" Andrew shouted. "Emeth. I have Helena. You help Griselde."

If there was a response he didn't hear it. As they neared the protruding boulder, Andrew reached out with the oar. He found a joint of leverage, felt the wood secure for an instant, then turned his body like a piston, driving the boat away from the rock, in toward the shore. The boat wallowed pitifully. It shuddered in the shallows, slammed against rock with a grinding of wood. Andrew felt the old planks breaking up under his feet. He grabbed Helena with one hand, feeling her arms squeezing his neck so tightly he could hardly breathe. With the other hand he grabbed a pack. "Jump!" he screamed. Emeth had already read his intention. He had his arm wrapped around Griselde's waist, helping her stumbling and pitching through the current toward shore.

They collapsed there in a heap, feet still dangling in the water.

The boat broke up into tattered pieces that twirled among the rocks then rapidly, very rapidly, cascaded downstream.

"Too bad," Andrew said as he caught his breath. "We could have used the wood for a fire."

"Too wet, anyway," Emeth muttered.

* * *

It grew painfully cold. Their clothing clung to their bodies, the night air pressing cruelly as they huddled together. Nothing was dry. There was no wood, no fire. From the little plateau where they huddled they listened to the roar of the rapids downstream. The water threw a constant spray into the cold air, and it settled on them like an icy mist.

Andrew awakened early from a fitful sleep. He sat upright on the cold rock, studying the mist-shrouded scene before him. It was impossible to tell how far away they were from the sheltered valley. As the lake narrowed between the mountain walls, the current had swept them downstream. Far downstream. But there had to be other ways in and out.

He fought to put out of his mind the freakish resemblances of the woman and the deformed man to Hadesseh and Gregor. Impossible. Why here? And what of the boy? *Just a trick of the mind,* he told himself. *Sometimes you can see the shape of the passing stranger, and you think how like this person I once knew—I once loved. It is a trick of one's longing, that is all. And besides, the woman looked like a wild thing—dressed in strange clothes, the leather strapping on her waist, the hawk settling there.*

Ah, but those eyes? Nothing. A trick of the mists and the light.

And the man? Well, of bent creatures there were many.

It was impossible. Barbarians. But weren't they the very people that they were seeking? Emeth had said they lived on the other side of the mountains. But surely some drifted south, just as their own people had forged caravan routes for trade to the north.

Andrew paced about the small plateau. The cold was cruel. He saw his companions huddled together, little Helena in the middle. Andrew moved to keep warm. He headed a short way back toward the valley, clambering up a fall of rock. It was wet, slippery. When he climbed a short way, hoping to spot a trail lying beyond, he grew dizzy from the roar of the river and slid back down. The path was too treacherous. There had to be a better way.

When he walked back, the others were stirring. Emeth was foraging for twigs among the rocks and had scraped together a pitifully small pile. In the lee of a rock he was striking flint. He shook his head. "Too wet," he muttered.

"Keep trying," Andrew said. "I want to find wood. I want to find shelter for us. We can't go on like this."

"But we should go together," Griselde protested.

"I can go more rapidly alone. See, there is enough wood to last the day if Emeth can get it lit. Stay here. If I find nothing, we will have to go back. Somehow. We have to get out of here," Andrew looked at Emeth. He paused, about to speak, then nodded. Neither dared say the words—there appeared to be no way back. They were stranded here. Instead, Andrew said, "Very well. Until this evening."

"Be careful," Emeth murmured.

The mist that had clung for days finally broke that morning before hard needles of rain. Suddenly the moisture-clogged sky wrung itself against the face of the mountain. A bothering, dismal rain—not the clean ferocity of storm, but the sad weight of drizzle. Nonetheless, it drove the mists back, and for the first time in days Andrew could take a better bearing of the place where they were. Not where, exactly, for he had no idea; but what kind of place.

At one point he climbed over some rocks and found a small copse of trees and brush alongside the path. He noted it carefully in order to gather wood on the return. If the fog returned they might easily walk right past.

The trail wound along the base of the mountain, following the course of the rapids that raged in a white froth. Gray stone flanked each side of the gorge as far as Andrew could see. The upper reaches of the mountains disappeared in rain and haze, gray rock ascending to gray heavens. The trail rose and fell, following the angles of the mountain, at times almost level with the river. Where the trail rose, sometimes a hundred feet above the current's rush, the sound of the river became a muted thunder among the rocks.

It was a treacherous path, with no discernible goal. It might wind for miles and miles this way through the mountains, cut once by animals, smoothed once, perhaps, by men, neglected by each now. Perhaps it emerged at some northern town. Perhaps it was no trail at all.

As the morning passed, Andrew became ever more convinced that they should try to turn back. Perhaps they could make it to the plain below and find shelter there, or perhaps try to set out to find the main road. He wondered if the others had started a fire. Emeth would wear himself out trying. It was good they had waited back there. How pointless to travel all this way. No, they must go back.

Survival was the goal now, not the mission. Hadesseh? It was all an illusion, a trick of the mists and his heart's bitter yearning. *It's not fair,* he thought. *I . . . we tried so hard.*

But there was no one to say it to.

Andrew paused at what he judged to be noon, under the shelter of an outcropping of rock, and quickly ate a cold lunch. The cheese was crusted and old, and so little of it. It tasted like sand in his mouth. The place exuded loneliness, the gray wash of rain slanting beyond the outcropping, the wind whipping cold spray across him. He turned back then, anxious to see the others if only with the news that they must all turn back. How, though?

Along the way he stopped to gather wood, bundling it on his back in the fashion of peasants. At one point he permitted himself a smile. Here I am, the one-time owner of Fontini Villa. Now on some desolate mountain path in the forsaken uplands. Lost and lonely, with no sense of a destination. A mission and divine calling? They were thwarted by fog and rain. So easily lost in a maze of mountains. Andrew bent under the load of firewood like a common serf, favoring a painful ankle, a rude cloak covering a rake-thin, scarred body, the cowl thrust over a face so pitted no Faenza trader would recognize him.

So it was Andrew arrived at the campsite with a wry smile thinking of the picture he presented. Arrived, and found the place empty.

Certainly this was the place. See the gutted remains of the fire. So Emeth had gotten it started; now grown cold and sodden. Andrew called out. He dropped the firewood and ran down the trail, still calling their names. *How could they leave without me? And how could they have managed the rock-strewn trail?*

Andrew trudged back to the cold fire pit. He did not light a fire. He waited, finally falling into a cold sleep.

During the night the rain changed to snow. Andrew felt it only as an oppressive cold and he huddled against the rock.

He awakened often, shivering, his only thought that he had been forsaken. *Outcast.* They had seen the whirl of death. Yes, they had wanted him to go ahead. To be gone! While they could slip away. Did they run as they left the affliction behind, as one would from the plague? Andrew wanted to weep for himself. So his half-sleeping, half-awake mind tormented him. A nightmare of loneliness.

He awakened in the morning with a start. He was wondering with his half-waking mind what it was that had so terrified Helena during these past days. Was it just the treachery of the mountain trail? It had started already when they climbed out of the lower valley. And it had grown as they went into the mountains. It had afflicted Griselde also. What did Helena mean? *It's still out there. It didn't go away.*

Even Emeth had been affected. Andrew saw it clearly now. Why had the knife been so important to him that he had been willing to climb down after it?

It was for me. I was afraid, he had said.

They had not forsaken him; they had been taken.

But how? What sign? These were wild places, the home of the wolf. But suppose the wolves had attacked on some signal. Whose? Griselde said she heard something. Were they trained to attack? If so, then by someone. Someone was out there! The attack had occurred when Andrew was gone. And now, once again, they disappeared when he was gone.

The questions stormed him; the answering silence was intolerable. The vacancy of this morning was haunted with questions.

And the air was cold, bitter cold this morning. The world outside his shelter wore a white mantle of snow. Little had been left in the camp. Some cooking utensils, now layered with wet flakes, heavy and sodden, weary with their own falling. It lay piled in some places, melting against the rock in others. The cold was not yet the penetrating cold of winter—the kind that eats into the heart of the rock, splitting it to the core like a knife's blow. Yet the cold deepened steadily. Andrew looked at the remaining implements of the camp, wrapped his cloak about him and left them behind as he walked back down the trail toward the valley.

Carefully Andrew scaled the rockfall, fighting the slickness of snow with each step. He climbed, wondering how on earth the others could have climbed it. Little Helena? Old Griselde? Impossible. Unless someone carried them? Or led them? Or, there was another trail? Andrew crested the fallen rocks. The snow was falling more heavily now, but he thought he could make out the winding of a trail on the other side.

The river roared like a brown beast, frothing and angry. Nearly inch by inch, Andrew climbed down the rockfall to the faint, winding trail. At first the snow gave him hope. They would leave marks, certainly. But if they had left—or been taken—in the morning, the snow would only cover any signs. It fell steadily now, the last wet traces of rock covering in ghostly silence. Wind sounds died. Only the ragged heave of Andrew's breath broke the air. His sandaled feet felt raw in the snow. He had to stop often to rub them. *I left the wood behind at the campsite! Fool. Never could I endure this for days and days until . . . what? I reach the valley? Find their bodies?*

Still he plodded on, stumbling often on the slick surface. As the snow accumulated the way grew less treacherous, but more tedious, each trudging step an effort. He sensed the rapids widening and began to believe he would reach the plain by the lake.

Andrew stumbled up the rock-strewn trail toward the valley, cloak wrapped around him to ward off the cold. The gray sky was as fatal as night. No sign appeared. Andrew moved like a blind man stroking a sea of bewilderment. And nearing collapse.

His despair arose anew as if from the black hole of the cistern; only the walls here were the rocks of the mountain. Dominic's laugh of mockery seemed still to echo among them. His face had filled the whole world above the cistern, and Andrew had looked up only to know his own weakness. He could not even end that!

"No!"

If they live, they need me.

And when Andrew saw the figure of a man, he shouted again, "No!"

* * *

Like a stubby pillar this man stood, and so he had been standing for some time. Snow lay an inch deep on his gray cowl and upon the coat wrapped about his body. His beard was latticed with ice. A gray pillar immobile in a white shroud. So still and silent he stood, Andrew thought at first the man was frozen there. Only the wisp of steam from his nostrils gave the sign of life.

Andrew approached him with caution.

"Where have they gone?" he asked.

"Gone. Where you cannot follow." The man's eyes fastened upon Andrew, the eyes of a man with nothing to fear.

"Where? Tell me."

If the words carried threat, the man was impervious, a pillar, a piece so long of mountain and wind and weather he was unmoved by threat. He was silent for a long time.

"Will you speak?" Andrew hissed. "Or do you taunt me? Would you like to taste the river?"

Yet Andrew could make no move against him. He looked over the length of the man's stubby body. His feet were anchored in fur boots. Andrew became mindful of the cold chafing of his own feet and ankles. The sandals had become ice-rimed; straps cut into the red skin.

"I have waited for you," said the man. His voice was like the chant of the wind.

"Why?"

"Waited since yesterday morning when your friends were taken." His voice was high and reedy, a voice like the wind.

"Where have they gone?"

"I expected you sooner. Yet you chose to sleep."

"I thought they had forsaken me."

"I know. That is why I waited. You know better now?"

"I must find them."

"You are in no condition to do so." He pointed at Andrew's feet. "You will come with me. And they are safe, your friends. For the moment."

Andrew followed him. His mind filled with questions. He was miserably cold. He followed.

He was an old man. Andrew saw that now. He was short from the hunched shrinking of age. He produced a walking stick from under the folds of his fur coat, turned and moved along a path through the gap in the mountain rock, Andrew in his trail like a trained hound, shivering, trembling. *They are safe. For the moment.*

They toiled along the trail, moving steadily upward. Snow deepened about them. The old man seemed to know the way as surely as if it were the path before his own home. Easily he picked the less perilous steps. Under the snow the rock was slick with moisture turning rapidly to ice.

As they moved around a bend he suddenly disappeared. Andrew walked past the bend, trailing the footprints, and stopped. "Here," the man said.

Andrew had missed this second rent in the rock altogether. The mountain's face must have twisted with dozens of such turnings. Andrew followed his voice. The passage was narrow, the rocky walls pressing so tightly he had to worm his way through. It wound upward like a serpent's back, snaking from ledge to ledge, sheer rock to each side. Andrew was utterly spent, shaking with cold. Yet the effort of the climb broke sweat under his cloak. Andrew could feel it run down his body, crystallize into ice on his calves where the wind whipped the skin raw. Snow seeped down into the passage in a gray cloud. Funneled by the sides, it accumulated steadily. It clung now to Andrew's ankles, to his calves in level places where it had begun to drift. Always the gray shape wisped before him, moving ahead resolutely. Several times Andrew was ready to call out, several times ready to berate himself for being a fool, but, whether through weariness or desolation, he continued in the man's trail.

After a long time, the gorge opened suddenly onto a small ledge, and Andrew gasped. They had climbed high into the mountains for hours. Far below them the rocks fell away into a gorge that seemed as deep as eternity. The snow hid its bottom. They stood on a narrow ledge, little more than a few square feet across. Directly opposite them, across the gorge, a plateau sprawled like a wide wrinkle on the face of the mountain. The gorge was spanned only by a rope bridge. The distance across was, perhaps, as far as Andrew could throw a stone, if he could have achieved the balance here to throw. The rope bridge, he saw, was the common knitting of three separate strands, two above and one below, the three linked by snow-encrusted ties. One might have seen such a contrivance spanning little streams near Faenza. If one fell there, one got slightly wet. This . . . this was a line flung across the sky. The bridge sagged fearfully, and swayed above the chasm.

"No," Andrew said automatically.

"You must," the man said. "You cannot go back. You have no place to go back to."

With that he stepped out onto the bridge. With his first step the thing swayed wildly and its layer of snow plummeted down. Andrew could not see into the bottom of the gorge, so thickly the snow was falling. The old man held one hand on each of the guy ropes, his feet balanced easily on the base of the triangle, his staff tucked through his belt. The ropes teetered wildly over the abyss.

"I can't do that." Andrew's mind spun at the very thought. A chill settled into his stomach, wove into the groin and legs. It begged no.

"But you must, and you can. Do not fight the motion. You must learn to live with it, to let the sway carry you rather than fighting against it."

No! Andrew would rather die than do this thing. His heart thudded wildly. It was hard to breathe.

"You will take one step," the old man said. "Then wait until I am across. You must wait. Two cannot cross at once. Then we would each fight each other, and so neither, or only I, would succeed. Live with the sway, and think only of the going. Watch the point across, where I will be waiting for you."

So saying he turned and walked out. The ropes bucked sharply, but the old man seemed to dance upon them. *He is doing it to mock me!* Andrew thought. *He brought me here to show me fear! Very well, and you have suc-ceeded, madman! And why should I follow you? I can still return.*

They are safe. For the moment.

Then Andrew noticed that the old man had been telling the truth; by his crazy dance he was showing a way. He gave in to the sway, precisely as he had said. He did not fight the ropes; he moved with them, stepping so that the very motion guided and lifted him across. He stood finally on the other side and called, "Now come. Live with the motion." His voice was thin across the abyss.

Andrew was already one step out on the ropes, his arms and legs trembling like water that fell down and down. He jerked his eyes up. *Look up! Do not think of it!* He wanted to turn back. But his knees refused to turn. His ankle throbbed terribly.

"One step," the old man said. "You do not go the whole way at once." His voice was gentle, a high, reedy flow of words carried on the wind. Not the slightest trace of urgency touched them. "You take one step, as you always do, as you have always done."

Andrew took the step. Feet shifted. He clung to the ropes with a rigid grasp, fists locked to them.

"Do not fight it," the old man ordered. "Relax your hands. That's it. One more step."

Andrew tried to relax his rigid fists, the locked knees. The rope beneath his feet was woven of many separate strands. His feet trembled on it.

"Do not look down. One more step."

Andrew could not break the lock of his wrists and knees. The slightest movement of the bridge seemed designed to fling him into the pit.

"We call this bridge the Crossway," the old man intoned. His voice was a soft, high flow of words. Hypnotic. "You can understand why. This bridge, so high in the mountain, crosses the deeper gorge, thus forming a sign of the cross. But also to cross the bridge, one must give up to it. One must be willing to *give oneself up* to it. One cannot cross by fighting it. Truly, it is also like that other cross. One step, now."

Andrew locked his eyes, burning with outrage, upon the old man. *He has me trapped.* Another step. The swaying brought a cyclone of dizziness. It pooled in his stomach and threatened to buckle his knees. *Defeat it!* How? By giving in. Relax. Another step. The eerie quiet of the snowfall was a mockery. How easy to fall, like the flakes. To drift down and down.

Another step. The tension in his knees eased. Andrew drove the command to them: Relax. Master it. Another step. The ropes swayed, back and forth like a swing. It is summer, not winter, he imagined. A rope swing. Ease the cramping in the wrists. See how the muscles have bulged like ropes themselves. Relax them, give in to the sway. Another step.

Andrew had been going down the arch of the rope, and now reached the nadir of its tension. He began to climb. He could see the old man above him. Another step. *You cannot go back. There is no place to go back to.* Another step. Muscles spasmed in his thighs. Trembling. Turn it to the motion of the ropes. Go now. Another step. And he was moving upward. On the swing. It is summer.

The old man's eyes widened. A smile cracked the latticed beard.

"Very good," he said as he reached out a hand to steady Andrew on the opposite ledge. "From fear to overcoming to defiance. Very good. Perhaps you will be so kind as to tell me your name."

"I am Andrew." Without thinking, he added, "Of Fontini Villa." Meaningless now and here. He did not notice the sudden light in the old man's eyes.

"Welcome, Andrew. I am an old man," he said. His face wrinkled into a smile. "But I am called Rafeo. Shelter is not far off."

The trail opened on a broad mountain meadow. After days of the press of rock all around on the river trail, the unfettered openness of the meadow struck with the force of benediction. The meadow was robed with the steadily falling snow, but it was free and unbroken to the edge of a distant drop-off. About a quarter of a mile wide, between mountain and drop-off, it stretched like a broad belt around the mountain as far as Andrew could see.

"It is large enough to keep a few sheep and a goat," Rafeo remarked. "And vegetables during the summer. But come. Upward is the shelter."

A series of dwellings was carefully niched in the mountain cliff, the gray rock of the walls mortared to the mountain itself. Somewhat like the chapel of Faenza, Andrew thought. A low line of dwellings ringed the mountain, the snow-filled meadow sprawling from its foundation. The dwellings were marked by wooden doors and small windows, spaced along an unbroken span of stonework. Despite his weariness, Andrew stopped and marveled.

"But where is everyone?" he asked.

"There are no others," said Rafeo. "But come. This is the central room. It is mine. Yes, master in a house full of ghosts. But we will have a fire soon, and then there will be two of us. We, and the ghosts."

He led Andrew into a room, bitingly cold. It was nonetheless a bright place. The rocky floor was partially covered with a carpet of woven wool dyed in a quilt of colors. Rafeo noted Andrew's surprise with approval.

"As I said, I keep a few sheep and a goat. In fact, they are probably in the stable. They have sense enough to come in out of the cold." He shot Andrew a glance as he stood in the open doorway. "Why don't you do the same?"

The hearth was built along the side wall, situated so as to warm two rooms at once. The bunk was against the rear wall, resting in an alcove carved out of the mountain's rock. It would be warm enough and snug. Rafeo busied himself starting the fire. He kindled it with twigs, then placed several hard, brown clumps on the flame. These caught and burned with a clean, bright flame.

"Goat dung," he explained. "Another reason for keeping them. I should have enough for the winter." He poured a cup of wine and handed it to Andrew.

Andrew sat down on the bunk to drink it.

"No, take off those clothes. I have a dry blanket for you."

Andrew wrapped himself in it, hugging the woolen cloth. It too bore a pattern of dyes. No doubt this was how the old man entertained himself, Andrew thought. He, his sheep and goat. A large pile of wool lay against a wall. On a forsaken mountain hermitage. Rafeo poured some water from a pot by the fire into a basin, tested it and toweled Andrew's swollen feet.

As Andrew sipped the wine, he felt a leaden weight drape behind his eyes. He was falling into a mist of weariness and capitulation. He fought it. "Now, old man," he said. "I want answers."

But the words sounded unconvincing even to Andrew. They seemed to say, "I will sleep. Sleep." Andrew fought the weight descending. His tongue tried to form other words, but it had grown too thick and heavy.

"Sleep well, Andrew," the old man said with a smile. He removed the cup from Andrew's hand. Andrew felt the old man lowering him to the bunk as he tried once again to insist on answers. But then the blanket had fallen inside his mind and he slept.

CHAPTER SIXTEEN

Andrew's eyes felt fuzzy, half-closed and unfocused.

The fire cast a warm glow over the rocky walls, their coruscations catching the light that glittered off flinty points. The room was snug, hardly a half-dozen paces across. By the hearth, cooking implements hung on pegs driven into holes drilled into the stone. A small stone oven beside the hearth issued the yeasty odor of baking bread. Across from the alcove where he lay snuggled in the woolen blanket, a narrow wooden desk on stone pedestals hugged the wall. A tallow lamp glowed upon it. Woolen garments were neatly stacked alongside; his own clothes, clean and folded, lay on top. Only one other piece of furniture adorned the room, an odd little three-legged stool on which Rafeo, like a bent elf, perched, busily operating a small, loomlike implement. He was weaving a boot. One stood completed by the stool, a knee-high boot woven to the sandals Andrew had worn. Rafeo's fingers danced like mating birds, in and out, the threads flying between them to the nestled boot.

Andrew lifted the blanket back, rose to one elbow.

Rafeo did not move, but asked with his back to Andrew, "And did you rest well?"

"How long?"

"Oh, a long time now. A long time. But not more than you needed."

"I feel like I have slept for days. You put something in the wine."

Rafeo chuckled. "You want to know how long you slept? Look outside."

Andrew rose slowly. It seemed impossible to move his body quickly. The soporific still clung to his nerves. Something inside him fought against it. There was some urgency—some reason he shouldn't sleep. Bit by bit the urgency forced wakefulness. *My comrades!*

Andrew flung the quilt back. His fingers fumbled with clothing.

He was startled to see what he had thought was the pile of wool move suddenly at his approach, then he saw a tail disengage itself and whack the floor with a thump, thump. The huge dog unwound and rumbled over to Andrew. He shoved it aside, the way one would heave a boulder. He opened the shutter of the one window and beheld a world gone strange with whiteness. Snow drifted nearly to the window's rim. The mountain wind hurled snow across the meadow, choking it in blinding sheets of white. Andrew slammed the shutter and pushed the holding peg down.

"How long have I been here?"

"We arrived at nightfall. It is now morning. Of the day following."

"Then they are lost. We have no chance of catching them in this."

"You are right. We have no chance of catching them." Rafeo paused to knot the boot he had been making. "Here. Try them on," he said.

The woolen boots were knit to the laces of Andrew's sandals and were perfectly sized. He snuggled his swollen feet into them, feeling a rush of warmth.

"But they are not lost," Rafeo said.

"Not?"

"No. But you cannot get to them." Rafeo's words stopped Andrew in midstep.

"Why not?"

Rafeo sighed, shrugging his shoulders. "The weather, for one thing. Who knows how long this will last. Understand, Andrew. I am an old man—"

"I will go alone."

"—and I have spent many years here. Most of them alone. Seldom does the snow come so early. But when it comes, even less seldom does it leave before spring. That is always late in the mountains. You see, you may be stuck with me some time."

"But you know where they are."

"I can guess."

"So tell me," Andrew demanded. "Tell me, old man."

"Old man? Yes." Rafeo chuckled. "Maybe too cautious?" He raised his hands as if to say, What can I do? He stood up and lifted the kettle by the hearth. "The water is hot. Let me serve you a hot drink—oh, it will not make you sleepy. Just the opposite." As he poured the drink into a metal cup, the room filled with its scent, like roses and lilacs mixed, pungent and sweet.

"So you want a story. Very well, I will tell you. Do you like the boots? Yes? That is good. Soon you will have a coat also. Ah, you will earn it. I see the look in your eyes. Now the story."

Rafeo was in no hurry. He sipped his own drink, eyes twinkling in the firelight.

"But I must take you back several years. And you must be patient. You are not a patient man, are you? No. Well, I think you may learn patience."

Andrew leaned back and sipped the warm amber drink. The old man would not be rushed, he understood, and he needed his knowledge.

"The awful power of Rome is doomed, I think. Has been for some time. Even here we get news, of course. While at the moment you may think yourself at the uttermost ends of the earth—"

"I am!" Andrew interrupted. "This has got to be . . . the ends of the earth." He paused. *How could the old man read my thoughts?*

Rafeo smiled. "Well, you may as well be, for this place and at this time. This is a forgotten place, and so a good place to be at this time."

"Enough riddles. You were going to tell me—"

"Yes, yes. I was. I was merely saying that we are not altogether so far removed from life as you may have guessed, Andrew. In fact, this place has served as a garrison outpost in the past—the far past. The caravan route lies east of us."

"Then we did miss it? There really is a way?"

"Oh, to be sure. These trails were made by people you've never heard of. Old tribes that tracked these routes ages ago. The genius of Rome, after all, has been to appropriate as their own what others achieved, and so too they did with these old passages, using them to establish trade routes with their northern territories."

Rafeo stood up and prodded the sleeping mound of the dog. He ushered it through the door. An icy blast invaded the room. The dog went out willingly enough, charging happily into the cold.

"He likes the snow," Rafeo explained as he closed the door. "He is bred for the mountains." He sat back down and sipped his drink. "Now where was I?

"Ah, yes. Right here." He grinned. "That is, how I got here. The madness of Rome.

"Well, we hear the news. The persecutions. But there is also great struggle to the north. Where the state no longer cares to go. There are several spots such as this, scattered here and there. Places from which the guardians of Rome once kept watch. Now these places—at least this one—can be a refuge and a starting point. To bring the gospel."

"People wouldn't come here willingly," Andrew observed. "It's too remote. No one can find it."

"Oh, that's not the point. The point is the necessity of solitude."

"Lonely. That's what this place is," Andrew said.

Rafeo reflected a few moments. "Some would say that. Indeed, yes. The difference between loneliness and solitude. Interesting. Loneliness—that's something one is driven to. It is feeling apart. Now solitude—that is something someone seeks. In order to go back out with direction, with something to do and say, one *seeks* solitude, hmm? That's all the difference in the world, Andrew, a difference of the heart.

"For the last few years there have been a number of people here seeking solitude. In fact, Andrew, some came here with your assistance."

"Mine!"

"Or, your family. Of Lycurgus and Doval. Elhrain and Taletha. You yourself. Through the fortune of Fontini Villa."

"You knew my parents?" Andrew was incredulous. This world seemed utterly removed from the fields of Fontini Villa. A world apart.

Rafeo's face wrinkled with delight. "Yes. I did," he said. "And even once, so many years ago when you were a mere boy, I knew you. But," he added, "back to the story. Those whose way your family paid, did you think they came to no end? Where did they go, Andrew?"

"I thought they were fleeing the persecution. Settling in new home-steads. To the north—"

"Aha! Yes. And north goes a long way, doesn't it? Yes, some settled in villages. Some took up new lives. A few, a very few, Andrew, kept going—to bring the good news to new lands. Oh, it can't be stopped,

Andrew. Even if it is so very young. We stand at the frontier of a new world—the kingdom of God."

Andrew looked at him a long time.

Rafeo merely nodded and continued. "There are two ways that people do this. Some settle in a community and bear witness by their lives. The way they live with others, help others, give of themselves to others is also a giving of Christ. They testify in deed, and in word as they are able.

"For others, the way of testament is the word itself. They bear the gift of tongues—they understand languages; they reveal the truth to others in language. In fact, our most recent resident here was one such."

"Joseph." The name slipped past Andrew's lips in a whisper.

Rafeo's eyebrows lifted. "You know the name? For such was a name he went by. With us he was called Brusca."

"Long ago, he had been with Emeth . . ."

"The other man with you?"

Andrew nodded. "A disciple. He had this, this gift you speak of. Emeth wanted to pursue his work. But how did you know—?"

"About what?"

"Us," said Andrew.

Rafeo chuckled. "Perhaps we *should* start there. I'm getting ahead of myself. More about Brusca, or Joseph, as you say, later.

"Very well," Rafeo continued. He leaned back, perilously so, on the little stool. "Once someone enters the maze of trails in the mountains, they are either fugitives from the law or fugitives seeking the Way. No one enters willingly, it seems. So, my job? To watch. I do it well, with the help of my dog.

"Several days ago I was watching from one of the high places."

"Why?" Andrew interrupted. "You mean you just stand out there and look?"

"Sometimes." Rafeo laughed quietly. "Oh, sometimes. But sometimes I feel signs too. One learns to listen in solitude."

"Listen to what?"

"The voice of God. Is that so strange? Only in solitude can one listen well. At least, that's the way it works for me. It is my calling."

Andrew shrugged.

"The fog had cleared for a few hours. I saw you on the lower trail."

"Before we found the lake?"

"Oh, yes. A dangerous place. You were lost, obviously. Many who come this way are. Not all. But I saw something else also. So I waited. Wondering how long it would be until I could help you."

"Something else? What did you see? What was that?"

"I saw the trackers." Rafeo's voice was quiet. He was not smiling now.

"Then . . . there *was* someone watching us?"

"Yes. Besides myself."

"Then Helena was right."

"She is the young one?"

Andrew nodded.

"They would have known your every footstep from the moment you left the valley far below. They watch. They prey. They are afraid of being found out."

"And the wolves?"

Rafeo nodded. "They have trained the wolves to watch with them. And to attack on command. As we trained the mountain dogs to give aid, they trained the wolf to gain power."

"Who is this . . . *they* you speak of?"

"Several years ago, one of your own people, a trader I believe, learned the devious routes of the mountains, and learned of this place also."

Andrew leaned forward, frowning.

"He is a man driven by a lust for power, yet afraid to show it. A criminal, I would say, for it is the nature of criminals to long to exhibit what they have gained. Their paradox is that they must do so in secret, else their criminal nature is revealed. So they are dangerous. All things that operate in secret are dangerous.

"So in time, he established himself there. In the valley of the lake. He is a man of terrible power, for he coerced the trackers, and their beasts, to his rule."

"Wait. You said he was one of my people. How do you know this?"

"He is not one of us, nor of the villages. He is a cruel man. How do I know this? This is my home. Is there anything in the mountains I do not know? I saw him bring slaves from the south to do his work. He has kept them there. Somehow he also bent the trackers to his will and has kept them under his control. Remarkable, really, for they were the original roamers of this land, and Rome with all its power never was able to subdue them.

"However, that time has gone, this much is certain. From his stone keep he plunders and manipulates, building his power. Wagons of goods come and go."

"Wagons can get there?"

"The stone keep, near the place where I found you, is some distance to the south. It guards the entrance to the mountains. The route you wandered—it winds into the mountains by another way altogether. Had you kept on you would have bypassed the valley altogether. Who knows where you may have wound up before I could get to you. But once entering the valley you were under his power. It's a wonder you escaped."

"A freak chance. I had gone for firewood."

Rafeo nodded. "Perhaps."

"And do you think he has my friends?"

"If they are alive, they are there."

"Then I will free them."

"Perhaps you will, but not now. There will be no travel here until the snow melts and that may not be, as I said, until the spring. You see, the only way out of here is the way you came in. And there will be no going out."

"We'll see. This man, this 'trader' as you call him. Do you know his name?"

"I don't. He is called by different names for he wears different faces. I have seen him only twice, and then from a great distance. A strong man. Hair, jet black. Handsome, but the kind who chills you, even from a distance. Perhaps you will know him yourself."

Andrew began pulling his cloak on over his undergarments.

"You won't get far," Rafeo said.

"I'll see for myself."

He sighed. "Yes, I suppose you'll do that."

* * *

The huge dog had carved a crooked trail from the door. Andrew followed its path a short distance, then struck out for what he remembered as the way out. The snow fought him each inch. It hugged his thighs, immediately rimming the cloak. Within fifty paces a hurtling fist of cold wind caught up with him. It sheered through cloak and undergarments. The snow gusted about madly so that Andrew had to duck his head under the cowl and push blindly in the direction of the pass.

Already he thought better of it. Maybe it would be easier in a week. If the snow were thigh-deep here in the meadow, the passes would be choked. In his mind's eye Andrew saw the frail rope bridge leading to . . . a canyon choked solid with snow. He pressed on.

Then the way became surprisingly easier. The snow cover was much thinner here. Wind had shorn the meadow, drifting the snow against the mountain's flanks. Andrew began to think that it would not be so bad after all.

But where the wind had lacerated the open space, it had left a treacherous coating of ice under the thin veil of snow. The clearing began to slant slightly so that Andrew had to struggle to stay erect. Ice shone beneath each step now, whipped by the wind into glassy perfection. Andrew stepped from small drift to drift simply to keep his balance.

A sudden desperation hit him. This was *too* slick. The booted sandals were sliding now. He stopped, knees weak. Even as he stood he seemed to slide. He tried to move backward, to regain the thigh-hugging grip of snow. His steps skittered. He couldn't gain any foothold. He stood a moment, bent over, trembling nervously. Then he tried to run back, thinking that by power alone, by the propulsion of the driving legs, he could make it to the safety of the deeper snow.

His feet gave way. Suddenly they flew out from under him and he landed with a bone-jarring impact. Body twisting, Andrew clawed at ice and snow. He kept sliding down the incline. He clawed helplessly at the ice. He managed to pull himself to a precarious stop. He felt he would keep going if he so much as twitched.

Suddenly the great dog, a white and brown bundle of fur and muscle, came hurtling along the ridge. His great shaggy head bent, he skidded to a stop by Andrew. His huge paws shredded the ice as he stopped. Andrew reached out to grab his fur and the dog shook away. It was as if he were saying, No! Lie still. He came back with huge jaws agape. Saliva dripped from the edges of its jaws. The animal looked like a wild thing of prey. Andrew lay still, trembling with fear. Cautiously the dog approached. The huge jaws lowered to Andrew's upper arm, where it lay stretched out, fingers still clawing at the ice. The jaws closed. Like a vise of enormous power they closed, and stopped just short of crushing the bone. Thus secured, it began, huge paws shredding the ice, to drag him. Andrew cast one fearful glance back at the ice and nearly screamed in terror. He had been within a few feet of the precipice.

The dog released him only when he was again on solid footing. Andrew began to stagger uphill. Suddenly the dog crashed into his side, shoving Andrew to the left. Again he staggered a few feet. The wind stung his eyes; he could see only a few yards ahead. He reeled dizzily. He wanted to go only upward, into the deeper, firmer snow. Again the dog shoved him. Andrew realized its intention. The animal was herding him. Bit by bit he steered him. Andrew found the tracks he had made coming out. The dog walked behind him then, to ensure his passage. And there was the wall of the mountain, a gray rim of stone.

Andrew stood there before Rafeo's dwelling, and felt like a fool. He finally raised his fist to the door to knock.

Rafeo answered, of course. His only words: "Perhaps you should wait until I have knitted your coat before you go out for a walk again."

The huge old dog lay down by the fire to dry out. Andrew stroked its ears and it whined with pleasure.

Andrew had no desire to repeat his adventure of the morning, but the small room was terribly confining to him. True, it was snug and warm. But Andrew had been for months in the open—through burning sun, mists, rain and now snow. He sat staring into the fire, letting its spell work on his nerves, then he would rise to pace back and forth. Rafeo could apparently sit contentedly for hours at his makeshift loom, fingers deftly shaping the woolen coat. Yet, suddenly he broke the silence.

"Very well," he said. "It is time for a tour. And to learn your chores."

"Chores?"

"Of course. I offered you shelter. But not ease. Come. Wrap the blanket around you if you wish."

Andrew did so and followed Rafeo outside. The huge dog merely shifted in place, knowing instinctively there was no need to go out.

There were several rooms built in a row, following the course nature provided by the shaping of the mountain. The rooms curved around the natural declivity, a shelter from the most fierce winds, open to the rising of the sun. Andrew studied the strange fracture in the mountain. Some great shifting at the world's making had thrust the rock awry and created these odd acres of meadowland suspended in space. Those acres were now a hard glistening of snow that spread toward the precipice. Andrew looked out and shivered.

Rafeo apparently lived in the central and largest chamber. Several smaller ones stretched along the declivity. They walked to the end, where a stable arched under the protection of the lower edge of the overhang—a deep, natural recess, unfenced, where the sheep and goats could roam at will. Grass from the meadow had been carefully stacked out of their reach on a rock ledge. Rafeo paused to knock down a forkful. The animals gathered quickly to it.

"That can be your first chore," he said. "The snow will give them ample water, but, as you can see, rock melt also runs into that pool over there. In the coldest weather we have to melt snow and ice over the fire for the animals. But for now, enough drips from the rock and gathers there."

"My job?"

Rafeo nodded.

"The larger task is to keep the rooms."

"For what?"

"Who knows? Did I know *you* would come here? But there you stand!" Rafeo shrugged as if to say, What can I do to get through to you? Then he turned slowly to face Andrew. His face was somber. "Maybe someone will have need when I'm gone. I buried the last of my brothers eighteen months ago. There were two of us who started here. Several have come and gone over the years. Perhaps the time is now coming when there will be no one left, or no need for us. Until that time we will keep it as if we expected visitors any day." He pointed to a bulge of snow-covered land by some scrubby, twisted pine trees. "There I buried Sanjeani, the last to go."

Andrew was silent a moment, reflecting on Rafeo's comments. But he also studied the stunted trees. "How do trees grow up here?" he finally asked.

Rafeo smiled. A simple question, perhaps. "The birds of course. They laid seeds of the flowers also. In the spring the meadow is full of them. The goats get drunk eating the flowers. The birds carried the seeds of the trees also."

They walked back to the first room in the row of dwellings. Rafeo paused before opening the door. His eyes sparkled with delight. His spirit was lively once again.

"You can see how ingeniously they were built," he said as he opened the door. "We give the Romans credit, of course. Every two rooms combine over a hearth. Each person could be alone in his room, but when he needed company he had only to sit by the hearth and talk with his neighbor. When the fire died down, they could set a game board on the hearth and play. So every two rooms adjoin."

They entered one, similar to Rafeo's, only smaller. It was bone-chillingly cold in the absence of fire. The alcove held woolen blankets. A small heap of firewood and dried goat dung lay piled by the hearth. On the desk lay an inkwell and quills.

"Sanjeani was the last to live here. He was a copyist, but a very poor one." Rafeo chuckled. "Mostly he made wine. Maybe that was why he was a poor copyist. The great work was being done by Brusca. We will come to that. Perhaps you will be interested."

"I didn't see any vineyards." Andrew's interest had quickened.

"Oh, they are around the curve of the mountain. Sanjeani selected his spot well. They are wonderful vineyards, catching the moisture and the right sunlight. And of course, he has fertile nutriment from the animals."

The next dwelling had long been uninhabited. It held casks and vats, piled along the walls, and a rack of clay bottles.

"The life work of Sanjeani!" Rafeo exclaimed. He burst into laughter.

"You said he was an excellent vintner. Let's prove it."

"Very well," said Rafeo. He plucked a clay bottle off the shelf and pried off its seal with the point of a knife. "No cups here. Try it."

The wine was like a graceful honey, sweet and gentle. Andrew swallowed carefully and let it lave his throat. "Ah. Never have I tasted such a wine." He thought of the delight this would have brought to his parents.

Rafeo laughed. "Save me some."

"Take your own bottle. There's plenty."

They continued the tour, appreciating Sanjeani's excellence as a vintner.

"This. Ah, this," said his guide, "is, or was, the dwelling of the copyist. Brusca. And it holds the one treasure of this whole forsaken place. Well," he said, raising the clay bottle, "the second treasure." He laughed as he undid the door. "I call his work a treasure only because I don't understand it. Such things make for good religion."

It was a spare room. The design was similar to the others, yet it held an intangible difference, an otherworldliness. The unlit hearth and the sleeping alcove were the same. The desk had been drawn closer to the fire for better lighting, and a blackened tallow lamp rested on the desk. It was the place of a man who worked steadily and late at night, unable to stop his work when the light passed from the window.

Along the wall where the desk would have stood was a narrow shelf holding several carefully wrapped packages. Rafeo began undoing one.

"These are the parchments. Perhaps Brusca's was the greatest task here. Maybe he just worked harder than anyone. He was a solitary man. One who kept silence, one for whom solitude was a habit, a way of life. His love was his work. He had the gift of languages, one of the great gifts, bestowed, as you may know, by our Lord himself. These are his parchments, his labor. Sometimes I thought he may have done well to spend a little time with Sanjeani, but . . ." He spread his hands.

Rafeo carefully lit the tallow lamp, then spread the crisp sheets before Andrew on the desk. The light was too poor to make out the work clearly. Rafeo began rewrapping the parchment, but Andrew stopped him.

"Wait. What exactly was he doing?"

"I don't know." Rafeo pointed to smaller packages on the shelves. "Sometimes I think he only made quills and ink. Once a year he would leave to supply himself. On his back he would strap a cask of Sanjeani's wine, walk many days to the distant villages below and trade for supplies. Sanjeani's wine was highly prized."

"I would like to study these," Andrew said.

"Feel free to do so," said Rafeo. "But perhaps tomorrow would be better. It is getting dark now."

*   *   *

Andrew did return in the morning, in part to avoid thinking of escape, for he felt like a prisoner here on the side of the mountain. His mind repeatedly crowded with images of his lost friends. Through them, over and over, also appeared the image of Hadesseh—now as a young girl, then as a young woman. Then too in the pinched images of the trees she had left on the parchments at the villa.

He daydreamed then—of sunny summer days when he frolicked with Hadesseh on the hills of Fontini Villa, and he woke bitterly to the realization that those days were as lost as the villa itself. He felt like a caged animal on the mountainside. He paced his room, driving the images from his mind, telling himself there was nothing he could do. Find Hadesseh?

Impossible now.

On the route north they had passed through many little towns and open fields. Everywhere he had sought even a glimpse of her, somehow believing if he looked hard enough at the people they passed one of them would turn out to be her.

And what, he asked himself, of the woman in the mountain valley? He knew it was a trick of light, of shadows and mists rather, but how he had wished! For one moment—a breath only—their eyes had met, but the hatred he felt was like a terrible blow. No, it had to be only coincidence. Besides, who could the little boy be? Just a trick of the imagination that mocked his longing.

So his thoughts tormented him as he paced the room. In time his heart would quiet, his thudding pulse dulling to an old ending: there is nothing you can do about it anyway. It is past.

No, his mind chanted over and over.

Suddenly his heart seemed to be breaking from loneliness. He wondered if he would ever see his friends again. He found himself pleading, begging with prayers. *Just once more, Lord. Let me see them one more time.* He vowed he would do anything to make that come true.

And as he turned to the parchments, he choked down his restlessness and anger.

The manuscripts were thus a diversion. The language was at first a cryptic mystery, and Andrew carried his knowledge of grammar and languages only as the dimmest recollection. One by one he unbound and studied the parchments, content to merely scan, to look, to let the runic signs seep into him. Yet when he met Rafeo in midafternoon of that next day for their meal, Rafeo observed the excitement in Andrew's eyes.

Rafeo had been working on Andrew's coat, now nearly finished. He lay aside the weaving implements, poured broth from the kettle by the hearth and broke a loaf of bread he had baked in the small stone oven. That and Sanjeani's wine were ample fare.

"Well, and what do you make of it?" he asked.

"I don't know," Andrew admitted. "That is, I'm not sure about it. Can you tell me anything of Brusca, his work, his background? Emeth didn't tell me much. Only that he wanted to bring the Word to the northern tribes."

Rafeo lifted his hands and shrugged. Andrew was becoming familiar with the gesture, partly self-deprecation, partly an opportunity to gather his thoughts.

"When Brusca came to us, I found him not far from where you were. He had been beaten, terribly so. I don't know by whom. The trackers? No, I don't think so. They would have killed him and fed his body to the wolves. Probably some outlaws seeking refuge in the mountains. My own guess? I think he was followed. He was coming *back*, you see. From the north countries, and there are people there who are jealous of their lands. They may have seen Brusca as a threat. To go forth into strange lands is always a risk.

"That is all I know. Whether by choice or accident, Brusca never spoke after that. Not at all.

"He may have been damaged somehow by the beating, but also he didn't appear to have any desire to speak. He did not live many years, either, but each day he lived, he lived for his parchments."

"I don't recognize the language," Andrew said.

"Nor do I. I think they were of a northern people. That's why I think he was coming back—to record the language.

"What good is it to record, if the people can't read anyway?"

"A good question. Perhaps we can assume that some people could read? Perhaps Brusca made it to some center of learning. Perhaps he was just beginning to organize the language he heard into written form." Again Rafeo shrugged, as if to say, It is beyond me.

"I would like to study them," said Andrew.

Rafeo nodded and smiled.

* * *

The manuscripts proved to be Andrew's tool for survival. Rafeo would not tell him anything more about the stone keep to the south. Nor would he speculate on the fate of Andrew's friends, no matter how pressed. "When the time comes," he would say. "What good would it do you now?" And that was true. In time Andrew's interest in the parchments became an obsession. With them, a new world opened.

Andrew also began to find a certain solace in his simple routine. It reminded him, in many ways, of the long months at the chapel of Faenza. The animals greeted him eagerly each morning—he learned the names and personality of each: gentle Lisabetta, the hard-hearted goat Simeon who thrust his burly head at Andrew's thighs. The lesser members of the small flock. Andrew often pummeled Simeon playfully out of the way so that others could eat.

From the stables he went to the copyist's room, kindled the small fire and went to work. He kept the fire small both to save precious fuel but also because he had grown accustomed to working in the cold with the tallow lamp spitting above his red hands. Every hour or so he would rise, pace the room, exercise and return to the desk. But when he turned to the script, it seemed body and mind separated; a trance of concentration took over. The mystery of the words lay like riddles, and Andrew attacked them from many angles at once. He identified problems, sought solutions.

In early afternoon, as if by a preconcerted signal, he laid the pen down, rose and joined Rafeo for a light meal. They sat in Rafeo's chamber then. And they knew no hurry, settling back with a bottle of wine from Sanjeani's capacious store. They let their minds roam free in conversation, sometimes talking so until darkness.

"The days grow longer," Rafeo said one afternoon. "Have you noticed?"

Indeed. Inch by inch the sun slid higher on the rock. Minute by minute the inches lingered longer. Andrew had kept watch.

"And one day you will begin your quest. But have you thought of what you will do?"

Andrew had not permitted himself that. He felt he would go insane with rage if he allowed his mind to dwell on it.

"You seek vengeance," Rafeo said knowingly. "You want retribution."

"Yes," Andrew replied after a moment. "If possible, I will have it."

"Are you at peace with it?"

"I don't know. I think," Andrew said slowly, "there are some whose lives are such a pestilence that it would be better for others if they no longer lived."

"Yet you might consider an alternative."

"There is none. If this person is who I think it is, he is pestilence, savaging the lives of those who cannot fight back. And some who are very dear to my heart."

"Wait. There may be an alternative. Perhaps more daring. That of forgiveness."

212

"Never."

"Think about it. At least consider the possibility."

"I cannot forgive. The wrong is too grievous."

"Therefore the greater risk. For forgiveness is a free gift, is it not? Defying what is deserved?"

Andrew sat back, smiled and let Rafeo work. He enjoyed the old man's mind at work, a rapier targeting possibilities, excluding insufficiencies. Very much, Andrew thought, like his own work with the parchments. "Very well, Rafeo. Explain. As you say, we have time."

"We understand," Rafeo said, "that only when freely given is forgiveness genuine. So too, then, only the individual who freely chooses to forgive is genuine. Because he has chosen, has been free to choose forgiveness or retribution, he himself is free. Genuinely free."

"Ah, but isn't retribution also a free choice?"

"So it would seem. But consider. Retribution is a taking, an exacting of some penalty."

"True. But the penalty is merited."

"Then justice is met. And justice, we believe, is a noble thing, a high thing. It is the very cornerstone of the philosopher. But is there something yet higher than justice? Higher than philosophy? If so, it must be the counter; not the step higher but the opposite, the exact, canceling opposite."

"Does it serve justice, then?"

"It must be higher yet than justice, an alternative action. So if retribution is taking what is merited, forgiveness is giving *what is not merited.*"

"Who is to say it is superior?"

"Consider further. What is the consolation of retribution?"

"We have just agreed. Justice is served."

"Yes, but for the individual who exacts retribution?"

"Satisfaction. Requital."

"Then nothing is changed. Satisfaction for what? A misdeed? Even a heinous misdeed? That does not change the original act. In fact, it asserts it more strongly. At best, retribution gains recompense; it can never match the deed itself."

"We must try. Else there is no justice."

"Consider how justice might be served another way. In forgiveness what is the action?"

"The person forgives."

"He freely chooses to do so?"

"Precisely. Else it is not forgiveness, but an abeyance of anger."

"Just so. By freely choosing he relinquishes not just the criminal, but also the misdeed. And the anger, and the anguish. Do you see? To freely choose to forgive is also to separate oneself from the injury."

"But I cannot see how justice would be served," Andrew protested.

"There is the paradox. If one separates oneself from the misdeed, from the injury, does justice have a claim?"

"Not if the evil is forgiven."

"Then forgiveness does not try to weigh in justice's scales an exact measure of retribution to crime?"

"No. It cannot. Not if the crime is forgiven and retribution forsaken."

"Do you see, then? The scales are no longer necessary at all. The crime is obliterated by the act of forgiveness."

"But the criminal deserves punishment."

"The one harmed by the criminal deserves freedom from the affliction. Is freedom ever the lesser good?"

"No. Nothing is higher than freedom. Else choice is impossible."

"That is the paradox, is it not? By obliterating, by going above justice, we free ourselves."

"But you ask me to forget the injury."

"That is the *action* of forgiveness. Without forgetting there is no forgiveness."

"But who can do this?"

"I don't know if anyone can! I have not suffered as I believe you have, Andrew. Nor, on the other hand, have I inflicted as you have. Oh, don't be angry. Quite often those who forgive are the most in need of forgiveness."

"I have been forgiven."

"When?"

"When Emeth baptized me."

"Is that the model, then? The dying and rising. But to what did you die if not retribution? To what were you born if not forgiveness?"

"Ah, but you forget, Rafeo. There is also judgment."

"But not yours."

"And why not? Is the judgment of the Lord a passive thing? A thing we wait on? Are we not instruments?"

"But that judgment is to come, isn't it? The model we have now is that of forgiveness. Are you afraid of it, of the risks?"

"Afraid? You do not know me well." Andrew shifted uncomfortably on the bench. Rafeo's eyes met his and held them.

"Perhaps too well," Rafeo said. "I don't have to know all your deeds to know you. Action isn't always courage. A dog will defend its home. It takes a man to give his home away."

"Hardly a just act," Andrew retorted. "What of his family?"

"Again that word *justice*. Would you really have justice? For everything? Weigh each good deed on the scale against each negative thought, word and deed?"

"No. No, I would not," he admitted.

"Think about it, Andrew."

"Oh, but I have, Rafeo. I have."

"I hope you have not missed my point altogether."

"I see your point. I don't accept it."

"Understand, Andrew, all this time I have not been talking only about forgiving your enemies. I have been talking also about your need to forgive yourself."

"Myself!"

"Forgiveness does not and cannot ignore the pain inflicted. Forgiveness calls it up from that bitter, buried memory and targets it. Here. This is the thing that hurt me so terribly, and this is the thing I now forgive." Even as he spoke, Rafeo's eyes seemed to target Andrew. His words struck Andrew like a raw force. "This," he said, "is the revolutionary act: to dredge once again that which we have spent so many years so carefully burying, tucking it safely away under the layers and layers of crafted forgetfulness. But it is a worm in there; it keeps turning. Why not call it forth then, recognize its unfairness, for this alone offers hope for healing. Until the worm is slain, there is no healing.

"For this reason one forgives: to heal oneself. To destroy that worm of bitterness which no matter how we try to layer it away, keeps insinuating its poison into the heart's flow. When we call it forth and name it, then dismiss it by the act of forgiveness—then we can embrace the hidden part of ourselves and call ourselves whole. But not until. Forgiveness ends in our own wholeness."

"Aren't there some human deeds that cannot be forgiven?"

"There are no such deeds, but there is such a one."

"Who?"

"The devil himself, because he is beyond the power of choice, having chosen for all time not to be forgiven."

"And God? Does one forgive God so easily?"

"For what?"

"For allowing the devil his freedom?"

"Then are you forgiving God or his permission?"

"Is there a difference?"

"All the difference in the world, Andrew. God permits, but the individual chooses. No deed is without consequence, even that first deed when the devil chose, for all eternity, *against* forgiveness. Perhaps God trusts the power of forgiveness more than we do, or more than we give God credit for. You see, that is the divine paradox, isn't it? The infinite risk of love, for love is nothing less than the act of forgiving."

Andrew had had enough. He shook his head and rose wearily. But as he reclined on his bed that night the thought struck him, needled to wakefulness by Rafeo's words. *Forgive myself? Perhaps. But one day there could be one of whom I would have to beg forgiveness.* He longed for the coming of spring.

CHAPTER
SEVENTEEN

T he puzzle of the parchments, the strange formula of the languages, continued to consume Andrew.

He knew well that every word carries suggestion in addition to definition—therein lie the mystery and power of language. It is as precise as mathematics; as inexact as life itself. The mystery of the parchments was that the whole thing was a shadow of suggestions.

Andrew recognized the language of one manuscript as Hebrew. The trouble was, he couldn't read it. Andrew surmised that it was the gospel account Emeth had spoken of. But why, then, wasn't it written in Greek? Andrew had been tutored in Latin and Greek since his earliest years. Other letters of the gospel were in Greek, he knew. The church in Rome had received one of them, from the Apostle himself, portions of which were copied and carried throughout the country.

* * *

At one of their afternoon meals Andrew speculated on the manuscripts to Rafeo. Rafeo himself had said little about them, content to let Andrew preoccupy himself as he wished.

"One of them," Andrew was saying, "is in Hebrew. I'm certain of it."

Rafeo nodded.

"My guess is that Brusca was translating some letter—probably a gospel account—into this northern tongue."

"Well, that wouldn't be so odd," Rafeo reflected. "Some of the early disciples might well have written in Hebrew to their fellow Israelites in distant lands."

"But I have only seen the gospel account in Greek," Andrew protested. "That's the problem. If I had a key text, I could compare it and maybe carry on the translation. Do you see what I mean?"

"Is that the only problem?" Rafeo asked. There was a twinkle in his eye.

"I suppose you're going to tell me you have a letter in Greek here?"

"No. Not at all. They are too precious to find their way to a place like this. Heavens! But I have read such a letter."

"Well, so have I. A copy of one of the Apostle's letters circulated widely around Rome. Emeth himself had made the copy and kept it for a long time before giving it over to a group starting a new church."

"Ah," said Rafeo. "Maybe it was the same I saw. The only thing is, I memorized it."

"Memorized!"

Rafeo nodded. "Something as precious as that, of course."

Within a week Rafeo had penned out a copy of the portions he could still remember. They were substantial. Andrew set himself to the hard labor of comparing grammars and patterns among the three written languages before him. For his own amusement, he began inventing sounds for the northern tongue, often reading the words aloud even when he didn't understand them. But in time he unlocked phrases, bits and pieces.

They were words about the Messiah—an accounting of his life.

Andrew lost himself in this new world, surprised at the recollections that washed over him.

The gospel of peace.

But at what a terrible price.

The stories that his parents once told seemed old now. A generation past. But what they lived for lived on. More than that—it grew. *How desperately the gospel is carried*, Andrew thought. *And what a price some people paid.* And still they kept coming, with their copies of sacred texts, their lessons, their letters. Often offering only themselves and the testament of their hearts and lips. The very vigor and commitment of these people bespoke the authenticity of the gospel they carried.

Andrew thought of the persecution in Rome, how mad Nero and others had made living toys of Christians for their entertainment. A mockery of all things sacred for the sake of sport. But it had not worked at all. The pressure itself spilled the Word outward, like oil pressed from olives in the vat. The purer essence flowed out, kept flowing.

Andrew shook his head in wonder. And his parents—they had been there, had seen the Messiah, had witnessed the price he paid. Andrew trembled at the thought of witnessing such an event, to bear witness to others.

* * *

The days passed. Layer upon layer of snow fell. Each morning, it seemed, Andrew had to carve anew the path to the stables. His relentless helper was the mountain of a dog who now became his companion. If Andrew slept late, he heard an indelicate paw scratching earnestly at the door. Its brute power seemed capable of caving the door in. Oh, but he had manners, this mammoth dog. Sleepily Andrew would admit him to his dwelling. While the dog watched Andrew dress, its tail hammered the floor. "Dustmop!" Andrew roared affectionately. A growl rumbled like thunder off the rock and urged his hurry.

Ill at ease between walls, this was a dog for moving through snow! He blasted out the open door, all haunch and wobble of flesh, his coat the color of snow stained by brown splotches. He parted the fresh snow on the way to the stables. By long custom he corralled the unwilling goat. Old broom-headed Simeon made a few obligatory kicks at the hurtling boulder of a dog, then settled down to his ration of feed.

When Andrew shut himself in Brusca's room, the shaggy dog ambled back to Rafeo, content to await the midday meal.

* * *

After weeks of blinding snow and cold so bitter it cut through the rock, a south wind rose and swept back the clouds. For days the sun shone unfettered by mist or cloud, a white brilliance that spat flame upon white meadows. This was the midwinter spring, the sudden blaze of light and ice that stirred the dulled roots of the spirit. Snow-melt glistened over the meadow on a surface packed hard. One could walk across its surface, feeling the ice give way occasionally, but with the giddy sensation of walking *on*, not through.

It was impossible to remain indoors long. One afternoon Rafeo located some walking sticks and, together with the shag-haired dog, who skittered playfully like an overblown pup on the ice, they went exploring. They hiked past the gardens still hidden under snow. Rafeo located Sanjeani's vineyard, its bulge of old vines discernible under the snow, the trellises now wearing transient blossoms of dazzling white. It had not been kept up since his death. The meadow ended in jagged snow-swept rock, becoming one with the mountain again. By careful climbing among the rocks, they found a place where they could look down into the awful emptiness. If one looked up from below, where the mountain rose in sheer rock, the lip of meadow would be scarcely discernible. But the view looking down made Andrew grow dizzy and he stepped back. The huge old dog frolicked among the rocks, and Andrew called him to still his own fear.

On the way back Andrew insisted that they pass by the gap to the rope bridge. Rafeo looked at him questioningly, but agreed. The meadow wound between huge boulders. They found the trail easily, but it was a mass of ice and snow piled among the rocks. The deception of the midwinter sun: the snow was there to stay until the spring rains.

Nonetheless, Andrew's thirst for answers and for the action that could lead to them was whetted. When they returned he took a blank parchment and brought it to Rafeo's dwelling. With little urging, Rafeo drew in the surrounding terrain, carefully tracing the route to the southern keep where he believed Andrew's companions were. Andrew thought of them, one by one, as Rafeo drew the map. Each face appeared before him in a way he hadn't permitted in months. Helena: her face wreathed in blond curls. Did she laugh or weep this day? Did she see sun or dungeon? Andrew recalled the first time he had seen her, there in the squalid hut in the village. How long ago that felt. And Emeth, with his hawklike features. How had they kept him these winter months? If he still lived. Why would they keep them alive at all—unless to lure him? And Griselde, too old to suffer indignity, she who had endured so much.

"This is the way," said Rafeo, handing over the map. "Understand, it will be weeks yet before you can travel. But . . ." He shrugged. "The time will come."

Andrew took the parchment and studied it. There was the trail they had followed, with the river as a demarcation. Andrew understood the symbols for elevation. A swirl of peaks, the long plain by the lake, then a craggy stone fortress drawn against the northern mountain. There appeared to be three trails. One, a long, looping circuit, followed the river they had traced coming north, circling down to the upper end of the valley lake, the point they had earlier crossed over into the valley. The second curved off the same trail, but wrapped around the valley itself, finally connecting with the raging rapids at the lower end. It was this path on which Rafeo had led Andrew to his mountain refuge. And a third more direct path twisted across treacherous passes from the valley to the mountain refuge itself. It was this trail that Rafeo had said met the tumbled boulders behind Sanjeani's vineyard.

"It is safest to return to the river trail," Rafeo said. "I have marked another way also. See," his finger etched the third line running to Sanjeani's vineyard.

"That's a trail?" Andrew asked.

"I have never taken it, but the watchers did. It is treacherous, Andrew. I have no idea if it is still there. Rockslides, you know. It would be best to think only of the river trail."

"But they would be watching that."

"It depends on when you go, how you travel. It is still many weeks before anyone would usually travel into the mountains. There is the risk, however."

Andrew rolled the parchment, determined to commit it to memory.

* * *

The weather changed slowly. After the brief fire of the midwinter sun, it snowed again. But then the temperature inched higher. Andrew went out one afternoon without his coat, savoring the warmth. The snow gradually loosened its hold on the earth. He awakened one night to the sound of rain, and prayed its onslaught. Toward morning the booming rumble of snowslides shook the earth.

Then one day the snow lay in soggy patches upon the meadow, broken by the hard heads of the first flowers, and Andrew knew it was nearly time.

He walked out in the meadow each day. Where he could find firm footing, he began to run in long, loping strides, feeling his winter-dulled muscles begin to respond. He walked often to the rope bridge. The ice among the rocks melted with interminable slowness. Melt water cut dozens of channels, forged a tunnel under the ice, slowly fissured its mass. When the day came that Andrew could set foot on the boulders themselves, he knew the exhilaration of escape. He clambered over the slick rocks to the rope bridge.

Andrew tested the ropes for damage. Snowslides could rip at the ropes, and he had no time for the intricate repairs that Rafeo had described. Strands had to be stripped away and new ropes, from a supply kept in the dwelling, knit to it. But, for all the harshness of the winter, the ropes seemed strong.

Impulsively, Andrew stepped out onto it. Surprising himself, he took another step. The swaying ropes carried no threat to him whatsoever. Andrew stood out on the precarious perch, swaying gently over the vast abyss, and felt absolutely no fear. On the contrary, he felt giddy with excitement. He stepped carefully all the way to the plummeting center, paused and looked down. The gorge fell like a throat, its gullet still choked with snow, the rock cascading with dozens of rushing rivulets that glistened with the sun's polishing. Andrew felt absolute awe, and he fought the urge to kneel.

He balanced there like one dangled on a thread from eternity. This was a beauty pure from the hand of God, wrought in nearly thorough silence. The wings of a distant eagle seemed audible, so still was the sky. Rivulets rang watery chimes against the rock. Beauty so pure, and so perilous— a thin rope stretched across a space no man was made to walk his way across. Solitude so thorough that he seemed to touch the hand of God. Or feel God's touch upon him. A still point, a flame with the blaze of glory.

He walked back, letting the natural spring of the ropes carry his steps. Like a swing.

I am free.

It was time to leave.

*   *   *

Rafeo walked with him to the foot of the bridge the next morning. He watched approvingly as Andrew strode across. Andrew paused on the ledge and waved to the old man, then walked into the narrow pass leading to the river trail. He wanted to walk the way he had walked before with his friends. He had directions now. The trail this way would be long, but he wanted to go this way, trying to feel the presence of his companions as he went. He wore the thick boots Rafeo had made. The leather thongs were laced tight to keep out mud and snowmelt that covered the trail. He wore a light jacket of softly tanned hide that he had found in Brusca's room. At his waist he had belted the sheathed knife.

Andrew camped without fire along the way. A steam of vapor rose from the thundering river beside him. Often he had to climb into the rocks to detour lower stretches where the trail lay underwater.

Another day and night passed. Having to climb above flooded portions of the trail slowed him terribly. He fought his impatience in order to nurture his strength. Sunlight of a third morning fired the trail. Andrew looked now for the juncture where the upper stream of the lake flowed out. According to Rafeo's map, he should have circled behind the mountain valley, affording entrance by the stream they had first crossed over into it. Then he would circle up through the rocks to the rear of the stone keep at the north end of the valley.

At midmorning he found the narrow gap in the rock. The water was deeper and faster than he remembered, a cataract now that thundered over the rocks in white foam. He went carefully, crawling from rock to rock, wary of the trackers. Once inside the valley, he immediately began to climb into the mountains surrounding it, hoping to circle and study the plain below.

All afternoon Andrew climbed among the mountains circling the width of the valley. At times he walked through riven walls of rock, at other times balanced on little more than a whisper of a trail on the side of the mountain. Often he hugged the stone, body moving crablike, looking out into infinite space broken only by distant peaks, their tops and flanks still draped by snow and yellowed ice. Sometimes he could look out over the valley, and he saw that the peaks fell away toward the south and the caravan routes. In this light, what had all been mist and fog before now appeared orderly.

The valley stretched between two mountain ridges, its length bisected by the narrow lake. Far in the distance Andrew could see the frothy plume of spray where the lake narrowed to a plunging torrent between the mountain flanks squeezing together. He hoped to catch a glimpse of the stone keep that Rafeo had spoken about, but he saw nothing like it. Nor did he see anyone. He could make out patches of farmed land. Wagon wheels had cut ruts down the plain and through a southern gap in the mountains, which before he had missed seeing altogether. That route would connect with the caravan routes, he thought. But he saw no one; it was as if he were by himself in a wilderness at the end of the world.

Andrew hoped that by this route he would arrive at the back of the keep and so gain the advantage of stealth. The path widened eventually. Andrew moved quickly now, hurrying against the setting sun.

*　*　*

At a turn in the path, Andrew paused to take a breath under an overhang.

They saw each other at the same instant: Andrew frozen in place, the wolf a sudden rumble of malice. The creature planted its legs in a crouch, ready to spring. The tracker stood behind it, his face broken by a smile of victory.

Options jarred Andrew's mind like heartbeats. The knife! No, too risky. And there were two of them, wolf and tracker. Evade. Deceive. The tracker growled a command at the beast. It catapulted, jaws agape. Andrew's fingers were already clawing for the jut of rock above his head. They gripped the cold rock. Just enough leverage. As the wolf leapt, he swung forward, driving his legs up and out, a rigid battering ram. He caught the beast in midair. Its body took the blow full force, and it twisted off balance. Scratching wildly at the loose rock at the edge of the trail, it caught Andrew's ankle in its jaws. Iron teeth locked down. They caught in the thick hide of Rafeo's boots. He felt the teeth piercing through, stopped finally by the tough hide and leather thongs. Andrew swung the wolf's body, jerking his leg, locked to a snarling madness. The wolf's hold broke. It clawed for balance, began sliding over the edge, broke loose with a howl that disappeared into the abyss.

Andrew wrenched his attention back to the tracker, his breath coming in raw heaves. The man was running, and he must not warn the others.

Andrew began to chase him, slowed painfully by his bad ankle. He stumbled along the rock, dizzy with the effort just to maintain balance, the pain of the wolf's bite rocketing along his leg. He reached for the knife. It was light in his hand, a natural extension—so light, so deadly. He drew his arm back, concentrated, prepared to throw. *Disable him*, Andrew thought.

The tracker looked back. That was his fatal mistake. He saw the knife and was raising one hand as if to ward off the throw when his feet skidded on a patch of icy rock. It sent him teetering near the edge, and he clawed in the air for balance. At the last moment Andrew ran forward, grasping one of the man's flailing hands. He could not . . .

Andrew felt the man's fingers slide through his own, saw the look of frozen fear settle on the man's face as he dropped. Soundlessly he twirled into space. Andrew pressed his hands against his ears to shut out the sound of impact.

He heard nothing. He bent to hands and knees and leaned over the edge. He saw nothing. Nothing but night shadows creeping up the rocks. He fell back, swallowing heavily, the blood pounding madly at his temples. He sheathed the knife at his waist with trembling hands.

It was several minutes before he rose and cautiously followed the path. He knew he could not afford being taken now. No matter the cost. But he had not wanted this—not death. He had to get in. And get his friends out. He moved through the evening shadows, trying to imagine the stone keep ahead, trying to put the plunge of the tracker out of his mind.

* * *

The trail wound around the mountain like a serpent's coil. As the trail wound downward it broadened. The sun stroked scarlet fingers across the rock, deepening quickly in the lower reaches. In this softness of sunset, he rounded a corner and saw it, much closer than he had thought. Its stone walls seemed a violation of the gentle evening light—implacable and dark. They rose from the side of the mountain, stone affixed to rock, roots sunk into the heart of the mountain itself. The thing was an ugly twist of snarling stone. Purple light touched its base, rode its thick flanks as Andrew studied it in awe.

To the south the mountain fell away in a series of broken fields to the valley far below, lost in darkness now. The very rock breathed cunning and deceit.

The tower he studied was built as a spiral of stone, broken by cupolas that dotted the stern walls. The sight unnerved him. It was eerily similar to his tower at Fontini Villa, but larger. Much larger. The base of the tower was girdled by a stone wall. Every stone of the thing sighed desolation. Andrew was dazed, wondering how to penetrate it. Then darkness fell.

The enormity of the task and his own insufficiency attacked him. From the courtyard the bone-chilling lamentation of a wolf arose, answered by others scattered in the distance. So this was it. There would be no need for fortification or guards when the tower was ringed by the hard teeth of predators and when trackers watched the passes. Andrew clung to the rock. He had to go down. But where? How to enter? His skills were dulled, instincts blunted; his body a pitted ruin dragged from a tomb—a cistern bloated by death and a charnel house of plague. He knew doubt. The rocks held him. A cold wind moaned. What had Rafeo said? One step at a time. A way would be given. He slipped from the rock.

Andrew approached the wall carefully, fearing there were wolves nearby. He had no desire to meet them. The pain at his ankle was testament to how close he had come. Silently he blessed Rafeo for the heavy boots. Without them the beast would have ripped his foot off. He moved on the downside of the keep. The stonework resonated threat; a cold, gray grimace in the darkness. Feeble light cast by the stars guided him through a maze of shadows.

When Andrew stumbled over fallen stonework in the dark, pitching into sharp rock, he nearly cried out. He lay in pain and studied the stone wall above him closely. Here it was—a way was given. Broken by winter storm or neglect, stones from the wall had fallen.

Testing the unsteady rock, Andrew began to climb. He emerged where the wall knit into the keep itself. It was a short distance now to a cupola. Probing carefully for ridges in the stonework, Andrew scaled the wall of the keep, found the lip of the cupola and hoisted himself into it. A shuttered window, as he had expected, confronted him. It could be easily enough overcome, but he waited in silence, studying the feel, the texture, the sounds of the place. He heard no voices, nothing.

The shutter was fixed from the inside. Andrew could not risk snapping the knife by prying it open. He probed the gap between shutter and rock with the blade, found the shutter peg. It lifted easily and the shutter swung open, creaking on its hinges with a dismal whine. Andrew stepped inside and shut it behind him. He froze, listening for voices, then moved into the darkness of the room like a swimmer underwater. As his eyes adjusted to the dark, he saw that the room, probably constructed for guards at one time, was vacant. He slipped across it like a shadow.

Andrew edged through the door and stared into the heart of the circular tower. Far below a hearth cast a flickering light across a vast floor. It had to be at least thirty feet down. Below ground level? Andrew wondered. No. It had been built to the slope of the mountain. The front door would open to the valley; the back had to be built directly into the stone of the mountain. It was a fortress, with the cupolas and turrets guarding its façade.

The entire place breathed vacancy—a shell of stone.

Andrew stepped out onto a circular staircase that wound upward along the inner wall. It was pockmarked by several doorways like the one he had just come through, no doubt leading to other chambers built into the outer wall. The stairwell wound up past him for another dozen feet or so, ending near a beamed ceiling.

The design perplexed him. It had been built by someone who lived in fear; nothing opened outward here, everything led inward.

Inward. Yes. Andrew stepped down the stairwell, wondering as he did so at the vacancy of the place. Then it struck him. The protection came from outside—the treacherous keepers of the passes. Whoever dwelt here now, whoever had appropriated this hulk of rock from its mysterious past, either had not the means or felt no need for defenders at the gates. Whoever lived here now exercised a control that extended much further, through the network of trackers.

Someone aggressive, someone with a lust for power, thought Andrew. It seemed that he could sense that someone lurking somewhere deep in this ruin. Words leaked into his mind—"I have my own villa to the north." But this was not a villa: it turned inward on hiding and deceit rather than turning outward to sky and fields.

As he stepped down the stairwell, his eyes probed the shadowy space below him. Yes, as he guessed. He spotted the doorways now, leading off the floor of the stone tower.

Andrew studied their positions, etching the plan of the place into his mind in case, in the hurry of flight, he had to be certain of his bearings. The way out was as necessary as the way in. The corridors lay below ground level, as Andrew judged the depth of the keep. Where then could these corridors lead? To subterranean rooms? How could someone live in such confinement! Andrew listened to the vacancy, alert for sounds. There was nothing. Someone must have fed the wolves outside; they were quiet now.

He stepped downward toward the floor and halted at a door oddly positioned a few feet above it. The rooms would be larger as the corridor moved down, the rooms lodged between this inner sanctum and the outer walls of the edifice. It was an ingenious design. If the central keep were ever stormed by an invading force, its protectors could fight from the inside, protected by this winding staircase, as well as from the outer cupolas.

Well designed—in a former age when men were bodies thrown at bodies in an endless game of power, when this one place of decision meant vast territories surrounding it. That had been the intention; now the only protection needed was the utter remoteness of the place itself.

Andrew heard the footsteps first. Then a laugh. Winding up one of the corridors to the chamber of the central keep. From which corridor? All sounds reverberated against the stone. There *were* voices. Louder now. Andrew froze. He wondered if he could make a rush for one of the corridors. He distinguished several voices now. He reached behind him for the door on the passageway, pressed against it, and slipped inside.

Unlike the spareness of the upper room through which he had entered, this chamber near the floor of the keep held all the opulence of the southern nobles. It dazzled. For a moment he would have guessed himself inside one of the estates of Faenza. Oil lamps hung on the walls spewed golden light over tapestry-draped walls. The golden light fell to rich carpets and silken pillows. It fell to the canopied bed. And to the woman who sat upon it, her eyes flashing in the light like a dark cry.

She had been combing her hair. It fell in raven coils about her coppery shoulders. Her fierce eyes sliced into Andrew, pierced him to the door.

"Hadesseh," he breathed. Andrew took one step toward her.

"You fool!" she hissed.

CHAPTER EIGHTEEN

ords fumbled in his throat like sick things, each dying in the effort. Her anger struck him like fists. It wasn't just the anger; it was the pure scorn she emanated that assailed him.

This close! After all these years. And now his body went rigid under her despite. Impotency slammed through him. His longing drained away like water.

"Well, what do you have to say for yourself, Fontini?"

She abused him with the name, using it like a curse. And Andrew felt like a child again, ready to weep. She pulled the nightgown around herself, a gesture made to look like an insult.

"I . . . have wondered about you a long time, Hadesseh." How foolish the words from his lips sounded.

"Oh, I can imagine." Her words were like ice. "Was it very lonely in your villa?"

She stood, her eyes flashing. All these years, Andrew had seen a young girl from his dreams. Here stood a woman; the same, yet wholly other.

"Look at you, Fontini!"

"Don't say it."

"Don't. Don't! How darc you command me. Look at you, you filthy pig."

"It wasn't how you think," Andrew stammered. "I never knew you had left until you were gone. I didn't know what happened."

"You're still a child pleading. Yes, I was 'gone.' With what choice? What you didn't know killed me."

The understanding shocked him—she knew him only as *that boy.* In all these years she had no inkling of Andrew's longing. This man before her, he understood, was nearly unrecognizable—this scarred, pitted derelict in filthy coat and peasant clothes. This one who stank of the wilderness. And one who had disappeared out of her life without warning or farewell. How could he begin to explain?

His hands folded about his body, and he huddled there, object of his own scorn. Weakness. She must deny him; this he saw now. How else could she have survived all these years?

What on earth or heaven ever made him think she would be the least interested in ever seeing him again? *I am the past she wanted to bury.*

"Hadesseh, forgive me," he murmured.

"What are you doing here? I thought you were dead."

"Please."

"Answer me!"

Her words were whips. Andrew shut his eyes. "What answer can I give?"

"Did you think I wouldn't recognize you? Why didn't you die, Fontini?"

"Andrew."

"What?"

"Please say my name."

"Get out. Get out of here and leave me alone."

He raised his eyes to her. "Is this what you want, then?"

"Don't you see? This is your doing. *I never had a choice!* It happened right under your nose, and you didn't even notice."

"What? Why didn't you tell me? I would have done something."

"Oh, I tried. Why didn't *you* listen? What was I to say? *Your* best friend crept in my room and . . . What could I *say!* You didn't care. I was just your . . . playmate. Like everything else. You played with life and I suffered for it. And then you were gone. And I had nothing—but *this.*"

"Hadesseh, can you try to understand? Since the day you left—"

"I left?"

"Since that day I have never stopped looking for you." But his own words fumbled. *I could not,* he wanted to say. *Plague! I was stricken, desecration, outcast.*

"You never should have tried." Her words cut through his fumbling like rapiers.

"Why?" Andrew pleaded. "Are you happy here? Who keeps you here, anyway?"

"You had a choice. I didn't." Her voice had risen to a chill of malice, her body rigid with spite.

You should know how I used her, Andrew.

The words were poison. *Used.* How could she abide it? Andrew fought to control himself. He stood up.

"Can you tell me this, at least?"

"I will tell you nothing."

"I was traveling with three companions—"

"And what is that to me? Were they your friends too?"

"A religious man, a little girl—"

"That's fitting."

"And the old woman, Griselde."

She stepped backward. She felt for the bed and sat down. For the first time her eyes shifted from their bitter malice.

Suddenly her face twisted. "Griselde," she said. "She was the one who . . ." Her voice trailed off.

"Who loved you? Yes. Where is she?"

"Beyond your reach. Or mine." Her voice hardened again, but Andrew had detected the uncertainty behind it.

"How so?" he asked quickly. "Where are they?"

"Don't ask."

"Tell me, Hadesseh. For their sake. Not mine."

"I cannot." She shook her head, the raven hair falling across her face. "Don't ask me about them!"

"Who runs this place?" And then he gave words to his worst fear. "Is it Dominic?"

"I am his queen," she spat suddenly. "And would you know how I hate him?" Her voice grew shrill. "Is that what you want? So you can think you still own me? Very well, Fontini. I hate him even more than you."

"Hadesseh. For their sake, please tell me. Are they prisoners?"

"The priest is."

"And Helena?"

"The little girl? What harm is she? She lives with the wives of the trackers."

"Can you tell me where Emeth is?"

"Who?" She responded dully now. Her anger seemed suddenly spent, uncertain. Her fingers twisted before her, knotting the loose fabric of her nightgown.

"The religious man."

"I'm not sure. Let me think. Anyway, you can do nothing now. Wait." She put her hands to her face as if to still her own thoughts. "Someone may come in. You must hide somewhere." She stood up and paced the room. "No, it must be here," she muttered. "Here," she pointed to an alcove, separated from the room by a draped curtain. "Lie down in here. No, don't talk. Just don't say anything." Her tone was peremptory, her face a mask. "Do what I say. Do not forget, you are in my power. If I do anything at all, it is for Griselde. Not you."

"Hadesseh," Andrew said, following her to the alcove. He turned and met her fierce eyes, bewildered before them. "I love you with all my heart."

"Don't say that," she hissed. "Especially don't say that. Because I hate you with all of mine."

"It was you, wasn't it? Last autumn. The girl with the hawk. The boy?"

"I wish I had shot the arrow into your heart," she hissed. "I could, you know. I'm very good with it. What else do I have here?" But the anger seemed again to drain from her eyes. Desolation stood in them like booted heels, scarring her memory.

Hadesseh pointed Andrew to the alcove. She covered him with loose cloths and pillows, draping them hurriedly, and closed the curtain.

* * *

Andrew fought against sleep with all his will. Weariness washed over him. He trembled under the blankets, lying against the wooden bench of the alcove. In his mind was Hadesseh's face. For years it had seemed impossibly distant; now it was just on the other side of the curtain. Andrew realized that for all those years he had been able to read no expression on that face he saw in his dreams. It was always too distant, an imagining, his longing imposed upon it. The face on the other side of

232

the curtain had looked with scorn on that longing, and thrust it back on him. Andrew saw himself through her eyes. The look made him shiver with a fear he had not known for years. The eyes held no mockery—only rejection. Clean and brutally final. Before that look he was nothing, nothing at all. With those eyes boring in upon him, his own eyes shuttered and he gave in to sleep.

He awakened once hearing voices. He wanted to leap up. Was it Dominic, here with his prize? Andrew's body relaxed when he remembered the others he had come for. He could not hear the words. Only soft murmuring. Then footsteps, and it was quiet. Still he waited.

Waited. He was the one beckoned now, the helpless one. Was this how she had felt? He remembered the times he would find her weeping softly, or lost in some vague loneliness he had thought was homesickness, a longing for her dead parents. Just so he waited now.

He had no idea what time it was. The keep was quiet, washed in the thorough solitude of deep night. He had not slept long, he thought. His body had given in to exhaustion, but not rest.

When she parted the curtains, Hadesseh wore a common shift, tightly belted at the waist, and slippers. Her coppery, lithe beauty was undimmed by the years. Her hair fell like a flight of ravens, dark wings flecked with auburn in the firelight. Only her large dark eyes, those mysterious pools, were shielded by bitterness and anger.

As if reading Andrew's thoughts, she said, "I will show you the way. If they wish to leave with you, they will have opportunity. If not, you will leave anyway. And never see me again."

The words were intended to be daggers, as if carefully rehearsed to be flung at him, but now escaping her lips they lacked the force of certainty. She did not move. Nor did Andrew.

"Do you promise me?" she insisted.

"Yes, I . . ."

"No more words. I don't want to listen to you." Still she did not move. She peered closely at Andrew, her eyes raking his pitted, scarred flesh. Andrew felt naked before her gaze. "You *have* suffered, haven't you?" she said softly.

He didn't know how to respond.

As quickly as her eyes had softened—if only for a moment—the cold mask veiled them again. Impenetrable. "Let us go," she rasped.

She hurried down the last few steps of the stone staircase, as if she could not get Andrew away quickly enough. Without pause she crossed the floor of the keep. Even hurrying as they were, Andrew was struck by the place. The fire had lowered to embers but cast its glow across a forest of tapestries hung against the cold stone walls. Pillows nestled against the walls. To the side of the room stood a large table, nearly lost in shadow. Its surface was set with shining goblets and ornate dinnerware. Hadesseh brushed by them and strode to one of the four corridors.

Its narrow passage dove downward. Hadesseh seized a torch from the wall, returned to the fire and lit it. While the torch caught she spoke, almost as if Andrew were not there. Solely to impart information he needed to survive the night.

"Prisoners are rare," she said tonelessly. "After all, the wolves have to be fed somehow. And meat is scarce during the winter months."

"Is that what happened to Griselde?" It was too brutal to imagine.

She whirled and thrust the glowing torch at Andrew's face. He recoiled. "Don't say a word about Griselde."

"What happened to her?" Andrew insisted.

She walked ahead in silence, her footsteps echoing off the hard steps of the passageway. It was so close he had to walk bent over. "I tried to stop him," she said. "When they took the girl from her, Griselde fought him. She clawed at him. He struck her. Hard. I could not stop him."

"That old woman? What had she ever done—"

"Don't ask any more questions," she snapped.

Andrew swallowed his rage. He vowed he would not leave without retribution.

The corridor wound down through the mountain of rock, twisting around sharp escarpments. At such points Andrew felt crushed, as if he would never get around . . . or back out. Hadesseh paused. Breathing was close and difficult. "The corridors lead to places under the mountain," she said while waiting to catch her breath. "In one opening the trackers live with their families. Oh, it is not like this. It leads a long way through the mountain to a cave that opens on the face of the valley. They have fields there. Some grow vegetables and grapes. The wives do, anyway.

"This," she said as she began walking down again, "this is just a hole in the ground. He may not even be here anymore."

The steps were slippery with ooze, the walls cold and glinting. Like the mustiness of a vault, the air grew hard to breathe. The walls glittered with scaly, metallic flakes.

"Is that the same material in the rock—" he began asking.

"Yes. So you remember, Andrew. Yes, it is. And if I had the proper compounds, I would blow this whole stinking place to bits. Forget it. This is not Faenza."

But the thought had entered her mind. *I would blow this whole stinking place to bits!*

They turned into a low grotto and confronted a series of cells, untended, kept in blackness, three on either side. The cells were sealed with wooden doors. The rock squeezed oppressively close, as if it would crush them with a will of its own. The place stunk with centuries of decay.

"He is in here?"

"This is the dungeon." She rammed the torch into a rack and stood back.

"Go ahead and look." She pointed indefinitely at the first cell.

"Emeth?" he called. He peered through the slitted window of the wooden door, into the gloom that the light feebly sliced. A pallet lay on the floor, surrounded by stagnant water. A blanket lay curled on the pallet, covering a body.

"He's in there?" Andrew asked angrily.

Hadesseh stood behind him. She had moved back against the wall. "Perhaps he is ill," she said. There was a coldness to her voice, the ice of cruelty that chilled Andrew. "The keeper may have taken a day off. Who knows?"

He lifted the heavy wooden bar and tried the door. It seemed to have been unused for ages, cobwebs and dust covering its surface like a coat. The wooden door swung noisily outward, groaning on its thick hinges. Andrew paused with it open an inch or two.

"Will anyone hear?"

"This is deep underground. The people who built this place did not like to be disturbed by the screams of the prisoners. No one will hear."

He glanced back at her cold form. Her face was cast as hard as stone. And Andrew knew fear in the pit of his stomach. *This is what she has become, what I have permitted her to become.* He swung the door open and entered. The dungeon held the odor of sick rot; the pool of water lay black. Andrew hurried to the pallet and ripped aside the blanket. He shrank back in terror, barely able to suppress the scream that tore at his throat. Lying there, yellowed teeth and hollow eyes gaping at the light, was the skeleton of a man. As he turned he heard the door closing.

Andrew sprang to the door, throwing his weight against it, and fell back sprawling in the fetid ooze.

"Go ahead, Andrew. Scream now for help. No one will hear." Her words issued in a manic rush, high and breathless. "Call as I once called. When you ignored me. Go ahead. As no one heard me, so too no one will hear you."

But he did not scream. He had to know. "Where is Emeth?" Andrew pleaded. He thrust his face at the slitted window, feeling wood shards against his skin. "Is *this* Emeth?"

"Emeth?" The name seemed somehow to shock her.

"My friend."

She was quiet a long time, as if fighting some internal warfare. "No, you fool. That skeleton has been there since ancient times."

Andrew turned to the pallet. The blanket was of a newer make. Within the last few years someone had thrust it over the bones. But the skeleton had been picked clean by centuries of vermin. Its pale bones shone in the light. It was of a person far shorter than Emeth.

"Then where is he?"

"You're in a cell, Andrew. I want you to scream! You are in my power!"

"Yes. I know. But will you tell me, is he alive?"

"He means that much to you?" Her voice was touched with incredulity.

Andrew did not respond. How could he tell her? Once before he had been in a cell, in a fetid, stinking cistern, and Emeth had come *down* to him.

Suddenly the mask of her set features shifted and broke. She sagged and would have fallen had she not leaned against the door. From the slitted window Andrew could barely see her profile, and the tears that ran from her squeezed eyes. She shook against the door, terrible deep sobs wracking her, as if exploding out of some prison they had too long been kept in.

"You didn't even scream," she cried. "What kind of person are you, that you wouldn't even scream?"

"Hadesseh." Spasms of weeping shook her body. "Hadesseh, you have suffered much. If you are willing, let me help you. And if I cannot, I believe Emeth can."

"*Me?* No one can help me."

"Hadesseh," Andrew pleaded.

"Shut up. Why don't you cry yourself?"

It was a foolish thing to say. Absurd. But it struck a chord of need that was undeniable.

"Hadesseh."

She rose, faced the door. "I wasn't going to leave you there," she said. Her voice was touched with fear. "I only wanted you to . . ."

"I understand."

"I wanted you to know what it is like. To be forsaken. Then I was going to let you go. Make you go. I wanted to make you afraid."

"Yes."

"You won't hurt me?"

"Hadesseh, I will not hurt you. Nor will I let you be hurt."

Cautiously she lifted the heavy bar. Andrew opened the door slowly, but she shrank back like a small animal, vulnerable, exposed. Andrew shut the door on the dark tomb.

"Will you tell me now where Emeth is?"

"He was never here. He's with the trackers. He and the girl work in their fields."

"Like slaves?"

"It is better than—this!" Her voice shook. "It would have been here, if I hadn't fought him."

"Let's get out of here." There was more to her story, but this was not the time for telling. Andrew took her hand. She recoiled from the touch, then permitted him. He held the torch with the other hand and hurriedly led her back up the steps.

* * *

That Emeth and Helena were with the trackers was an act of grace—Hadesseh's. In her room she told Andrew how it happened. When the three had been brought to the keep, Dominic had ordered all of them to the dungeon. The trackers had dragged them across the keep, Hadesseh watching from the stair. She had recognized the old woman, shouted her name. When Dominic's men carried Helena toward the stairs, Griselde had gone insane with fury. She pleaded with Hadesseh. Dominic had laughed in her face, ordering them down the stairs. Breaking the hold of a tracker, Griselde had flung herself on Dominic, clawing at his face. He slammed her back, blood streaming down his cheek. Dominic seized a whip from one of the trackers, reversed it in his hand and struck Griselde across the forehead with its heavy, bludgeon grip. The old woman fell.

Dominic ordered her body to be thrown to the wolves. Nothing Hadesseh could do, none of her beseeching words, could avert his command. He was livid with rage. And so they had thrown her unconscious into the courtyard where the wolves had torn her. Then the fury died out of Dominic, and Hadesseh's pleas for the others prevailed. Because of her, Helena and Emeth were put in the care of the trackers to work as their slaves.

"They expected you to follow," Hadesseh concluded. "I think that is the real reason they were kept alive. As bait. To lure you. For days they watched the trail, wanting to take you by surprise. When the snows kept coming, they concluded that you had perished on the trail."

She was sitting on the bed, telling Andrew this, while he paced the room, all the while plotting a way to free them. It had to be by stealth. The trackers were too many. Yet he could not find a way. Suddenly she surprised him by asking, "Why are you so dangerous?"

"What?"

"What makes Dominic fear you so?"

Andrew pondered it. No, he decided. He could not tell her his story now. No matter how he longed to. No matter how he hoped it would restore her trust. To do so now would be leverage, a manipulation, and she had suffered enough. She must choose herself, according to her own evidence. Yet he could not resist tempting her choice. "Perhaps because he fears losing you," he said.

"Hah! I am nothing to him. His kept woman."

"Is he here now?"

"No. Do you think I would have taken you through his keep if he were?"

"Do you think I would have minded?"

She paused, in that way of reflection she had always had, as if probing inwardly before committing herself to words.

"You are no longer Fontini, are you?"

"The Fontini Villa no longer exists," Andrew answered. "But where is he?"

"He does not confide in me. I would guess he has left on some business.

To oversee the first transport, possibly. He is sometimes gone for weeks at a time. Then again, he may be back in the morning."

There was urgency, then. Andrew walked to the shuttered window and opened the covering. The room faced the west, but the dimmest sheen of morning light could be seen. There, hanging in the northwestern sky lay a bright star.

"Look."

She rose and came to his side. He sensed an easing of her revulsion. "Your name means 'the Star,' " he murmured. "So I have followed."

She looked at him strangely, then murmured, "My name is all I kept."

"Will you tell me how to get to them? Then I will leave. And I will follow you no more. You too have chosen."

"Yes," she said. "Don't forget it." But her voice was bereft of assurance. "Only, you cannot go to them now. Wait until nightfall. See, it is almost morning."

"I'll go now, I think."

"No." Her voice was adamant. "There are a dozen or more trackers. They are wild men, born here in the mountains. Even Dominic doesn't fully trust them. This place was theirs before it was his."

"A way will be given."

"Don't be a fool. Think about it. Emeth and Helena are not you! They will need cover of darkness to escape. And you need rest. Look at yourself. Besides, one more day will make no difference."

"What if Dominic returns?"

"Then he returns. Isn't that what you really want?"

She seized his arm, roughly, but the touch sent a shiver the length of his body. Once more he let her lead him to the alcove. Andrew lay down and fell almost immediately into an exhausted sleep.

* * *

He awakened the instant the curtain parted. The slightest motion of the air drove him into recoiling. Again Hadesseh peered at him with those wide, startled eyes.

"It has been arranged," she said hurriedly. "I have sent orders to the trackers that I have need for the two. They should be here within the hour."

"The trackers obey you?" She *was* queen of this keep, Andrew reminded himself. Yet she had said they were independent, not even Dominic's tools. Her order could have stirred curiosity, since it doubtlessly contravened Dominic's own commands.

"Apparently," she said, as if surprised herself. "Dominic is not here, and I gave them no opportunity to discuss it. Anyway, it would have been impossible for you to take them from the trackers themselves. They and their . . ." She shuddered.

"The wolves?"

"The trackers are beasts themselves. There is no difference. I ordered that the two be brought to the central keep. But first, I have food for you."

"Thank you." Andrew realized that he was famished.

"And," she said, eyeing him disdainfully, "water. You may bathe first."

His laughter must have surprised her. His peasant clothes were worn and baggy. Blood from the wolf's fangs lay caked with mud on his legs. She pointed to the water basin and turned her back on him, pretending to find something of interest out the window.

Quickly Andrew stripped off his shirt and began washing. The water was frigid. He scrubbed furiously. From the light he judged it as late afternoon. The bath was refreshing, the icy water tingling the flesh like needles.

"What is that scar from?" she asked. She had turned to watch him without his knowing it. Andrew was reaching for his shirt. He twisted so that she would not see the knife at his back. "It is nothing. An accident."

"It looks like a snake," she said.

"Yes. I guess it does."

Quickly he pulled the shirt on.

"Why do you wear a knife at your back?"

So she had seen! "You ask too many questions, Hadesseh. You always did."

Suddenly she too laughed. For the first time. How long had it been? "And you are always too short of answers. It is the knife of the Kwaljin. It is a sacred knife. How did you come by it?"

"I know nothing of the Kwaljin."

"But I do. I know many things you don't, Andrew." Her eyes glittered dangerously.

Is she mocking me? he wondered. For a moment she seemed once more

240

the young Hadesseh, eyes bright and teasing, a hauteur in her knowledge.

"Such a knife is never found," she said. "It is only given."

"How do you know this? It is not of your people."

"No. It certainly isn't. But they did know weapons. And they knew of the Kwaljin, the warrior priests from the eastern deserts. Answer me, Andrew." There was urgency in her tone.

"I cannot. I swear I cannot. I found it among my father's things. I have no idea how he came by it, or what it meant to him. It would have been better had you not seen it."

"Very well." But her eyes beheld him differently. For the first time, it seemed, they studied him. And Andrew grew uncomfortable under her probing gaze.

"How did you hurt your ankle?"

"I fell."

"I don't mean that. Any fool can tell it was broken at one time. And poorly set. I meant the bite. It is a wolf bite, isn't it? The skin is torn."

"A tracker. On the way in. With his wolf."

"And?"

"They are dead."

She fixed him with her gaze, as if testing the truth of his words. "Why don't you eat, Andrew? I have food for you."

He stood anxiously by the small table, eating hurriedly of the vegetables and bread she had brought. He left a round of cheese untouched. The wine tasted like a vintage near Faenza. Andrew was surprised to find that he preferred the robust vigor of Sanjeani's wine now.

"When will they be here?"

"A little while yet. I asked that they be presentable. And fed. When they come, you are to leave at the first sign of darkness."

"And never return?"

"Precisely, Andrew. It is finished."

"Has he been that good to you?"

"It's none of your business. But I told you. I hate him."

"Why do you stay?"

"I have no choice."

"You can come away with me. I can find a safe place for you."

"For what? Where? To be *your* kept thing rather than his?"

Andrew had no answer. He had nothing to offer. "Will you tell me what happened? How you left?"

"No."

"He told me he had abused you."

She was silent. Andrew heard her sit down on the bed behind him. He turned to her. "Will you tell me, Hadesseh? Tell me and I'll leave. Understand, it is for your sake that I ask."

"There's nothing to tell." She averted her eyes. Her fingers toyed nervously with the bed covering. Over and over the trembling fingers twisted its edge.

"Hadesseh," Andrew said softly. "I cannot leave without knowing you are at peace. Then I will leave gladly."

"You want me to have suffered, don't you? You want me to *need* you."

"I think your courage prevents you from admitting your need. That is a dangerous thing. That is the thing I fear. Once I found myself at that same point."

"And?"

"Someone showed me the courage to die for me."

"Emeth?"

"Yes."

"No wonder then about your loyalty to him. But, you see, I have no such one. Perhaps only those who have suffered greatly possess the courage not to speak of their suffering. Who can stand the whine and sniffling of the weak?"

"But do you *want* to speak of it? That is the question. Not whether you dare."

"No." The hard cast of her beautiful face shifted, came close to breaking. She denied him the gift of tears. "No. It is done."

"Silence is a kind of protection, isn't it?" He knelt before her.

"Yes." She trembled. "Yes."

"Silence is the grave in which one buries fear."

"I know that. Don't torment me."

"Only it is not dead. It must be drawn out and confronted. One must learn to live with it, to name it, to understand it. And thereby to master it."

"I cannot."

"Yet you can begin by telling me. Is there anyone else, Hadesseh, who will listen?"

"I don't want to tell you."

"Believe that I want to hear. For one moment set aside your hatred. Speak only to my ears, not my person. And I will listen."

Her breath came in quiet gasps, as if she were drowning in the very air she breathed. She trembled, then, in a spasm, went rigid. "I am his queen," she spat. She trembled under the words, loathing the taste of them, then pressed her hands savagely into her face and wept.

Andrew reached out, touched her hand. She permitted him. And then she did this incredible thing. She lifted her hand to his own ravaged cheek, let her hand slip behind his neck and drew him to her. He trembled on her breast like a child, while she clung to him.

"What are you doing!"

The sharp voice whipped Andrew around like a leash. His body involuntarily went tense, fists ready to strike. He leapt from the bedside. Hadesseh flung her hand to his shoulder as he whirled, her fearful cry brushed aside.

The speaker did not move. He stood before Andrew—this wild man in peasant clothes—as if studying a thing, his eyes level and bold.

"Answer me," he insisted. He made no threat to call guards or trackers. He simply insisted with an adamancy that could not be denied.

Seeing it was a boy, a very young boy, Andrew forced his body to relax. Andrew took one step forward, and the boy did not move. His black hair wreathed an unperturbed face of coppery hue. The eyes . . . those pitiless eyes insisted on answers. The shock of them stunned Andrew like a blow. That face! He had seen it. It was in Hadesseh's parchments! A face she had seen before he was born. The blow of recognition staggered Andrew, driving him back.

"He is a friend," Hadesseh said guardedly.

"Friend?" The boy looked at the couch with disbelieving eyes. He couldn't have been more than four or five, yet he bore an air of maturity that disturbed Andrew profoundly.

He peered intently at Andrew. Those eyes would not break off. There was no denying the stubborn pride in his bearing.

"Believe me."

"Tell me," the boy insisted.

"No!" Hadesseh said. "No questions now."

"Then I'll tell my father." He turned and left.

CHAPTER NINETEEN

ndrew turned to Hadesseh slowly, as if weights rooted his body to rock. She sat bowed on the couch, hands wrung to her forehead.

"Father?"

She nodded, still holding up her hands as if shielding herself. "That was the bargain."

"Your life for his."

"Yes." Her voice was toneless, a raw scraping in her throat. "So now you know," she sighed. "He gave the boy a name. Me a home. A life."

A *home*. The word ripped at Andrew's heart. She was the unhomed.

Hadesseh sat weeping, the only sound in the room, a sound which scraped Andrew's heart. The raven hair cascaded about coppery shoulders, like black rain poured over her face.

Andrew took one step toward her—poised on a rope bridge over a chasm of pain—and was stopped by the knocking at the door.

Hadesseh made no motion to answer. She was beyond caring. Again that knock. Insistent. Demanding. Was it the boy returning? Or Emeth and Helena! Andrew turned back to the door and opened it.

The tracker looked at him with a spasm of surprise, for a moment undecided whether to fight or flee. He was not undecided long. A smile worked over his thick features, rubbery lips peeling back over broken teeth. Andrew moved first. He caught the man's arm, wrenching it behind his back. But he had no leverage in the narrow doorway. By brute force the tracker carried Andrew on his back into the stairwell. Andrew could feel the huge muscles on the man's squat body bunching. The tracker twisted around. Andrew was no match for his strength, and he could not let him escape. He released his hold and tried to place a foot blow. The kick landed on the rigid muscle of the tracker's thigh and rebounded as if it had struck rock.

The man had no intention of fleeing now. He sensed the opportunity, and moved in with the instincts of a predator. The grin on his face shone now with pure malice. Tiny eyes glowed in his face. A slip of saliva clung to his whiskered chin. Andrew backed off, gave him room. He was conscious of Hadesseh standing in the doorway and hissed a warning at her. Andrew wanted to take this man alive. He wanted answers. Where were Emeth and Helena? He backed across the doorway and feigned a stumble.

The man's lunge was clumsy, but dangerous as a wolf's. The huge legs rocked forward. Andrew sidestepped, twisted, hammered him behind the ear with a blow that had all his power in it. Power, but not the lethal force of leverage. The man sprawled, staggered into the room, lost balance, skidded across the floor and slammed into the bed. He raised his shaggy head, shook it with a befuddled expression. The slitted eyes found Andrew.

Again that powerful body hurtled. Again Andrew tried to sidestep. His stumbling was not feigned this time. As he moved, his foot caught on the wrinkled rug. He felt his legs going, fought for balance. The tracker snagged one huge arm around him and flung him into the stone wall. Then those massive arms locked around him, the eyes growing wide with delight. His grin widened as he measured Andrew's pain. He bit on his own tongue with the effort to crush.

Andrew flailed at his face, trying to drive his thumbs toward those slitted eyes. Feeble efforts. Defeated. Andrew could no longer see what he struck at. He found a black curtain rushing, falling, covering his own eyes.

Then the hold suddenly relaxed. Andrew saw the tracker's eyes again; they narrowed. The pupils suddenly rolled upward. Slowly the body collapsed.

Andrew bent heaving for breath, fighting the fire that raged along his ribs. He looked up and saw Hadesseh standing before him. The iron poker that was in her hand fell, clattering on the stone floor. She raised her hands to her mouth in fear.

"Did I kill him?" she whispered.

Andrew knelt to him. The pulse raced under the ropes of neck muscle.

"No." Andrew said. "I need him. But first . . ." He ripped loose a tie from the curtains, a thick piece of braided silk, and bound the man securely at wrists and ankles. Then he threw the soiled bath water, with a certain degree of pleasure, in the man's face.

"Is he the one you talked to?" Andrew asked. The man's eyes were rolling. He began to struggle against the bonds even before he was fully conscious.

"Yes. He's their leader. I don't know his name, though."

"Would the boy have told him I was here? If so, there will be others."

"No. He wouldn't. I don't know."

Andrew slapped the man sharply across the face. "Why didn't he bring them? Emeth and Helena?"

"I don't know." Then as if she could not help herself, "Andrew, I'm afraid."

"Don't be. You're his queen." Andrew hadn't intended the remark cruelly. Simply as a statement of fact. Still, she shrank back from him.

"No, I'm not, I'm a prisoner too. Don't you understand?"

"We'll get the truth out of him."

"Then what?"

"Then I'll get Emeth and Helena."

"Just like that? Andrew, you can't. You see what he did to you. He was about to kill you."

I was taken by surprise, Andrew was about to say. *I was thinking of you; not of the threat.* How could he explain? He had to believe he could succeed, by force if necessary. Take them all. Either that or give up now. Andrew fought through his own doubt to a core of outrage. He allowed himself to be succored by anger. Who did Dominic think he was! He slapped the man again, harder.

The tracker was fully awake now, struggling against the ropes.

"Why didn't you take the captives?"

"I don't take orders from . . . *her,*" and with a sneer he spat at Hadesseh. Andrew snapped his fingers to the man's throat. The tracker's eyes were torches glowing with hatred.

"Where are they?"

Before the tracker could spit at him too, Andrew squeezed on his windpipe. The thick body began to writhe.

He felt Hadesseh's hand on his shoulder, shook it off. He increased the pressure, slipping fingers down to the artery.

"Talk!"

The tracker nodded, his face dark red.

"They wait in the cave," he gasped. "For the master only. Not you."

"Guarded?"

He nodded.

Andrew pressed down. "How many?" He loosened his grip. "It doesn't matter," he muttered, and released his hold.

Andrew knew he had to act quickly. The other trackers would know the man was gone, and why. He couldn't stay here. Andrew pivoted the man to his feet. He wavered unsteadily with wrists and ankles bound. Andrew drove his fingers into the pressure point at the nape of his neck, remembering Catillo's final lessons. As the man went limp, Andrew shifted him over his shoulder. Without a word to Hadesseh he walked down the stairs, across the floor of the keep and toward the dungeon corridor, balancing the tracker's weight clumsily over his shoulders.

Urgency fueled each step. Through the window at the front of the keep Andrew saw shades of evening settling. A distant motion caught his eye. With the heavy body still draped over his shoulder, Andrew stepped toward the window and peered into the uncertain light. Far down the road came a horseman. Leading a laden wagon. They were distant, too far to see clearly. But he felt it in the very insolence with which the horseman approached. It was Dominic.

Andrew's first impulse was to get the tracker down to the dungeon and then find his way to the cavern. He hurried to the door, but stopped again. Things were happening too fast. Out of control. How would he free the others? Or find them? The tracker had to be the key.

Andrew called out to Hadesseh.

She appeared at the door of her room.

"Which corridor do I take?"

"Where?" Her voice was faint, bewildered.

"To the trackers."

"You cannot fight them. They are too many."

"Will you tell me, Hadesseh? Even now he approaches the gate. There's not a moment to lose." There was no need to identify the *he*.

She pointed toward the easternmost corridor.

"There. It opens into a cave on the face of the mountain. As I told you."

Could he trust her? Andrew remembered her slamming the dungeon door on him. *I want you to scream.* He had no choice. He ran toward the corridor, leaving her call to him echoing at his back.

Don't follow, he pleaded silently. *Act. Disguise. Keep him occupied.*

How much time do I have? Andrew went cautiously now, partly because the corridor was absolutely dark—the trackers knew this rock as their home and had no need for torches. He could not risk being caught by surprise.

It would take Dominic some time to make his way up the winding road. Would he oversee the unloading of the wagon? Would it be too dark? Would he talk to Hadesseh?

Andrew staggered under the weight of the tracker. He set him down. The only sound was the ragged heaving of his own breath. He felt for the man's ankles and sliced the cord with his knife. Andrew reached for the man's face to slap him awake, and sensed the flicker of movement. His jaws snapped at Andrew's hand. The tracker writhed to free himself, but in an instant the point of the knife rode the ridge of his jaw. Before the tracker could scream Andrew hissed him to silence.

"Not one word, not a sound without my command. Is that understood?"

Silence. Andrew could sense the struggle of will. He pressed the knife point again.

"Understood?"

The man growled assent. Andrew relieved the pressure.

"Here's what we're going to do. You will walk ahead of me. Slowly. One motion to run and I'll . . ." He left it unfinished. "Lead me to them. And there you will order their release, in the name of Dominic. Understand?" Andrew hissed.

His outrage was at Dominic, not the tracker. Dominic was responsible for this . . . this travesty of secrecy and opulence. For the death of Griselde. For the bartering with Hadesseh for the life of a young boy. But

Andrew let the tracker feel his anger for Dominic; perhaps a little fear on his part could at least help free Emeth and Helena.

As they moved down the corridor, Andrew saw the flickering of light. "Are we nearing the opening?"

The tracker muttered assent.

"You know what to do." It was a command.

But nearing the mouth of the cave, Andrew hesitated. "Wait," he said to the tracker.

The man stopped obediently. In the dull light Andrew saw a smile inch across his face. Andrew wished he could read his thoughts. He needed a plan. The worst thing he could do was to rush into the tracker's domain, perhaps becoming vulnerable to *his* plans. But even now Dominic could be in his keep. Asking questions.

And Emeth and Helena waited. What was he to do once he had them? How would they escape? Vainly he ransacked his memory of Rafeo's maps. They had shown nothing of this part of the mountain.

The fingers of light fumbled into the darkness from the tunnel's mouth. There were at once too few and too many options. Too many unknowns.

He prodded the tracker ahead of him, reminding him none too gently of the bite of the knife.

The corridor broadened gradually. The light grew. The air stirred. They emerged on a slight plateau, above a winding stair crudely cut into the rock. The cave below was vast enough to hold individual houses plastered of rock to the stone walls of the cave. A small village lay in the shelter of the cave's entrance. Cooking fires spumed; here and there children ran among the hovels. Women moved from fires to houses. Andrew counted ten such dwellings ringing the floor.

The light came from the cooking fires. Beyond the mouth of the cave, which opened upon a vast stretch of fields, night had settled. It had taken longer to travel the corridor than Andrew guessed. He could see a small group of men gathering outside the entrance to the cave.

He saw none inside the cave. Some, he told himself, would be doing their duty, watching the trails. Or they would be off-loading the wagon. Andrew studied the patch of huts below. His eye caught a splash of blond curls among the dusky figures. He nearly cried out. Helena was wearing a mere rag of clothing, poor guard against the increasing chill of night. The men from the field approached the cave. Emeth was not among them.

"Where is he? The man?"

The tracker pointed. Andrew spotted a hut at the end of the hovels. It was a cone-shaped structure, windowless, standing by itself like some animal pen. The door was barred.

"In there?"

The man nodded.

"Bound?"

He shrugged.

How far can I use this man? Andrew wondered. Not far. He was caged, waiting. His humiliation burned in him. Andrew wondered if he could keep him under control long enough to return through the corridor. Night would be on the keep now. He had to find the trail he knew. He wished he had Rafeo's maps with him. They seemed to blur in memory to a hopeless maze.

"You will do this if you wish to live," Andrew snapped. Again a dull, cunning smile crept across the man's face. His eyes avoided Andrew. "You will stand and call out these words. And these only: Release the captives. The master requires them. Send them up to me."

The tracker moved to the head of the stair.

"Not there. Over here. By the wall." Andrew stood behind him in the shadows, the knife poised against his neck. "One mistake and you're the first to go."

The tracker turned to the circle of huts below. His voice thundered out Andrew's words.

The people stopped their activity, stunned to silence. Everyone stood in place.

"Tell them to move!"

"They don't understand the words."

"What?"

"Only I speak with the tongue of the south." The man turned his head, grinning evilly at Andrew.

Andrew saw the trackers by the cave entrance milling uncertainly. They recognized the leader's voice, not the words. *If necessary, I can take them!* Andrew thought. *All of them.*

"Then speak their language. Remember." He pressed with the point of the knife. There could be no mistakes now. The tracker winced at the bite on his neck. Andrew read the struggle on every inch of the man's face—

250

how he wanted to deceive. But the price would be his own life, a price too costly. Only madmen and martyrs do this freely, and the tracker was neither.

Words roared forth from him, and Andrew was strangely shaken by them. He had a strange sensation that he knew those words. Where? How? He remembered the crude attempts he had made at pronouncing the words on Brusca's parchments, with absolutely no sense of the sound of the language. He was certain of it: these were the words of the parchment. Of course, he thought. These were the survivors of some earlier invading force from the north. They had adapted to the mountains, living cut off from their former life. They had made their home here, and for them a long-past war never ended.

Andrew didn't understand the words the man used. He had to pretend, enough so to convince the man against deceit.

The language wandered confusedly in his mind. All those hours! If only he had mastered the language. Had the appropriate sounds to match the meanings. The sounds he had made were gibberish in his own ears. *Keep it simple,* he commanded himself. *One word, one phrase. No more.*

As best he could, Andrew voiced remembered words from the gospel account.

"Tell them: 'Make haste.' "

The tracker swung half-around, eyes blazing, confused. Andrew barely restrained him. Only the point of the knife kept the man from exploding into action. The tension was physical; Andrew could feel it, uncertain how it would go. He tensed his arm to plunge the knife. *Yes. I will,* he told himself.

The tracker recognized it. He thundered the words back at the village. The others below scurried together.

Again Andrew commanded the tracker. "Let the child come unto me, and the man. Do not hinder them."

The man spoke the words, but too quickly and too angrily for Andrew to follow. Confusion!

Someone looked about for Helena. An old woman, who came running with Helena, pointed upward. Helena looked about befuddled. They dragged Emeth from the hut—a gaunt, feeble shadow. They shoved the two toward the stairs and stood back, milling about anxiously.

As Emeth and Helena stumbled to the stairs the four men below surrounded them in a loose phalanx. Andrew read the deceit in the tracker's words. He was helpless before it. They were using Helena and Emeth as hostages. One of them grinned evilly and drew a knife. They stepped forward slowly, Emeth and Helena caught in their midst.

No options. Andrew's grip tightened on the tracker. He felt the man's muscles harden to resist. It was hopeless.

* * *

A fumbling, grotesque figure shambled into the mouth of the trackers' cavern. He made harsh rumbling sounds in his massive chest, sounds that ripped through the tension of the stony silence.

He shuffled in sideways, arms swinging, huge shoulders rolling. Hair fell over his face, nearly shutting out the eyes. The crooked mouth gaped. A noise broke through the rubbery lips.

The people turned, falling back nervously before the deformed creature.

Gregor lifted his massive head and shook it like some enraged animal. He shook his arms. Again the noises fumbled through his lips. They were, Andrew realized, in the language of the trackers. Gregor shook his head wildly as he grunted sounds, his eyes running over the people.

A few of the women prostrated themselves, faces to the floor, hands out in supplication.

The men fell back, reaching for weapons. Andrew felt the man in his grip suddenly fall to his knees, and Andrew was powerless to do anything about it. His own body seemed to turn numb.

Gregor shuffled into the cavern, striding in his awkward, shambling gait toward Emeth and Helena. They did not move.

One tracker foolishly darted toward Gregor, knife drawn. Gregor whipped one huge arm out like a battering ram, catching the man and flinging him back against the wall. But not before the man's knife drew a long gash down Gregor's arm. He shuffled forward, unmindful of the blood dripping from outstretched fingers.

Gregor stopped before Emeth and Helena. He bent forward, extending one hand in a beckoning motion, his thick lips muttering unintelligible sounds.

Helena—brave Helena—stepped toward that hand.

Andrew nearly shouted out, No!

But with infinite tenderness Gregor scooped her up. She clung to his neck, blond head against his tangled mass of hair.

Gregor reached out his dripping arm and wrapped it around Emeth, then half-carried him up the stairs.

He stood then before Andrew. The tracker scuttled sideways against the rock. Gregor's eyes slid off to him, then tried to focus on Andrew, who stood there like one frozen. At last Gregor's eyes met his. Gregor bent down, released Emeth and Helena, then straightened. His massive shoulders hunched over; his head was at the level of Andrew's chest. But the eyes held him, looking long and deeply into Andrew's. Gregor blinked once. His lips twitched in what may have been a smile. He muttered a sound that sounded like, "Go."

"Come with us," Andrew said.

Gregor shook his head violently. Hair fell into his eyes. "Go," he said. And he turned his back on them, facing out toward the trackers. They had regrouped. Several had found wooden spears. They stood cautiously at the bottom of the stairs. One pointed up at him. They babbled angrily. Blood pumped in steady spurts down Gregor's arm. Once more, he rumbled, "Go."

Andrew picked Helena up and carried her, forgetting how heavy a young child can be as she squeezed his neck and buried her face in his long hair. His mind was racing. If the keep was quiet they could climb the stairs and leave by the same guardroom through which Andrew had entered. Hadesseh's room would be closer to the ground outside, but he wanted to avoid her. She had exacted the promise from him.

They went as quickly as they could along the crypt-black corridor. After the first turning they heard something like the sound of a roar at their backs. Then they were deep in the mountain's belly. Andrew kept the lead with Helena in one arm, hand out to feel the damp wall for guidance. Emeth hobbled behind. Freedom was the spur to him. He sensed it, forcing himself along, calling up diminished reserves.

Andrew thought he saw a change of the darkness and slowed his pace. How long had they been gone? Would Dominic be waiting? Light crept into the corridor. Perhaps Dominic had not yet entered. Perhaps he had come and knew nothing of the day's events. That was impossible! The boy would tell him. Or the trackers. Maybe even now they sped through the corridor behind them. No. Andrew thought of Gregor, the faithful, final protector of Fontini Villa, standing atop the stairs, huge fists clenched even as the blood pooled about him.

He hurried on.

They emerged at the floor of the keep. A fire had been lit at the hearth, but Andrew neither sensed nor saw any movement, or any sign of people. Where were they?

Cautiously he stepped out, signaling Emeth and Helena to silence. He put Helena down and pointed to the staircase. They moved ahead of him, Andrew following to guard against any attack. They were crossing the keep, quickly now, toward the staircase. Andrew's instincts were so tensely strung that he sensed the slight disturbance before seeing anything. Behind me! At the pillar by the corridor they had just come from. Andrew sprung like the serpent striking as the figure emerged. He had committed himself to a lethal blow, was moving, could no longer stop, even as he saw in a flash of horror that his target was the boy, his eyes started in terror. Andrew collided heavily against him, turning his body in the last instant so that he absorbed the impact as he slammed into the pillar, dragging the boy behind him.

Andrew sprang to his feet, lifting the boy. About to ask if he was all right, Andrew noticed his face—bruised, battered. The boy's eyelids were swollen to mere slits.

"Is it you?" the boy asked fearfully. "She told me to wait here."

"Who?"

"My mother. I'm afraid."

"Who beat you?"

He trembled, fought tears.

"Never mind. What is it?"

"He has hit me before." His voice was plaintive, as if something had cracked and broken in his world. "Not as bad as this. He wanted to hurt me. Mother told me to wait for you. That you would come back."

Andrew dropped to one knee, holding the boy's trembling shoulders. He swayed forward into Andrew's arms.

"What is it? Tell me."

"Help us."

"Is that what your mother wants?"

"She asked if you would come to her room. She said you would come back this way. I've been waiting. But when I saw the others with you . . .

I didn't dare."

Andrew picked him up and ran to the stairs where Emeth and Helena stood. He brushed past them, into Hadesseh's room. He saw her, but saw no one he recognized. She had been brutally beaten, one lip broken open. She clung to him, shivering like a caged animal.

"He did this?"

She nodded.

"Why?"

She pulled away from him, looked nervously at the door where Emeth and Helena stood. She crossed to close the door.

"He knows you're here."

"How?"

"I can't tell you."

But Andrew knew. *I'll tell my father!*

"Where is he?"

"He went with the trackers to the cave."

"We didn't see him. Why not through the corridors? You knew I was there."

She nodded. "I told him you were fleeing from the cave. And . . . and," she looked at Andrew as if he would not believe her, "he is afraid of the corridors. He never enters them." She suddenly began laughing—a manic, high laugh like a cry. "He is afraid of dark places." The laughter broke in tears.

"Mother," the boy whimpered. Emeth held him.

"I believe you," Andrew said. He searched her eyes and found the hollow depths of loneliness and desperation there.

"He asked me where you would take them."

"And?"

"I said back to Faenza."

"He believed that?"

"That was when he beat me."

"And the boy?"

"Yes." She looked at him, bewildered. "Will you take us with you?"

Andrew was tempted to press her, to ask her if she were certain, but his heart leapt at her question, and all he could do was gently stroke her tangled hair.

"Quickly. Gather what you need."

"We have all we need. I don't want anything of his."

"The boy too?"

"Yes. Especially. He can't survive here, not like this."

Andrew nodded. "Take coats," he said, retrieving his own from the alcove. "It will be cold at night."

Quickly Hadesseh opened a trunk. She found enough outer garments for the others.

"Out your window then. To the back trail. Quickly."

He glanced back at the room as they left. The golden goblets, the opulent tapestries and silken pillows. Unhomed. But this time she had chosen. On impulse he returned, swept the remains of their earlier meal, the round of cheese, some vegetables and dried meat, into his pockets.

He needed nothing else.

CHAPTER
TWENTY

I t had started to snow again. Impossible. Andrew wanted to shout at the sky: Not now!

The flakes grew quickly in intensity. Climbing down the fallen rock to the outside level, their feet slipped dangerously. None of them was in condition to hurry, Andrew thought. None of them was able to. *This is monstrous.* A horrible mistake, a mad comedy of slipping and stumbling among the rocks. He grabbed hands, steadied bodies, as they climbed toward the mountain trail.

Precisely as they reached it, and huddled there gasping for breath, they heard the eerie ululation of wolves far in the distance.

"They are far away," Andrew assured. "Don't worry. Single file now and stay close to the mountain."

The order was needless. Almost immediately, as they moved out around the trail, the gorge yawned in the darkness—a black hole filled with blowing snow, a vast emptiness. Andrew followed them at the rear, ears tuned to the night sounds, desperately afraid to hear the howl again.

Hadesseh had picked up Helena and was carrying her at the front of the small file. Following her came the boy, then Emeth. Andrew realized suddenly that he was relying on her. Could he trust her leading? Did she sense that he had to remain at the rear?

He remembered her old sense of all things of earth and sky, her familiarity with nature. Was it still there? She was no longer the same young girl Andrew knew as they plodded into the night.

Nor was he Fontini any longer.

He had his own work now. He must stand guard, like Gregor. The image of the man moved pitifully through Andrew's mind. The sacrifice! They had to make it! Too many had sacrificed too much.

The snow fell more heavily in great white flakes, occasionally twisted by a plume of wind. A blessing after all, Andrew realized. It would cover their tracks.

Dominic too had to make choices. Would he believe they had fled south? It would make sense. Or did he, in his cunning, guess the truth? There was no home anymore. Dominic had made sure of that.

For the first time it occurred to him *who* had burned the villa. How Dominic must have hated him. When did friendship turn to this? What kind of devil lived in his heart? Even now, Andrew believed, there had to be at least one spark of regret in Dominic. Then he remembered the face looking down at his as he lay in the cistern, a face of absolute scorn and rejection. A face ravaged by a lust for power and envy.

No. He was coming. Andrew felt it with a chill deeper than the night air. He was coming.

But what trail would he take if he came north? Did he know of Rafeo's retreat? Andrew prayed he did not.

Andrew tried to keep the group moving as quickly as possible. The one sound he did not want to hear—the howl of tracking wolves—was blessedly absent. But he was still uneasy.

If they were tracking—trained as they were—they would do so silently!

* * *

Andrew called a brief halt when he saw Emeth stumble. They huddled in the lee of a rock along the narrow ledge, gathering strength from their common need. Although Hadesseh sat slightly apart with her son, as if still distrustful, Andrew felt her draw toward them. Rapidly Andrew told Emeth and Helena of his rescue by Rafeo and the winter months on his mountain. He gave them rough directions on how to reach it, but did not give the reason. *If I am taken, they must still break free. I am the one Dominic wants.*

Emeth was panting weakly. Throughout the winter he had been forced out like a pack mule to gather firewood. He had been the beast of burden, carrying loads on his back. Since the first thaw he had labored in the fields, only to return each night to the tiny hut, where he received scraps from the evening meal. The labor had not bowed him; near starvation had. Helena had seen his need and, given free run of the compound, had managed to slip bits of food into his hut during the day. Daily he found something from her, sometimes only a thick lump of suet, secreted behind the door. And so he survived.

"They began to believe that I was a god," he laughed. "To survive on the gruel and bones they gave me. In another month they would have worshiped me."

"Or buried you," Hadesseh added. She had been listening intently. "But you owe *me* something," she said as she turned to Andrew. "How does the son of Fontini Villa come to be here at all?" Andrew sensed that she had not meant the comment jeeringly. Her voice was level and firm. She wanted answers.

"But I am *not* the son of Fontini Villa," Andrew began to say carefully. "If I learned anything from my parents, and it took me so terribly long to learn this at all, it is that I was only the keeper of the estate. And I did that poorly. I became the prisoner of what I once owned . . ."

"Once?"

"It is destroyed. Entirely. But I am not, thanks in part to Emeth. Now I am only the son of—"

"The last Magus on earth?" she finished.

Again Andrew searched her words for a note of mockery. There was none. He nodded. "And son of Taletha," he added quietly. "Of the liberation. But that too is past, and I'm at peace with it. I've spent all my life coming to terms with it."

Emeth leaned against the mountain rock. His breathing seemed strangled. "Some are starting to call us Christians," he said. "A good term. Sons and daughters of the Messiah."

"There isn't time now," Andrew interrupted. "We have to be on our way. Some distance below us the trail enters a gap before merging with the river trail. We can rest there."

They roused themselves and fell into their assumed order along the trail. They marched steadily, but terribly slowly, through the night. Andrew thought of the sheer precipice falling from this thin ridge they clung to on the side of the mountain. In the darkness, the others were aware only of the place where they walked. Or were they? he wondered. Surely Hadesseh sensed the abyss below. Helena had fallen asleep with her head on Hadesseh's shoulder. Andrew was going to call out to relieve her, but stopped. Hadesseh needed the touch as much as Helena.

They were nearing the gap that led toward the river trail when Andrew heard the long, chilling howl of the wolf. It still seemed distant, as if coming from across the vast abyss itself. But close enough that Andrew wanted to force his comrades on to the river trail that night.

Their footsteps dragged. The boy plodded, head down, legs moving like weights. How young he still was, Andrew thought; how vulnerable to suffer the knowledge he had. Emeth walked with one hand raised, touching the mountain wall for security. He too sensed the danger only footsteps away.

When they arrived at the gap Andrew found a sheltered overhang and stopped them. The boy sank against the rock and fell asleep in an instant. Hadesseh laid the girl gently by his side and wrapped their coats snugly about them.

Andrew headed back up the trail.

"Where are you going?" Emeth called.

"I want to watch the back trail for a few minutes."

"I'll go with you."

"No. Please stay here with the others. I'll only be gone a few minutes."

Andrew walked back further than he intended, probing the darkness carefully. Snow was falling heavily now, effacing their steps, collecting in drifts among the rocks. Once more Andrew thought he heard a distant howl, but it was from a great distance and it may have been only the wind. Sound travels many miles in these mountains, he reminded himself. He waited, silent in the numbing cold. The snow layered on his hair. Finally he turned back. It was now deep night. Soon they would have to leave again. If they could, Andrew would have traveled all night.

As he approached the shelter Andrew was conscious of low voices. The boy and girl slept huddled among the stones like stones themselves. A white quilt enfolded them. But Emeth and Hadesseh sat together, voices murmuring in a soft stream of words. Her head was bent. They were leaning together, heads nearly touching. Andrew approached them quietly, but when they looked up, they were not startled. In the darkness it seemed that Emeth was smiling.

"I'll try to sleep now," Hadesseh said. It cut off Andrew's questions. She nestled close to the girl.

"What was that about?" Andrew asked Emeth.

"We were talking, Andrew. When there are many questions, and too few answers that suffice, there must be story. Isn't that true? And also we ate. There is food for you too."

"No thanks. I want to watch awhile yet."

"Then I will sleep. We are in good hands."

"I hope so. I'll keep watch."

"Yes. Yours too are good. Good night."

And he was alone in the night, watching them sleep as peacefully in the falling snow as if they were on silken beds. But it was the sleep of exhaustion that permitted no delusions.

Andrew climbed above them to a point in the rocks from which he could see, as well as possible in the blowing snow and darkness, both the trail ahead and behind. He weighed the possibilities—and found them slim. If Dominic had believed Hadesseh, he may be looking to the south. Even if they discovered their error, it may be sufficient advantage to give them time. But surely the trackers would tell Dominic that Andrew had returned through the corridor.

How long could Gregor have held them off? Andrew found himself hoping that Emeth had told Hadesseh about Gregor's bravery. But he also thought that Hadesseh somehow already knew.

If Dominic came north, did he know which trail? What of the wolves they had heard in the far distance? Were they hunting them? One thing was certain. At this moment, at least, they were alone. *Relish it then. Know a moment of peace.*

The night and the loneliness, the cold, the high point among the rocks were seductive. Andrew gave in and slept a few hours.

*   *   *

The distant cry of a wolf, high and piercing as a wail of grief, jerked Andrew awake. Standing up, he shook off a layer of snow several inches deep. And still it snowed. In the half-light of dawn, the gray rocks glistened with white coats. The air crackled with cold. Andrew tried to place the howl he had heard, listening intently. If he were to trust his senses, it came now from the trail behind them. The animals had picked up the scent even through the snow.

He hurried down the slippery rocks and found the others already up, stamping their feet for warmth, looking down the trail for him. Their faces were etched with tiredness. The few hours of sleep were desperately little, but it would be long before they got more. If they got more. Emeth especially looked haggard.

Again Andrew heard the howling, as if the predators raged at their heels. They *were* behind them now, on the trail.

Nonetheless, relief showed on their faces when Andrew came tumbling down from the rocks.

"I heard it," Helena said abruptly.

"Yes," said Andrew. "You hear everything don't you, little lady?" He chucked her under her pointed chin. He marveled at the serenity of those blue eyes. "They are a long way behind us though. Are you ready to go?"

She turned, grasping Emeth's hand.

Hadesseh did not move. She looked back up the trail, frozen in place.

"Come, Hadesseh."

Still she would not look at Andrew. With averted face, she began to say, "I thought you had . . ."

"That I had gone?"

"Yes."

"I was up in the rocks. Watching."

Her eyes shot around at him. "Like a guardian?"

She turned and strode to the head of the procession. The others followed. Except the boy. He lagged behind, watching Andrew with averted glance as they walked. He seemed to want to question Andrew, but Andrew didn't know how to invite him. They walked on in silence. Until the eerie howl drifted again. It was answered this time from the far distance.

"They're closer," said the boy in a thin voice. "The wolves are closer."

"Yes." Andrew had been studying the rock ahead. "Yes, they are." He thought he saw a plan, shaping tangibly in the pillars of rock that overhung the trail. He could use help. No. He shut it out of his mind. He could not involve the boy. Yet it was his life!

"Wait," Andrew said. "No. Listen, go ahead with the others. See those rocks there?" The boy followed his pointing and nodded. "I'm going to try to loosen them on the trackers. If you hear a loud noise like that, I want you to tell the others to run. It will slow the trackers, not stop them. It depends on how many there are. But you have to make the river trail. Then turn north. Go now. I will catch up."

Andrew watched until the boy caught up with the others, then he began climbing. The trail they had been following was about four paces wide through the mountain gap. Its floor was littered with fallen rock, slippery from the snow. As Andrew climbed, well beyond the point he had selected and careful to leave as little sign as possible, he could see his companions forging ahead slowly. Their effort to hurry was a shambles. Time was urgent. If this failed they would be overtaken before they reached the river trail.

He circled back behind the jut of rock he had noted. He stepped behind protruding rocks, seeking windswept surfaces to hide his trail. Now if the rock he wanted was only loose and not sunk down into the mountain. If he could topple it at precisely the right moment! It would not suffice to block the trackers; it had to be *upon* them. And for that Andrew had to depend on too many things. That the rock could be jarred loose. That it would wrench others loose as it fell. That he could time the motion of the trackers. That they would be intent upon the trail and not spot him above them. Too many things. Too much risk. But it had to be done.

He hacked at the base of the rock, digging through a layer of ice that had built around it. He almost shouted approval. It had been blocked in lesser stone. Carefully he tested its huge weight, feeling it give slightly. If he could topple it, it would carry a rockslide down on the trackers. The drop here was nearly sheer. It could work. Had to work. He waited, apprehension hammering at his temples.

They came around a bend, heads down. There were three, the lead tracker restraining a wolf that lunged against a thick leather strap. They moved quickly. Too quickly, and Andrew had not provided himself enough time to gauge their pace. And they were spread out, the lead tracker several paces ahead of the others as the wolf dragged him along. *Slow down*, Andrew wanted to scream. He heaved his shoulder into the rock.

Even as he did so, feeling its weight give way beyond stopping, he saw the boy suddenly appear ahead on the trail. Why had he come back? At the same instant the lead tracker saw him, lifted his head to gloat over his prey. He heard the sudden rumble of the rock. The wolf sprang back on its heels, colliding with the tracker. All this occurred in an instant, and that was all it took for the rock to pummel downward. The boulder missed its mark completely, falling ahead of the tracker and the wolf, but they were caught in the secondary slide, a cascade of lesser rocks ripped loose by the fall.

The wolf offered a howl of pain at the sky as a rock smashed against his body. It tangled the leash, pulling the tracker off balance. Rocks ripped into them, burying them under a cloud of snow.

Andrew had no time to see if they would recover. He was racing back down the steep cliff, tumbling from rock to rock, behind the other two trackers. He had to take them before they saw the boy. Now while their attention was riveted on the rockslide, while they still believed a whim of nature had tricked them. Reaching the floor of the gap, Andrew ran forward. He saw them, pawing at the rocks that littered the lead tracker. Beyond the pile of rock Andrew saw the boy frozen in fear. "Run!" Andrew screamed. Ludicrously, the trackers thought he had challenged them, and they did not understand the command. They looked at each other in puzzlement, then turned together to take him, confident in their paired strength.

Andrew's run never stopped; instinct gathered strength, a leap, the hurtle, the rigid foot taking one tracker high in the chest. Andrew saw his eyes open wide in astonishment before the blow fell, saw the eyes shutter as the blow struck home. Even as Andrew fell he came around, smashing another blow into him. The other tracker turned to run. He began scrambling over the loose rock ahead of Andrew. He saw the boy now. Saw a way out.

The snow built up by the rockslide slowed Andrew's pursuit. He clawed at the rock. As he crested its mound, the tracker was nearly upon the boy who stood there, a thin, uncertain, vulnerable child. "Lie down!" Andrew shouted. "Down." The boy shot him one bewildered glance. Andrew was poised above the mound of rock, throwing arm cocked with the knife ready. It was a long and desperate throw. To Andrew's relief, the boy obeyed. The uncoiling was automatic. The whip and reflex of the strike. The blade cut a blue streak in the rigid air, a shining among the gray rock.

Andrew had aimed at the blur of the man's legs, not daring the risk of striking his thick coat at this distance. The blade struck the man's thigh; his leg spasmed and his own force bowled him over, rolling past the boy. Andrew raced down the fallen rock. Andrew was nearly upon him as the tracker groped behind and turned on him with the knife brandished awkwardly, inexpertly, yet dangerously. His breath came in clouds of steam.

The man's mistake was to reach for the boy. It diverted his attention. Andrew sprang forward, hammering blows.

He twisted the knife from the man's grip, held it ready to plunge. But the tracker lay unconscious in the snow. Andrew groaned at the desecration before this boy. *Here I am! This is what I made of myself. I am no better than any of them.* The boy's eyes stared at him, full of what? Wonder? Fear? Awe? Andrew was afraid of what he saw there.

"Why did you come back?" he asked roughly.

"I . . . thought I should help you."

The words nearly broke Andrew's heart. *Help me?* Did he laugh or cry? *Don't you understand, boy? It was to free you.*

"After this, do what you're told," Andrew said. Yet, he admired the boy. He wanted to find other words. Words of praise.

"I will," the boy said quickly. But he didn't flinch, did not waver, did not falter in that bleakly studied look.

Andrew grabbed the man's coat and began dragging him back to the rock pile.

"What are you doing?"

"If others come, I want it to look like they were all caught in the rockslide."

The wolf had had its back broken by the first rock. The lead tracker had been buried in the rubble. Andrew laid the two unconscious trackers nearby, threw loose stones over them, and left them. A cave-in, nothing more. So, he hoped, it would appear. He thought of that eerie howl he had heard in the far distance. There would be others. But they were safe for the moment.

"Quickly now," he said to the boy. "We have to catch up with the others." Andrew noticed that the boy insisted on walking at his side, no matter how fast he went. "It would be better," Andrew added, "if nothing were said about this."

* * *

They trudged steadily all day along the river trail. Finding no signs of pursuit during his many back treks, Andrew called an early halt and, protected by a large outcropping of rock, permitted a fire. There they ate the last of their food.

"We should be with Rafeo tomorrow," Andrew said to the silent group. Heads were bent forward wearily; shoulders shook with cold as they huddled close to the fire. Its blue and orange flames, flickering in the draft and burning unevenly on the damp wood Andrew had gathered during the day, were a nourishment to them. "And there will be plenty of food there," Andrew said. "He has some of the best wine ever vinted. The grapes of his meadow taste like the sky itself."

Helena laughed aloud. "Taste the sky!"

"Yes. And a dog so huge you could ride him. A monster of a dog, but gentle as a lamb. Ah, Helena. Wait until you see this dog."

"Will the wine make me big too?" She turned her blue eyes toward him. For the first time she smiled.

"Big? Wine makes you big?"

"Like the monster. The dog. I want to grow big."

"Don't be in too much of a hurry, Helena. You can drink water. It has the taste of stars."

"That's fine," she said, giving her curls a shake of emphasis.

The others were too weary to take notice. Staring with spent eyes into the stingy fire, their faces were etched with shadows. Andrew saw himself, for a moment, as they would have seen him. That face he saw in the pond of Faenza's chapel; the scarred and twisted features. No wonder the boy watched him with such mixed emotion: what manner of man or monster was this? But for the first time he felt the stirring of hope. And freedom. There had been no sign of pursuit all day. As if reading his thoughts, Hadesseh lifted her face and smiled at him across the flames.

It was snug there under the lee of the rock, although an occasional gust of wind tossed in a few foolish flakes of snow that melted by the fire. Here was respite from the bitter cold that had deepened its grip on them hour after hour.

When Helena fell asleep on Hadesseh's lap, she rose with the girl, lay down by the warmed rock and fell asleep.

"Why don't you sleep too?" Andrew asked Emeth.

He stared at the fire as if entranced. "I'm not ready yet," he said after a moment. "This is precious. I'll enjoy it."

"Yes. I know what you mean."

The boy got up and fed a few twigs into the fire. He kicked at a smoldering branch and darted back from the shower of sparks. He was nimble, quick.

The boy walked around the fire and sat a few feet from Andrew. In the glow, his black hair shimmered with strange red highlights. So much like Hadesseh. He sat holding his knees, staring into the fire.

"Are you cold?" Andrew asked him.

"Not now."

"Thank you for wanting to help me."

"That's all right. I was in the way."

"Oh?"

"I'm always in the way." He reflected. "How do you do that?" he asked. "It seemed so easy for you."

"What?"

"Those men. There were three of them. I'm afraid of the trackers."

"You needn't be afraid anymore. Do you understand that?"

"Yes. I think so."

"And how can you be in the way? You're not even close to me." Andrew patted the ground by his side, hoping the boy would come. With a shrug he slid over, his body tense despite the feigned nonchalance. He held himself carefully away from Andrew.

So they sat, watching the fire, without further words. When the boy fell asleep, Andrew held him to keep him from falling over. Then to hold him close. His head fell against Andrew's shoulder. He stroked the boy's hair, feeling its softness against his cheek. So too he slept.

During the night the boy rolled off and Andrew laid him in a more comfortable position.

* * *

With one of those surprising twists of mountain weather, the morning shot rays of penetrating brilliance along the mountain trail. Beyond the lee of rock where they lay, light poured into the canyon. The snow lay a foot or more deep, carved into eerie shapes. The wind had fallen silent now, as if holding its breath from the bitter cold. The only motion was the spume of the river that twisted in a bed of steam. It flung droplets that frothed against the new snow, draping it with a lacework of diamond-sharp ice. It reflected in blue points against a white mantle. It was so cold they felt each breath in the pit of the chest, but the overpowering brightness spun a false spell of warmth, light so pure and clean that one almost felt able to dance upon it.

They did not light another fire. There was no food and the fire would tantalize them with the thought. The sunlight was its own fire, glittering off countless points and throwing on them illusive heat that touched the spirit if not the body.

Hunger became the spur. At noon they rested briefly, but Andrew spent the time encouraging his companions with descriptions of Rafeo's lodgings. He debated again whether to tell them of the rope bridge, remembering well his own terror the first time he saw that flimsy lifeline stretched across the abyss. He told them.

"Well," said Emeth, "if we're going to cross, we might as well do it in daylight."

Andrew agreed. More than anything, their bodies cried for rest. Their spirits also. Andrew knew this as he studied them. Yes, Hadesseh had chosen, but she also knew the pain that choice entails. Choice isn't freedom alone, Andrew now understood; it's commitment to a way no matter what the way brings. And the boy, ripped from a way of life that was all he had known, what did he feel? *I'm always in the way.* No. In all his life Andrew would never forget that moment by the fire when, already sleeping, the boy laid his head on Andrew's breast.

Andrew watched them walking before him now as they set out again. Only Helena, her golden hair adazzle with daylight, seemed impervious to hunger and weariness. She had grown even in these months. Swathed in clothes too large for her, she skittered along, now to Emeth, now to Hadesseh, occasionally walking alongside the boy. Andrew felt oddly out of place watching them.

They still moved slowly, legs pumping against the snow. At midafternoon Andrew found Rafeo's gap in the mountain and breathed a sigh of relief. It was miracle enough that they had not been followed on the river trail. Within hours now, they would be safe. For the first time Andrew took the lead, picking the easiest route along the rugged uphill climb.

When they reached the head of the gorge, panting and with legs nearly spent, Andrew felt the urge to shout for pure joy. His companions saw the expression on his face and hurried to catch up to him. Andrew flung an arm outward in the direction of the refuge. The white quilt of the snow was stroked by a million points of light from the lowering sun. The refuge itself was girdled in shadow. Andrew wanted them to enjoy it. He turned back to them, and saw the blank masks.

"What is it?" he cried.

"We have to cross that?" Helena said. "I don't think so."

"Why, you can cross it. Pretend you're on a swing."

"A swing!" Hadesseh exclaimed. "A swing." Carefully, hand out to balance herself, she peered into the gorge and fell back gasping.

"Very well," Andrew said, "then I'll have to carry you across." He moved playfully toward her, thinking—*it has been done.*

"No!" she said. "Just let me get used to it a minute."

"Here," he laughed. "Let me show you. Actually only one can cross at a time, unless I carry you, which I will for those two." He pointed at Helena and the boy who stood gawking at the ropes. "If there are two, they will fight each other's motion."

Andrew stepped out onto the rope. "I'll go across. Watch." He went a few steps. He remembered Rafeo's words to him. "See how you move with the motion of the rope. Don't fight it. The rope will carry you."

Winding thinly across the distant meadow, he heard a shout. Ah! There was Rafeo himself. A small figure disengaging himself from his dwelling. Rafeo paused, seemingly to fasten his coat. Behind him the huge old dog bolted free, legs pummeling the snow into a cloud. He danced in circles, jumped in the air.

"A wolf!" Helena cried.

"No, no. It's the dog. A mountain of a dog for all that, but all dog. He's my friend. See how happy he is to see us."

"Oh," she said. "Let's go see him. Can I play with him?"

"I'll carry you across first. You can ride on my back. Just like the old mule. Remember the mule?"

Andrew was turning back toward her when he heard the sound that chilled him to the bone. Suddenly his legs trembled on the rope. "No," he breathed. The high, eerie shrilling of the wolf sliced undeniably through the air. He whipped his glance across the meadow's length.

They came through the tumbled boulders at the southern edge. Sanjeani's trail! The back trail that they weren't supposed to know about! Clambering through the rocks came two figures, small at this distance. Two men. Running. Being tugged by two wolves. Now Andrew could see the heave and surge of their shoulders, straining at the leashes. The two men ran clumsily behind then. They came with frightening speed.

The man in the lead straightened. Andrew saw him clearly now. He stood upright, lifted one fist in the air and shrieked words that the wind whipped away. Andrew recognized the figure, and all the energy seemed to leak out of his body. Dominic.

Someone whimpered behind Andrew. No. Not now! Not so close. It's not right.

The tracker lunged across the meadow behind Dominic. Even from this distance, closing rapidly, Andrew could feel the violence seething in him.

At the very moment when they broke into view from Sanjeani's trail, Rafeo emerged from the north, behind the two men. Andrew shouted at him, "No! Get back." Dominic took it for himself. His laugh was a demented shriek.

"It will do you no good, Andrew. I have you. Scream! Scream all you can!"

Rafeo broke into a stumbling run toward them.

The wolves broke free, trailing their leather leashes across the meadow, pumping, heads down to attack. They were like arrows, targeted toward the chasm.

Behind them the great dog at Rafeo's side stiffened momentarily. It lifted its nose like a prayer, sorting through the savage odors. He shook his mammoth head and exploded across the meadow, bounding like an awkward boulder. The great dog emitted a fierce bray as it ran. It was the first time Andrew had ever heard him bellow. The sound thundered like a challenge across the meadow.

He was upon the lead wolf in a moment, catching its neck in mighty jaws. Andrew saw the body flip in the air. The dog flung the body aside like a toy. The other wolf was quicker, lethal in its quickness. It struck, fangs buried deep in the woolly hide. They tumbled over and over, a snarling madness.

Andrew's body unlocked. He had to act—intervene. He drove himself forward on the rope bridge. *You can't fight it!* Desperately he struggled against the ropes, silently urging Rafeo back. *Don't interfere. Let me handle this!* His progress was terribly slow as he fought the ropes. The bridge swayed and bucked crazily, a catapult poised above the abyss. There was a terrible moment when Andrew reached its nadir and the meadow above slipped from view. He flung himself up the ropes. Slipped. Found footing and began climbing. He could see them again. The tracker had stopped, torn between helping Dominic or his beloved wolf. He kicked at the snarling mass. Howls ripped from the wolf, met by the rumble of growling from the mountain dog. Brute power conflicted with cunning agility.

Dominic wasted no time. Now Andrew could clearly see his face, and the venom in the look chilled him, just as it had when he was in the cistern. His black eyes burned like coals. The glare of hatred fell on Andrew like a blow.

His gloating eyes never leaving Andrew, Dominic drew a knife and bent to the ropes. He paused, shook the knife at Andrew, and laughed. "From one trap to another, Andrew. Look down! There's no escaping me!"

Hadesseh screamed at him, "Dominic, no! Please, no!"

He raged at her, "You were the trap. Nothing more. Do you think I don't know the mind of Fontini? It is as simple as a map. I knew he wasn't dead. I know everything!"

"If not for yourself," Hadesseh pleaded, "then for your son. Don't do this to him!"

Dominic flung his head back and laughed. "Son! A whore's son." He slashed at the upper rope. One of the two guide ropes snapped loose. He bent to the heavy, braided central rope.

Like a little scarecrow blown stumbling across the meadow, Rafeo scuttled forward. Andrew attacked the upward climb, commanding his body to move. There was no time! And no way to hurry. The going was so slow. He saw a strand fray dangerously. *Rafeo!* he wanted to call out, *stop!*

He was paralyzed with his own sense of dying. Watching it creep up on him step by step. He felt the ropes twist under the cutting.

Rafeo didn't stop. With a shriek he flung his little body on Dominic. The little bearded man clung to Dominic's back like a leech. Rafeo pummeled feeble, awkward blows with one hand on the back of Dominic's head.

Andrew reached to his waist. The knife sprang to his hand. He tried to steady himself with one hand clutching the swaying ropes. Tried to find a target. The two whirled at the edge of the abyss. Twisted. "Rafeo, let go!" he shouted.

But he would not. Dominic slashed blindly behind him with his own knife. Rafeo shrieked as the blade hit home, buried in his thigh. Still he held on with a grim embrace, his fingers clenched futilely to Dominic's neck.

Behind them the tracker lunged forward. He seized a rock, running with it uplifted. He would smash Rafeo as easily as one does a insect. The knife spurted from Andrew's hand. He couldn't see if it struck. The rope bridge swung wildly and he had to bend down to regain his balance. The tracker screamed, flung his hands upward. On the icy slope he could not stop his motion. His legs tangled. He slid. Andrew saw him make a wild grab for the ropes as he toppled, then in a long, soundless spiral the man fell. Andrew could not pry his eyes from the body as it plummeted. There was no sound, not one, as he disappeared hundreds of feet below.

Andrew's hands trembled on the ropes. He had bent to one knee, his stomach convulsing. *Once again*, he thought. *What else could I do?*

When he looked upward, Dominic's eyes were turned toward him, glazed and dulled. Behind him Rafeo lay, his fingers trembling at the grip of the knife buried in his thigh. With one desperate effort he wrenched the blade free and flung it into the chasm. He fell back, whimpering quietly.

Dominic's glazed eyes targeted Andrew. His hand reached out for the one remaining guide rope. "You!" he hissed. "You demon. Why do you want to destroy me?"

"I never wanted to destroy you," Andrew rasped. He fought through his vertigo, standing unsteadily on the rope. He felt Dominic jerking the remaining guide rope. Andrew's hands shook on it. He stood there, about a dozen paces from the ledge now, so near safety. "You were my friend. Why, Dominic?" He shouted madly, "Why?"

"You wanted to destroy me, belittle me." Dominic's voice was a crazed shriek. "I'm stronger than you, Andrew." He took one step onto the bridge.

Andrew quailed, shaking his head. Dominic seemed to have reverted to a little boy, voicing an outrage he had carried so long. *An outrage that I never knew*, Andrew thought. *Where did it come from?*

Dominic's eyes glittered madly now. "Remember, Andrew. When you knocked me out of my tree fort?"

"I didn't knock you out. We fell."

"Oh no. You knocked me down. Right then I swore I'd get back at you. You should have died a thousand times."

"Dominic, I—"

"Silence, fool." He took another step.

He is mad, Andrew thought. *I can't reason with him.*

"Well, this time, this time Andrew, I'll show you what it's like."

He stepped out fully onto the bridge. Suddenly he shook the ropes madly, bouncing them up and down. "See," he screamed. "See what it's like."

"Dominic," Andrew cried. "There's still time. Still a way. I forgive you, Dominic."

"Forgive!" Dominic's eyes were like a furnace. "Never." He stepped forward.

"Don't," Andrew pleaded. "Two can't be on this thing. One of us . . ."

"Yes! *One* of us will fall. You!"

Andrew was turning. He could not meet Dominic, not like this. Struggling back toward the far ledge, he felt the ropes bucking wildly behind him. Dominic was following, coming *down* the rope toward its low point at the center of the gorge.

"Run, Andrew," Dominic screamed. "You'll never get away from me. I'm better than you."

"No," Andrew croaked. The ropes swung dizzily. He struggled toward the nadir, feeling Dominic coming in the wild bucking motion. He turned.

Dominic's hand fastened on his collar, jerking him, pulling him backward.

Andrew went down on one knee. He clung desperately to the guide rope. Dominic twisted at his collar, choking him, pulling him back. It seemed a terrified silence had fallen on the gorge. No sound. The sun was graying in Andrew's eyes. Dominic twisted the collar viciously, cutting off his oxygen. Andrew slashed backward with one elbow, catching Dominic just inside the knee. He felt the limb tremble, buckle.

Dominic gave a low growl, like that of a cornered animal as he felt his feet slipping. Andrew twisted his head upward against the chokehold. Dominic's eyes were wide, anguished, as if he suddenly realized where he was. He struggled to regain his balance, still clinging to the collar of Andrew's coat. Time seemed suspended.

The sudden weight as Dominic fell jerked Andrew's head down, as if his neck were breaking. Andrew clung desperately to the guide rope. He wrapped his legs around the lower rope.

For a second, Dominic tried to regain the rope with his own feet. His free hand clutched desperately, missed. He toppled, the other hand still clenched to Andrew's collar, pulling his head down toward the chasm. Held so, Andrew looked directly down into Dominic's eyes. The madness was gone, replaced by stark terror as Dominic clung to Andrew's collar.

Andrew was choking. He tried to twist an arm around to grab Dominic's hand. He couldn't. Clinging to the ropes with one hand and with his legs twined around the rope, he could not reach him.

"Dominic," he rasped through his constricted throat, "try to grab my coat with your other hand. You're choking me. I can't reach you to help you like this."

Dominic's eyes seemed empty. "I'm . . . beyond reach." For the first time there was a note of sanity in his voice.

"No," Andrew said. "Try it. I can save you."

Dominic shook his head slowly. "Andrew," he whispered. "Forgive me."

Andrew looked down into Dominic's eyes. A red cloud seemed to be forming behind his own eyes. Head down, choked, he found his own grip loosening. The words could hardly come. "I forgive you."

Dominic closed his eyes and let go.

Andrew shut his own eyes. Tightly. He sucked greedily for air.

When he looked again he could barely see the plume of snow drifting in the wind far, far below.

Carefully he pulled himself upright on the rope bridge. He knelt there a long time, balanced on one knee, holding the guide rope, his head bent, before he dared rise.

"Andrew," Hadesseh called. "Are you all right?"

He looked up. She was several paces out on the rope. Some instinct had guided her, at that terrible moment, to step out to help. Suddenly aware of where she was, she looked down.

"Don't look," Andrew said sharply. "You can't stop now. Let me get across. I'll test the rope and guide you up."

She nodded courageously, the ropes trembling under her hands.

CHAPTER
TWENTY-ONE

Andrew knelt on the ledge by the rope bridge. He studied the hacking marks Dominic had made at the remaining guide rope. He tested its strength. It had to hold! As he did so his eyes peered past the rope, down and down into the cavernous reaches of the abyss. He could see nothing. Yet in his mind's eye he saw many things, and he struggled to keep from weeping.

Not now, he insisted. *They have to get across.*

Rafeo lay moaning gently behind him. He had fought to a sitting position. Hands clenched to his thigh. He nodded at Andrew, his old gray beard trembling.

In one swift movement Andrew ungirdled the sheath from around his waist and dropped it into the canyon. It fell a very long time, as if it had grown wings and floated. The bottom of the gorge lay in shadow now, the brilliance of the snow tinged by a strange violet light reflected off the rocks.

The sun will rise again, he thought. *Will melt the snow. A thousand rivulets will gather and, like wet hands, lift the bodies, carrying them—where? Downstream to the river, past the lake, to the valleys below.* By then the bodies would no longer be recognizable—broken to bits by the power of the river.

Hadesseh called softly.

Andrew looked up in surprise. She was still standing there, balanced over the crosswise bridge. But there was no fear in her eyes.

"Help me."

In the same way that Rafeo had once talked Andrew over that dangerous chasm, so Andrew spoke peace into Hadesseh. Precisely as Rafeo had done to him, he led her out, then up, painting pictures of a summer day. She stepped nervously forward. When she neared the ledge he reached out his hand and led her the last steps.

"Oh, no," she said as she looked past Andrew.

The huge old dog had stumbled across the meadow and now lay obediently behind them, his head cradled in Rafeo's lap. He whimpered painfully, thick fur stained terribly. His legs jerked spasmodically, as if it were a pup again and, sensing a meadow in springtime, wanted to romp among the flowers. A dog of rocks and clouds now lay dying.

Hadesseh bent to Rafeo. He smiled up at her. His old coat seemed to have absorbed much of the impact of Dominic's knife. Nonetheless, he felt too weak to care for the dog. He looked gratefully at Hadesseh as she lifted the animal's huge head, careful of its wounds. She cradled him in her lap, for the moment unmindful of everything but the suffering of the great old animal. The dog turned its deep brown eyes on her. One ear was torn and flopped awkwardly along its cheek. Carefully Hadesseh pressed it back, stroking the fur, murmuring into the brown eyes. Then the dog found the strength to lift its mammoth head an inch, two inches, and brushed Hadesseh's cheek once with its warm tongue. It sighed heavily, and lay back in her lap.

*   *   *

Andrew stood up. "I'll get them," he murmured.

"I don't think I can watch," Hadesseh said. She lifted her face to him. "But I'll trust you."

Andrew nodded. He turned to the rope bridge and crossed once more to the other side. Emeth stood between the boy and the girl, who huddled against him, squeezing his hands.

"It's all over," he said as he came up toward them. "It is really over now."

Andrew knelt so that Helena could climb onto his back. She squeezed his neck as tightly as she could. He carried her across, certain that her eyes were shut as tightly as her arms around him.

He returned for the boy.

"I want to do it myself," he said. Then he whispered, "Please?" There was no hauteur in his voice. Only a strange longing. Andrew hesitated. The boy had grown up in the mountains, among the rocks and high places. And he wanted to do this thing.

"Very well," Andrew said. "Just relax and let the ropes carry you."

"I never had a swing," he said. He stepped out on the bridge. He was a small and precious thing walking that span, and Andrew's heart hammered for the bravery of this boy.

Across the gap Hadesseh stood rigidly, watching now. She knew. Her son had to do this thing. She understood. He did it for her. Her and Andrew and himself. And he succeeded.

Emeth hesitated, then threw back his cowl and unsteadily made his way across. He went hurriedly with little shuffling steps, like a man with nothing more to lose, a man not at all fearful of dying. When he made it across, his face was grim and he shook his head as if to say, Never again.

When they all stood on the ledge, Andrew pointed across the meadow toward the refuge. Rafeo was standing now, favoring his wounded leg. Hadesseh had belted a bandage over the knife wound, stopping the bleeding. Rafeo leaned on her, his face gray and drawn.

After Andrew had settled them in the refuge, he pulled the boy aside. "I wonder if you could help me a minute?"

The boy nodded. His eyes were still partly swollen, the skin discolored. He didn't hesitate. He pulled on his coat and followed Andrew outside.

They stood above the old dog, the limp body all matted and stained. Andrew shook his head sadly. Something noble had passed.

"He saved my life once," he murmured to the boy.

The boy looked at him with searching eyes. Andrew shook his head and bent to the large body. Together they seized the massive legs and half-dragged, half-carried the ponderous weight up the meadow. Andrew knew the spot. By the vineyard lay the rude cemetery. They placed him there, scraping the snow away and then covering the body with a cairn of rocks. They piled the last of them by the light of a little pale disk of moon and a heaven littered with a million distant stars.

* * *

They gathered in Rafeo's dwelling because it was the largest. After eating, Andrew prepared fires in two other dwellings. Emeth could stay with the boy in one room, Hadesseh with Helena in another. Andrew saw to it that the rooms were warm, that there were plenty of woolen blankets for the rough bunks and that food and wine were available. They needed rest and food to restore their bodies.

He didn't think there would be other trackers following. They protected their territory *against* invasion and likely did not go out, especially with their leaders gone, into the territory of others.

Andrew returned to his old dwelling. The fireplace warmed it quickly. It felt like a home to him. The parchments still lay rolled by the table in their oilskin cases. The quills, the inks lay nearby. He was too worn to look at them, even to think of them. He felt empty, completely flagged. But he did think, for a moment, of that instant in the trackers' cave when the words came to his lips. And then Gregor was there. Gregor! The outcast, the hero. Truly he had never forsaken. The picture of him standing there, buying them the time to escape at the cost of his life's blood, seemed formed in fire in Andrew's mind.

He could not sleep, even as darkness settled across the meadow and deepened to night. When he lay down his mind kept racing, as if it had a will of its own, seeking some connections that he had been missing. He finally sat up on the bunk, leaned against the rock wall and watched the flames burn steadily in the hearth.

He stirred slightly when the door opened, his body suddenly tense. Hadesseh slipped through, wrapped in a large woolen coat. She shut the door and leaned against it, her eyes probing Andrew's.

He stood up and walked to her.

"I'm sorry," he said. "So very sorry."

Hadesseh raised two fingers to his lips and pressed them. "If we start apologizing," she said softly, "we may never end."

He looked long into her eyes, lost himself in their depths. He was about to speak.

"Shh." She hushed him, as if reading his thoughts. "If we can't put it behind us, right now, it will always be there. So let's end it."

"We can't go back. Oh, how I wish I could undo . . ."

Again she hushed him. "It is what we do now," she said. "Not what we want to undo. Do you think the Lord would have led us all this way, through all this merely to have us reflect on our sorrows?"

Andrew choked. "It wouldn't be hard," he admitted. "Dominic—I keep thinking there had to be something I could have done, or something I shouldn't have done . . ." His words fell like weights.

Hadesseh shook her head. "Nothing, Andrew," she said softly. "You can't make choices for another person, nor bear the consequences of his choice."

"And yet they say that is precisely what the Messiah did. Bore the consequences."

But she looked at him with need in her own eyes, looked at him and whispered, "Andrew. Please, just hold me a minute. I haven't had anyone just hold me for so very long."

* * *

Andrew felt almost afraid to touch her at first. He was trembling as she leaned toward him, his hands rising awkwardly, fearfully, to embrace her. They sat back on the bench, leaning against the wall. They watched the light of the fire leaping; then it slowed and diminished, and there were only bright glowing coals staring back at their closed eyes.

Before they fell asleep Andrew managed these few words. His mind was already shutting down, but he had to know one thing. Through thickened lips he asked, "The boy?"

"Yes." Her words were a whisper, a sigh.

Andrew felt her raven hair brush his cheek and felt as if his heart was breaking. "I don't know his name," he whispered.

"John," she said. Her words were muted with weariness. "His name is John. It means 'Beloved by God.' "

But then Andrew, seated on the bench before the fire with Hadesseh leaning against his shoulder, was himself falling asleep, and he was also thinking, *Beloved. For the first time in so very long, I feel safe.*

* * *

Andrew awakened the next morning to the bright crackling of the fire. The window shutters were ajar, and sunlight cascaded into the cold room. Hadesseh knelt by the fire, holding something in her hands.

"I found a bit of wood, but what on earth is *this*?"

"Dried goat's dung," Andrew replied with a smile.

"Dried . . ." She flipped it into the fire. "Oh well."

Andrew laughed. "Up here wood is precious. Somehow the dung keeps coming."

Hadesseh laughed with him. "Helena and John have already met them. That cranky one—"

"Simeon," Andrew supplied.

"So he has a name too."

"What are you doing up so early?"

"Not all of us can lie around all day, Andrew. The children wanted to explore. It's beautiful outside."

"It is. But they have to be careful. The old dog once saved . . ." He stopped. That story could come later. "Where are they now?"

"Emeth's getting food ready. They're famished. He sent me to try to awaken you."

"The children. Will they be all right?"

Hadesseh sat for a moment, studying the fire. "Yes," she said softly. "They will be all right. Now."

Andrew shifted to the edge of the bench. He felt stiff and sore from sleeping leaning against the stone wall. He could not remember Hadesseh leaving during the night. He reached for his woolen boots and began strapping them on. "Will you tell me one thing?"

"I'm not sure," she said with a smile. "Why don't you just ask me?"

"You said, last night, that John means 'Beloved of God.' Your name, Hadesseh. I think that means 'star.' Somewhere I got that idea. Did you tell me that?"

"No. I didn't. Hadesseh means 'myrtle.' Like the tree. The myrtle tree. The name is an honor among my people."

Andrew was puzzled. Then another thought struck him. "Those parchments. You drew pictures . . ."

Hadesseh gasped. "You found those? Do you have them?"

Andrew shook his head. "No. But I hid them."

"I'm not going back, Andrew."

He looked at her. "I know. What I wanted to ask was . . . the trees. The trees you drew. That was you?"

"That's the way I felt then," she said. "It's long ago. I really don't want to talk about it now." She stood and held her hand out to him.

* * *

It was later that Andrew, remembering the source, talked with Emeth about Hadesseh's name.

Emeth arched an eyebrow laconically. "You've been studying languages?" he asked in that ironic way he sometimes took. Andrew was glad to see it; it signaled the start of Emeth's return to health. "Perhaps you have never heard of the Hebrew name Esther. It is the equivalent of the Persian name Hadesseh. Esther means 'star.' "

"Odd that a people would use a foreign name for one of their own," Andrew observed.

"Oh, not at all," Emeth replied. "Esther, under her Persian name Hadesseh, was the queen who dared death and the wrath of a king to save her loved ones."

"Did she succeed?"

"Oh, indeed she did."

* * *

They stayed at the mountain hermitage for several weeks. They all needed to recover their strength, for one thing. And, for another, they had to wait out the turning of the seasons.

Spring came slowly to these high mountain regions, but as it came it brought a rare splendor that held them in awe. Grasses groped along thawing puddles of ice, renewing their strength. The sun warmed the dormant earth. The sheep paraded about led by old Simeon, giddy with the freshness of spring. Then the rains came again, gentle and steady, and the flowers spread like colored quilts. And yet they remained at the refuge.

For this reason also.

Andrew found Hadesseh one evening probing among Brusca's parchments. When he entered, her face was lit with excitement.

"What is it? What do you see?" For he knew she had found something that had eluded his best efforts.

"It's simple really." She explained Brusca's grammar, pointing out the parallels. Once he was shown, it made perfect sense to Andrew. But he had spent months laboring over it; Hadesseh had solved it in a matter of hours.

"But it was easy," she insisted. "You see, I heard the language almost daily among the trackers and their families. I can speak it."

"You can!" Andrew remembered his own fumbling attempts. And also he understood Hadesseh's excitement. Yes, the parchments were a treasure, but only if opened to the people for whom they were designed. It was where Emeth's quest had always led.

That evening Emeth led them in prayers, then remarked, "The sign of a promise. And the promise must be fulfilled."

Their restlessness grew then. They pored over Rafeo's maps. They spent hours practicing the language until the words felt natural on their tongues.

In the end, it was harder to leave than they expected. The mountain refuge had become home to them.

"We can always come back," Emeth said.

They agreed, knowing in their hearts that they never would. They had plotted a course to the north, to find the people who corresponded to the language. They located and pinpointed a village on Rafeo's map as a place to start.

But when they left, there were only the five of them—Andrew and Emeth, Hadesseh, John, and Helena. During recent days Rafeo had grown reflective. He walked with a limp from his wound. While his spirit was irrepressible, his body was not. He had decided to stay on his beloved mountain refuge.

"I'm afraid I'm letting you down," he said. "In all the world's corners, it is strange that the Lord has called me to this place. But it is my place."

Andrew nodded. When he hugged the old man goodby he felt the frailty of his body and he understood. Yes, this was Rafeo's place—this slip of land hung between heaven and earth on the side of the mountain. A home among clouds and sunlight. He knew that Rafeo would never be crossing the rope bridge again.

They left them—Rafeo, his sheep, old Simeon—to their mountain meadow. They left the rooms clean swept, kindling and dried dung stacked neatly by the hearths.

When they turned toward the gorge and the rope bridge, Simeon actually trotted a few paces after them, as if to follow. Then he turned and ran back to his ewes, butting them none too tenderly in their flanks. They stood chewing, their large soft eyes watching the wanderers leave.

EPILOGUE

John lay awake on his bunk. A cold wind whistled across the thatch roof, sneaking through chinks to snap at his skin. But it was not the cold that kept him awake. He had grown accustomed to it.

He sat up on the bunk and pulled the old woolen blanket around his shoulders. Although he knew he was too old to do so, he let his fingers brush the softly worn wool against his cheek. He breathed the comforting odor of the blanket and pulled it tighter around him.

He wanted to get up, but he knew he was too old now for that also. He wanted to look at the man whom he had learned to call father, after the things he had heard that night.

It would be easy. His parents slept just across the central room, on the other side of Helena's. The woven blanket that covered his doorway wouldn't make a sound. The hearth in the central room of the circular hut still glowed, sending a little warmth into the rooms. It was quiet there now, after the noise and congestion of the meeting. He could do it.

John thought of his friend Albert. What would he do? John wondered, unconsciously rubbing the blanket over his cheek. Albert wouldn't even be thinking about it. He would be sleeping soundly. Nothing worried Albert, except whether he could beat John at a wrestling match. John grinned. He hadn't yet.

Albert had been at the meeting. It had been his first time. He came with his parents.

There were more there each time. It was a good time. They sang songs together. They prayed together. Then one of his parents talked, and then, finally, they ate the big meal together.

It had taken so long for the people to start coming.

It was his mother who started it. One of the other mothers had a sick baby. His father and Emeth had gone to their hut, to pray over the baby. But it was his mother who had gone into the hills, alone in those wild hills where, he heard, there were wolves. She had been gone a long time, but she came back with a basket filled with some strange, weedy plants. She washed them and stirred them and did something with them to the baby.

They were the first people to come to the meeting—the mother and the baby, and then some time later the father. They always came now. But there were so many now. They were going to build another hut just to meet in.

But it had been tonight's meeting where John had heard the things that kept him awake.

Afterward, while the others were leaving, he and Albert had gone to his room to play. They had cleared a space and were setting up stones and little wooden figures for a war. They were very careful with their wars, each wooden peg set exactly right before the battle started.

But tonight, Albert fell asleep. John looked up after a long silence, and there he was. Sleeping!

Well, Albert was a year younger than he was. Maybe he would tease him in the morning.

John had sat there by himself, playing. But also listening to the voices from the next room. And as the others left he heard his mother's voice through the woven blanket, talking with Albert's parents. He didn't know where his father had gone. Perhaps to walk back with some of the others. Helena had been sleeping for a long time. But that was expected. Not Albert.

John looked at his sleeping friend as he listened. He felt he was eavesdropping. *They think I'm asleep too*, he thought.

"But how do you know it's true?" asked Albert's father.

He had heard his mother's voice, and he sat stiff, hardly breathing, as she told the story. He knew some of the names by now. Elhrain and

Taletha. But he hadn't know about their long search over the desert for the Messiah. What did she call Elhrain? A Magus? And Doval and Lycurgus. He a Roman general. They saw the Messiah's death? And the other stories set his mind spinning.

And she talked about his father.

At times his father seemed in pain. John knew his body sometimes hurt him. There were scars. He had seen them with his own eyes, and wondered about them. But these things . . .

They had talked a long time and John was starting to drowse when Albert's parents walked in, laughing to find their son sound asleep. His mother was surprised he was still awake. She tucked him in, as she always did.

But then he couldn't get back to sleep as the house fell silent and the night deepened. He heard his father come in, heard low voices from their room, then the long quiet fell. And still he could not sleep.

John stared at the light that trickled through the shuttered window. He wished he had a dog. His father had told him long ago that he might have one. It was just—they wanted the right kind. Like the mountain dog.

He remembered that his mother had once trained hawks. How he loved to see them roam. She knew so much! She knew plants and animals—not just as things but as if . . . as if they were alive. How he loved the long walks they took out into the hills.

Especially when his father was busy during the planting season. He had helped people, teaching them many things about planting and harvest.

But John felt more like his mother. He wanted to know the secrets of things—how they were what they were and how they came to be that way.

It would be nice to have a dog, though.

I'm not very much like Father, he thought. Sometimes he was gay and happy, then suddenly he could be . . . lost. Still there but gone.

"It's just the way he is," his mother had said once when he asked her about it. "He loves you just the same, all the time."

John had nodded. But after what he heard tonight, he wondered. So many questions. Tentatively he set his feet on the cold ground. *Maybe just a look*, he told himself. That wouldn't be babyish—to just look and then come back. To know everything is the same.

He froze.

He heard the footsteps softly approach the woven blanket. *Someone's there*, he thought.

He toppled back onto the bunk and pulled the blanket about him, feigning sleep.

The blanket brushed aside, softly, in a whisper of motion. Footsteps glided toward the bed. John squeezed his eyes.

He felt the hand reach out and brush his hair. Gently it stroked his temples, his cheek. He opened his eyes. His father was leaning over him.

"Couldn't sleep?" he asked quietly. His voice was a whisper. He sat down on the edge of the bed. His arm fell along John's body. It felt strong; it felt comforting.

John shook his head. "No," he whispered. "I can't sleep."

"I know how it is," his father murmured.

A long silence followed. His father was in no hurry to leave. The fingertips gently massaged John's temples.

"Father," he said sleepily. "Will you . . . tell me about yourself?"

Was it a chuckle? John couldn't tell.

"Yes," his father said. "Of course I will. Sometime. But right now you should sleep. I have something more important to tell you."

"What?" John murmured.

"I love you, son. With all my heart I love you."

"I love you too," John whispered.

Author's Note

The spread of the gospel during the first century presents one of those mysteries of grace that baffles the human mind. How did this relatively small band of believers centered in Palestine spread the redemptive message so that it inched, slowly but powerfully, over the known Western world?

There were more, of course, than the little band of Jesus' disciples who picked up the cause and pursued the mandate of the Great Commission. Jesus preached to thousands; thousands of others were anointed by the Holy Spirit at Pentecost. What happened to them all? How did they go forth? Here history is largely silent. The heroes of faith disappeared, but their message did not.

St. Paul, foremost among them, probably never fulfilled his dream of bringing the gospel to Spain. A victim of the singular madness of Nero, Paul died around A.D. 64. But by then he had been instrumental in starting or furthering dozens of tiny congregations scattered about the Mediterranean Sea. His biblical letters only give a tiny glimpse of the historical reality of this powerful missionary. Surely others were affected by his zeal. They too pledged their allegiance to the cause of Christ. Some scholars of church history have speculated that by the end of the first century there were nearly a half million Christians in the kingdom of God.

Such allegiance did not come without cost.

When Rome burned in A.D. 64, and accusations began to turn on Nero himself, the madman found a convenient scapegoat in the new Christians. Politically powerless, primarily from the social underclass, they were a susceptible target. And Nero made the most of it, parading their deaths in his coliseum for the entertainment of a jaded and perverse citizenry.

Spreading the gospel was often a violent and frightful enterprise. No book can capture the brutal reality. Often under suspicion at home, the new converts moved out to a world in which territorial and clan warfare were facts of everyday life. Every stranger was under suspicion.

Out of such terrible suffering, such unspeakable bravery, innumerable legends were born. And often, where history is silent, legends are all we have. Some are doubtful, of course. One legend had the gospel brought to England by the end of the first century. Possibly. One doesn't know for sure. Such is the fabric of legends.

Persecution, suffering and despair were the price of allegiance. Fame and glory? Not here.

But those who wielded the persecution forgot this: Those brave souls—those men and women who carried the gospel in their hearts, on their lips and sometimes in the parchments of letters—went under the power and authority of the everlasting God, the risen Christ and the Holy Spirit.

Their efforts were not in vain. They are indeed our spiritual ancestors. They held allegiance to their God, no matter how fearful the price of the gospel of peace.